Praise for Mary Louise Kelly

THE BULLET

"Nonstop pacing, a touch of romance, and a heroine who's full of surprises combine to create great thriller escapism for the Harlan Coben set."

—*Booklist Online*

"As much a portrait of metamorphosis as it is a thriller, and it owes less to the likes of Lee Child—or Alfred Hitchcock—than to Albert Camus."

—*The Washington Post*

"Written with style and intelligence, the clever plot gains velocity until the final page."

—Valerie Plame, former CIA covert ops officer
and author of *Burned*

"Mary Louise Kelly's *The Bullet* has an irresistible hook and a run of fantastic twists that pulls you breathlessly through to the last pages where all is revealed with a sure, steady hand. It's having your cake and closure too—and it's very satisfying. I'd kind of like a time machine so that I could have the wonderful premise of this book for my own!"

—Jamie Mason, author of *Monday's Lie*
and *Three Graves Full*

"With an extremely likable narrator and twists and turns galore, *The Bullet* is at once a thriller, a medical mystery, and a study of how well we really know the people we love."

—Alice LaPlante, author of *Turn of Mind*

"Mary Louise Kelly's *The Bullet* is right on target with a riveting, twisty tale of a woman whose search for her own identity leads her to seek vengeance against the killer who stole it from her."

— Hallie Ephron, author of *Night Night, Sleep Tight*

ANONYMOUS SOURCES

"Kelly's years as a political writer and intelligence correspondent covering wars, terrorism, and nuclear powers have served her well, and she portrays James with authority in a smart, fun voice that will stir lust and envy among readers. The author leaves open a window on the final page that suggests a sequel, much to the reader's delight."

— *Publishers Weekly*

"Mystery and thriller readers will happily delve into this fast-paced story featuring a feisty protagonist whom one hopes will have further adventures."

— *Library Journal*

"In Mary Louise Kelly's entertaining new novel, a smart, sexy reporter wanders into the midst of a truly scary terrorist plot. In the manner of an Alfred Hitchcock thriller, Kelly's heroine has to outfox the conspirators to escape. This book is great fun, from beginning to end."

— David Ignatius, columnist for *The Washington Post* and author of *Bloodmoney*

"One of the most genuinely chilling plots I've ever read. A scenario that will haunt anyone who's ever read a newspaper. I couldn't put this book down."

— Allison Leotta, author of *Speak of the Devil*

Also by Mary Louise Kelly

Anonymous Sources

MARY LOUISE KELLY

THE BULLET

POCKET BOOKS

New York   London   Toronto   Sydney   New Delhi

Pocket Books
An Imprint of Simon & Schuster, Inc.
1230 Avenue of the Americas
New York, NY 10020

This book is a work of fiction. Any references to historical events, real people, or real places are used fictitiously. Other names, characters, places, and events are products of the author's imagination, and any resemblance to actual events or places or persons, living or dead, is entirely coincidental.

First Pocket Books paperback edition October 2016

POCKET and colophon are registered trademarks of Simon & Schuster, Inc.

For information about special discounts for bulk purchases, please contact Simon & Schuster Special Sales at 1-866-506-1949 or business@simonandschuster.com.

The Simon & Schuster Speakers Bureau can bring authors to your live event. For more information or to book an event contact the Simon & Schuster Speakers Bureau at 1-866-248-3049 or visit our website at www.simonspeakers.com.

Interior design by Davina Mock-Maniscalco

Manufactured in the United States of America

10 9 8 7 6 5 4 3 2 1

ISBN 978-1-5011-4243-7
ISBN 978-1-4767-6984-4 (ebook)

*For my mother, who has
always believed I could do anything.*

*And for my father, who has worked hard his whole life,
to give me opportunities to try to prove her right.*

And what we students of history always learn is that the human being is a very complicated contraption and that they are not good or bad but are good and bad and the good comes out of the bad and the bad out of the good, and the devil take the hindmost.

—Robert Penn Warren, *All the King's Men*

You think you know people when you grow up with them. When they've been beside you your whole life. You know their voices, the curves of their hands, what makes them laugh. You know their hearts.

But it turns out you don't know their thoughts. Not truly, not in full. All people have their secrets, and not just things they keep from you, but secrets *about* you. Things they hope you'll never learn. You can share your home with someone, share all the silly, little details of life, share the soap, the sugar bowl, shoes—and you would never guess.

You think you know someone.

Then one day you find yourself running. Really running, lungs burning, legs churning. Too frightened to stop and look back. It turns out I have been running my whole life. I just never knew it.

Let me tell you what it's like to run.

Let me tell you a story about fear.

PART ONE

Washington

One

My name is Caroline Cashion, and I am the unlikely heroine of this story. Given all the violence to come, you were probably expecting someone different. A Lara Croft type. Young and gorgeous, sporting taut biceps and a thigh holster, right? Admit it.

Yes, all right, fine, I am pretty enough. I have long, dark hair and liquid, chocolate eyes and hourglass hips. I see the way men stare. But there's no holster strapped to these thighs. For starters, I am thirty-seven years old. Not old, not yet, but old enough to know better.

Then there is the matter of how I spend my days. That would be in the library, studying the work of dead white men. I am an academic, a professor on Georgetown University's Faculty of Languages and Linguistics. My specialty is nineteenth-century France: Balzac, Flaubert, Stendhal, Zola. The university is generous enough to fly me to Paris every year or so, but most of the time you'll find me in the main campus library, glasses sliding down my nose, buried in old books. Every few hours I'll stir, cross the quad to deliver a lecture, scold a student requesting extra time for an assignment—and then I return to my books. I read with my legs tucked beneath me, in a soft, blue armchair in a sunny corner of my office nook on the fourth floor. Most nights you will also find me there, sipping tea, typing away, grading papers. Are you getting a sense for the rhythm of my days? I lead as stodgy a life as you can imagine.

But it was by doing just this, by following this exact routine, that I came to schedule the medical appointment that changed everything.

For months, my wrist had hurt. It began as an occasional tingling. That changed to a sharp pain that shot down my fingers. The pain got worse and worse until my fingers turned so clumsy, my grip so weak, that I could barely carry my bags. My doctor diagnosed too much typing. Too much hunching over books. To be precise—I like to be precise—he diagnosed CTS. Carpal tunnel syndrome. He suggested wearing a wrist splint at night and elevating my keyboard. That helped, but not much.

And so it was that I found myself one morning in the waiting room of Washington Radiology Associates. I was scheduled for an MRI, to "rule out arthritis and get to the bottom of what's going on," as my doctor put it.

It was the morning of Wednesday, October 9. The morning it all began.

Two

The waiting room for Washington Radiology was a strange place. It featured the standard doctor's-office rack of well-thumbed magazines, the usual box of tissues and oversize pump bottle of Purell. But because of the radiation in use, the door leading to the exam rooms was constructed of solid steel. A large sign read DANGER! RESTRICTED ACCESS—STRONG MAGNETIC FIELD—SERIOUS INJURY MAY RESULT. Just to make sure you got the point, this was accompanied by an illustration of a huge magnet surrounded by sizzling lightning bolts. Sitting there waiting to be called felt a bit like waiting to be escorted into a nuclear power plant.

I leafed through a brochure. The clinic offered mammograms, ultrasounds, biopsies, and something ominously named nuclear medicine. And then there was magnetic resonance imaging. What I was here for.

"Ms. Cashion?"

I stood up.

A young woman in scrubs ushered me past the steel door and into a changing room. "Take everything off," she instructed. "It ties in front." She handed me a folded paper gown and bootees, then disappeared.

I began to unpeel my clothes. Layers of cashmere and suede. An old boyfriend once told me I was born to wear winter clothes, that even naked I moved as though I were wearing velvet. He had a point. I dress year-round in shades of plum and tobacco and wine. Rich colors. I don't do pastels.

The technician reappeared and explained how the procedure would work. I would lie back on a narrow cot, she would slide me inside the giant tube of the scanner, and then I was to stay still for forty minutes. No squirming, no blinking. I was to resist even taking a deep breath. She handed me earplugs and a panic button in case I felt claustrophobic.

No need. Getting an MRI was heavenly. What's not to like about stealing forty minutes from a weekday morning in order to rest motionless in a warm, enclosed space? The machine hummed with a loud, rhythmic, tapping noise. I nearly drifted off to sleep.

Afterward, the technician showed me back to the changing room. She cleared her throat and stared at me. "So, we'll get those images sent over to Will Zartman. He's your regular doctor, right?"

I nodded. She was still staring, naked curiosity on her face. "Was there anything else?"

"No, no." She giggled shyly. "I just—I mean, how did you get it?" Her hand reached up to brush the back of her neck.

"Get what?"

"The . . . you know, here." Again, the hand reaching up.

"Sorry, I'm not sure what you're talking about."

"The bullet," she said. "How did you get that bullet in your neck?"

EXTRAORDINARY, ISN'T IT? How your life can change, just like that, with a few words from a stranger? Later, you look back and think—that was it. That was the moment when life cleaved into two chapters, "Before I Knew" and "After."

But I wasn't there yet. I was still firmly living in "Before."

I was walking up K Street, back toward campus, a nice stroll on a crisp autumn day. It would take half an hour to get back to the library. No hurry. I didn't have class until after lunch. The encounter with the MRI technician had left me more amused than concerned. Because, obviously, I did not have a bullet in my neck. That would require my having been shot. Which had, obviously, never happened. It's not the kind of thing you would forget. The technician must have been inexperienced. She must have mistaken a shadow on the image, or something like that. Still, it would make for a great story one night at a dinner party.

I pulled out my phone to share the news with my doctor. I liked Will Zartman. He belonged to a rare breed of physicians: he took my calls, listened carefully, and most of the time phoned in a prescription without ever making me come see him. It probably helped that I was never sick and thus rarely troubled him. Before this pain in my wrist started, I hadn't talked to him in months.

Now he did his usual careful listening, then he asked me to wait. When he returned to the line a few minutes later, he sounded thoughtful. "I'm looking at your MRI now. They already e-mailed it over. There is . . . she's right, there is something there."

"Like a shadow, you mean?"

"No, like a . . . like something metal."

"There can't be. "

"It's lodged up against your spine. Bit tricky to make out. Did you ever have surgery on your neck or shoulders?"

"What? No."

"Things get dropped, you know. Surgical instruments, clamps, that sort of thing. The surgeon never even notices and stitches it right up. Happens occasionally. Anyway, I wouldn't worry. We'll be able to get a better idea from the X-ray."

"I need an X-ray now?" I sighed.

"Think we'd better. I'll set it up."

I thanked him and said good-bye. My wrist ached; I rubbed little circles against my inside pulse point as I walked. It was a nuisance to carve out time for another medical visit. Appointments that were supposed to last an hour could somehow expand to eat up half your day. Still, I wasn't teaching a terribly heavy course load this semester. I could find the time. And despite myself, I couldn't help but feel curious.

THAT NIGHT I went to my parents' house for dinner.

That happens more often than it probably should, for a grown woman of thirty-seven years. My parents and I are close. We speak every day, sometimes more than once. Most mornings I call my mother as I potter around my kitchen, brewing a first cup of tea. We swap views on the day's headlines and whatever book we fell asleep reading the night before.

You see, I live alone. I am a spinster. The word is not fashionable, but it is accurate. I'm not married, never have been. I never found anyone I liked enough. This state of affairs is fine by me; I keep my own counsel. I am not shy, on the contrary. But I am an introvert. Few people understand the difference.

Instead of a husband, I have cultivated a close circle of girlfriends. I take lovers when I feel like it. Another old-fashioned expression, I suppose, but again—accurate. And I see my parents. They live nearby in Cleveland Park, a neighborhood of wide sidewalks and genteel old houses that's home to journalists and lawyers and other members of Washington's chattering classes. My parents' house is yellow clapboard, with a shady porch and views out over the stone towers of the National Cathedral. It's the house my brothers and I grew up in, one block from the school where all three of us learned to read and write. My brothers are in their forties now, my parents well into their seventies. But they show no signs of wanting to downsize. I think they like watching my brothers' children rampage around the house, cracking lacrosse sticks and baseball bats against the same scarred doorframes that bore my brothers' abuse. An upstairs bathroom counter has a burn mark, from my own teenage years, when I incinerated a curling iron by cranking it to high heat before absentmindedly sailing out the door to a sleepover party. My parents' house, in short, still feels like home.

There's that, and there's the fact that I enjoy their company, but a not insignificant reason that I eat dinner there several nights a week is my mother's cooking. She cooks with flagrant disregard for cholesterol warnings or calorie counts, serving large helpings of casseroles from recipe books that went of print in the 1970s. Tonight she pulled from the oven a chicken potpie. I knew from long experience that it contained both an entire bag of frozen carrot-and-pea medley and lashings of Crisco, and that it would taste divine.

I waited until we were seated and the wine was poured before launching into my story. "So, you won't believe what happened at the doctor's office this morning. The strangest thing."

"Oh, not for your wrist again, was it?" asked my mother. "Is it feeling any better?"

"No. But they're trying to figure out what's going on, why the splint didn't help. I got an MRI this morning—"

"Which wrist is it again?" my father interrupted.

"The right." I held up my hand. "But they take the MRI of your whole upper body, to see where there's swelling, what's out of alignment, that type of thing. And when I got up to leave, the technician came running after me, all excited. She asked me—how crazy is this?— she asked, 'How did you get that bullet in your neck?'" I paused for dramatic effect. "A *bullet in my neck*. Can you imagine?"

You would have to know my father well to have noticed him flinch. His jaw tightened, the faintest flicker of a movement. I glanced at my mother. She was staring down, intently focused on her potpie, chasing peas around the plate with her fork.

They were silent. Not the reaction I'd expected.

"Goodness," my father managed finally. "What did you say?"

I gave him a strange look. "I said she must be mistaken, of course. You're supposed to stay still while they scan you. But I must have twitched. Maybe that shows up as a blur or a shadow on the image."

He nodded. "Right. Well, sounds like you had an adventure." He turned to my mother. "Chicken's delicious. Pass me a bit more?"

They sat chewing.

"That's it?" I demanded. "That's your reaction? I thought you two would be falling over laughing."

"Well, you said yourself, the likely explanation is the technician made an error," said my father.

"Darling, we're just concerned," my mother added. "I don't like the idea of you being in pain. I keep hoping this whole wrist issue will go away."

I sighed. "So do I. And now I have to go back and get x-rayed. I'll be in a full-body cast before they're through with me."

My parents exchanged a look.

"That was a joke. I'm *fine*."

My mother opened her mouth to say something, then changed her mind. Dinner proceeded. The conversation turned to an old Brando movie they'd just watched. But my father's hand trembled as he topped up our wineglasses. He saw me register it and pretended to lean down to pat the dog. "Old age," he said, grimacing as he sat back up. "Senility will set in soon."

As we stood up from the table, another look passed between my mother and father. Long-married couples develop a language all their own, one that requires no words to communicate. I couldn't decipher everything they were saying to each other. Just enough to know that they were choosing not to tell me something.

Three

The X-ray was striking.

Unlike my older brothers, I had been a calm child, not prone to broken bones and late-night emergency-room visits. I do not ski or mountain bike or ride horses or, indeed, partake in any dangerous activity whatsoever, if I can avoid it. I told you, I'm no Lara Croft. And so—aside from dental checkups and the resulting blurry images of my molars—I had never been x-rayed, never glimpsed the interior architecture of my body.

I found it fascinating, the play of dark and light, shades of silver and charcoal and chalk. You could see the long, forked roots of my teeth. They were outlined more sharply than in the images I'd viewed at the dentist's; this must be a superior-quality machine. Farther down came the fragile curve of my neck, vertebrae stacked neatly. The soft tissue of my skin and muscles appeared as a ghostly haze. The X-ray, in its way, was lovely.

It was also unambiguous. I had still not set eyes on yesterday's MRI, so I couldn't compare the two. But that MRI technician had been utterly, unassailably correct.

The bullet glowed. It glowed bright white, brighter even than the metal fillings in my teeth. The denser an object, the brighter it appears on an X-ray. And the bullet was presumably made of lead. It looked about half an inch long, tapered at one end. The tip pointed down toward my shoulders. The flat end was lodged near the base of my skull.

I studied the image in disbelief. It simply was not possible. Over and over I blinked, looked away, looked back—and there it still was, glowing luridly. My mind flailed through loops of Cartesian logic. That's the French scholar in me: *Je pense, donc je suis.* I think, therefore I am. I doubt the bullet is there, therefore it must be. No, that wasn't right. But I was too addled to figure it out. René Descartes never tried to practice philosophy with a bullet embedded dangerously close to his brain.

A bullet. Good God. I was sitting on an examining table on the second floor of a medical-office building on M Street. It's the same building where Dr. Zartman practices; he had called a radiologist friend and wangled a lunchtime appointment for me. Now the radiologist was glancing back and forth between me and my X-ray, illuminated on a flatscreen monitor hanging on the wall. His eyes were wide, his face lit with a mixture of excitement and horror.

"You really had no idea it was there?"

"No."

"Did you say you got an MRI already? Do you have that image with you?"

"No." I frowned. "Dr. Zartman has it. We can ask him to—"

"Come to think of it, don't do that again."

"What?"

"Don't get an MRI again. The machine's a giant magnet. That's what the *M* stands for. And you've got a slug of metal in your neck. Then again . . . lead isn't magnetic." He cocked his head, considering. "Still, if it's an alloy . . . or if you've got metallic fragments . . ."

He inspected the X-ray again. "No, not worth the risk. The bullet's right up against your spinal cord. Major blood vessels all around it. You don't want it to move."

I swallowed. The room felt as if it were closing in.

"May I?" He placed his hand on my neck. Prodded gently up and down. "There's no bump. No subcutaneous scar tissue that I can feel. Where was the entrance wound?"

"I don't know."

"Maybe around here?" His fingers inched higher, kneading the base of my scalp.

"I said, I don't know. I didn't know it was there in the first place."

"So you don't know how long it's been in there?"

"No idea. I have no idea. I don't know what to say."

His eyes narrowed. "It's awfully . . . unusual. Getting shot would seem to be a memorable event. Getting shot in the neck, especially so."

"I agree. What's your point?"

"Just that—forgive me, how to put this?—I'm finding it hard to believe you really had no idea you've been walking around with a bullet in your neck."

I glared at him. "Well, that makes two of us then. Two of us who think that this"—I rapped my fingers against the flatscreen—"that this here makes absolutely no sense."

"WELL, I DON'T know a damn thing about guns. Or ammunition. But that's sure as hell no surgical clip that got dropped."

Will Zartman and I were sitting side by side in his office, our eyes glued to the image of my neck on his desktop computer screen. He was youngish for a doctor, not much older than me. I didn't know him well. But I felt comforted by his reaction. He seemed as bewildered as I was, unsure whether the appropriate response was to panic and race to the emergency room, or to giggle at the absurdity of the situation.

"You're saying you really didn't know it was there?"

I was getting the feeling that I would be hearing this question a lot. "No, I really didn't."

"And you've never felt any pain? Any stiffness turning your neck, any tingling?"

"Well . . ." I lifted my right hand and gingerly flexed it up and down. "You know about the wrist. I don't know if it's related."

"No, me neither." He turned back to the screen. "I suppose the question is going to be, do we try to remove the bullet? I can think of all sorts of risks involved with that. On the other hand, I can think of all sorts of risks involved with leaving it in there. Lead poisoning, for one." He scribbled something on a notepad. "I think the next step is for you to see a neurosurgeon. Meanwhile, let me take a look."

He brushed the dark waves of hair off my neck and leaned close. "There's no scar."

"I know."

"And I know I already asked, but you've never had surgery? Anywhere above the waist?"

"No. I've never had any surgery, period. Not that I can think of. And I'll answer what's probably your next question: no, I've never been shot, either. As your radiologist friend was kind enough to point out, that would tend to be a memorable event in one's life."

Dr. Zartman took a deep breath and sat back. "I've never seen anything like it. I mean, bullets don't appear out of thin air. Somehow this one found its way to the middle of your neck. You really don't know how?"

"You can keep asking. The answer's still no."

"What do your parents say?"

"They—" I hesitated. "They don't seem to know."

He must have heard something in my voice because he looked up. "What do you mean, they 'don't seem' to know?"

"Well, I did mention it to them last night. That the MRI had picked up something that looked like a bullet. It seemed so ludicrous. Their reaction was—I guess it was a little strange."

"How so?"

I thought for a moment, trying to capture the right word. "Uneasy. They seemed uneasy. But that's normal, right?" I felt suddenly protective. "It would be normal for parents to feel uneasy when their daughter is in pain and is forced to undergo medical tests, and then tells them she got weird results. I mean, how would *your* mom and dad react if you told them you might have a bullet in your neck?"

He nodded. "Point taken. Still. Someone has to know what happened. You should talk to them again."

I DROVE TO my parents' house filled with trepidation.

The conversation I was about to have with them could go either of two ways, as I saw it. It was possible—probable, surely—that they knew nothing. But this was small comfort. After all, there *was* a bullet in my neck. If my parents didn't know how it got there, who would?

The even more disturbing possibility was that they did know something. I remembered how my dad's hand had trembled at dinner. How my mother had chased peas around her plate, refusing to meet my eyes. There could be no good-news story, no happy version of how a bullet had wedged itself inside my neck. But how terrible could it be? Whatever had happened, I appeared to have suffered no lasting harm. So why would they not have dared to tell me?

The only even remotely plausible explanation I could conjure up involved my brothers. Today they're both respectably married pillars of the country-club set. Six kids between them, plus mortgages and stock portfolios and regular tee times—all the trappings of middle-class middle age. But as boys, they had been wild. To this day, our across-the-street neighbor won't speak to them; she has nursed a grudge for thirty-five years. That's how long it's been since they shot out her bedroom window. I was a toddler at the time, so I have no memory of the episode. But as my brothers tell it, one of our uncles had unwisely given them BB guns for Christmas. They were both rotten shots, and they had been trying to improve through target practice on a squirrel living in the magnolia tree outside their window. (According to the version of the story that has descended through family lore, their aim got better, they eventually shot the squirrel, and left it—supposedly as a token of contrition—on our neighbor's front-door mat. Perhaps she was shrewd to have stayed out of their way all these years.) But—to return to the question at hand—was it possible that they had shot me, too? Back when I was too small to remember?

Unlikely. If they hadn't gotten away with shooting out a neighbor's window, they would never have gotten away with shooting their sister. It would have become family legend, the kind of story that gets retold and embellished upon at wedding-rehearsal dinners and fortieth-birthday parties. There's no way I wouldn't have known. And then there was the bullet itself. I probably knew even less than Dr. Zartman about guns and ammo, but the slug in my neck looked a lot bigger and more lethal than what you would load into a child's gun.

Driving toward Cleveland Park, I kept stopping to look at it. The radiologist had e-mailed a JPEG version of my X-ray. At every traffic light, I braked the car and stared at my phone. You could zoom in until the bullet filled the entire screen. Then zoom back out, until it was just a tiny white light nestled between slivers of gray vertebrae.

It was late afternoon when I pulled into the driveway. Daylight was fading. I locked the car and entered my parents' home in my usual way: a perfunctory knock, even as I turned my key in the door.

My father was sitting at the kitchen table, bent over a crossword puzzle. His beagle, Hunt, ignored me as usual. But Dad's face brightened. "Caroline! I was hoping you would swing by. What's a seven-letter synonym for—"

"Dad." My voice caught. I didn't know how to ask him. Instead I held out my phone, let him glimpse the e-mailed image of the X-ray.

His eyes told me what I needed to know. "Oh, sweet Jesus. Darling girl. We didn't know it was still there."

Four

You're thinking that I don't seem appropriately distressed, aren't you? That a woman who has just learned she is walking around with a bullet in her neck, that she has perhaps been *shot*, would be a bit more hysterical.

Well, here you go.

Standing there in the kitchen, my father fussing over me ("Darling, please sit down. Let me make tea—"), I lost it.

"What do you mean, you didn't know it was *still there*?" I screeched. "What *did* you know? Why didn't you tell me?"

"We didn't—we just—we assumed that they removed it. We never thought to ask."

"Never thought to ask who? What are you talking about?" I half picked up one of the chairs and slammed it down hard against the table. "Dad? What are you *saying*?"

I am not prone to outbursts, not a volatile person. But my father's evasiveness felt more alarming than the images from the X-ray and the MRI. They had seemed unreal, like props in a strange dream from which I was surely about to wake. Whereas my father . . . I had come here expecting him to dismiss the whole situation as risible. I had expected to share a good laugh, then have him solve the mystery of how my X-ray had gotten mixed up with someone else's, some poor soul walking around with (cue laugh track!) a *bullet in her neck*.

Instead he was fumbling with his phone keypad, mumbling about calling my mother.

"Dad—"

He held his finger up, signaling me to wait. "Frannie, Caroline's here. Come home, please. . . . Mm-hmm. Yes." He hung up. "She'll be here in twenty minutes."

"Dad, whatever it is, please just tell me."

"You know what? To hell with tea." He pulled two glasses from a cabinet and a bottle of Scotch from beside the fridge.

"I don't want whisky!" I swatted the bottle away. "I *want* you to tell me what's going on. How could you have known—"

"Drink," he ordered, and wrapped my fingers back around the glass. His hand shook as he poured. "It'll calm you down. I'm sorry this has come as such a shock. As soon as Mom gets here . . . I suppose we should call your brothers, too."

"Why? Was it them?"

"Was it who?"

"Martin and Tony. Is that who shot me?"

He looked confused.

"With their old BB guns. Like the squirrel?"

A surprised smile passed over his face. "No. It wasn't your brothers. Though Lord help us, they probably tried." The smile faded and his eyes turned serious again. "You really don't remember? Not anything?"

"What should I remember?"

"From when you were little."

I shook my head, waited.

"We always wondered. Never wanted to ask. They told us to let sleeping dogs lie."

"Dad. You're scaring me."

"Please don't judge us too harshly, Caroline. We love you. We always will. No matter what, you are our daughter."

I stared at him. Those were the most frightening words I'd heard yet.

AN HOUR LATER, my family was assembled in the living room.

Allow me to make the introductions:

You've already met my mother, Frannie Cashion. Attractive, lively. Busy with the Flower Guild at church, and with bossing around her daughters-in-law and their ever-expanding broods of children.

My father, Thomas Cashion. He's retired from practicing law, but he still consults occasionally and has developed a new, rather tiresome addiction to crosswords. He also runs three miles daily, which he claims is the best defense against my mother's onslaught of casseroles.

My middle brother, Anthony. He's a lawyer like Dad. The loudest and most obnoxious of us three kids. Now he was playing true to form, stomping around complaining that there was never beer in the house, and that this family powwow better not take longer than an hour, because he had dinner reservations at Rasika at eight, and did we know how hard those were to get?

As usual, my oldest brother, Martin, told him to shut up. Martin works in finance. Real estate investment banking. He has repeatedly tried to explain what he does, but my eyes always glaze over when he launches into the benefits of maximizing liquidity through joint-venture recapitalization and tax-syndication equity. *Are you still speaking English?* I want to ask. A similarly glazed expression creeps over his face when I prattle on about how you can't read Balzac without applying Roland Barthes's semiotic code and accepting the plurality of the text. It's safe to say we have different interests. Fortunately, Martin and I really like each other.

Now he plunked himself down next to me on the sofa. "Sis? You okay? You look like hell."

"Martin, please." My mother.

"Fine, but seriously, what's up? Why the sudden summit? And why isn't Sis talking?"

I stared pointedly at my father, waiting for him to speak.

He cleared his throat. "Your sister got some news today." Dad's voice was low, soothing. The voice he must have cultivated to command respect in the courtroom. I rarely heard him use it at home. "It's news she wasn't expecting, and that frankly your mother and I weren't expecting. And it leads to some questions, and to a conversation best had as a family."

My mother nodded. Martin leaned forward, frowning. Even Tony stopped pacing and sat down.

"Caroline got an X-ray today. And it revealed"—Dad patted his neck—"it revealed right here—"

"It revealed this," I snapped, and held my phone out to Martin. He examined the photo, used his fingers to zoom in and out a few times.

"What is it?"

"My neck."

He drew the screen closer to his face and squinted. "Your neck?"

Tony leaned over and grabbed the phone. "But what's that?" He pointed toward the lower left corner of the screen.

"That would appear to be a bullet."

Both my brothers looked up at me as if I were insane.

Dad attempted to regain control of the conversation. "It is a bullet." He swooped down and took the phone. "And I'm sorry, we are so sorry"—he gestured at my mom—"that you're finding out this way. We didn't know it was there. But we did know . . ." He took a deep breath. "We did know that you were shot. When you were three years old."

Silence. Then Tony spoke. "Where? How?"

My mother crossed the room, knelt in front of me, and took my hands. "Before you came to us. Before you came to be our beautiful angel girl." A tear slid down her cheek.

I still didn't understand. "Before I came to you? What are you talking about—*before I came to you*? Dad said, when I was three. I'd been here for three years."

"Ohhh." Martin exhaled the word slowly. "Was that why, Mom?"

She ignored him, kept her eyes fixed on mine. "We

adopted you, Caroline. Your parents had—had died. We promised to love you and raise you as our own. And we have. We do." She squeezed my hands tightly. "You'll have so many questions, I know. We'll do our best to answer them. But you need to understand: within this room, within this family, nothing changes. Nothing. You are our daughter. You are their sister. Period."

She shot my brothers a fierce look that meant *Say something*.

Martin cleared his throat and shifted awkwardly on the sofa to face me. "Right. Absolutely. Nothing changes." He glanced at Tony for support.

"Sure, right." Tony sat blinking incredulously. "I haven't thought about all this in ages, to be honest. We were so little when you came. But, Mom and Dad, I have to say, this is a hell of a way to break it to Sis—"

"You knew?" I stared at him. "And you?" I turned to Martin.

Of course they had. I quickly did the math. Tony would have been seven, Martin already nine, when I arrived.

Does it sound strange to say that at that precise moment this felt like the more painful betrayal? Not the shock of learning—at thirty-seven—that I was adopted, that I was not and had never been who I'd thought I was. But that my brothers had known and kept it from me. They had kept a secret from me, kept it so long they had nearly forgotten it themselves. Then again—*Jesus*—they were not really my brothers.

I began to shake.

My father reached for me.

But I was lurching backward, scrambling over the top of the sofa, then running, desperate to get out of that room.

I SPENT THE next two hours locked in my old bathroom. I threw up, then sat shivering on the edge of the bathtub, a towel wrapped around my shoulders.

From downstairs I could hear noises, footsteps as people moved from room to room. I imagined my mother crying, and my brothers calling home to their wives, explaining that a family crisis was under way and they would be late. Actually, that was an interesting point—did their wives know about my history? Did *everyone* in this family know except me?

I searched my memory. Nothing stood out. My childhood had felt normal, or as normal as I suppose anyone's ever does. I did think now to question the lack of baby pictures. Above the fireplace in the room I had just fled stood a row of silver frames, snapshots of family milestones. My parents' wedding picture, my brothers' weddings, a triple frame to hold portraits of each of my brothers and me at our respective college graduations. On the left side of the mantel, Anthony and Martin were both displayed as plump, bald babies in christening gowns. My mother had brushed me off when I'd asked where my own baby photo was: "Third-child syndrome. I was too busy chasing your brothers to snap pictures of you."

Now I felt like an idiot.

Outside the bathroom door someone moved, and then came a knock.

"Feel like talking?"

Martin. I frowned at the door.

He stood there a minute, then tried again. "Sis?" The door handle rattled. The lock held. I heard him lean against the door and slide heavily down to sit on the floor of the upstairs landing.

"I would be completely freaked out, too, if I were you. For what it's worth. This stuff coming out after all these years."

I said nothing, focused on radiating hostility through the door. Minutes passed.

"I can sit here all night, you know. Always did like this landing. Mind you, I've got the whisky on this side of the door. Hear that?" A clinking sound, ice in tumblers. "I'm betting you could use some right about now."

I began to weaken. "Go away. I don't like whisky."

"Fine. Pretend it's champagne. Or Bordeaux, or Sancerre or something. Whatever you froggy Francophile types prefer to drink."

"Please just go away."

We sat awhile, and then he said, "You know, I think the last time I remember you locking yourself in this bathroom to sulk, it was over that loser. What was his name? The chubby one?"

"Shut up, Martin."

"No, come on. What was that, your sophomore year? You were mad as hell because he'd cheated on you with some blonde. Josh something, wasn't it? Or Jack?"

"Jeff Benton." I couldn't help myself.

"That's right. God, what a tool. What was the deal? He bailed on taking you to prom?"

"Yeah." A long pause. "Yeah, he did. So you and Tony slashed his tires and spelled out the word *dickwad* in liquid fertilizer on his front lawn."

"Well, that's what brothers are for."

Brothers. My stomach twisted. I pulled the towel tighter around myself.

"Caroline. How about coming out now?"

"No."

In the narrow gap under the door, four fingertips appeared.

"Don't," I warned.

The fingers wiggled farther in. "Come on. Before I get splinters all down the back of my knuckles."

"Or I could just stomp on them."

"Don't do that. I have to play squash this weekend."

This finally made me laugh. It came out more a croak than laughter, but it released something in me. "Martin?" I hesitated. "What happened to my parents? My—my real parents?"

"Your birth parents," he corrected. "I don't know. What I remember is being told we were getting a baby sister, and then one day there you were. Mom and Dad seemed happy about it, so we were, too. I don't remember them ever using that word, *adopted*. It just seemed normal. Like . . . there had been two Cashion kids, and now there were three. Same as any other family when a third child comes along. Tony's right, we kind of forgot about it. The circumstances of how you arrived. Honestly. It's not like we've been sitting around for years gossiping behind your back."

I wasn't sure I believed that, but I relented. Stood up and opened the door.

Martin pulled himself to his feet.

I eyed my rail-thin, blond, blue-eyed brother. "You know, I look nothing like you."

"This only just dawned on you?"

"No, but I mean, why didn't it ever strike me as odd?"

"I don't know. I have plenty of friends who look nothing like their siblings."

"Right, but you and Tony look like twins. Aryan male models in a Brooks Brothers ad—"

"Oh, come on!"

"Whereas I . . . I look like Salma Hayek if she were a few inches taller and had better cleavage."

He snorted. "Don't think I'm letting you get away with that just because you're having an atrocious day. Your girls got nothing on Salma's cleavage."

I punched his shoulder.

It felt like a resumption of our usual banter, yet hollow. As if something precious had been lost.

Five

The story gets worse from here.

The blackest, most terrible bits did not emerge until nearly midnight.

The five of us huddled back in the living room, my brothers installed protectively on either side of me on the sofa. My father and they had kicked back the bottle of whisky and opened a second. Mom and I nursed mugs of tea. I figured I was already a wreck, my inhibitions plenty loosened as it was without adding whisky to the equation. But there was no suitable state—drunk, sober, or anywhere in between—in which to receive the story that Dad proceeded to unleash.

He told me that I had been born in Atlanta.

My parents were a young, married couple named Boone and Sadie Rawson Smith. Boone was a pilot for Delta; Sadie Rawson stayed home to raise me. They were college sweethearts. They had moved to Atlanta from Charlotte, shortly before I was born. These details were included in the newspaper obituaries.

They died together, shot cleanly and at close range. Boone through the head, Sadie Rawson through the heart. Murdered. My parents had been murdered in the autumn of 1979. They were both twenty-six years old. Their bodies were found in the kitchen of the white brick house they owned, on a pleasant street in a neighborhood called Buckhead.

I was with them in the white brick house. I was shot, too. Shot in the neck and nearly died. When police kicked in the door, they found me blue-lipped and barely breathing on the kitchen floor. I was rushed to the hospital, given blood, stitched up. A miraculous recovery. But the case was never solved. The killer was never caught. Boone and Sadie Rawson Smith were buried, the house was sold, and I was sent to live in Washington.

"That's pretty much all we know," my father concluded. "When you came to us, the police investigation was still active. They wouldn't tell us much more than what was in the papers. And then time passed . . . years passed . . . and it no longer seemed to matter so much." He had been speaking with an air of grim determination; now his voice softened. "You were so frightened when you came to us, Caroline. You wouldn't talk the first few weeks."

"Our doctor was worried you might have suffered brain damage," whispered my mother. (*My mother.* I suppose I'll have to start being more specific. My mother, meaning Frannie Cashion. The woman in the room with me now.) She shook her head. "I knew he was wrong. I could look in your eyes and see that you were bright. Really bright. You just needed time."

"And we think that you might still have been in pain," Dad added. (*Dad.* By whom I mean, Thomas Cashion.

The dad I had grown up with. God, this was strange.) "You had been badly wounded. They told us you'd had two surgeries, that you'd barely . . . barely made it. But none of the medical records we received ever indicated that it might still be in your neck. We just"—he glanced helplessly at my mother—"we assumed that the bullet had been removed during one of those operations."

"But I don't have a scar." It was the first time I'd spoken in nearly an hour.

"You did. You used to have a scar." My mother leaned forward and touched the base of my skull, half an inch to the left of the raised ridge of my spine. "We could see it through your hair. But your hair grew in thicker every year. And you got sick with chicken pox when you were six, and after that you had scars everywhere. I lost track of which were which. Then they all faded. Even this one." For a moment her finger pressed hard against my skull, then she drew back and clasped her hands tightly on her lap.

I turned to Dad. "It's bizarre that the doctors didn't tell you they left the bullet in. I mean, wouldn't that be pertinent information to know, about a child you were adopting?"

"It's outrageous," he said. "Both from a medical and a legal standpoint. But, Caroline, you were under Georgia state protective custody. Your records—they—everything was sealed. Because of the criminal investigation. We were never allowed to meet your surgeons. Maybe they were calculating that the bullet didn't pose an urgent threat to your health by the time we were signing the adoption papers, so we didn't need to know. And after that—I don't know. Maybe it fell between the cracks, when Georgia handed off your files to DC."

"I suppose we could have lodged an appeal to get your medical chart," said Mom. "Especially once the investigation quieted down. But . . . Dad's right. Months went by, and then years, and you were happy here. Thriving. You seemed fully healed. We weren't focused on digging around for old charts."

It was too much to take in. I couldn't absorb it. Instead I found myself latching onto small, concrete details. Such as my lack of a scar. Or the name of a city.

"Atlanta," I heard myself say. "I've never even been there." The name conjured up scenes from *Gone with the Wind*, Scarlett O'Hara flouncing around in a hoopskirt made from curtains. What else? Coca-Cola. Coke corporate headquarters were there. And the Olympics. Atlanta had hosted the Olympics, back when I was in college. I remembered the US team dominating, Michael Johnson sprinting off with two golds. But I had no mental picture of the city. Apparently, though, I had indeed been to Atlanta. I had lived there, for several years, and then forgotten every second of them.

Martin seemed to read my thoughts. "You don't remember any of this? About your . . . about the Smiths? Or about coming to live with us?"

No, I didn't.

"It would be remarkable if she did," Dad put in. "We did some research on this. Few children remember anything from before age four. If they do, it's often not a real memory, but a narrative they've created for themselves, from being shown photographs or told stories about a place or a person. And we deliberately never talked about anything that happened before Caroline came to us. We certainly didn't have photos to show."

"On top of that, you'd been through such trauma." Mom looked at me. "Even an older child might have blocked it out."

I nodded. That sounded reasonable. They both sounded just like their usual reasonable and reassuring selves, if you set aside the sheer insanity of this scene. The insanity of the entirely rewritten life history that I had been handed, a history that included a double homicide and two sets of parents and a bullet burrowed beneath my skin. Mom was right: I should have so many questions. But at that moment they eluded me. My wrist ached, more sharply than usual. All I wanted was to lie down and close my eyes.

"Dad." The word seemed to charge the room, like a lie that we were all waiting for someone to challenge. I forced myself to repeat it. "Dad, would it be all right if I slept here tonight?"

"Well, of course, darling."

I walked over and kissed the top of his head. Then I kissed my mother and stretched my lips into a weak smile at my brothers. They would all start talking about me the minute I left the room. I didn't care. I turned and climbed the stairs to my old bedroom, cradling my wrist in my good hand.

Six

Remarkably, I slept. It is a small mercy that the body is capable of overriding the brain, forcing it to shut down in times of crisis. I slept for five obliterating hours before my eyes snapped open. I have never been one to wake up disoriented, and now, even in the predawn darkness, I knew exactly where I was and why.

Of the many questions that must have percolated while I was asleep, the one that woke me up was this: *Was my name really Caroline?*

I crept downstairs.

In the kitchen, looking as though they had not fared so well in the sleep department, stood my mother and Tony. Mom wore a blue flannel nightgown and robe. Tony had changed into stretched-out, gray sweats emblazoned with the logo of his high school wrestling team. He must have found them folded in the back of a dresser drawer, forgotten for the twenty-odd years since he'd last shambled in from practice and dropped them, stained and sweaty, in a hamper for our mother to wash.

They stopped talking when they saw me in the doorway.

"What's my real name?" I asked without preamble.

"Your real name?" my mother repeated.

"Is my name really Caroline?"

"Oh, I see. Yes. Yes, it is."

"But not Caroline Cashion."

"No. Well, that is, of course it is. That's your legal name now. But you were born Caroline Smith. We decided to keep it. The name Caroline fit you. So graceful. And it sounds pretty with Cashion, and . . . we thought it might be less disruptive for you, emotionally. To be called by the name that you were used to."

I thought about this. "Do you have my birth certificate?"

"Yes." She gestured vaguely toward the ceiling. "It's upstairs in the files. We had to have that and the adoption papers to get your first passport. You can see it, if you want."

"Sure. Yes."

I chewed my lip. Tony stood and poured a cup of coffee. Then he excused himself. He needed to get home, get showered, say hi to the kids before work. He gave my shoulder a squeeze. "Hang in there. I'll call you later, okay?"

"Yep. Nice sweats, by the way."

He looked down. "High school glory days."

"Good times. Go Bulldogs."

He looked unsure whether to rise to this. Then old habit kicked in, reflexes honed over a lifetime of sibling bickering. "I'll remind you that my senior year we nearly won the Mid-Atlantic Prep Championship tournament."

"You *nearly* won?"

"That's right."

"You mean, you came in second."

"Third. A mere detail."

"Wow. No wonder the ladies couldn't resist."

He grinned and pulled me to him in a real hug. "My smart-ass sister. Sorry about all this. I'll call you."

He slammed the kitchen door shut. My mother turned and started cracking eggs into a bowl. She rustled around in the fridge, pulled out bacon and bread. An uncomfortable silence grew between us.

"What about the rest of my family?" I ventured after a while. "I mean, not to sound ungrateful, but didn't I have grandparents? Why didn't they take me?"

"I asked that same question. Before we signed the papers. For selfish reasons, I confess. I didn't want anyone to show up later and try to claim you back once you were ours. We were told there was no immediate family to take you. Your father's parents were already dead. And your mother's—I gather they were separated, and not in particularly good health themselves. Not the ideal home life for a traumatized little girl. So the decision was made to find you a new family. It was quick. They cut through all the red tape; no one wanted to see you stuck in bureaucratic limbo."

"But didn't they ever try to visit me? My own grandparents?"

"Once." Mom lowered her eyes. "Your grandmother wrote once. Asking to see you. We thought it was too soon. That seeing her might confuse you. She didn't have any legal rights, not after we finalized the adoption."

Mom hesitated. "I did write to her, some years after that. The letter was returned, unopened. She and your grandfather had both passed away by then."

I winced. A minute went by before I could speak again. "And why—why you? Why did I come here?"

Mom glanced at me sideways. "You know I had trouble delivering Anthony?"

"Yes." I couldn't think how I knew this; it wasn't something I could remember ever being openly discussed.

"I was unwell for a long time after his birth. We both stayed in the hospital for several weeks. It's all fine now, of course, but the end result was we couldn't have another child. It was physically impossible for me to carry a baby again. And we so badly wanted a girl. *I* so badly wanted a girl." She smiled. "So we signed up with an adoption agency. We weren't sure it would lead to anything, and for a couple of years it didn't. We knew we were low priority; we already had two healthy children. But it turned out, in your case, that that was helpful. It bumped us to the top of the list. The social workers wanted experienced parents. A happy, stable family that you could slot right into. I showed them pictures, how I had a girl's room all done up in pink, just in case. A week later, we got the call."

I remembered the pink room. It was a little girl's dream. The centerpiece was a lace canopy bed worthy of Cinderella. Beside it on the carpet had stood a matching miniature bed for my favorite doll. My plastic Fisher-Price record player had a real needle to play vinyl 45s, and my lightbulb-powered Holly Hobbie oven had singed a hole in the carpet (burn marks apparently being a signature of my childhood). What I could not summon now, for the life of me, was any memory of seeing that room for the first time. I had never given it much thought, but I suppose I'd always assumed that before the canopy bed, a baby's crib had stood there. My crib. That was the logical evolution, just as the canopy bed had given way at some point in my teenage years to the queen-size mattress and headboard that now dominated the room. I had slept in that queen bed last night. The burned carpet had been replaced, the pink walls long since repainted a tasteful shade of taupe.

Mom slid into a chair beside me and set two plates on the table. While I was wallowing in nostalgia, she had whipped up an omelet. Bacon, eggs, grated cheese. She knows I love bacon. Pork in all forms. I have been known to go well out of my way for good chorizo. But when I took a bite, I spit it right back out.

My mother looked mildly offended.

"I'm sorry. It tastes like cardboard."

"Ah." She touched my hand. "That can happen when you've had a shock."

I stared at my plate in surprise. "I thought that was just something people said. Or, you know, literary license. Lazy writers always make grieving characters lose their appetite and complain how everything tastes like cardboard. I had no idea it was true." My mouth felt filthy. I crossed to the sink and spat again. Scooped cold water and splashed my face over and over, until my hair was matted and water dripped onto the tiled floor. I stood there trembling. My mother rose and rested her hand on my back while I shook.

After a long time I straightened. "Why didn't you and Dad tell me?"

"How could we? What happened to you was so awful. More than any child could bear."

"But what about later? When I was an adult? I'm thirty-seven years old, for God's sake!"

"We—they advised us not to. The adoption counselors. They said it would confuse you. And, Caroline, that's the way it was done back then. Adoptions were nearly always closed. Even children with less . . . less dramatic histories never learned who their birth parents were. Lots of children grew up not knowing they were adopted."

I pulled away from her. "You should have told me."

For the first time she looked impatient. "Sweet girl, would it have made you happy? What good would it have done?"

LATER THAT MORNING I taught my Friday class as usual. FREN 388, the Novel in Nineteenth-Century France. It's frowned upon to call in sick, and it turned out to be a relief to pass an hour focused on something I understood, a subject that I had mastered.

Today's assignment was Flaubert's *Madame Bovary*, a book I always look forward to teaching. The portrait of a woman trapped in a dull marriage, it is a groundbreaking work for feminists. It was scandalous back in its day: in 1857, Flaubert was put on trial for obscenity and "crimes against public morality." This because of the disgraceful behavior of his protagonist, Emma Bovary. She lies to her husband and lavishes a cigar case and a silver-handled riding crop on her lover. Still, she has her charms, and usually I take the time with my students to savor her seductions, her little vanities. Today, though, I felt impatient. Her sins felt tame set against the revelations of my last twenty-four hours. Emma Bovary thought *she* had problems? At least she knew who her parents were, and no one had murdered them, and she wasn't running around with a bullet jammed against her spine.

With considerable effort I managed to stick with my prepared lecture notes. I even ended with a flourish, about how provocatively Flaubert had illuminated the turbulent social and political landscape of 1850s France. My students seemed to like this; they all diligently scribbled it down. I rewarded them by ending class a few minutes early. Then I gathered my notes, switched off the lights, and stepped into the quiet hallway. What now? According to my usual Friday routine, I should retire to my fourth-floor library nook for an exciting afternoon of grading papers and sipping herbal tea. I pictured my blue armchair, my electric kettle, my I ♥ NPR mug, neatly rinsed and left to dry. I couldn't face them. Instead I headed toward the White-Gravenor building's wide staircase.

Outside, the lawn of the main quad was busy. Students throwing Frisbees, calling to friends, making weekend plans. The day was pretty but cool. I began to walk, with no particular direction in mind. I just needed to move. I was near the main university gates and the John Carroll statue when my legs folded. One moment I was walking, and the next I was on the ground. I had eaten nothing since yesterday morning, but this wasn't a faint. Nothing so dainty. I just . . . gave out. The body overriding the brain.

Here is something I did not know before but was about to learn. When a person receives a great shock, that person both continues to function and doesn't. Let me explain: At that moment I could not stand up. But I was capable of sitting there on the cold sidewalk and registering quite clearly how I must look. My legs splayed, my hair askew, my bag strewn behind me. Some tiny part of me relished the spectacle. Students were cutting me a wide berth. I calculated what they must be thinking, how long it would take before someone bent down to ask if I was all right.

What would my answer be?

Seven

It was Saturday morning when the bullet began to throb. Not a steady ache, like my wrist. This felt more ragged, more demanding. The pain came and went, but when it was there it was hot. I imagined the bullet pulsing, like an organ.

Back when I was a girl, the whole country was caught up in the frenzy for the *Star Wars* movies. I was a baby when the first one came out, but I do remember weeping on the morning that *Return of the Jedi* hit the theaters. I must have been six or seven by then. Tony and Martin were allowed to go see it; I was deemed too young and ordered to stay home. It seemed an unbearable injustice. Afterward, my brothers annoyed me for weeks by conversing in garbled Yoda syntax ("Told you I did, the potatoes please pass"). They also joked about sensing a Disturbance in the Force. It sounds hokey, but thirty years later, this is the phrase that now came to mind. I did sense something like a Disturbance. As though the bullet wielded some force that was disturbing the normal rhythms of my body.

I thought about the veins and muscles in my neck. How for years they must have grown and pushed and curved around the lead, like the roots of a tree when they meet resistance from a stone.

I had been three years old when I was shot.

Three.

That meant the bullet had been inside my body for longer than my teeth.

I CALLED MY doctor late that afternoon.

Was it possible? I asked him. That an ancient wound could start hurting, just like that?

"Unlikely," he replied. "But describe the pain?"

I thought about it. "Hot. Like it's radiating heat or something."

"Well, it's definitely not doing that. Unless it's gotten infected, but I didn't see any sign of that when I examined you this week."

"Okay, but it really is . . . throbbing. I can feel the metal. The physical weight of it. Like it's jabbing me."

"I suspect that might be psychosomatic."

"I am not imagining this, Dr. Zartman."

"Call me Will. And I'm not suggesting you are. It would be an entirely normal reaction. Now that you know it's there, you're going to feel it. I suppose it's also possible that the bullet has shifted. Perhaps it's pressing on a nerve that it wasn't before."

"Why would it shift?"

"That I don't know."

"And would that be why my wrist started aching?"

A long pause. "I don't know that either. Half the patients I see seem to be suffering from mild cases of carpal tunnel. It's almost always because they spend too much time in front of their keyboards. So that was my natural assumption in your case. But if—if that bullet is pressing on a nerve—then, sure. Symptoms might be presenting in your wrist."

"And maybe I really am feeling pain in my neck, too."

He ignored this. "I'll call and hassle the lab again. Try to hurry them up on your blood work. I'd like to see your blood lead level. They work seven days a week over there. Maybe they'll have something by tomorrow."

"Thank you."

"And I should hear back on Monday from Marshall Gellert. The neurosurgeon. I couldn't track him down yesterday, but he's the best in town. I'll ask him to see you right away."

"And then what?"

"We'll have to see what he says. Meanwhile, what did you find out from your parents? Can they help with figuring out how it got there?"

I made a sound somewhere between a laugh and a bark. "You were right. They knew."

"And?"

I laugh-barked again. "How much time have you got?"

He listened for nearly an hour. After we hung up, I stepped out my front door and went for a long walk through the streets of Georgetown. No collapses this time. Just the steady beat of my boots hitting brick. And in my neck the dark mass of the bullet, throbbing, pulsing, keeping time.

• • •

THE TOMBS IS a Georgetown institution. A big, dark, brick cellar one block from campus. There's a bar on one end and a noisy restaurant packed with undergrads on the other. It is the kind of place where students meet their roommates for happy-hour pitchers and buffalo wings on a Saturday night, then return hungover the next morning, to meet their parents for an eggs-Benedict brunch. It's tradition to come to the door at midnight on your twenty-first birthday. They stamp you on the head and pour your first legal beer on the house.

I did think twice about turning up on Saturday night. I might bump into someone I knew from the university, and I wasn't in the mood for chitchat. But the thought of staying home was too depressing. Plus the Tombs is right around the corner from me, and I couldn't be bothered dressing up and heading anywhere swanky. So I called Martin and told him to meet me.

We settled ourselves in a leather booth in the back corner and sat staring at each other. Martin knows me too well to bother with small talk. Instead he flagged down a waiter, ordered the artichoke dip and a beer for himself, and a glass of white wine for me.

It is not quite true what I said earlier, about not liking whisky. I like rye whiskey fine. I can't stand Scotch, but a few years back I was seeing a man from Kentucky. He liked to drink Sazeracs, mixed with rye from a distillery near where he grew up. Rye tastes like bourbon but better. More peppery and less sweet. I acquired the taste and still drink it on the rare occasion when I am drinking to get drunk.

Martin knows this. He raised an eyebrow when I canceled the wine and requested instead a double Bulleit, neat.

All he said, though, was "Make it two."

We sipped in silence for a bit. Then he said, "Irritating, isn't it? How it's become all fashionable lately?"

"What?"

"Rye."

"It's fashionable?"

"Don't you ever go out? It's the hip thing. Laura and I actually got invited to a rye tasting the other night. All these fortysomethings who never drink anything but seventy-five-dollar-a-bottle Bordeaux, sipping and pretending to detect notes of green apple and tobacco."

"I just like the taste."

"See, that's the fashionable thing to say. Very authentic of you." He took another sip, then looked into my eyes. "You used to have nightmares, when you first came. You would crawl into my bed and curl up against me, hot and all wet with tears. When I woke up in the morning, you were always gone. Do you remember?"

"God, I'm getting sick of people asking me that."

He looked hurt.

"I'm sorry. Martin? I'm sorry. But you know, you're one of the worst parts of all this." I pointed at him. "You and me. Finding out that—that you're not really my brother."

"I am really your brother."

"You know what I mean."

"You mean we aren't related by blood."

I nodded.

"I thought about that, too." He glanced around, then

picked up a steak knife lying on the table. He held out his finger and drew the serrated blade across it. Drops of blood sprang out.

He reached across the table. "Your turn."

I must have looked aghast.

"Come on, trust me. Give me your hand."

I did as he said. The blade hurt more than you would think as it sank into my flesh.

He set down the knife and pressed his finger against mine. "Now I am. Your blood brother."

For the first time since this all began, I started to cry. I knew it was only a gesture, but at that moment it felt like the kindest thing anyone had ever done for me. We sat there, hands clasped, tears running down my face. He wrapped a napkin around our fingers and held it tight.

"Martin, I didn't mean—"

"Shush. You don't have to say anything."

He caught our waiter's eye and mouthed, *Two more*.

The waiter looked at me with misgiving, no doubt thinking I was enough of a mess as it was. But he trotted off. The drinks went down easy. We were on our third round when suddenly I grinned.

"What?" asked Martin.

"We're drinking Bulleit."

"So?"

"Pronounced *bull-it*. And I've got a bullet in my neck!"

"Not funny."

"Oh, come on, it's hilarious." I clinked my glass against his.

Slowly he smiled. "Technically, you know, we're drinking shots of Bulleit. Get it? Bullet shots?"

"Okay, *that* was lame," I said, but I started to laugh.

We were both laughing and laughing, and it was around that time that the room began to spin.

At some point Martin must have paid and bundled me up the Tombs' steep stairs, out onto Thirty-Sixth Street, and then home and into my own bed. Brothers are good for things like that.

Eight

If you have ever been run down and flattened by a bus, then you have some idea how I felt the next morning. I doubt I would have crawled out of bed at all if the phone hadn't rung.

"Did I wake you?" asked Will Zartman.

"No, no, I was just . . . Actually, yes. What time is it?"

"Coming up to eleven o'clock."

"Christ. Right. I had—I guess I had a big night last night."

"Oh. Out at a party?"

"Just a bar." I groaned. "I think I drank half my body weight in rye."

"Very trendy."

"So I'm told. I'd rather never see the stuff again."

"Hair of the dog," he said.

"Sorry?"

"Go fix yourself a Bloody Mary. You'll feel better. Only hangover cure I've ever tried that works. Mind you, that's just me talking. As your doctor, I suggest you make a pot of coffee and go back to bed. And of course never,

ever, consume more than four units of alcohol in a single session again."

"Right."

"So who were you out with?" he asked casually. "Some girlfriends?"

Was I imagining it, or was something more than purely medical solicitousness in his voice?

"My brother."

"Oh. Fun." He must also have sensed he'd crossed a line, because he cleared his throat and adopted a more clinical tone. "Anyway, sorry to have disturbed you on a Sunday morning. And I hate to be the bearer of bad news. But I got your results from the lab this morning. Nothing we need to be majorly alarmed about at this point, but your blood lead level is quite high."

"How high?"

"Twenty-nine. That's micrograms of lead per deciliter of blood. For adults, anything over twenty-five is considered elevated. That's when people start showing symptoms. Headache, irritability, delayed reaction time, that type thing."

"Great," I said miserably. "I needed something else to worry about."

"Of course, it could be completely unrelated. Where do you live?"

"Georgetown."

"Ah. Old house?"

"Eighteen fifty-nine." Georgetown is a historic district; almost all the houses are a hundred years old or more.

"Well, there you go. You could have lead paint on the walls. Or lead pipes. Do you drink DC tap water?"

"Every day."

"Ghastly stuff. Swimming with critters you don't even want to imagine. And of course, for years it was contaminated with dangerous levels of lead. But listen, put this out of your mind for now. We'll cross that bridge when we have to. It's just one more factor in the mix."

"In what mix?"

"In the mix as we make a decision. On whether to schedule surgery to try to get that bullet out."

A GOOGLE SEARCH turned up little.

I had finally dragged myself out of bed and brewed a pot of tea. Then I settled myself with my laptop on the living-room sofa and tried to ferret out any information I could find about Sadie Rawson and Boone Smith.

It was strange. These days even the dullest person would generate a dozen search hits, if only from friends tagging him in photos. But my birth parents had died fifteen years before the Internet became widespread. You couldn't google them.

The main newspaper in Atlanta, the *Journal-Constitution*, must have reported on the murders. Crime was worse back then in big American cities, but surely a double homicide and the near-fatal wounding of a child would have drawn media attention. But the *Journal-Constitution*'s online archives were only digitized back to 1990. Everything older was presumably on microfiche, gathering dust somewhere.

The only hit I got was for a class of 1974 "In Memoriam List," on the website for the University of North

Carolina at Chapel Hill. It had been updated this past spring, in advance of a fortieth-reunion gathering planned for next year. The list was titled "In memory of those classmates who have passed away since graduation" and included dozens of names. Both Boone and Sadie Rawson were on it. There was no other information, not even the date of their deaths.

That was it. No wedding announcement, no work-related press releases, no photographs.

I pulled out the birth certificate that my mother, Frannie, had fetched from the upstairs files for me. It stated that I had been delivered at Piedmont Hospital in Atlanta. The home address it gave for Boone and Sadie Rawson Smith was Eulalia Road, in the northeast of the city.

I plugged that into Google Maps and selected the street-view option. A minute later I was staring at their old house. Eulalia Road appeared to be a short, quiet, residential street. My first home had been in the middle of the block, a one-story brick house with a separate, detached garage farther up the driveway. The grass lawn in front had a big tree, which blocked my view of the front door itself. But you could see that the house was well kept, the brick and shutters freshly painted.

I had no way of knowing if this was the house in which my birth mother and father died. They were murdered three years after they had brought me home from the hospital. They might have moved. Still, I couldn't stop staring. The zoom function was frustratingly blurry; the picture wasn't sharp enough to let me see in the windows. Yes, I knew the interior would have been redecorated. The owners might have changed many times since

1979. No trace of me or of my first family would remain in that pretty, little house.

But all day long I kept wandering back to my laptop, hitting refresh on the image, and imagining a small girl, turning somersaults on that lawn.

I AM NOT known for rash decisions. I tend to drive my friends crazy, thinking and rethinking choices for weeks before finally staking out a course of action. It's the way I'm hardwired, the way I move physically as well: slowly, methodically, like a dancer moving through deep water. I think this is why, in my work, I'm drawn to the literature of centuries past. I *like* that Marcel Proust spends thirty pages describing how his character tosses and turns in bed before falling asleep. And that's the action-packed part of his masterpiece, *In Search of Lost Time*. Proust meanders for a further six volumes before wrapping things up. It's a gorgeous book. By comparison, contemporary literature feels too frenetic.

Suffice to say, I am not a taker of spur-of-the-moment trips. But that evening, my thoughts kept circling back to the house in Atlanta. I wondered what color the shutters had been painted when my birth parents lived there. I wondered how tall the tree out front had stood, what kind of car they had parked in the garage. I wanted to see it. I wanted to go there, see the house, and find whatever remained of my first life.

It felt urgent. The more I thought about it, the more certain I was that I would be too distracted to go through the motions of my normal routine tomorrow. I never miss work; I couldn't remember taking a sick day in all the years I'd worked at the university. But surely this counted as a personal emergency? And I actually was unwell, I thought, touching my neck. It would be tricky: Fall semester was in full swing. I had four lectures to teach in the week ahead. But the next break in the academic calendar wasn't until Thanksgiving. The end of next month. I would go crazy if I waited that long.

I thought for a while, rubbing circles up and down my wrist. Then I checked the clock—9:00 p.m., not yet too late to call—and looked up the phone number for Madame Aubuchon.

Hélène Aubuchon is the formidable head of Georgetown's French Department. She is in her seventies, but her posture (not to mention her legs) puts students four decades younger to shame. The French use an acronym, CPCH, to describe a certain type of aristocratic woman. It stands for *Collier de Perles, Carré Hermès*—meaning, a lady too well bred to leave the house without her pearl necklace and Hermès scarf. Hélène must have perfected the look in Paris back in the 1960s, and she'd remained immaculately pulled together ever since. I respected her, and I was also a little afraid of her.

She answered on the fourth ring. *"Allô?"*

"Bonsoir, Madame Aubuchon? Je suis désolée de vous déranger . . ." We had worked together for years now, but I still addressed her with the formal *vous*. Hélène Aubuchon, in my experience, was not prone to informality.

"I'm so sorry to bother you at home," I continued in rapid French. "But I've had a bit of a family emergency. I'm going to need to take a few days off."

"Ah. When were you thinking?"

"Well, ideally, starting tomorrow."

"Non. Tout à fait impossible," she said sternly. "But you know this. Not in the middle of the term."

"I've just found out I was adopted. When I was very young. I never knew."

"Oh là là. Ma chère. That must have been a shock. However, I need you to run the study-abroad session on Wednesday evening. And you are needed in the classroom, that sophomore tutorial *surtout*—"

"The reason I was adopted is that my mother and father were murdered."

Silence.

"And may I tell you how I learned all this? It's because doctors discovered a bullet in my neck. Right up against my spine. It was fired there by whoever murdered my parents. They shot me, too."

More silence. Then: *"Mais je ne comprends pas."* I don't understand. "A bullet?"

"Yes. In my neck."

"But—you don't—you don't mean it's still there?"

"It is. I can send you the X-ray if you like. The bullet glows bright white."

"And your parents were—you said they were *murdered*?"

"My birth parents, yes."

She let out a little poof of air. *"Oh là là là là là là."* I imagined her loosening the Hermès and fanning herself. *"Je m'excuse.* Take as much time as you need."

• • •

A QUICK CHECK online revealed that flights departed Reagan National Airport for Atlanta nearly every hour tomorrow. They weren't prohibitively expensive, either. I picked a midmorning departure, Delta flight 1139.

Then I opened a small suitcase and began tossing in sweaters, leggings, a caramel-colored suede skirt. What did one pack for such a trip? What passed for an appropriate wardrobe for an outing to lay flowers on the graves of a mother and a father you had never known? When I had booked my plane ticket, the computer asked whether I was traveling for business or pleasure. Umm, neither. Not even remotely.

I jotted down a list of everyone I should remember to tell that I was leaving town. My family, obviously. A student for whom I'd agreed to serve as thesis adviser. Also, Will Zartman. His name gave me pause. I was supposed to go see his neurosurgeon colleague next week. I reached up and touched my neck. The pain was less intense today. Will was probably right: I was only imagining I could feel something. The neurosurgery consult could wait. That bullet had been in my neck for thirty-four years; another few days wouldn't hurt.

It occurred to me that there must be knock-on effects from this week's surreal developments that hadn't even dawned on me yet. Yesterday, for example, after hanging up with Will, I reflected that all my life I had blithely filled in medical forms claiming no family history of diabetes or heart disease. Whereas, for all I knew, all four of my biological grandparents had dropped dead from massive coronaries. I had no clue what my family medical history was.

I felt a stab of fury toward my parents. My *adoptive* parents, if that was the right term. By what right had they kept so much from me? How could they have thought I would not want to know? What made it worse was that I was closer to my parents than to anyone else in the world. They could both read me like a book. I had assumed the reverse was true as well.

Now I felt a shift. A fracturing. The decoupling of souls.

You think you know people when you grow up with them. When you believe they've been beside you your whole life. You know their voices, the curves of their hands, what makes them laugh. You know their hearts.

But it turns out you don't know their thoughts. Not truly, not in full. All people have their secrets, and not just things they keep from you, but secrets *about* you. Things they hope you'll never learn. You can share your home with someone, share all the silly, little details of life, share the soap, the sugar bowl, shoes—and you would never guess.

You think you know someone.

Then, at the age of thirty-seven, you grow up.

Nine

I woke up hungry, which—considering I hadn't eaten in four days—seemed a good sign.

My favorite breakfast is a ham-and-cheese croissant from Pâtisserie Poupon on Wisconsin Avenue. This pleasant spot is cramped but sunny, and the only place in Washington that produces croissants and baguettes that taste remotely the way they do in Paris. They also bake a bacon quiche that—trust me on this—will change your life. Amazing what a pastry chef unafraid to embrace obscene quantities of butter, salt, and pork can achieve. I suspect the same formula is at work in the *croissant jambon fromage*, which is why, for the sake of my thighs, I try to limit myself to stopping by no more than twice a week.

Pâtisserie Poupon is only a few minutes' walk from my house. I could head there for a croissant and tea, swing back home for my suitcase, and still make it to the airport in plenty of time. When I got there, though, I was greeted with a locked door and a CLOSED ON MONDAYS sign. No, no, no. I always forgot this inconvenient detail. I pressed my nose against the glass and squinted, desperate enough to beg an off-duty employee to open up and sell me yesterday's remnants. But the bakery was deserted, swept clean, chairs neatly stacked on tables, sunlight glinting off empty display cases. Not a croissant in sight.

Discouraged, I retraced my steps home. I would have to settle for a gluey bagel at the airport. More taste of cardboard. Although wasn't there a café that sold decent prosciutto paninis, right after the security line? Which terminal was that again? I was trying to recall as I rounded the corner onto my block and spotted a man standing on my front step.

I stopped in my tracks.

It was Will Zartman. My doctor, leaning on my doorbell and looking agitated.

"Dr. Zartman? Is that you? What on earth are you doing here?" I glanced at my watch; it was not yet nine o'clock.

"Caroline! Hi. Hi there. I told you, call me Will." He heaved a deep breath. "I thought I'd missed you."

"You did, nearly. I'm just grabbing my bag. But why are you—"

"I got your message when I woke up. I've been trying to call. I must have tried you five times. Don't you ever answer your phone?"

I considered this. I'd left my cell phone in the house, propped on top of my suitcase. I often wander out without it. Not out of forgetfulness, but because I spend too much time around teenage students who can't conduct a five-minute, face-to-face conversation without twitching for their phones. I like my friends as much as the next person, but I don't feel the need to tweet them my thoughts a dozen times a day. And anyone who needs to reach me can probably wait an hour or two. I don't have the kind of job that demands urgent responses. So, no— on an early walk for my morning croissant, I don't ever answer my phone.

"Why are you here? Is something wrong?"

"Is something *wrong*? You mean, aside from your experiencing a burning sensation in your neck, and the fact that an X-ray just confirmed there's a bullet in there? I thought we'd agreed that you would see Marshall this week. The surgeon. You need to talk to him."

"I will. As soon as I get back. I just need a couple of days."

"No. Leaving town is a bad idea. That's why I kept calling. You shouldn't be traveling. I'm worried that you—"

"But *why* are you worried? A week ago you barely knew who I was, and now here you—"

"I knew who you were. Any man under the age of ninety and still in full possession of his faculties would notice who you were."

I raised my eyebrows.

To my surprise, he did not blush or back down. Instead he leaned forward and gripped my right wrist. "Look, you need to take this seriously. A bullet rubbing against your spine is not something to mess around with." He turned my arm over, studied it. "You're not wearing your wrist guard."

"It's been feeling better."

"No, I'll bet it hasn't."

"Oh my God! I know whether my own wrist hurts.

And anyway, whether it hurts or not is none of your—" I clamped my mouth shut. Whether my wrist hurt was of course precisely his business. "I'm going to be late," I said, changing tack. "I promise I'll go see your friend Marshall. Later this week, if you like. Now excuse me."

I unlocked the door, plucked my phone and suitcase from the front hall, and pulled the door shut again.

Will was still standing there. "How are you getting to the airport?"

"Taxi. I'll get one on M Street."

"You'll be lucky to catch one in rush hour." He pulled out his phone, glanced at the time. "My first patient isn't booked until ten. My car's right here. I'll drive you."

"Across the river? To National Airport?" It wasn't far, maybe twenty minutes' drive. Still. "I'll be fine."

"For God's sake, get in the car."

So I did. He was right; traffic was terrible. We inched along in silence. An accident had narrowed Memorial Bridge down to one lane for cars crossing into Virginia. Beneath us the river flowed sullenly, the water choppy and brown.

Will's Jeep had a baseball glove and tennis rackets thrown in the back. The radio was tuned to NPR. We listened as the *Morning Edition* anchors delivered gloomy updates on the latest horrors in Mali, in Syria, on Capitol Hill. Strangely, my mood lifted as they forged on. So many people in the world had worse problems than I did. By the time the newscasters introduced a story about an oil spill and the resulting environmental catastrophe off the coast of Norway, I broke into a grin.

Will glanced over. "Oil spills are funny?"

"No, but honestly, are you listening to this?" I shook my head. "If we don't all die from toxic oil fumes, we'll be overwhelmed by rising Islamist militants from the Middle East. There's no hope."

He grinned, too. "I was only playing NPR to impress you. Want music instead?"

"Sure. Whatever you like to listen to is fine."

He hesitated. "Country, actually. You probably think it's corny. But, yeah, I love it. Waylon Jennings, Johnny Cash, Hank Williams, all the old honky-tonk stuff. Garth Brooks isn't bad."

"No. Seriously? Garth Brooks?"

"Well, but mostly I listen to C-SPAN radio. Obviously. Unlike you, I find there's nothing like live coverage of a House Agriculture subcommittee to get a guy going in the morning."

I smiled. We fell quiet again, but the silence was more amiable now. I studied his hands on the steering wheel. No wedding ring.

Will Zartman was not my type. I tend to go for undernourished, slightly tragic-looking academics. You know the sort: pale, artsy guys who chain-smoke while wearing skinny jeans and black turtlenecks. It's a pathology, I know. Too much time spent studying abroad in Paris during my formative romantic years. My penchant for the Euro look has provided endless amusement for my brothers over the years; they excuse themselves to the kitchen and break out in the "Sprockets" routine from *Saturday Night Live* whenever I bring a new boyfriend home. Tony in particular has perfected Mike Myers's mincing hip wriggle ("Now is ze time vhen ve dance!").

Annoyingly, I had the feeling that Tony and Martin would like Will. He looked both robustly healthy and robustly American. He was into country music, of all things. Definitely not my type.

Will pulled up to the curb at airport departures exactly fifty-two minutes before my flight was scheduled to take off. I didn't have luggage to check; I should just make it.

"Thanks for the ride. It was awfully nice of you." I reached for the car door. He saw me flinch as I jerked at the handle with my right hand.

"Hang on." He put the car in park, jumped out, ran around, and opened my door from the outside. "Door-to-door service. There you go."

I felt simultaneously charmed and irritated. "Okay. Well. Thanks again."

"I'm going to make that appointment for you with Marshall Gellert. How about the end of this week?"

"Fine."

"But will you back here by then?" He searched my face.

I nodded. "By Wednesday or Thursday, I would think. I need a few days down in Atlanta. To try to make peace with things. And to see their old house and whatever else is left to see, which I'm guessing isn't much."

"Right. But, Caroline, if that bullet is pressing down on a nerve . . . if that's what has inflamed your wrist . . . then you really need to get it checked. Before there's any further damage. Promise."

"Cross my heart."

Then, before I quite understood what was happening,

he stepped close. I smelled soap and coffee and something else, an animal scent, as though he'd recently been in the company of a warm dog. He lifted a lock of my hair. His fingers slid down the dark curl, then closed around it and held still for a moment. My breath caught. The gesture was astonishingly intimate.

He dropped the curl lightly on my shoulder and stepped back. "Be careful. Take care of yourself."

"I will." I couldn't think what else to say, so I turned and walked toward the bright lights of the terminal. Glass doors slid open and then sealed shut behind me. I did not look back, and for two days I did not again think of Will Zartman.

PART TWO

Atlanta

Ten

I wish that I could report a dramatic development the first time I stood outside that house on Eulalia Road.

It was early afternoon on Monday when I pulled my rental car up to the curb. The front of the house was in shadow, and the street was quiet. Either few children lived on this block or else they were not yet home from school. Wind rustled the leaves of the graceful elm tree that dominated the front yard. How old must that tree be? Fifty years old? Seventy-five? It was stout enough that it must already have been well established when the Smiths lived here. I must have played under these branches, must have tried to wrap chubby little arms around this trunk. I waited for an epiphany. For some ancient shard of memory to dislodge itself and come rushing back to me.

But no: it was just a tree. The house was just a house. I felt nothing.

I crossed the lawn, climbed five brick steps to the front porch, and knocked.

No answer.

I knocked again and was about to conclude the house was empty when the door cracked open.

"Yes?" An older woman's voice. I could see a patch of gray hair above the safety chain, which remained fastened.

"Hello, forgive me for disturbing you. My name's Caroline Cashion, and I used to live in this house, when I was a child."

Silence.

I fished in my handbag and produced my business card, embossed with the university seal and indicating my status as a member of the faculty. I'd found that pulling rank as a professor could prove useful. Even in Washington, where the average government intern probably wields more actual power than I do, the title commands respect. It's as if people hear *professor* and are transported back to their student days, a period in their lives when teachers represented ultimate authority.

Sure enough, the chain dropped and the door swung open.

Inside, the scrawny, nervous-looking woman introduced herself as Nan Dorminy. She loved the house, she told me. Great morning light. She'd bought it nine years ago, when her husband left her. He was a good man, she insisted, misinterpreting my startled look. I shouldn't think otherwise. He just needed his space.

I nodded politely. Were Southerners always this forthcoming around strangers? "Men can be like that," I offered, hoping this was an appropriate response.

Apparently it was, because Nan Dorminy clasped her hands together as though a point of disagreement had been settled. Now then, she asked, when exactly had I lived here, and what could she help me with?

"Thirty-four years ago," I told her.

"Oh, I've no idea who was living here then."

"My parents were the Smiths. Boone and Sadie Rawson Smith." I watched for a sign that she recognized the name. Surely it would have been notorious for a while in this neighborhood.

But she shook her head.

I tried again. "They were—it's a terrible story. But they died in this house, I think. They were killed. Back in the seventies."

Her chin jerked up. "Oh. Oh, yes. Old Mrs. Carter told me something about that. Years ago, when I moved in. There was a whole nice family that died. A little girl, too. But the property's changed hands several times since then."

"No, that's just it. The little girl was me. I was—I was injured, when they died. But I survived. I moved away."

"Good heavens." Her hand fluttered to her heart.

We stood without speaking for a moment.

Then I asked, "This Mrs. Carter you mentioned. Is she a neighbor? Did it sound like she knew my parents?"

"She might have. But I'm afraid she's dead now, too. She passed away last summer. Or was it two summers ago? Her niece got the house." Mrs. Dorminy frowned. "I can't think of anyone on Eulalia who goes back that far. Thirty-four years. A long time."

She agreed to show me around, in case anything jogged my memory. But she was right. Thirty-four years is a long time. The house had been renovated. She pointed proudly to where previous owners had blown out the back to build an eat-in kitchen, and how she herself had knocked two bedrooms together to make space for a master bath. The old pantry had been converted to a laundry room. None of the internal walls were where they used to be.

There was only one moment, when I asked what lay behind a door off the main hallway.

"Oh, that's just the attic," she sniffed. "Hot as Hades up there in the summertime." She opened the door to reveal a dark staircase leading up. The steps were worn wood, stacked with paint cans piled three and four high. An assortment of dried-out paintbrushes and mixing pans clogged the remaining surfaces. She appeared to use the staircase as shelving, storage for tools for half-forgotten home-improvement projects. But something about the slant of the stairs, and the sharp smell of dust and unfinished wood, tugged at me. I closed my eyes and breathed in. Something flickered. It felt as if there should be a light switch, on the left, not a modern flip switch, but the old-fashioned kind, a metal chain you have to yank. When I peered into the dim opening, there it was.

But Mrs. Dorminy was already pulling me back. "It's been cleared out up there, if that's what you're wondering," she said, not unkindly. "It's only my old clothes up there now. I'm not the kind of person who would move into a house filled with other people's things."

She shut the door and the moment passed.

Afterward I sat in the rental car, staring at the elm tree. It was still just a tree. Just bark and branches, no epiphanies hiding there. Faulkner's famous line came to me: *The past is never dead. It's not even past.* William Faulkner would know. Southern writers feel the weight of the past more heavily, capture it more precisely, than those from anywhere else. Not even Proust, not even Joyce, can touch them.

In this case, though, Faulkner had missed the mark.

The past was past. Whatever love or laughter or fear or sorrow I had known in that house remained lost to me. The girl who had once climbed those attic stairs was a ghost, nothing but a ghost.

Eleven

My appointment at the *Atlanta Journal-Constitution* was both productive and painful.

I had reasoned that the newspaper might be a source of names. The coverage back in 1979 must have quoted people who knew the Smiths, friends of the family and that type of thing. I had the vague sense that if I could find someone who had once looked my parents in the eyes, who could share a few old stories about them, it would provide me some sense of closure. If that failed, at least the archives might contain details that would help fill in my sketchy understanding of how—not to mention why—my birth parents had died.

But as I've mentioned, the paper's website only went back to 1990. So yesterday, after leaving Eulalia Road, I had called the main number. The newspaper proved impenetrable in that hostile way unique to bureaucracies that are allegedly eager to interact with their readers and community. I was disconnected twice and transferred to voice mail more times than I can count, before I finally found myself speaking to one Jessica Yeo.

Initially, she was also unhelpful. Any request for articles from the 1970s would take some time, Jessica informed me. The best thing would be to e-mail my specific query to customerquestions@ajc.com. Someone would get back to me. Given my recent attempt to navigate the switchboard, I doubted that. I tried to clarify that my query involved a private matter that might better be explained in person. She sounded even less interested. All kinds of kooks must call the newsroom, claiming hot news tips they needed to pass on in person.

"Look," I said finally, when I sensed she was about to hang up on me, "I'm only in town for a day or two. If it matters, I'm calling from Georgetown University. I'm on faculty there and—"

"You're faculty at Georgetown?"

"Yes. It's Professor Caroline Cashion."

Ah, the old professorial passe-partout. It worked like a charm. She sighed and allowed that she might have a few minutes if I could swing by the next day, first thing.

So this morning at nine I had pulled up outside the black, glass box of a building that housed the *Journal-Constitution*. Surprisingly, the newspaper was not downtown, but in the suburbs, set deep in one of those bland office-park mazes that are ubiquitous these days across America. Only one small, easy-to-miss sign identified the headquarters of Atlanta's venerable newspaper. For a moment I wondered whether I'd come to a satellite office, perhaps where the printing presses or the sales team resided, rather than the news hub. I checked the address: Perimeter Center Parkway. This was definitely it.

When she appeared in the lobby, Jessica Yeo also

looked nothing like I'd expected. I had expected the
newspaper librarian to look more . . . well, more like a librarian. Sensible shoes, reading glasses hanging from a
neck chain, maybe a prairie skirt. But Jessica Yeo might
have just stepped out of a boho coffee shop in Berkeley.
She was young and wore a floaty, flowered hippie dress
utterly ill-suited to the autumn weather outside. This was
accessorized by blue nail polish, nose and eyebrow pierc-
ings, and a wild cloud of frizzy, dark hair.

From the way she eyed me, I guessed I didn't fit her
image of an academic, either. I was wearing a black,
leather dress over leggings and stiletto boots. The black
matched my mood, the boots lent me confidence, and
again—if there was such a thing as an appropriate wardrobe for this project, I was damned if I could figure it
out. We sized each other up and shook hands, then she
led me across the lobby.

She was not in fact a librarian but a research assistant
for the news department. This meant helping reporters
check facts, find sources, and track down phone numbers. She walked fast, her cowboy boots clacking over the
tiled floor, explaining over her shoulder that she only had
a few minutes. Things would get busy after the 9:30 a.m.
editorial meeting. At the end of a hallway she waved her
ID badge at a scanner, and a door clicked open. We
stepped into an ugly, beige room stacked floor to ceiling
with newspapers and mismatched filing cabinets.

"The archives room. Such as it is," said Jessica. "So,
what dates are we talking?"

"Fall of 1979. October or November, I think. The

names to search for would be Boone Smith and his wife, Sadie Rawson."

"Mmm. Smith is too common a name. There'll be a zillion stories. But we might get somewhere with Boone and—what was the other name? Rawson?"

"That's right. Sadie Rawson."

"And it's just one article you're trying to find?"

"I don't know, actually. I'm hoping there might be several. They might be spread out over a few weeks."

She sighed and turned toward a shelf stuffed with large, navy, clothbound books. Near the far end were two labeled 1979. The spines were held together by Scotch tape.

"Our incredibly high-tech index," she sniffed, yanking out a swivel chair with caster wheels and plopping down. "Theoretically, everybody mentioned in the newspaper should be in here. Theoretically, mind you." She began flipping through yellowed pages. They looked as though they'd been produced on a typewriter; the letters had faded to reddish brown.

Jessica was right. There were a zillion entries for Smith. But toward the bottom of the list, under *Smith, Sadie Rawson and Boone*, there was a date. Actually, four dates, along with notations of which pages and sections the articles had run in. The first had appeared on November 7, 1979.

"Bingo!" crowed Jessica. "All righty then, let's see what we've got."

She began riffling through drawers, pulling out boxes of microfilm. Then she dug the scuffed cowboy boots into the carpet and rolled herself, still seated, across the room. She stopped in front of an enormous machine that must have represented cutting-edge technology around the time that story was written in 1979. Jessica kicked one boot absentmindedly against a metal cabinet as she threaded the film and began to fast-forward. Minutes passed. You could practically hear the machine groan with the effort of dredging up names that had lain forgotten for so long.

At last the correct edition came into focus. The story bore a simple headline: "Buckhead Couple Shot, Killed." She zoomed in, and we began to read.

ATLANTA—A Delta Airlines pilot and his wife were shot and killed Tuesday afternoon in their Buckhead home, and authorities said they were searching for clues as to why the couple may have been attacked.

Boone and Sadie Rawson Smith, both 26, were shot sometime after 3 p.m., Atlanta police said.

"This may have been a robbery that escalated into a shooting," said Lt. Steve Meadows, commander of the Atlanta Police Department's homicide unit. "We're working all angles right now."

Investigators had made no arrests as of Tuesday night, Meadows said. He urged the public to come forward with tips about the shooting on Eulalia Road, just south of Peachtree Road in northeast Atlanta.

Jessica bit her lip. "You said you needed this for personal reasons. Did you know them?"

I had a hard lump in my throat. "They were my parents."

She jerked around in her chair and stared at me in horror. "Your *parents*?"

"Yeah."

"Jesus Christ. I'm so sorry."

"It's okay. I mean, obviously, it's not okay. But I was really young. I don't remember it." I coughed. "I grew up somewhere else and only just found out about all this, to be honest. Long, strange story."

"Jesus."

"Anyway." I avoided her gaze. "Anyway, I wanted to see what had been written about them. Could you print me a copy of that?"

"Sure."

"And check for the other articles?"

She found all four of the stories that mentioned my birth parents. The next day, November 8, 1979, a follow-up story had appeared. It divulged no new details on the police investigation. But the reporter had done some digging and learned that the Smiths had been college sweethearts in Chapel Hill, North Carolina, and had been the parents of a three-year-old daughter. No mention of her name, or what had happened to her. What had happened to me.

The third story had run the following Monday, November 12. The day of the funeral. Several neighbors and family friends were quoted. But it was the photograph that made me gasp. A grainy but large photo, showing a young couple, arms around each other's waists, standing beside a backyard barbecue grill. The man had tongs in one hand and a grin on his face. He looked pleasant. I did not recognize him. But her. God, *her*. I felt the dizzying sensation of looking into a trick mirror. The kind you find in the dressing rooms of discount stores that reflect you either ten pounds lighter or ten pounds heavier than your true self and distort your features just enough that you appear both recognizably yourself and disconcertingly foreign.

Or perhaps that is too cryptic a description. The simple fact is, she looked just like me. Her hair was different—darker than mine, and sculpted into *Charlie's Angels* wings, which would have been the rage back then. She might have been a few inches shorter, too, although it was hard to tell. The eyes, though. The lips, the smile. Identical. The curves, too, on display in a tube top and bell-bottom jeans. You could show this photo to any of my friends today, and at first glance their only questions would be why I was dressed for a seventies theme party, and who was the guy beside me flipping burgers.

I reached up and touched the screen. "I've never seen them before," I whispered.

"She looks like you. Or I guess, you look like her. You really do."

I began to cry. Quietly at first and then great, wrenching sobs. I had perhaps not believed it until that moment. There is a difference between knowing something in your mind and knowing it in your heart. I had by now seen my original birth certificate, and the MRI and the X-ray. But they had not packed the visceral punch of staring at a face nearly identical to my own. My mother. My flesh and blood, undeniable, her eyes smiling up at me for the first time in more than thirty years.

• • •

JESSICA HUSTLED ME into a conference room down the hall and brought coffee. It was scalding and carried the saccharine whiff of artificial sweetener, but I drank it anyway. I blew my nose on a paper napkin.

"You okay now?"

"Yes. Sorry. I didn't intend to start blubbering."

"Don't be silly."

"I wasn't prepared for that photo."

"How could you be? How could anyone? I can't imagine."

Jessica patted my leg and told me to sit tight for a minute. When she reappeared, she was carrying several printed sheets of paper. The archived articles.

"There was only one more." She handed them to me. "From a few days after the funeral. Odds and ends about the investigation, how a suspect had been questioned and released. They don't give his name. And there's a little more about you. They don't give your name, either. It just talks about how the daughter was injured in the shooting, and how she was still recovering."

I flipped through the stack.

"Maybe read them later?" she asked gently. She had been gracious, but clearly she needed to get back to work.

"Sure. It's just—it's not much, is it?"

"What do you mean?"

"Well, I know they weren't famous or rich or anything. But four short articles? That doesn't seem like much. Wouldn't this have been a pretty sensational crime? A handsome couple and their cute toddler, shot in cold blood in their own home? In a nice neighborhood? I'm surprised there wasn't more coverage."

Jessica considered this. "Bear in mind the police would have wanted to keep a lid on how much information they gave out. Anything that gets in the paper can tip off the perpetrator. That's always the way. Reporters tend to know a lot more than they're allowed to print. And look at the date." She tapped a blue fingernail against the top printout. "Nineteen seventy-nine. They were dealing with, like, two dozen murders a month back then. Atlanta was the murder capital of the country."

"Really?" I had no idea.

"Oh, yeah. You must remember the Atlanta child murders. The bodies of children kept turning up in the woods, then in the river. Awful stuff. We did a big anniversary feature reminding people about it, right after I started working here. When was that?" She counted on her fingers. "Four years ago. Right. And the story was pegged to the thirtieth anniversary. So there you go! Nineteen seventy-nine."

She looked pleased with herself for figuring this out. "We dug up some unbelievable archive photos to run with that story. Totally gruesome. But it does help answer your question. The cops were probably overwhelmed. They would have had a massive backlog of cases, and the child murders were making national headlines. Investigators would have been focused on the kids. Maybe your parents got a little lost in the shuffle."

"Maybe." I thought about this. "You think the reporters covering crime might have been overwhelmed, too? That would explain why there aren't many stories."

"I guess. Who was it that covered your parents?" She

reached for the articles. "Huh! Funny I didn't notice. I don't know her." She pointed at the byline on the first story, someone named Janice Fleming. "But this one. Leland Brett. He's one of our managing editors."

"What, you mean still?"

"He's worked here forever. Leland's probably upstairs on the sixth floor right now."

THE NEWSROOM WAS disconcertingly bright and modern.

I wanted it to look the way the *Washington Post* does in *All the President's Men*: a warren of chipped desks, drowning under piles of paper and clattering typewriters and flasks of whiskey. A place where unshaven reporters plied their trade, weaseling news tips out of shady sources. The way newspapers are supposed to look. But the *Journal-Constitution* newsroom could have passed for a travel agency. Or a suburban bank. Cheerful blue-and-orange color scheme, glass internal walls, Aeron chairs. Everything looked sleek and sterile and anatomically correct.

Everything, except Leland Brett's office.

He seemed to have missed the memo. His desk was parked in a ratty, stale-smelling corner. Ancient, pink *While You Were Out* . . . phone messages scrawled in fading ink were taped two and three deep on the windows and glass walls, blocking out most natural light. Jessica had knocked and shoved me through his door with only the briefest of introductions ("She's a professor up at Georgetown; you wrote about her family ages ago") and then disappeared. I was left clutching the sheaf of papers and wondering where to begin. What exactly did I want to know from this man?

Fortunately, he made a great show of politeness, ushering me in and pulling up a chair across from me. I resisted the urge to brush off the upholstery before taking a seat.

"So, what do we have here, pretty lady?" Brett was short and puffy, with blond hair that had thinned to just a few pale tuffets, dotted across his scalp. He looked about sixty. He adjusted reading glasses on his nose and reached for the articles, brushing his hand along my leg as he took them from me. Pretty lady? And touching my thigh? Surely they didn't still do things that way down in Georgia. Or maybe they did. I frowned and explained as succinctly as I could that my birth parents had been killed in Atlanta in 1979, that I had been adopted and had only just found out about the murders, and that he had written the original stories for the *Journal-Constitution*.

"I would have written them for the *Journal*," he corrected me. "We didn't merge newsrooms until a few years after that. The *Journal* was the evening paper; the *Constitution* came out every morning. But let's see what you've got."

He scanned the first two articles with an air of concentration, then glanced up. "I can't say I remember this. I've written a lot of murder stories over the years, sorry to say. You say these people were your folks?"

"Yes."

"Awful shame. What a pity."

He turned back to reading. When he got to the third story—the one with the photograph—something sparked in his eyes. "You know, I think maybe I do remember them. Good-looking kids. They never caught the guy, did they?"

He ran his finger down the pages. "That's right. That's right. They had a baby girl. I'm guessing that must have been you, am I right?" His gaze met mine and then wandered down appreciatively.

Oh, dear. So the thigh brush had not been accidental. "It was me. Mr. Brett, would you have any idea how to reach these people you quoted? It looks like you interviewed a couple of neighbors, and also someone you identify as a close friend of Sadie Rawson Smith's. I'd love to talk to them."

"No idea." He scratched his head, puffing up the blond tufts until a clump of them stood on end. "You could certainly check if the neighbors are still living in their same houses. And as for the friend . . . what was her name?"

I pointed to a quote in the third article, attributed to a woman named Cheral Rooney.

"Cheral Rooney . . . Nope, no, ma'am, doesn't ring a bell."

"Might you still have old notes that you've kept? I suppose they would be on paper, not computer, from back then."

He looked over at a cardboard box dumped in a corner, overflowing with small, spiral-bound notebooks. "I do keep them. But not as far back as that. We moved headquarters three years ago. I threw most everything out."

I was impressed, despite myself, that he'd managed to

accumulate so much clutter in a mere three years. "What about the investigation itself? I'd love to get some insight into why the Smiths were killed. There's a cop quoted who suggests it might have been a burglary gone wrong."

"Sounds likely. I don't recollect any whiff of their being mixed up in any trouble. Nothing that might have got them killed."

"You talked to a cop who told you they brought a suspect in for questioning—"

"Did I?"

I showed Brett the relevant paragraph. "See, right here. But they let him go."

"Well, they probably brought in lots of people for questioning. I honestly don't remember. And let me level with you. I was a kid then. I must have been—let's see—twenty-four, twenty-five years old. Covering general-assignment stories, whatever the editors decided to throw at me that morning. I didn't have police sources. I swallowed whatever they told me and wrote it up."

"But this commander you quoted . . ." I searched the copy for the name. " 'Steve Meadows, commander of the Atlanta Police Department's homicide unit.' You must have talked to him."

"I'm sure I did. But that was *thirty-four years ago*. Who knows? It's possible I lifted that quote from a briefing, or a press release. I wish I could tell you that I had a direct pipeline to the homicide chief, I really do. Not that it would have done me much good. The Atlanta PD was even more screwed up back in those days than it is now. Understaffed, same as today. The guys working homicide could barely keep their heads above water. Meadows or whatever his name was likely didn't have a damn clue who took out your parents."

That seemed a rather indelicate way of putting things, and I shot Brett a dirty look.

"Sorry. But it's the truth."

I took a deep breath and willed myself to keep going. "Your colleague Jessica"—I cocked my head back toward the newsroom—"Jessica said reporters often know more than they're able to print."

"She's right. But whatever I might have once known about this story, I've forgotten long ago. I'm sorry, sweetheart."

He leaned back and flicked his gaze up and down my legs again. "I tell you what. I'll have one of the interns look at this today. See if they can track down a phone number for one of those neighbors who used to know your mom and dad. And meanwhile, I've had a thought."

I waited.

"What I'm thinking is, you're a great story, in and of yourself. We could interview you. Write up a profile. About your coming back to Atlanta, coming home after all these years, trying to find out about your family. It could be a sweet little update."

I shook my head no.

"Now, hang on, hear me out. There might be readers out there who remember your folks. Certainly our older readers still remember that period in the city in general. Terrible time. Late seventies, early eighties, new murders rolling in every other day. It would be great if one of them turned out to have a happy ending after all this time."

"A happy ending? My parents died."

"True. My apologies, didn't mean to sound disrespectful. But what I was fixing to say was that you turned out so well. After everything your family suffered. A college professor, and a beauty to boot."

"No," I said firmly.

"We could talk about it over dinner."

"No, thank you." I narrowed my eyes in a way intended to signal that my refusal covered both the story proposal and the dinner invitation.

"As you like. But think about it this way. Friends of the family might see the story and want to get in touch. Or old work colleagues of your dad's. Who knows who might be out there? If my interns don't turn up anything, it's your best shot at locating people who knew your parents."

He had a point. I pressed my lips together. "Thanks for the offer. I'll think about it."

I DROVE FROM the newsroom to the cemetery.

The obituary that Leland Brett had written that ran the day of the funerals mentioned the burial location. Arlington Memorial Park was in a neighborhood called Sandy Springs, just a ten-minute drive from the newspaper. A pretty cemetery. Tasteful fountains, small, landscaped lakes. If it weren't for all the mausoleums and marble, the place could have passed for an upscale golf course.

I stopped at the front office, housed in a squat building inside the gates.

"Hi," I greeted the woman behind the desk. "I'm trying to find a specific grave."

"Write the deceased's name down here," she said. "I'll see if anyone's free to do a location lookup."

Five minutes later another woman appeared, wearing a black pantsuit and carrying a pink-highlighted map. I reached out my hand for it.

"Did you drive?" This second woman had a harsh, nasal accent. New York maybe, or New Jersey.

"I did, yes."

"Easier if you just follow me then. The sections aren't well marked. People get lost, drive around for an hour looking. I was ready for a smoke break anyway."

I hopped back in my Mazda rental car and followed. She led for five minutes along smooth, paved roads lined with pine and magnolia trees. Birdsong came to me; a pair of robins flitted between our cars. Eventually she pulled over and rolled down her window.

"Should be right over there." She pointed down one of several rows marked by small, circular stones set flush in the ground. "Want me to get out and find it with you?"

"No, I'll be fine. Thanks. Thanks very much."

The day had warmed up considerably since I'd left my hotel this morning. An unseasonably mild breeze ruffled my hair as I climbed out of the car. Bright sunshine glinted off the asphalt. I shed my jacket, unwound my scarf, and threw them both on the front seat. I picked up the roses I had purchased en route and started walking.

Their graves, when I found them, were modest but well kept. Boone and Sadie Rawson Smith were buried side by side under a single granite marker. It listed their names, dates of birth, and dates of death. Nothing else, no epitaph. I crouched down and ran my fingers over the lettering. I'd asked the florist to tie together two dozen white roses with a pink satin ribbon—pink, for the little girl who had loved this couple once, who had taken three decades to find her way back to their side. I laid the flowers on the grass and stood back.

I had expected this to be the toughest moment in my journey to Atlanta. I had expected to weep. But I was all cried out from my morning in the newsroom. Instead I felt empty. And suddenly, embarrassingly, hungry. My stomach growled.

I stood around a bit longer, waiting to be felled by overwhelming emotion. It didn't happen. The photograph of my mother's face had hit me harder than this sunny, peaceful spot. Within a few minutes I felt ready to leave. I touched my fingers to my lips and then spread them one last time across the cool stone where my parents' names were carved.

If it was closure I was looking for in Atlanta, I wouldn't find it here.

Twelve

Leland Brett called my mobile just as I was stepping back into my hotel.

I'd booked a room at the St. Regis, an imposingly posh establishment that far exceeded my usual travel budget. The clientele was mostly expense-account types, business travelers who glided through the lobby wearing bespoke suits and brandishing platinum AmEx cards. But I was justifying the indulgence on the grounds that I'd suffered a terrible shock and therefore deserved a little pampering. I was spending my waking hours performing mournful chores, visiting graves and poring over obituaries. The only thing keeping me going was the prospect of returning in the evening to a good hotel with high-thread-count sheets.

Leland caught me as I handed the rental-car key to a valet and pushed through the front doors. I leaned against the wall by the elevators, pressed the phone to my ear, and listened as he made his pitch.

"More I think about it, more I love the idea of telling your story for our readers," he drawled. "And it's a grand opportunity for you, too. What about I swing by after work, buy you a drink, and we can ponder it further? Where are you staying?"

The man was persistent, you had to give him that. No doubt a valuable quality in a reporter. But sipping cocktails across from him while he "accidentally" pressed his leg against mine under the table was the last thing I felt like doing.

"I'd love to," I lied, "but I have plans tonight." Another lie. "And I'm leaning against this whole profile idea." That, at least, was the truth.

"Well, that's a shame. But while you cogitate on it, here's a little favor I've done for you. I've found you a phone number for Cheral Rooney. Your mama's friend. Turns out she still lives in town. She's a teacher, retired from one of the big private schools. Got a pen handy?" He read out a home phone number and an address. "I reckon if I were to ask the interns to keep working on this, they maybe could find numbers for other folks. Other old neighbors and family friends and whatnot. And of course, there's no way of knowing who might come forward if we were to run a story about you." He paused, then blew out a soft, low whistle. "No, sirree. Just can't know until you try."

The rat. This was blatant and despicable manipulation. What made it even more annoying was that he was right.

"What exactly would you need from me?" I asked warily.

After that, he knew he had me.

I did hold steadfast in my refusal to meet him tonight. But he talked me into having breakfast with him in the morning at eight, at the hotel restaurant. The interview would take an hour.

"One other arrangement we ought to iron out," he said. "We'll need a picture of you. The staff photographers will want to do it at the golden hour. That's right before sunset, the best light. Let's take it in front of your parents' old house. Where was that again?"

"Eulalia Road. Near Lenox." I was learning the lingo of Atlanta neighborhoods; Lenox Square was a huge shopping mall that everyone seemed to know.

"Wonderful. What's the house number? We'll need to call the current owners, let them know what we're up to."

"Oh, it's a Mrs. Dorminy. I met her yesterday. She gave me a tour."

"Did she? So she already knows who you are. Hopefully she won't mind a staff photog taking a few snaps with her house as backdrop. Technically, mind you, we can shoot from the street, never set foot on her property. But it never hurts to be courteous."

"Are you sure you need my picture, though?"

"My dear, your picture is going to be the best thing about this story. The caption practically writes itself: " 'Dark beauty, haunted by tragedy . . .' " Readers will eat it up. Now, you have a good night, and I'll see you in the morning."

Thirteen

I pause here to mention the state of my wrist and neck. Nothing is more tiresome than listening to people go on about their medical woes, so I've spared you the minute-by-minute updates. Suffice to say that my wrist hurt, nearly all the time.

I had come, though, to feel it as a sort of background noise, a chronic nuisance that I was learning to work around. You can learn to live with almost anything, I suppose. Driving with one hand was easy. Shampooing, less so. Cutting steak or anything else requiring a knife and fork wasn't pretty, though it could be done. The one thing I could not manage with one hand was typing. But here I had apparently gotten lucky. Typing—the very activity that provokes the carpal tunnel symptoms of most sufferers—did not bother me in the least. I could type all day without a twinge.

As for my neck, it had stopped hurting. No, that's not quite right. It hadn't stopped hurting, but the hot pulsing had retreated, like a wild animal that has tired and decided, for now, to rest. The important thing was to keep still. The pain nipped when I turned my head, especially to the right, so I learned not to do this. If I needed to glance sideways, I swiveled my whole torso. I probably looked like a geriatric constrained by an invisible neck brace, but it helped.

My most pressing physical complaint, late on that Tuesday afternoon, was that I was ravenous. Five days without a proper meal had proved my limit. I dialed room service and ordered enough food to feed a family of four. Then I sat back to make a few phone calls. First, my mother. I knew instinctively that it would crush her to learn that Sadie Rawson Smith could have passed for my sister. I didn't think my mother would feel jealous, exactly. More . . . left out. Excluded. So I glossed over my newsroom visit and focused instead on the cemetery, how pretty it had been, how peaceful. I told Mom about laying the flowers and running my fingers over the granite names. She offered, for the hundredth time, to fly down to be with me.

"Just to keep you company," she pleaded. My sweet mom. It was tempting to say yes. But she would slow me down, and this pilgrimage felt like something I needed to do on my own. I assured her that I was fine. I would wrap up here tomorrow, I told her, and probably fly back to Washington on Thursday morning.

Next I left a message for Martin. Finally, I steeled myself and dialed the number that Leland had produced for Cheral Rooney. Again, no answer. Just a recording of a pleasant-sounding man's voice, telling me to leave a message for Rick and Cheral. Lord, where to begin? I hung up, thought for a moment, then called back and left a short message stating my name, phone number, and that the matter was in regard to an old friend of hers.

When the room-service trolley arrived, I asked the waiter to set everything out on the coffee table. He did so, along with two starched napkins and two sets of cutlery, having quite reasonably assumed that I couldn't be planning to eat all this myself. It was a ridiculous spread: Caesar salad, tomato-and-basil soup, fresh fruit, a basket of warm rolls, a side of fries, a slice of pie. And a cheeseburger. To be precise, a glorious bacon double cheeseburger, dripping with mustard and grease. I wolfed it down and wished I'd ordered a second. Instead I contented myself with polishing off the rest of the food. It was delicious. Not a single bite tasted like cardboard.

Does it sound callous to eat with such gusto given recent events? Given the bleak reason for my mission to Atlanta? It felt that way. As though I were being disrespectful. I pulled out the photograph that Jessica had printed for me and studied it. My birth parents looked so happy, laughing and flipping burgers on the grill. The sun was beating down on them, and she appeared to be batting smoke out of her eyes. On a table behind them you could make out jars of mustard and mayonnaise, a platter of buns. All of a sudden, I broke into a grin. This must have been why I'd been craving a cheeseburger all day. I'd seen the photograph this morning, and the suggestion of flame-grilled beef had insinuated itself somewhere in my subconscious.

It was funny, now that I thought about it, but we Cashions never made burgers when I was growing up. Tony and Martin preferred steak or barbecued chicken, hands down. Mom did, too, and Dad is a casserole man. But Boone and Sadie Rawson Smith had apparently liked a good quarter-pounder, and they'd passed on the taste to their only daughter. It was such a silly thing, but I felt a connection to them, zinging back over the decades and the loss and all the things that might have been. I decided that if they could see me now, licking grease off my fingers, they wouldn't find it disrespectful. No, they'd want me to eat a burger or two for them.

I was still smiling to myself an hour later when I crawled into bed and fell into a deep sleep, snuggled beneath the high-thread-count sheets.

Fourteen

It was on Wednesday that things began to happen fast. Leland Brett showed up for breakfast right on time, and to give him his due, he conducted a detailed and thorough interview. He'd asked me to bring along a copy of my adoption papers, proving that I really had once been Caroline Smith, daughter of Boone and Sadie Rawson. He studied this until he seemed satisfied, then questioned me about my work, my hobbies, my family up in Washington. What sports did I like? (Um, none.) What kind of music did I listen to? (Classical. Hip-hop. Aerosmith. Everything really, except country.) Leland had done his homework, reading up on me on the university website. He wanted to know how I'd learned French and how often I made it to Paris. I got the sense he was warming me up. Pitching softball questions, waiting for me to relax and drop my guard before he broached the real subject at hand. When the food arrived, we hadn't yet touched on the events of 1979.

Incredibly, I was starving again. I'd ordered the signature sweet-potato pancakes, served with hot bourbon sauce, candied pecans, and a side of sausage.

Leland looked impressed. "I see you've got a healthy appetite." He eyed both me and my pancakes hungrily. "I like that in a woman."

God, here we went again. I frowned. "Leland, in case I've somehow given you the wrong impression, I should make clear . . . this is a business meeting, okay? I'm here to help with the article. Period."

He feigned innocence. "Well, of course. And I'm just here doing my job, which at the moment includes enjoying breakfast with a fine-looking woman. That's no crime, is it?"

"No," I agreed through gritted teeth.

"But that does make a good segue. You married?"

"For God's sake."

"For the story, that's why I'm asking!" I was about to push back my chair and walk out when he chuckled. "Calm down, hon. I don't bite. Just having a little fun with you. A little bit of fun. Otherwise this whole business is downright morbid, you have to agree."

"It's morbid whether I agree or not," I snapped.

"That is the truth. Now, have yourself a bite of those pancakes, and then I want you to tell me about why you decided to come back to Atlanta now, after all these years."

I glared at him but complied. He looked surprised to hear that I'd only recently learned my birth parents had been murdered.

"But what did you think had happened to them? Car crash or something?"

"No, you misunderstand. I'd never heard of them. I didn't know I was adopted."

"Good Lord in heaven. Your parents—the Cashions, I mean—they never told you?"

"No. They thought it best—how did Dad put it? Best to 'let sleeping dogs lie.' I'd never heard of Boone and Sadie Rawson Smith before last Thursday."

Leland opened his eyes wide in astonishment.

"It's been . . . something of a shock."

"I should think so." He shook his head. "Imagine that. Did they say why they chose to tell you now?"

I'd known we would end up here. We'd been tiptoeing around the bullet this whole conversation; Leland Brett just hadn't known it. I felt uncomfortable talking about my neck. I don't like being the center of attention at the best of times, and the thought that everything I confided now would end up printed in the newspaper . . . it was enough to give even a more extroverted person pause. But, hell, we'd come this far. And going public did seem my best chance to connect with people who had once known my family. So I told Leland about the carpal tunnel in my wrist, about getting an MRI, and finally about what the X-ray had shown.

He dropped his fork. "You're not saying it's still in there?"

I nodded.

"A bullet? *A bullet?* From the day your parents were shot?"

I nodded again. "Apparently it's been in there all this time. Thirty-four years. It never bothered me. There's no scar."

"Christ Almighty." He was scribbling furiously in his notebook. "You're sure? You have a copy of that X-ray?"

"On my phone. If you need to see it."

"Christ Almighty," he repeated. "That's the craziest story I ever heard. And I've heard a few." He was firing questions at me, trying to reconstruct the exact sequence of how I'd learned about the bullet, when my phone rang.

I squinted down. Will Zartman, calling from his office. He would be trying to firm up the appointment with that neurosurgeon. I sent the call to voice mail; I'd call him later.

I turned back to Leland. "Sorry, where were we?"

"I was saying, I've got a few more questions. Why don't I give you a ride over to the newsroom? We can finish up there, and—"

"Can't. I'm going over to Cheral Rooney's after this."

"Oh, so that phone number worked?"

"Mm-hmm. She called me back this morning, right before I came down to meet you. I don't think she could get her head around what I was telling her. Poor woman. She sounded even more stunned by all this than you are."

"MY GOD, YOU'RE so like her. Same eyes. There's not an ounce of Boone in you."

Cheral Rooney sat studying me across her living room. She had given me directions to her home, a compact, gray stucco house that backed up to the Chatta-hoochee River. "I was going to ask you for ID before I let you in. There's a lot of crazies in the world. But when I saw you walking up the driveway, I realized—no need. Like watching Sadie Rawson herself walk through my front door."

"You knew them both, then? Both my birth parents?"

"Your *birth* parents?" She cocked her head. "Yes, I suppose that's how you would think of them. But look at me, I've forgotten my manners. Would you care for coffee?"

"No, thank you."

"Are you sure? I've just brewed a pot."

"I'm not much of a coffee drinker. But I'd love some tea, if it's not too much trouble."

She bustled off and returned a few minutes later, carrying a tray. It held a plate of cookies, a mug of steaming coffee, and a tall crystal goblet filled with ice and pale brown liquid. I took a cautious sip. Iced tea. I'd heard this, how Southerners remain loyal to cold tea no matter how chilly the weather outside.

I set down my glass and met her eyes. "The newspaper identified you as a close friend of my birth . . . of my mother's. How did you know her?"

"We lived in the house next door. Moved there in '74 and stayed more than twenty years. Until we bought this." She swept her hand to indicate the room where we were sitting. "Eulalia was a great street for young families. Starter homes, you know. Although too expensive for that now. Did you know a house down on the Lenox end just sold for one point six million dollars? Incredible. We paid fifty-five thousand dollars when we first bought."

I shook my head. "It's a lovely street. So you were already living there when the Smiths moved in?"

"We were. We were glad to get a nice young couple next door. The four of us got to be good friends. And then when John and you came along, your mother and I spent nearly every morning together."

I tried to follow this. "John is—your son?"

She pointed at a framed photograph on a side table beside the sofa. It showed a pudgy man in a golf shirt and khakis. "My oldest. You're older than him, but only by a couple of months. You and he were great pals as toddlers. You don't remember him?"

"I'm afraid I don't remember anything from those years."

"The two of you used to play together, in a playpen we would set up in the kitchen and fill with balls and toys. Sadie Rawson and I would drink coffee and bake together. That girl could burn things, I tell you. She had a true talent for it. She'd roll out dough and pop it in the oven, get to talking, and forget all about it. Next thing you knew, your kitchen was filled with smoke." Cheral smiled. "And we went for walks. Endless walks. There wasn't much to do back then when you stayed home with a baby. None of these play groups and Gymboree classes that young mothers do today."

I was hanging on her every word. "What was she—like? I mean, was she quiet, or funny, or—"

"Funny, yes. And about as far from quiet as a person can get. She was the life of the party. Boone was the serious, steady one. They played off each other. I guess all couples do."

"Sounds like I take after my father."

"Not in the looks department, you don't. It's incredible, how you favor her. She was a pretty, pretty girl. Bedroom eyes and shiny, lip-glossy lips. We'd be out pushing baby strollers, just walking around the block in our housedresses, and you'd see the men's heads snap when they drove past. Sades would just laugh and wave."

A cloud passed over Cheral's face. She was no beauty, didn't look as if she had ever been. Late middle age had scored her mouth with dry lines, and her hair was bleached and brittle. But surely that wasn't jealousy I detected? Not after all these years.

"She sounds like she must have been a handful. I thought so. I thought she must have been feisty. Keeping her maiden name, and all."

Cheral looked confused. "No, she went by Smith."

"Right, but Sadie *Rawson* Smith. Like Hillary Rodham Clinton. That must have been progressive, for Georgia in the 1970s."

"No, no, it wasn't a Hillary Rodham thing. Sadie Rawson was her first name. You know, like . . . Mary Belle. Or Georgia Ruth. Lots of girls down here used double-barreled names. Still do."

"Oh. Quite a mouthful."

She shrugged. "Sadie Rawson has the same number of syllables as Elizabeth, if you think about it. And nobody thinks that's too long a name."

We fell silent.

"It must be very upsetting for you," she ventured after a bit. "Learning about all this now." I'd told her the broad outlines of what I knew and when I'd come to know it, on the phone this morning. I left out the bullet details.

"It's been strange. It's good to meet you, though. I love hearing what the Smiths were like. My parents—the

Cashions—don't seem to know much. And the newspaper accounts about what happened are pretty bare-bones. The paper ran four stories and then . . . it seemed to fall off the radar."

She nodded.

"The police must have talked to you. Did they ever let anything slip? I mean, could you tell if they ever had a good lead?"

"They interviewed us twice. Rick and me. We hadn't heard or seen anything out of the ordinary that day. We told them everything we could. To be honest, I wasn't that impressed with the efforts of the Atlanta police. They were convinced from day one that it must have been a burglar who got surprised by your parents and started shooting. But they never did catch him."

"I don't understand how that happens. A burglar breaks in, kills two people, and the police just . . . let it drop."

"Well, it was an unusual case. No physical evidence, at least not that I could gather. There weren't any fingerprints in the house that weren't supposed to be there. And they never found a murder weapon. All they had was an eyewitness."

"There was an eyewitness?"

"Of course, honey. You."

Fifteen

Before I left, Cheral Rooney pressed a pair of gold earrings into my hands. "They were your mom's. Only thing I have of hers. They've been sitting in my jewelry box all these years—I never could bring myself to wear them."

The earrings were enormous, finely braided hoops. They had a vaguely Gypsy quality to them, delicate and gaudy at once. Not the kind of thing I would ever wear. But then, I hadn't been a fashionable young woman in the 1970s.

"They were the height of fashion back then," said Cheral, reading my mind. "I'd borrowed them to wear to a party, only reason I have them. After your parents died the whole house was a crime scene. Police tape everywhere. I wasn't allowed in to try to scoop up anything else of hers. Then one day, movers appeared. Boxed everything up and the house was sold."

"Thank you for keeping these."

"She had beautiful jewelry. And clothes. With her figure, she could wear anything. She had this green coat, so chic, with matching green suede boots. . . ." Cheral smiled sadly. "You'd have loved her taste."

I nodded.

"I would have come to visit you. I would have liked to stay in touch. Your mother would have wanted that. But afterwards the doctors wouldn't let me see you. You were in intensive care for weeks. And I assume the police were trying to question you during that time."

"Do you know if I—if I saw anything? Was I able to tell them anything that helped?"

She shook her head. "I've no idea. You don't remember?"

"No. Not anything."

"Probably for the best. You were a baby, Caroline, barely more than a baby. I didn't mean to suggest otherwise when I said that, about you being an eyewitness. Who knows what you saw or didn't?" She patted my shoulder. "Anyway, after a time the social services must have gotten involved. Next thing I heard, you'd been adopted by a new family. We never had word again; it was like you'd just been spirited away. I hope they were kind to you. The couple that adopted you, I mean."

"Very kind." I felt my voice tighten with love. "The kindest family ever. I couldn't have asked for a more loving home."

"I'm glad." Cheral touched my shoulder again. "Mercy, it's brought back some memories, seeing you. To think that you're older now than Sadie Rawson and Boone when they died. Such a nice man, your daddy. Didn't deserve what he got."

"Neither of them did."

She blinked, then nodded. Tears were in her eyes as she closed the door. Tears, and something else. A hint of jealousy again? Or some other emotion? I couldn't tell, could only sense it twitching, a sour undercurrent beneath the surface.

SOMETHING CHERAL ROONEY had said was nagging at me. Something, some detail, didn't sit right. I couldn't put my finger on it, and the more I tried to catch it, the more it eluded me, like a kitten batting at a piece of yarn.

I was parked back on Eulalia Road for my appointment with the *Journal-Constitution* photographer. I was not looking forward to it, was already regretting my decision to participate in this entire exercise. It felt tacky. As though I were exploiting a long-ago tragedy to seize fifteen minutes of fame. That was the farthest thing from the truth, but still, people would judge. I pulled out a compact and reapplied my lipstick. My brothers would have something to say if they could see me sitting here, primping for pictures to accompany the presumably breathless article that Leland Brett would be typing up right now ("Dark Beauty Still Distressed by Bullet in Neck!"). The only question was whether Martin and Tony would be appalled or doubled over with laughter.

I glanced at my watch. The photographer was late. He had insisted we meet at five o'clock, to get set up in plenty of time for the golden-hour light. I decided to wait another fifteen minutes, then I was out of here. A few cars rumbled by. Across the street two boys kicked a ball back and forth in their yard. The smaller boy kept missing and sending the ball rolling dangerously close to the street; the older one managed to pounce and catch it each time, just before it bounced over the curb.

I leaned back in the front seat and imagined a young Cheral Rooney and my mother pushing baby strollers along this same block on a late-afternoon stroll. What would they have chatted about? I pictured Sadie Rawson wearing the sassy green coat and suede boots that Cheral had described. Now, those I would have liked to inherit.

I sat up. That was it. Where had they gone? The coat, the boots, the allegedly fabulous wardrobe? Cheral said everything had been boxed up and carted away. But to where? The clothes must have been donated to charity long ago. Books and knickknacks, too. That left my mother's jewelry, though. I fingered the gold, braided hoops, wondered what necklaces and bracelets she used to slip on to match. Now that I thought about it, where were my parents' wedding rings? Had they been buried in them, or had everything been sold off? They must have had a car. They might have had life insurance. My thoughts raced along these lines for several minutes, before my gaze swung toward the brick house in front of me. This house had once belonged to Boone and Sadie Rawson. Where had the money gone when it was sold?

The question of an inheritance had not crossed my mind before. There was no indication the Smiths had been rich, and in any case I wasn't hurting for money. Still. Normal married people write wills leaving everything to each other. Failing that, they leave everything to their surviving children. I was the Smiths' surviving daughter. So how must things have unfolded? What on earth happens when a couple is murdered, and their heir is three years old, and she ends up being raised with no contact with her past, not even the same last name?

I had no idea how one might go about tracing such things, but I knew someone who might. Jessica Yeo. The newspaper researcher. Her job was to help track down information and people. Plus, she knew Atlanta.

I picked up my phone and dialed.

"That is so bizarre," she answered. "I was about to call you. Literally, I was about to pick up the phone, and here your number shows up on my caller ID. Since I've got you now, is it *Frannie* with an *i-e* or with a *y*?"

"Sorry, what?"

"Your mom. Mrs. Cashion. Does she spell it F-R-A-N-N—"

"Oh. With *i-e*. Why are you—"

"Leland's got me fact-checking your profile." Clicking sounds came down the phone line; I pictured her blue fingernails flying over the keyboard. "It's also kind of confusing, the way he's written the section about the bullet. Did you get the MRI first or the X-ray?"

"The MRI. But listen—"

"I knew it!" she chirped. "You would think he could get the details straight. He was probably too busy ogling your chest to pay attention to the chronology."

That stopped me short. "Wow."

"Sorry. Sorry, sorry, sorry. I didn't just say that. He is my boss, technically. But you are a woman, and you're alive, which pretty much qualifies you as fair game in Leland's world. *Damn it!* I didn't just say that, either."

"He, umm . . . he must be an interesting guy to work for."

The typing ceased. "He didn't really put the moves on you, did he? Not when he was interviewing you for a news story?"

"He did. In a harmless kind of way."

"The bastard. His poor wife. But that's exactly right: Leland's so obviously harmless that it's hard to get too riled up." The clicking resumed. "Just a couple more questions. Did he get right that you haven't been back to Atlanta to visit, anytime between 1979 and now?"

"That's right. Hang on, though. I've got a question for *you*. Is there a way to figure out what my birth parents' Social Security numbers would have been?"

"I'm sure there must be. Why?"

"I'm sitting here parked in front of their old house. Waiting for your photographer, who's late, by the way. And it occurs to me that the Smiths used to own this house. When they died, it must have been sold, and I have no idea where the money went."

"Oooh." Jessica sounded intrigued. "I like it. You think there's some nest egg out there with your name on it, that's been racking up interest all these years?"

"I'm not asking out of greediness. I'm mainly interested in where their possessions went. You know, if there's a chance of getting back any personal items that might be meaningful."

"Sure, sure. You could check the property deeds. See who sold the house on behalf of your parents. Fulton County would keep those records, I think."

I hadn't thought of that. "Do you know how to access them?"

"Yep. Tell you what. Let me finish up this article for Leland. First thing tomorrow, I'll nose around for you."

I exhaled. "That would be terrific. I'll pay you for your time. And I'd be grateful if you could keep this between us, for now. No need to mention it to Leland."

"No problem. Let's see what I turn up. It'll be interesting. Very Watergate."

"Watergate?"

"You know. Follow the money."

WILL ZARTMAN WAS livid by the time he reached me. "Don't you *ever* answer your phone?" he demanded. "Or is it just my calls that you ignore?"

"I'm not ignoring you! I've been running around all day, and I was going to call you back tonight—"

"I've left two messages, Caroline. I was getting worried that something had happened to you."

"I'm fine. Totally fine. I—"

"No, actually, you're not. That's why I've been trying to reach you. Part of why I've been trying to reach you." He cleared his throat. "I set things up with Dr. Gellert. The neurosurgeon. He can squeeze you in Friday afternoon. That works, right? You're still flying back to DC tomorrow?"

"Absolutely."

"Good. I also showed your X-ray and MRI to an orthopedic surgeon, an old friend of mine from med school. He agreed that your original doctors must have decided against removing the bullet because it was jammed so tight in there, against so many important nerves."

"Makes sense."

"But his question was, what if the bullet has shifted? He thinks your wrist pain is almost certainly related. And that didn't start until a few months ago. Which means something is pressing down in a way that it didn't used to. Do you have a family history of osteoporosis?"

"Will. For God's sake. You of all people should know I have no idea what my family medical history is."

He sucked in his breath. "Of course. Sorry. The reason I ask is, as we age, our bodies change. The spine compresses. Most people lose about half an inch in height, every decade. That begins in our late thirties. How old are you exactly?"

"Not old enough for my spine to be buckling, thank you very much."

"I can pull your chart, if you prefer."

"Thirty-seven," I said disagreeably.

"So you're on the young side, but that's around when it starts. Think of your disks as jelly-filled pads between your vertebrae. Over the years they lose fluid and flatten out. Like a house settling on its foundation."

"Oh, that's a lovely image. My body, a collapsing old house . . ."

"That's not what I meant. Your body is a lot of things, but old and collapsing would not be the words that spring to mind."

I absorbed that. My face felt hot. I was blushing.

"That was inappropriate," he said after a long moment. "I apologize. I don't know what came over me." He cleared his throat again, more ferociously this time. "I've lost my train of thought. I—oh, yes. My point was that if your spine has compressed—even by a millimeter—that's a problem. We need to jump on it. My med school buddy suggested you get a three-hundred-and-sixty-degree X-ray taken, to give us a better idea what's going on. What time does your flight get in tomorrow?"

"I'm not sure yet. I need to sort out my reservation tonight."

"Do you actually have a ticket booked?" he asked suspiciously.

"Yes, but I paid for a flexible fare. I wasn't sure how long I would want down here."

"Would you e-mail me your itinerary once you nail it down?"

"Why?" It was my turn to sound suspicious.

"Because, Caroline," retorted Will, "we're not messing around here. There's a piece of metal buried in your neck. Your symptoms suggest that it may have shifted. I don't mean to scare you, but you can't put this off. Do you understand? You could risk paralysis."

"Oh," I said in a small voice.

"All I mean to say," he added more gently, "is that at a certain point, the risk of doing nothing begins to outweigh the risk of surgery. I think we may be nearing that point."

Sixteen

The picture that ran on the front page of the *Journal-Constitution* was arresting.

The photographer had screeched up half an hour late, ranting about traffic and bad directions. He whipped out his camera and positioned me hurriedly on Mrs. Dorminy's lawn, swearing the whole time. But his timing was exquisite. The portrait was saturated with golden light. My lips stood out, a slash of scarlet across pale skin. The angle of the shot made me appear smaller than I am, fragile even. The effect was haunting, even before you got to the caption: *Caroline Cashion standing in front of the house where she lived with her parents until she was three years old* . . . On the inside pages, they ran the X-ray image, cropped to emphasize the bullet glowing inside my neck.

It was surreal, reading Leland's account of how I had returned to Atlanta. He told the story chronologically, and he got the facts more or less correct, yet the article felt somehow disconnected from me. I wondered if this is how celebrities feel when they see glossy profiles of themselves. There was nothing per se to quibble with; it just read like an account of someone else's life.

In any case, Leland Brett had been right. The article immediately produced results. Two phone calls. The first rang through the hotel switchboard to the phone beside my bed.

"Hello, Caroline?" said a deep voice.

"Yes?"

"This is Ethan Sinclare. I was a friend of your father's."

"Oh! Hi."

"Forgive me for calling so early. I'm staring at your picture in this morning's paper. What a shock."

"It's okay. But—can I ask how you got this number?" I was irritated with Leland. He had no business telling people where I was staying, not without checking first with me.

It turned out, though, that Sinclare had figured it out on his own. "Lucky guess. It says in the article that you granted an interview over breakfast at the St. Regis. That's not a place that *AJC* reporters typically frequent, I wouldn't think. So it seemed reasonable to assume that's where you must be staying."

"Ah, I see."

"I always wondered what had happened to you. The police wouldn't tell friends of the family anything. It's a relief to know everything worked out for you."

"Thank you. So how did you know Boone Smith?"

"We were tennis buddies. Same ALTA team. That's the league here."

"I didn't know he played."

"Oh, sure. Boone was pretty good. He played varsity

at Chapel Hill. We used to whack a ball around in the evenings, after work. We ended up doubles partners for a while."

"And you knew Sadie Rawson, too?"

"Of course. Great couple. Both so proud of you. Listen, I'd love to meet you, if you've got the time. I don't know how long you're planning to stay in Atlanta—"

"I'm flying back to Washington today, actually."

"Glad I caught you, then. I live just over in Brookhaven. How about breakfast? I could be at your hotel in an hour."

ETHAN SINCLARE CROSSED the room as if he owned it. Tall and powerfully built, he had the lithe body of a man who still put in regular hours on the tennis court. Sinclare wore a dark suit and gleaming cuff links. He fit right in with the expense-account crowd now polishing off breakfast in the St. Regis.

"Thank you so much for seeing me." He took both my hands in his huge ones and gave them a squeeze, before taking his seat. "I couldn't believe my eyes when I saw the article this morning. Usually I don't see the paper until I get to the gym. Betsy—my wife—she reads the copy that comes to the house. But she was up early today, walking the dog, and the front page was already spread out on the kitchen counter when I came downstairs. It took my breath away."

He unfolded a white linen napkin across his lap. I saw now that he was older than he'd appeared from a distance. Salt-and-pepper hair, and a patrician face, tanned and deeply lined. He must have been sixty-five, maybe older. He sat studying me, too.

"You're very like her."

I nodded. "So I've been told."

"You really are. You've got her smile. She was tinier, though. Petite." His eyes roamed over me, but not in a salacious, Leland-esque way. This did not feel sexual. "It's jarring, seeing your face. Trying to reconcile it, you know, with Sadie Rawson's. I didn't know her all that well. And it's been a long, long time. But the resemblance is unmistakable."

The waiter bustled up. "Good morning, sir. Madam." He winked at me. "What may I bring you this morning? Your favorite sweet-potato pancakes?" God, they were good at these high-end hotels. This poor man must have served dozens of people yesterday, and here he remembered my order.

"No, thank you, just the yogurt and fruit today. And . . . umm, maybe a side of bacon."

"Very good." He bowed. "And for you, sir? Might I suggest the lobster frittata? Served with fingerling potatoes, fresh horseradish—"

Sinclare, who had not so much as glanced at the menu, waved him off. "Two eggs, please, scrambled. With a whole-wheat bagel, toasted, no butter. Sriracha sauce on the side."

"Sir-rotch . . . sorry?"

"Sriracha sauce. They'll have it. Thanks so much." Sinclare turned back to me and smiled. "Gives a bit of kick to the eggs."

"Ah. I'll have to try it sometime."

"It's come to me, now that we're talking food. Why you look familiar. You do look like your mother, no question, but also a bit like that woman with the cooking show. The Englishwoman, looks Italian? Always licking frosting off her fingers."

"Nigella Lawson."

"That's the one!"

"I'm trying to remember exactly what she looks like. Whether I should feel flattered or insulted."

"Oh, feel flattered. The camera doesn't zoom in and linger on all that frosting-licking for nothing. Betsy adores her show. But I gather you're in a different line of work than the lovely Nigella. A professor, was it? French lit?"

"That's right. Up in Washington. And you? Are you a pilot?"

"A pilot?" He looked confused. "Oh, you mean, because Boone was? No, that's not how we met. I'm an attorney. Securities claims, broker-dealer arbitrations, that sort of thing. The litigation side of things. Meaning lawsuits rather than corporate deals."

"I know what litigators do. My dad and brother are both lawyers."

"Your dad?" He shot me a strange look.

"My dad, meaning the man who raised me. Thomas Cashion."

"Of course, of course. The article made it sound as though you don't remember much about Boone and Sadie Rawson."

"Nothing at all, unfortunately."

"I suppose you were so young."

"I thought being back here might jog some memories. Seeing my old house, and all that."

"And has it worked?"

"Not so far. The newspaper archives had an old photograph of my parents, and seeing it was . . . jarring, to use your word. But I can't say I would have recognized them."

"Mmm. I might have a few pictures of your dad kicking around the house. I'll have a nose through the old albums this weekend. Maybe some of us posing in our tennis whites. I'll mail them to you, if I find any."

"That's kind of you."

"And the bullet?" He lowered his voice. "Did you really not know it was there?"

I shook my head no.

"You poor girl." He patted my hand across the white tablecloth. "What a thing to learn, after all this time. That X-ray is unbelievable. There's no way they can operate and cut it out?"

"The doctors aren't sure."

"Well, if you decide you want another opinion, probably the best neurosurgeon in the Southeast is an old friend. Mike's over at Emory now. I'd be happy to put you two in touch."

"Thank you."

"Just say the word. It's no trouble. You don't want to mess around with someone who's not top-notch. But I assume you're talking with good doctors up in Washington?"

"Not really," I hedged. "I've been too caught up with coming down here, and processing everything that's happened, to give the bullet much thought." Ethan Sinclare seemed like a nice man, but I didn't feel like discussing my medical symptoms or my private life with him. It was exhausting enough trying to keep up with them myself.

Sinclare insisted on picking up the check. As he walked me out, he pressed his business card into my palm and made me promise to keep in touch. "I don't blog or do Facebook or any of that nonsense. But if you ever need anything, anything at all, call me. My cell number is on there. It would be an honor to help out the daughter of Boone Smith."

I TOOK THE elevator back upstairs to pack.

I'd booked an afternoon flight from Atlanta to Washington. I needed to get home to meet the neurosurgeon tomorrow, and meanwhile Madame Aubuchon had e-mailed from the French Department to inquire whether I felt inclined to teach my regular Friday-morning class. Her tone was polite, but there was no mistaking that the correct answer would be yes. I wrote back to confirm that I would indeed be there.

I was looking forward to getting home. To resuming my normal life. I missed my campus routine, my hours in the library. And I was finished here. I had not achieved closure, whatever that meant. But it had been strangely comforting to sit at breakfast this morning, spooning up yogurt and listening to Mr. Sinclare rave about my birth father's backhand. Apparently Boone had employed a weird grip, one hand so high up the racket it practically rested on the strings. Sinclare swore that it resembled a drunk man playing air guitar. But it had produced a ferocious topspin that left their opponents spitting with frustration, every time. I loved that detail. Not because I gave a damn about Boone's tennis grip, but because I could glimpse him as a real person. I'd felt the same way when Cheral Rooney shared Sadie Rawson's talent for scorching cookies. It was a relief to meet people who had known the Smiths, known them as funny, flawed, normal people—and not just as victims of a tragedy.

I started brainstorming whether there might be some way to honor my birth family. Perhaps a donation to a charity they might have supported? If any sort of inheritance ever did turn up, I could direct it there. Cheral might know whether Sadie Rawson had embraced any particular cause. It cheered me to have a plan. These last seven days had been wretched. So painful. But perhaps I was through the worst.

I began to hum as I threw the last sweater into my suitcase. "Sweet Emotion." Aerosmith is hard to beat when you need perking up. Steven Tyler's screech is too infectious. When had that song first come out? Mid-seventies, I was pretty sure. The radio stations would have played it nonstop. Boone and Sadie Rawson had probably owned the album on eight-track tape. They might have played it at parties, Boone playing air guitar for real, Sadie Rawson dancing so hard the gold Gypsy hoops flew off her ears. I stood grinning at the thought.

Then my cell phone rang.

THIS TIME IT was Leland Brett. People had been calling the newsroom in response to the story about me.

"Some real nut jobs out there," reported Leland. "Not

that that comes as any surprise after forty years in the news business. One lady says she's a psychic, she can help you contact your parents beyond the grave."

"Hah! That would be useful."

"Yeah. So would winning the lottery, but that's not gonna happen either, is it? But listen. This one guy. Says his name is Beamer Beasley."

"Beamer Beasley?"

"Now, don't laugh, sweetheart. It's not such an unusual name for Georgia. His middle name's probably Bubba. Anyway, he says he's a cop. Says he worked homicides for the Atlanta PD back in '79."

"Why did he call?"

"He says he worked your mama and daddy's case. I had Jessica check him out. He sounds legit."

"And . . . did he seem to know anything that might be relevant?"

"I don't know. He wants to speak to you personally. Asked me to pass the message along."

I glanced at the clock. I had a couple hours before I needed to leave for the airport. I'd been planning to return a few phone calls, then go for a walk.

"Maybe I could meet him."

"Sure. Why not? Tell you what. How about you meet him here, at the newspaper? Nice, neutral territory for you both. I could find you a quiet meeting room to use. And afterward, I'll take you out for lunch."

"Absolutely not. Not least because I'll be racing straight to the airport to catch my flight."

"Meet him here anyway." Leland sounded disappointed. "Maybe he'll agree to an interview after you and he are done talking. There might be material there for a follow-up story."

AN HOUR LATER Beamer Beasley and I were seated across from each other in a small conference room.

He was African-American, older, perhaps in his seventies, with grizzled hair cropped close against his skull. Time had thickened him around the middle and left him stooped. But his eyes were clear and gray and intelligent. Beamer Beasley had a stillness about him. You sensed that he'd seen an awful lot in his years on this earth, and that there wasn't much left in the repertoire of human depravity that might faze him.

"I came here to say two things," he said, after Leland had finally been persuaded to leave us alone and shut the door behind him.

"I'm listening."

"The first is that I'm sorry. For failing you. You deserved justice after what happened to you and your family. You deserved that. And we tried hard, but we failed you and I failed you."

"I'm sure you tried your best—"

He held up his hand to hush me. "Please. Let me finish. When you work law enforcement for as long as I have, you learn to forget most of the wickedness you come across. You learn to leave it at the office, put it out of your mind. Only way you can keep on getting up in the morning. But some cases—you carry them here." He pressed his hand over his heart. "I've been carrying yours for a long time. I always hoped to get the chance to tell you that. I wanted to tell you that I'm sorry and ask for your forgiveness."

A tear sprang to my eye. I was genuinely touched. "Thank you. It was brave of you to come here and say that."

"Not brave at all. Wish I'd been able to say it thirty years ago."

"Well, I appreciate your saying it now." We sat in silence for a moment, then I leaned forward. "May I ask you a question?"

"Go ahead."

"I did wonder . . . how a case like that was never solved. A double homicide and a child shot. It's such a dramatic crime. But the newspaper made it sound like you guys just gave up."

He flinched.

"I don't mean to sound rude."

"No, you've got every right to ask. We didn't give up. But you have to understand what was going on in the city." He frowned and shifted in his seat. "You ever hear of a man named Marc Tetalman?"

I shook my head.

"I expect his name is lost to the history books. He was a doctor, visiting Atlanta from out of town, for a convention. He got shot down and killed by robbers trying to steal his wallet. This was a few months before your parents died."

I waited.

"I was on duty that night. We were interviewing his wife, down at Grady Hospital, when the surgeon came out and told her he'd died. It was their wedding anniversary. Eleven years married. That's why they'd left the hotel and gone out to dinner that night."

Beasley swung his head from side to side sadly. "Marc Tetalman's death caused a big old scandal because he was well-off and white and everybody worried the publicity would hurt the city's convention business. It did, too. After that, everybody decided they'd rather go to Houston or Miami. But what stuck in my head was that Tetalman was the one hundred and twelfth homicide that year in Atlanta. The one hundred and twelfth. And he died in *June*, Ms. Cashion. One hundred and twelve people killed, and we weren't even into the hot part of summer yet. Do you understand what I'm telling you? We were dealing with a new murder nearly every day."

I remembered what Jessica Yeo had said. "Somebody told me Atlanta had the worst murder rate of any city in America."

"That's right. Not even Detroit could keep up. Nobody knew why. And then, when you thought things couldn't get worse, little boys started turning up strangled."

"The child murders."

"Yes, ma'am. On top of everything else we had a genuine serial killer running around the city, murdering black kids and throwing their bodies in the woods or in the river. You can't imagine. Folks were scared to let their kids ride bikes down their own street. And the politicians, they were blaming us. The old governor came out and said we cops ought to show 'less jawbone and more backbone.' His exact words, I never forgot them."

Anger flashed across Beasley's gray eyes. "Worst of it was, Governor Sanders was right. You had black cops— not all of us, but some—whispering that maybe it was the Klan, the KKK, that was killing the kids. You had a lot of white cops who just up and quit the force. And then to top it off, the courts went and ordered a hiring freeze. Said the police department was racist, the hiring policies were racist, and we needed to stop hiring new cops altogether for a while. You can guess how much that helped things."

He puffed the air out of his cheeks and leaned back. "I'm going on too long. I don't imagine you care much about the sorry history of the Atlanta PD. But you asked me why we let your family's case drop, and that's the only way I know how to answer you."

"You're saying, basically, that it was a bad time for the city. Too many murders to investigate and not enough of you to do it."

"In our defense, we did try. Your case got under a lot of people's skin, not just mine. A young couple gunned down with their daughter watching. You didn't see that every day, not even back in 1979. And I hate to say it, but you all were white, and that meant folks paid more attention. But there wasn't much to go on. No murder weapon, no witnesses."

"Except me."

"Except you. But I gather you don't remember anything, and I don't think you were old enough to understand what you'd seen back then, either."

I hesitated. I wasn't sure I wanted to know the answer to my next question. But I might not get the chance to ask again. "Would you describe for me exactly what happened that day? As best as you all were able to reconstruct it? I would like to know the details of how they died."

"Hmm. You sure about that?"

"I think so."

"Once you get an image in your mind, it can be hard to shake it back out. The way your parents died wasn't pretty. You know the basics of what happened, don't you? Might be best to leave it at that."

Again I hesitated, then made up my mind. "I'd like to know."

The gray eyes searched mine. "All right, then. I expected you might ask. I read through the old incident report before I drove over, to refresh my memory."

"I'd love to get a copy of that report, if possible."

"All right. I don't have it on me, but I can do that."

I bit my lip, then prompted him, "I know from the newspaper account that they died in the kitchen, and that it was late afternoon."

"That's right. Neighbors heard a commotion and called it in. There was no sign of forced entry. The first responders had to kick in the door. They found you three together on the floor."

"But they were—my parents were already dead when police got there?"

"They would have died instantly. The nature of their wounds suggested that, and the autopsy results were consistent. They wouldn't have suffered."

"It's so strange," I murmured. "Why I lived, and they didn't. I mean, if we were all shot at once, three bullets from the same gun. You'd think it would have gone the other way, since I was smaller and weaker. Was it—was it just the location of their wounds?"

Beasley looked at me. "I told you when we started that I wanted to say two things."

"You did, that's right."

"We're treading close to the second one now." A look of grim determination settled on his face. "You sure you want to do this?"

"Yes."'

"Then I'm going to walk you through the sequence of what we think happened. Let me get through it, and then I'll answer your questions as best as I can."

"Sure. Okay."

"We believe your father was shot first. That's based on the way he was found positioned on the floor. And it makes sense, if you think about a man trying to defend his family. He would have tried to put himself between the gun, and your mother and you. So the shooter would have hit him first."

I shuddered. Took a breath to steady myself. Then nodded at Beasley to go on.

"Your father, as you may know, was shot in the head. Shot at close range, ten feet or less. The bullet passed right through. It came out the back of his head and lodged in the wood of the doorframe. But the shooter dug it out and took it with him. The wood was splintered and broken from where he'd hacked at it."

I frowned. "That doesn't sound like something a random burglar would do."

"What do you mean?"

"The old newspaper articles, the ones that Leland Brett wrote." I motioned at the closed door of the conference room, and the newsroom beyond. "He quoted a cop who thought the shootings were an accident. A burglary gone wrong. But wouldn't a burglar have panicked and run?"

"And not stuck around to dig a bullet out of a wooden

doorframe?" Beasley completed my thought. "You're right; it's odd. But people are odd. They do all kinds of things that don't make sense."

"At any rate, you never recovered the bullet."

"We never did."

"And my mother. She was shot in the chest?"

"She was," he said carefully. "She was trying to protect you, too. She had pushed you down behind her."

Tears sprang again to my eyes. I tried and failed to keep my voice steady. "So . . . you're saying . . . what, that the guy shot her and then pushed her aside to get to me? What kind of person does that? What kind of a person shoots two people and then aims a third bullet at a defenseless *three-year-old child*?"

"No, Ms. Cashion." Beasley leaned forward and folded my trembling hands into his. "There was no third bullet. The bullet that killed your mama passed right through her, too."

"I don't—I don't understand."

"The reason you didn't die was that bullet was going slower by the time it got to you. Your mama did protect you. She slowed it down."

I blinked at him.

It took a moment for the full, sickening significance of what he was saying to hit home. Then my hands flew to my neck, and I began to claw.

Seventeen

In the wild, a mother tiger will fight to the death to defend her young. She will knock down an animal four times her size, will attack and kill even a male tiger. When she senses a threat to her cubs, she growls. Then she flattens her ears and bares her canines, the corners of her open mouth pulled back. That snarl is the last thing a would-be predator ever sees.

Human mothers share the instinct. Most of us know at some raw, unspoken level that our mothers would fight like a tigress to protect us, would give their lives to save our own. But it is one thing to believe, in the abstract, that your mother would take a bullet for you. It is quite another to learn that she has literally done so.

Beasley had to pin my arms to my sides to prevent me from opening my skin. He must have been twice my age, but he was still strong, and I was no match for him. I thrashed for a minute, then went limp.

The bullet throbbed. A hot, white pulse through my neck and shoulders. It defied belief: the same bullet. The very same piece of metal had passed through Sadie Rawson's breast, through her heart, on its way to me.

"I want to rip it out," I whispered.

"I know." Instead Beasley made me focus on taking shallow, jagged breaths. He held me upright.

Gradually, my breathing slowed. When I could speak, I asked, "Was that the second thing you wanted to tell me? Please say there isn't more. I don't think I can take it."

"That's the worst of it." He extended a handkerchief and I blew my nose.

"Thank you. I'm sorry. Sorry for going crazy like that."

"No need to apologize."

"Just that every time I think I've heard the worst of it, there's some new revelation that knocks me flat. *The bullet that's in my neck is the same one that killed my mother?* That's—that's—I don't even know what it is."

"It's gruesome."

"Gruesome. Yes. That it certainly is." I shivered. Pain was shooting down my wrist now, too. I folded my right arm tight across my chest and cradled it, hunched over like a broken bird.

"Ms. Cashion." He was looking at me sideways. "I have to ask. Has coming back here triggered any memories? Going back to look at your old house? Or hearing me describe the details of what happened that day?"

"No. Nothing. I'd hoped it might."

"Probably wouldn't have been admissible anyway. In court, I mean, if you'd remembered anything relevant. But I had to ask."

A thought occurred to me. "Were you one of the detectives who questioned me? After I was shot?"

"Yes." His voice was neutral, quiet. "You were heartbreaking. Tiny little girl, all bandaged up. The doctors didn't want us anywhere near you, but we had our jobs to do. I didn't talk to you myself. They brought in a child psychiatrist, a lady trained to deal with kids who've experienced trauma. But they allowed a couple of us to watch from the corner."

"And—what did I say?"

"Oh, you wouldn't talk. You were barely more than a baby, barely talking as it was. I never heard you say a word. But we hoped you might remember what the guy looked like. The shrink showed you photographs, and you pointed at one. She shuffled 'em, and you pointed at it again. Same one. But two days later when we could organize a lineup, you wouldn't ID him. Wouldn't point at anybody at all."

I thought about this. "How did you know what pictures to show me? I mean, were they random? Or did you have a suspect?"

"We had a few. We questioned the man who used to clean your parents' gutters. He couldn't keep his story straight about where he'd been that afternoon. Turned out he spent it blind drunk in a bar, didn't want his wife to know." Beasley shrugged. "More promising, there was a guy who'd done a few burglaries around your neighborhood. We picked him up when he tried to off-load silverware and jewelry he'd lifted from a house on Cantrell Road."

"The random-burglar theory."

"Exactly. And there *was* jewelry missing. Apparently your mama had a particular necklace she favored, that she never took off. It was gone. Never did turn up. But . . . there was nothing to indicate the Cantrell Road guy ever set foot inside your house."

I shook my head in confusion. "So whose picture was it that I picked out?"

"We also had—we had a statement from a neighbor. Directing us towards someone."

"What neighbor? The Rooneys?"

Beasley screwed up his face in concentration. "Can't say I remember the name. She was a teacher. Lived next door."

"That's Cheral Rooney. I met her yesterday."

He looked wary. "And what did she say?"

"Nothing about a suspect! She just talked about what the neighborhood used to look like, what my mom was like. She gave me an old pair of Sadie Rawson's earrings."

"Uh-huh. Well, she was under the impression—I'm sorry if this comes as yet another shock—but she was under the impression that your mama had been having an affair. And she thought this other man was someone we should question. So we did, and we thought we might be onto something, because that's the picture you pointed at. His picture. But we couldn't make it stick."

I tried to take in this latest piece of information. "Was it true? Was she having an affair?"

"Who knows?" Beasley shrugged. "He denied it, and there wasn't any evidence. So maybe it was true, or maybe it wasn't. Maybe the neighbor just didn't like your mama. Or maybe she was jealous. Women can be vindictive. No offense."

"The newspaper said police arrested a suspect and let him go. Was that—"

"No, no, we never arrested anybody. We questioned him and then we let him go. He had an alibi. Airtight. And we had no physical evidence, not a scrap. We couldn't hold him."

IN THE PARKING lot outside the newspaper building, a chilly rain was falling. I pulled my jacket over my head and dashed for the Mazda. Wet and panting, I climbed in and flicked on the heat and the windshield wipers. They were old and made a squeaky, scraping sound each time they shuddered across the glass. Every two seconds, they cleared a glimpse of the gray world outside, then the rain sluiced down to blur it again. I forced myself to concentrate on the wipers, to use them as a metronome. Steady. Deep breath. Everything will be okay. I willed even the throb in my neck to obey the commanding rhythm. *Scrape, throb, breathe*. Don't think. *Scrape, throb, breathe.*

I'm not sure how long I sat like that, staring at the half-fogged windows. I knew I needed to step on it if I was to make it to the airport with any hope of catching my flight. But I couldn't muster the energy to shift the car into drive. When the throb had quieted to a manageable level of pain, I twisted around in my seat belt, reached for my phone, and dialed Martin.

"Sis! How are you? Where are you? Still in Atlanta?" His voice sounded so normal, so unburdened, it seemed to come from a different world.

"Yes," I said dully. "Still in Atlanta. I'm—"

"Would you do me a favor and phone Mom? She's completely freaked-out, says you didn't call yesterday."

"Sure. I will. It's been crazy down here."

"Seriously, Sis. Call her. And listen, can I call you right back? I've got an investor on the other line, we're trying to close on a deal this week."

"Martin." I pressed the phone closer to my ear. "Hang up on him and talk to me."

"Sure, okay, but he's in Abu Dhabi. We're recapitalizing his properties in Manhattan, I'm talking hundreds of millions in office/flex—"

"You know I have no idea what you're talking about. Please." My voice cracked. "I need—I need you to tell me what to do."

Martin is too much the classic oldest child to resist such a plea. He has always exhibited an almost parental sense of responsibility toward Tony and me. It seems to coexist easily alongside the pleasure he takes in teasing and tormenting us (and in Tony's case, actually giving him a physical pounding from time to time). I could picture him now, pulling his shoulders back, preparing to launch into full older-brother, let-me-tell-you-how-to-fix-your-problem mode.

Except that my current problems were not easily fixed.

He listened in silence as I told him about Beamer Beasley and everything that I had learned.

"Wow," he muttered when I had finished.

"Yeah."

"That's insane about the bullet in your neck being the same one that . . ." He broke off. "It's hideous, actually. It's . . . Christ, I don't even know what it is."

"That's what I said when I found out."

"But aren't you thinking that maybe you could have the bullet removed? You're going to go see a surgeon, right?"

"I'm supposed to do that tomorrow. Will set it up."

"Who's Will?"

"My regular doctor."

"On a first-name basis, are we?" asked Martin suspiciously. "How old is he?"

"I don't know. Fortyish."

"Married?"

"Martin, for God's sake."

"I repeat, married?"

"I don't think so."

"I knew it. Next you're going to tell me he wears black, skinny jeans and that he chain-smokes Gitanes. Where do you find these guys?"

"Very funny. If you're trying to cheer me up, it won't work."

"Not at all. Farthest thing from my mind. I am curious, though, whether Dr. Sprockets has taken you techno dancing yet?"

Despite myself, I smiled. "Trust me, he's not the skinny-jeans type."

"Or should I call him Dieter?"

"Martin! He drives a Jeep and he listens to Johnny Cash."

"Aha! So you've been in his car? Front seat or back?"

"Will you listen?" I exploded. "I'm not dating him. I'm trying to have a serious conversation with you about a serious subject—"

"Fine. Want to know what I think you should do?"

"I'm beginning to regret asking, but yes. Go ahead."

"I think you should get your butt on a plane back up here and go see that surgeon. The one Dr. Sprockets has hooked you up with. Personally, I would have done that before jetting off to Atlanta, but whatever. Go see him and schedule the surgery to get the bullet removed. And before you do any of that, for chrissake, call Mom."

I sighed. "I know. It's just—I thought I was finished down here, and suddenly it feels like I'm not. Think about it: I've found out more about my parents since I woke up this morning than I have in the last thirty-four years combined—"

"Your birth parents."

"My what?"

"Your birth parents. Not your parents. Because that would be Mom and Dad."

"Of course," I said more gently. "My birth parents. That's what I meant. But that kind of underscores my point. My whole life I've thought that we had this idyllic, perfect childhood—"

"We did, basically."

"No. You did. I think we can agree that mine turns out to have been quite a bit darker than that."

"But hang on, how does it—"

"Could you shut up and listen for a minute without getting defensive? I'm saying I always believed I had the perfect childhood in Washington, and it turns out that that was a mirage. And then I come down here to Atlanta, and—and I guess I constructed another version. That my birth parents were this storybook couple, gorgeous and in love, and tragically cut down in their youth. And now it emerges that maybe that wasn't true, either."

"Why not? Because *maybe* Sadie Rawson had an affair?"

"Yes."

"But who cares if she did? Who cares if she wasn't an angel? I mean, not to sound harsh, but does it matter at this point?"

He was right, but I was still upset. I struggled to find the words to make him understand. "The cop—Beasley—he said Sadie Rawson pushed me down behind her. That it looked like she had tried to protect me."

"Well, it sounds like she did."

"Right, but what if it was from a threat that *she* brought into our home? Don't you see, Martin?"

"Not really."

"The neighbor told police that she was cheating on my dad, and that they should question the man she was sleeping with. And then apparently I pointed at a picture of the same guy. The same guy! If it's true, and if it's in any way related to the shooting . . . then sure, she protected me," I said bitterly. "Kind of like a mother hawk protecting her young from a live snake that she herself has dropped into the nest."

Eighteen

Cheral Rooney looked surprised to find me on her doorstep again.

After hanging up with Martin, I had checked my watch and calculated that I might yet make my flight if I floored it to the airport. That would be the sensible thing to do. My brother was right: I needed to get home, get my neck seen to, and forget about the past. But I couldn't do it. Not yet. Instead I backed out of the newspaper parking lot, pointed the car toward Cheral's house, and stepped on the gas.

From the car I made two phone calls to Washington. The first was to my mother, to reassure her that I was still alive. The second was to Will Zartman, to let him know I wouldn't be on the flight this afternoon after all. His response was uncharacteristically subdued. He didn't protest and he didn't ask why. He merely inquired into how I was feeling, and whether I needed a refill on painkillers. He hung up before I'd even said good-bye. Strange. I wondered whether I'd misread his intentions. The way he had touched my hair the other day, and that comment about my body. I'd been sure he was building up to something. But today, he could not have sounded less interested.

Cheral Rooney, by contrast, lit up when she saw me.

"Caroline!" She pulled me in out of the rain. "Come in, come in. You'll get soaked out there." She stood back and inspected me. "I wasn't expecting to see you again. I thought you'd already left town? Let me put on a pot of coffee. Or, no, you're partial to tea, aren't you?"

"Cheral. Leave the drinks for a minute. Come here and sit down." I led her back into the living room where she'd received me yesterday.

"Did you see the article in this morning's paper?"

She nodded.

"Apparently a lot of people did. And one of them told me some things about Sadie Rawson that I didn't know. Some not very nice things. He told me that before she died, she might have been having an affair."

Cheral stiffened. "Who told you that?"

"One of the cops who investigated the murders. He said *you* were the source for that. That you were the one who told police about it. Is that true?"

She was looking strangely at me. "Does it matter? Why would that even come up now?"

"Because I was asking him about suspects. So, is it true?"

She pursed her lips in apparent annoyance. "Well, I can't think why a police officer would want to dredge all this up. Why he would want to tarnish a daughter's memory of her mother. You want to know what's true? Sadie Rawson was beautiful, she was funny, she loved you. Everything I told you, it's all true. I really think that's all you need to know, Caroline."

I reached forward and touched her knee. "Thank you. For trying to be kind. But I'd rather know the whole story, all of it, even the bad parts."

Cheral stared into the corner of the room for a long moment. "Oh, I don't know what the right thing is to do," she murmured.

"Look, you said yourself, none of this probably matters now. But since I'm here, and since I'm asking, I think I deserve an answer."

Several seconds passed, then Cheral began to speak. "I didn't know your mother before she was married. I knew her type, though, and so do you. You only had to talk to her for five minutes before you guessed that she'd been the prom queen, and the prettiest girl in her sorority, and that a dozen boys had dropped down to one knee and begged her to marry them, before she picked your daddy. She had that way about her, you know? A mystique."

I nodded.

"I was flattered that she wanted to be my friend, if you want to know the truth. I mean, it was only because we were next-door neighbors. Her best friends were still her sorority sisters. They were mostly up in North Carolina, though, and she was down here and stuck home with a baby."

"And so this other man—" I interrupted, hoping to hurry her along.

"But it was like she couldn't stop," said Cheral, ignoring me. "She was so used to having men buzzing around her. Like flies drawn to honey. The four of us—Rick and me and your parents—we would go to a party together, and she would be dancing and flirting and carrying on.

She wasn't happy unless every man in the room fell a tiny bit in love with her by the end of the night. Scarlett O'Hara had nothing on your mother, I tell you that."

"She was young."

"She was old enough to have a husband and a child. She was old enough to know better." Cheral heaved a deep breath. "Sadie Rawson did love you, she really did. She was sweet when she was pregnant with you. She wanted a girl. She wasn't much better at sewing than she was at baking, God knows, but she stitched together dresses for the two of you. Red and white gingham, with fancy, red bows at the waist. Mother-daughter dresses, so you two could be all matchy-matchy. Before she even knew whether you would be a boy or a girl! She just knew she wanted a girl, and Sadie Rawson *always* got what she wanted."

The bitterness in Cheral's voice was now unmistakable. "Wouldn't you know she bounced right back, got her figure back in about four seconds flat? And I don't know exactly when, but sometime after that, somewhere around the time you learned to walk, she started carrying on with Tank."

"Tank?"

"He was a football star in high school. Notorious for rolling over the other team like a tank. I guess the nickname stuck." Cheral rolled her eyes. "He and Sadie Rawson used to flirt like crazy. I'm sure it drove Tank's wife nuts. But then, after a while, I noticed Sadie Rawson was ignoring him. We'd all go out, and she wouldn't talk to him, wouldn't even make eye contact with him."

"And so you assumed something must have happened between them?"

"She seemed to think it was a game," spat Cheral. "That having an affair was a great big funny game. She didn't seem to get that what she was doing was . . . *wrong*. That she was hurting people."

So this was the sour undercurrent I had sensed. Cheral had watched my mother cheating and had disapproved. Maybe she felt protective of my father and me. Or maybe she was jealous, as Beamer Beasley had suggested.

"But are you sure something happened, something more than flirting?" I pressed.

"Oh, honey. They were in love. They were discreet enough, but sometimes I'd see his car parked in your driveway. He'd pull all the way up, so you couldn't see the car from the street. But my upstairs window looked right out over your parents' backyard."

I pictured Cheral scowling out her window at the driveway next door. Tried not to picture what must have been going on inside Sadie Rawson's bedroom, with me asleep in my crib down the hall. "Do you have a photo of him? I want to see what he looked like."

"Maybe somewhere." Cheral shrugged. "Our old albums are boxed up in the storage unit. I keep meaning to clean it out."

I pressed my fingers to my lips, thinking. "What about Boone? Did he know?"

"I'm not a hundred percent sure, but I don't think so. I never saw the car except on nights when your daddy was flying overnight somewhere. And Sadie Rawson kept her mouth zipped shut. She didn't talk about it, not even to me, not until after she ended it."

"Ended it—you mean, ended the affair?"

Cheral nodded yes. "She eventually came to her senses, decided she wanted to try to make things work with your daddy. I'll give her that."

Relief washed over me. I couldn't tell you why it mattered, but it did, to know that at the end my mother might have been faithful to Boone. To believe that, maybe, at the end they had been happy.

Then Cheral spoke again. "She was terrified, that's why she talked to me. Scared out of her mind."

"Scared? Of what?"

"Of Tank! He wanted them to run away together. Wanted her to leave Boone, and he was going to leave his wife, and they would run away. But Sadie Rawson wouldn't do it. She could be so damn stubborn, your mother. When she broke things off for good, he went crazy."

"Crazy how? Threatening to tell Boone?"

"Oh, worse than that. He hit her. He was a big guy, as the name suggests."

"He *hit* her?"

"That's when she finally told me everything. She came over and sat down in my kitchen and cried and cried. She didn't know what to do. I told her she'd made her bed, literally"—a sad laugh escaped Cheral's lips—"she made her bed, and now she had to lie in it. But she was scared."

I felt sick.

"I've thought about this, so many times. Whether there was something I could have done. Somebody I should have told. But I don't think even Sadie Rawson believed he would really harm her."

I frowned in confusion. "You said he hit her. It sounds like he harmed her plenty."

"He said he would kill her," Cheral whispered. "Tank said he would kill her before he would lose her. And then she was dead." Tears began to fall down Cheral's cheeks. "She was dead, and I knew he had kept his word."

Nineteen

There is a ring road that circles Atlanta. It functions like the Beltway in Washington, separating the core of the city from its surrounding suburbs. In Atlanta, this road is called I-285. Locals refer to it as the Perimeter. I had learned this at the Hertz desk three days ago, when I picked up my rental car, and the agent instructed me to avoid the Perimeter like the plague at rush hour.

"Un-frigging-believable that a sixteen-lane highway can get backed up, but it does," he'd advised. "Better to take Georgia 400. Otherwise you'll be stuck in mind-numbing traffic *forever*, wishing you could slit your wrists."

I had made a mental note and kept away.

But as I drove away from Cheral Rooney's house, I noticed a sign marking an I-285 entrance ramp, and on a whim, I took it. Frankly, mind-numbing traffic sounded appealing. Mind-numbing anything, for that matter. I was desperate not to think about what I'd just heard. I steered down the ramp and into the stream of cars, which—sure enough—was barely crawling.

By the time I had completed a full circle around the Perimeter—two hours in the late-afternoon traffic—my mind began to clear. I decided I'd had enough. Enough with chasing phantoms. I could try to find this Tank, confront him, demand to know what had happened that day back in 1979. But what good would it do? It wouldn't bring back Boone and Sadie Rawson. What had happened to them—what had happened to me—was unspeakable. It would be a long time before I got over the shock of seeing Sadie Rawson's face in that photograph. But you can feel only so much sorrow for a person whom you physically resemble, but can't actually remember. Enough. It was time to go home.

Dusk was falling. I had nearly finished another loop around the city. The car needed gas and I needed a drink.

Out of habit, I headed back to the St. Regis. I had handed in my room key this morning, to discover that Ethan Sinclare had picked up the tab for my entire stay. Three nights, plus (I cringed to think of him seeing this) the gargantuan bill for my room-service cheeseburger frenzy. He must have circled back and handed the manager his credit card after we'd finished breakfast together this morning. He had left a handwritten note at the front desk:

Caroline—

   Such a pleasure to meet you. Hope you don't mind my doing this. Betsy and I would love to take you to dinner if you ever find yourself in Atlanta again. I like to think that somehow, Boone is watching over you, and that he knows his friends are looking after his baby girl.

Yours truly,
Ethan

What a nice man. No wonder Boone had liked him. And thanks to his thoughtfulness, this trip had now cost me a fraction of what I had budgeted. I could afford to stay put tonight, catch my breath, and fly back to Washington first thing tomorrow.

Soon I was stepping out of the Mazda and onto the stone driveway of the hotel. The elegant lobby was hushed, only a few people milling around, a piano tinkling somewhere out of sight. A familiar-looking bellhop scurried over to take my suitcase. I was headed toward the front desk when I froze. Did a double take. Felt my heart skip.

Standing there, beside the elevators, was Will Zartman.

WE STARED AT each other for a long moment.

Then Will held up a hand and waved.

I crossed the lobby to where he stood. "What are you *doing* here?"

"Hey, Caroline. Nice to see you, too." He smiled, waited.

But I wasn't in the mood for routine pleasantries. "What are you doing here?" I demanded again.

"I was worried. You sounded awful on the phone."

"Did I? Well, it's been a hell of a day. I didn't think—you didn't sound very interested when I called."

"I was interested." His voice was both determined and a little shy. "I was starting to think the only way to get you back to Washington was if I came down and dragged you back myself."

"If you came down and dragged me back? And so—so you just went and jumped on a plane this afternoon?"

"You need to keep your appointment with the surgeon tomorrow, Caroline. Either that, or let me connect you with one down here."

I stared at him, trying to take this in. "How did you find me?"

"You told me where you were staying. Remember? And I did try to reach you this afternoon, to tell you I was coming. As you would know if you ever, just once in a while, answered your phone."

"But I checked out of the St. Regis this morning. How did you know I would come back here? I didn't decide myself until a few minutes ago."

He shrugged. "Lucky guess. Where else would you go?"

"Well. This is—it's incredibly sweet of you. But don't you have, like, a job? Patients you're supposed to be seeing?"

"Look, if you want me to turn around and go home, just say the word." Will sounded offended.

"It's not that, I just—"

"And actually, caring for patients *is* my job," he continued huffily. "Although you'd be amazed how helpful it is when they do what I tell them. To take a wild example, when I've wrangled an appointment with one of the most respected surgeons in Washington, it's helpful when my patients bother to show up. As opposed to, say, embarrassing me, ignoring my medical advice, and carrying on in a way that is, frankly, reckless."

I held up my hands. "Touché."

"To answer your original question, I don't see patients on Fridays. It's my writing day. I don't see patients after lunch on Thursdays, either. But thanks for your concern about my practice."

"Okay, okay. Sorry."

He stepped back, crossed his arms on his chest, and regarded me with an expression that was half-angry, half-sheepish. "Another thing I don't usually do is fly around the country chasing down disobedient patients. But you . . . you sounded like you were in trouble. I feel responsible."

"Responsible? Why? What does all this—"

"I screwed up. I told you to slap on a wrist brace and you'd be fine. I should have taken your wrist pain more seriously, should have ordered an MRI months ago. I wouldn't blame you if you sued me for malpractice. But I'm trying to put things right, so here I am."

"So here you are."

We stood facing each other awkwardly. Did he expect me to thank him? To reach out and shake his hand? Lean in for an embrace? This encounter was clearly beyond the remit of the typical doctor-patient relationship. But what otherwise *was* our relationship? Unspoken words hung in the air.

"Hungry?"

"God, yes," I said, grateful to have the silence broken. And I was hungry. I hadn't eaten since Ethan Sinclare had bought me breakfast this morning. "I could do with a drink, too."

He glanced around. "Where's the bar?"

"I'm not actually sure. There's a restaurant upstairs, but . . . you know, I don't think I've eaten anywhere besides this hotel in three days. I keep ordering room service. Would you mind if we went out?"

It didn't take long for the concierge to size us up. He

recommended two places nearby; one was high-end sushi and the other, a steak house. He probably got a cut for every reservation he steered their way. When I insisted we didn't need fancy, that my primary concern was an icy pitcher of margaritas, he relented and directed us to a place called the Georgia Grille.

"Order the jalapeño poppers," he said. "Trust me on this."

Fifteen minutes later, it seemed that trusting him might have been a mistake.

The Georgia Grille was one of the least inviting restaurants I'd ever seen. Set in the back corner of a bland strip mall, it was squashed between a dry cleaner's and the parking lot. Neon letters spelled out the name across a grimy stucco wall. You couldn't see inside; there were no windows. No way to tell if the place was even open.

"This can't be right," I said, checking the piece of paper where the concierge had scribbled the name. "What was he thinking? It looks awful."

"It does," agreed Will. "If it's as bad inside as out here, let's maybe try that steak house after all."

He held open the door; we stood squinting on the threshold. Once our eyes adjusted to the darkness inside, we decided to stay. The place was packed. An old wormwood bar slouched across one wall. The walls were painted tawny butterscotch, and candles glowed on every surface. The scents of roasted pork and fresh tortillas hung in the air. It was hard to imagine a starker contrast with the dingy exterior.

We slid onto two seats at the bar. I peeled off my jacket and looked around.

"Y'all look like you wouldn't say no to a couple of margaritas." The bartender peered at us.

"You read my mind."

"Y'all plannin' to eat, too? Want to look at a menu or just let me tell you what's good?" He salted the rims of two glasses. "Lobster enchilada's the best thing on the menu."

"Sold," said Will.

"I should clarify. It's the best thing on the menu unless it's a Thursday night. Which I believe you'll find it is. In which case, what you want is the cowboy shrimp special."

"I don't know," I said. "I'm not a big shrimp eater."

"Fat, juicy babies grilled up on a bed of grits, with bacon and white beans and spinach—"

"I take it back. You had me at bacon."

"Smart girl."

"Oh, and the jalapeño—what was it we're supposed to ask for?" I looked at Will. "The fritters?"

"The poppers." The bartender set down our drinks. "That went without saying."

I was beginning to feel better. Funny how a large margarita and the prospect of a good meal can do that. I downed my drink in two long swallows and signaled for another.

Will raised his eyebrows. "I guess you needed that."

"Like I said. It's been a hell of a day."

"Just so long as you stay away from the rye. Not that I wouldn't enjoy having to throw you over my shoulder and carry you home."

I pretended to scowl. Will was tall and broad-shouldered;

he would have no trouble slinging me over his shoulder and carting me off. Tonight he looked annoyingly good. He wore a camel-colored cashmere sweater and boot-cut Levi's.

"May I ask you a personal question?" I asked.

"Uh, sure. Shoot."

"Have you ever owned a pair of black, skinny jeans?"

"Skinny jeans? You mean like mall-rat teenage girls wear?"

I laughed. "I guess so."

"Umm, no. I'm afraid that's a glaring omission from my wardrobe. Why?"

The tequila was hitting my bloodstream. I smiled at him. "No reason."

He gave me a quizzical look, then cleared his throat. "Look, Caroline. At the risk of embarrassing myself, can I say something? I meant what I said before. If you want me to walk away tonight and never bother you again, I will. Okay? The last thing I want to do is make you uncomfortable, especially with everything else you're dealing with. And Lord knows my own life doesn't need any more complications. But I—I really like you. I do. I have for a while." His eyes held mine. "I'd like to help you, if you'll let me."

I felt something soften inside me.

"I'd like that, too. And I . . . I'm glad you flew down." The words spilled out before I had time to think. I was surprised to realize they were true. My cheeks burned, and I busied myself tracing my finger around the rim of my glass and licking off the salt.

"You're blushing."

"Am not."

He swiped his hand across his mouth to hide a grin. "Fine. Change of subject then. Want to tell me about your day from hell?"

"Oh, it's been the longest day ever." I sighed. "The phone started ringing before I even got out of bed. First this guy who used to play tennis with my dad. With Boone Smith, I mean. And then this cop called—"

"Hang on, hang on. Why were these people calling you? How do they even—"

"Because of the newspaper story."

Will looked blank.

"The *Journal-Constitution* wrote a profile, about me coming back to Atlanta. It's on the front page today."

"You're on the *front page* of today's paper? Seriously?"

"Yeah."

"Jesus. I must have walked right past it at the airport."

"Well, every single other person in Atlanta seemed to see it." I described for Will how I'd met Beamer Beasley in the newsroom, and what he'd told me about the day of the murders. Eventually, I arrived at what Beasley had told me about the bullet itself.

Will went pale and touched my hand. "That must have been awful to hear."

"Yes. I—I wanted to claw it out right there. I still do." I shuddered.

"I don't blame you."

We were both still. Then, suddenly, Will sucked in his breath. "Tell me again what exactly the cop wanted to know about the bullet? When he asked whether you could feel it in your neck?"

"That was pretty much it, I think." My forehead wrinkled with concentration. "Beasley was walking me downstairs, and he asked whether the bullet hurt. Whether I'd ever explored getting it surgically removed."

Will threw me a sharp look. "You see why he was asking that? It sounds like your case preyed on him, all these years. He never solved it. No wonder he wanted to meet with you."

"What are you talking about?"

"He told you there was no physical evidence, right? Don't you think the police would have liked to get their hands on the bullets? Then they might have figured out what type of gun was used. Maybe they could even have identified the actual murder weapon; I'm not sure how these things work. But Beasley said the bullet that hit your father disappeared, right? And the other one was off-limits to police, because it was sewn up inside a hurt little girl. Inside you, Caroline. You're walking around with the evidence in your neck."

SOMEHOW THIS PRECISE point had not occurred to me. I'd been so caught up with the horror of that bullet having traveled through Sadie Rawson's flesh that I hadn't stopped to consider its potential utility as forensic evidence.

"Do you think that's why Beasley wanted to see me?" I asked Will. "To find out if there was any chance of extracting it?"

Will shrugged. "I don't know. But imagine if you were him, and you unfolded your morning paper to find a case that had haunted you your whole career, plastered across the front page? He must have choked on his coffee. Of course he'd want to question you. Does the article mention that the bullet is still intact and in your neck?"

I shrank down. "Yes. They ran the image of the X-ray."

"That was in the *newspaper*?" Will looked aghast.

"They wanted proof that I wasn't making all this up!"

"Okay, okay." He took a deep breath. "To speak to your question, I have no idea whether Atlanta police would have the resources, or indeed the interest, in reopening a case that's sat cold for thirtysomething years. But Beasley wouldn't be much of a cop if he hadn't asked, would he?"

"He also asked whether coming back here had jogged any memories."

"Yeah. That would be the other thing I would want to know, if I were in his shoes."

"I told him it hadn't."

"Nothing at all? Even going back to visit your old house?"

I shook my head. "There was a moment—I thought I remembered where a light switch should be, and there it was. On the stairs leading up to the attic. But no, nothing about my family, or how they died."

"I'm glad, actually. Glad you don't have to relive that day." My right arm had been resting on the bar, and now he laid his arm against it. We were barely touching, but where his skin brushed mine, the hairs stood up, instantly electric.

"How's your wrist?"

"The same," I managed.

"I've seen you drawing circles, like this. Does that help?" His finger traced a slow circle on the white skin inside my wrist.

I nodded. Closed my eyes. The room tilted.

His finger circled again, more firmly now.

I was finding it hard to breathe. "You're not my type."

"That's a shame." Another circle. "For what it's worth, you're not my type either."

My eyelids fluttered open. "I'm not? Why?"

"Well, for starters, I usually steer clear of women who set off metal detectors even when fully undressed."

I smiled.

He smiled.

Then he stretched out his leg until it pressed against mine. Hip against hip, knee against knee. You could feel hard muscle outlined beneath his Levi's, could feel the heat rising off his skin.

Later, in a dark corner of the parking lot, he leaned me back against a doorway. With one hand he gently braced my neck. With the other, he traced the same, slow circle over my blouse, around the tips of my breasts. He took his time. Slow, then slower still. His fingers circled and curved and teased until I was dizzy, until I heard myself moan. Until—for the first time in days—the throbbing in my body was nowhere near my neck.

Twenty

G ood morning, madam."
My usual waiter greeted us at breakfast. He eyed
Will and me with an uneasy expression, as though he
wasn't quite sure what to do with us. I checked my
watch; it was barely seven o'clock. Perhaps the restaurant
wasn't yet open for business? Will had dragged me out of
bed half an hour ago, adamant that we needed to get to
the airport and talk our way onto an early flight home. I
had agreed on the condition that we grab a decent breakfast first.

The waiter eventually turned, beckoned us to follow,
and showed us to a secluded table behind a gigantic, pot-
ted plant. He presented the menus with a flourish. "Now
then. The kitchen's just getting going. Fresh orange juice?
Are you leaning towards the yogurt, or the sweet-potato
pancakes today?"

I smiled. The man had memorized my breakfast pref-
erences while I hadn't even learned his name. I made a
mental note to leave a big tip. "The pancakes again. You
have an astonishing memory."

"Thank you. I also recall that you prefer the pancakes with a side of sausage?"

Make that a really big tip. "You recall correctly, thanks."

"Very good. How about for your—err—friend?" The uneasy look again.

"Just coffee and toast. Whole wheat, please," Will told him.

The waiter nodded, glanced at me again, hesitated. Then, as if he couldn't help himself: "And will any of your other friends be joining you for breakfast?"

It took a second, and then I got it. Even luxury hotels such as the St. Regis must see their share of the world's oldest professionals. I had now waltzed in with a different man on my arm three mornings in a row. And today, Will and I were no doubt radiating the rumpled glow of two people who've just enjoyed great sex and little sleep. My poor waiter probably assumed I was a high-end hooker. A hooker whose services included a weird ritual of making her clients buy her pancakes afterward.

"Your other friends?" Will asked after the waiter walked away.

"Don't worry about it."

Will raised his eyebrows, then let it drop. "How's your neck?" he said instead.

"Fine." It was nearly true.

"And your wrist?"

I flexed it up and down. "The same. Sore."

He reached across the table and lifted my right arm to examine it. His fingers laced through mine, rotating my wrist in one direction and then the other. Tiny needles of pain shot out.

"Ow. I told you. It's sore."

"Just checking your range of motion." He slid his hand out of mine, rested my arm back on the table, and traced a slow circle inside my wrist. "I gather this feels better."

"Mmm. Don't start that again, or we'll wind up back upstairs."

"Where you could demonstrate again for me what an astonishing range of motion you enjoy in other parts of your body."

I swatted him with my good hand. "Shhh!"

"Sorry," he said, not looking sorry at all. "So. Let's see. We could talk about . . ." He drummed his fingers on the tabletop. "It's a shame, actually, that we have to race back to Washington. I keep meaning to check out Turner Field one of these days."

"What's that?"

"The Braves, silly. Home field for the Braves. The baseball team here in Atlanta."

I stifled a yawn. "They're pretty good, right?"

Will lit up. "Yeah, not bad. Just won their division."

"Did they win the World Series this year?" I asked by way of making conversation.

"Did they win the World Series this year?" repeated Will, sitting back and staring at me in disbelief. "Tell me you didn't just ask that. The World Series hasn't happened yet. It starts next week. The Cards play the Dodgers tonight in St. Louis. And then tomorrow's the American league, Red Sox versus the Tigers in Boston. Huge game. How can you not know that?"

"But isn't baseball a summer sport? Shouldn't this be

the off-season?" This time I could not hold back a yawn. Baseball. Johnny Cash. Was there no end to the topics that animated this man and bored me senseless?

Will was now gaping at me as if I were an alien just landed from Mars. "Are you actually American? Or do they brainwash you before they let you join the French Department, make you swear only to follow, I don't know—competitive cheese eating? Escargot racing?"

"The French are excellent at soccer. And tennis. Formula One racing. And . . . let's see . . . *pétanque*."

"What the hell is *pétanque*?"

"It's, you know, like *boules*. You have metal balls, and you try to roll them as close as possible to a wooden ball, the *cochonnet*."

Will snorted. "I stand corrected. That sounds gripping."

"Oh, you're impossible."

"Tell you what. How about, as a special treat, sort of a remedial educational service, we watch the World Series together? The opening game is on Wednesday. I'll explain everything, teach you the mechanics of the game."

"Wow. That sounds . . . tempting." My brothers have tried episodically over the years to educate me about baseball. They share a block of season tickets for the Nationals, Washington's wildly popular franchise. Every once in a while—when enough time has elapsed that I've forgotten what torture it is to sit through nine innings—they persuade me to come along. Tony buys the beer while Martin devotes himself to explaining, for the umpteenth time, the difference between a player's batting average and his on-base percentage. I remind him that I haven't even mastered which is left field and which is right field. The only useful piece of information I've picked up is that section 109 is home to an outpost of Ben's Chili Bowl, which sells a mean Half-Smoke.

"So we're on for Wednesday?" Will was waiting for an answer.

"Sure. Okay. But not at some sports bar. Your place?"

"No, let's say yours."

"Deal." Yes, that would be better. I could cook. I'd still be stuck watching baseball, but at least we would eat well.

"I'll bring scorecards, show you how to track all the stats."

"Now you're pushing it."

He grinned and pushed back from the table. "At the risk of boring you further, would you excuse me a second? I've got a few voice mails I need to respond to. Be right back."

I watched him walk away with some relief. I needed a moment alone, to collect myself. What on earth was I doing here? With Will Zartman? With my physician, for God's sake, in an Atlanta hotel, flirting over predawn pancakes? Clearly I was not myself. The last twenty-four hours had brought a tumult of contradictory emotions: one minute found me weeping; the next, gobbling up jalapeño poppers and giggling like a schoolgirl. I wasn't sure what I felt anymore, other than raw. It would take time to process everything I'd learned yesterday.

And now this thing with Will. It was true: he wasn't my type. But that didn't seem to be preventing my feeling attracted to him. Will, the earnest, solicitous doctor in Washington? Him, I could resist. But this less predictable man, who'd flown to Atlanta on a whim and then kept me up all night—well, he was intriguing. I studied him as he wove through the restaurant, absorbed in his phone conversation. He was wearing the same Levi's and cashmere sweater as before. The jeans hugged him in interesting places; maybe I liked the boot-cut look after all. This would be a ludicrous time to start a relationship. My whole world had just been upended. But no one ever argued that laws of reason and logic apply to the chemistry between a man and a woman. Will caught my eye from across the room and winked, held up one finger to indicate he would be just another minute.

I winked back. It had been a while since I'd had a crush. You would think I'd be too old for such nonsense, that at thirty-seven I would have graduated to responding less like a teenage girl and more like a sensible woman approaching middle age.

It was a pleasure to discover this was not the case.

PART THREE

Washington

Twenty-one

Sibley Hospital is a gleaming, state-of-the-art facility set deep in well-tended lawns. It's the kind of place that makes you grateful to live in twenty-first-century America. No one wants to suffer dire illness or injury, but should it happen—it's reassuring to know that the best medical care money can buy exists right up the street.

I'd never visited Sibley before. The elevator deposited me on the fifth floor. Hushed, carpeted corridors. A closed-in smell of disinfectant and dust, as though the air had been recycled many times. It must have been years since someone had thought to throw open a window. I found my way to the Division of Neurological Surgery, where the dimly lit, blue-and-green waiting room felt vaguely aquatic and was presumably meant to be calming. At three o'clock sharp a sturdy-looking nurse in scrubs called my name. We went through the usual routine, checking my weight (steady, despite the cheeseburger frenzy), my blood pressure, my temperature.

"All right, then." She peeled the pressure cuff off my arm and indicated for me to climb down from the examination table. "Let's get this CT scan done and then you can relax a bit, while Dr. Gellert reads the results."

I looked up, startled. "A CT scan? Do I really need that?"

"Yes, ma'am. Apparently you do." She was already holding open the door to the hallway.

"But . . . hang on. I already got an MRI."

"CT's different. Uses X-rays."

"I already got an X-ray, too."

"Not like this, you didn't. This one, you lie flat and slide in. Then they take loads and loads of pictures. Slices. The doctors stack the slices on top of each other, and we can see your whole head in three-D. It's cool, you'll see."

I felt a stab of frustration. The afternoon would slip away; I had a pile of mail waiting at home for me, not to mention piles of laundry and no food in my fridge. "How long will it take?"

"You're gonna like this."

"I doubt that," I whined.

"Thirty seconds."

"Thirty *seconds*?"

"New machine. I told you, it's cool."

THE THIRTY-SECOND ESTIMATE, of course, referred only to the time needed to perform the CT scan. The time needed to review the results was another matter. My nurse assured me that I'd been tagged an urgent priority. Still, it was pushing 5:30 p.m. and I had read *Vogue* cover to cover, called my mother, and placed an

online grocery order with Safeway by the time Marshall
Gellert strolled in.

He was a slight, intense man in his fifties. He perched
on the edge of a stool, scrutinizing me with hawklike eyes
colored an almost-otherworldly shade of blue. But what
you noticed were his hands. They never ceased moving.
As he spoke, they danced up and down his thighs, darted
into his pocket, produced a pen, and twirled it across his
knuckles in tight, precise loops. He seemed unaware. I
couldn't take my eyes off them. Those fingers might soon
be slicing a scalpel into my neck.

"Dr. Zartman was adamant that I should see you immediately."

"He can be pushy that way."

The hawk eyes bore down. "I'll admit it's an extraordinary case. The survival rate for being shot in the head
would be one in several thousand, at best."

I nodded. What could one say?

"Extraordinary that your brain stem wasn't injured.
I've got your whole file." He opened a purple folder on
his lap. The profile from yesterday's *Journal-Constitution*
peeked out from near the bottom. He'd done his homework. "The cranial computed tomography indicates no
neural damage. The foreign body is just below the left
side of the foramen magnum—"

I held up my hands. "In plain English, please?"

"Sorry. The bullet's one point three centimeters long.
Roughly half an inch. Lodged below the opening where
your spinal cord passes through and connects to your
brain. Here we go." Mounted on the wall beside us was a
flatscreen monitor. Dr. Gellert reached over to flick it on.

After a moment, the sharpest image I'd yet seen came into focus. A stark outline of my skull, my teeth, and the bullet, glowing white as usual.

"What's unclear is why it may have shifted after all these years. If indeed it has."

"Will thinks my spine has compressed."

"Will?"

"Dr. Zartman, I mean." I let my hair fall across my face to hide my blush.

"Well, that's a decent theory. At any rate, your symptoms certainly suggest movement of some sort. Which makes you a more urgent candidate for intervention than if it were causing you no trouble."

"Your advice, then, is to go ahead and remove it? But I've been told it's surrounded by nerves and blood vessels." I frowned at the screen. "Even to my untrained eye, it looks awfully close to my spinal cord."

"It couldn't get much closer," he agreed, a tad cheerfully for my liking. "Ms. Cashion, the truth is that with an injury like this, there are considerable risks to any course of action. Including leaving it put." He flipped the pen behind his ear, wiggled and stretched his fingers. "I always like to look at comparables. Tricky in your case. As I said, the odds are maybe—*maybe*—one in five thousand that you should even be alive and walking this earth. Still, there are documented cases of people surviving gunshots to the neck or skull. I pulled some recent ones that may be instructive."

He plucked a photograph from the folder. It showed teenage boys in yellow jerseys, kicking a ball around a scrubby field. "A soccer team? I don't follow."

"Bear with me. This is one of my favorites. It's from June. This past summer. Those boys are playing on a field in Bosnia. Same field where an unfortunate goalkeeper was playing when he started complaining that his head hurt. Article cites a Sarajevo newspaper, says the goalie completed the match, but—I'm quoting here—'He soon complained of a stiff arm and had difficulty speaking. He was driven to a local hospital, where doctors were shocked to see that a nine-millimeter bullet was clearly lodged in his skull.'

"The good news is, he's fine." Dr. Gellert held the article out to me. "They got it out. But here's my favorite detail: Local police arrested a guest at a nearby wedding. Guy thought it would be a good idea to celebrate by firing his pistol into the air. They found another twelve shells scattered around the soccer field. Could have wiped out the entire team. God love the Balkans."

I smiled politely and handed back the paper.

He started stuffing it into the folder, then froze. "Hang on, I take it back. That's not even the best bit. Listen to the kicker: 'For the record, Krtalica only conceded one goal while playing with a bullet in his head.' One goal! Can you beat that?" Dr. Gellert was clearly enjoying himself.

I tried to steer the conversation back to my predicament. "Of course, that's a totally different scenario from mine—"

"Of course, of course." Gellert cleared his throat. "And check the source: Yahoo News New Zealand. Perhaps not a paragon of accurate medical reporting. That's the problem with most of the cases I turned up. They tend to happen in rural China, or the favelas of Rio de Janeiro. Impossible to authenticate. But, this one." He shuffled through the folder again. "This one is interesting."

On the page before him were two black-and-white images that looked remarkably like the CT scan of my own head. A bright-white bullet, unmistakable, resting atop a neat stack of vertebrae.

"*New England Journal of Medicine,*" said Gellert. "As reputable as you can get. Three years ago, this guy walks into a cardiology clinic in Moscow. He's eighty-five years old, needs treatment for heart disease. The doctors spot something odd and ask him about it. The patient reveals that at the age of three, his older brother accidentally shot him with a pistol."

"Three? That's the same age as I was."

"Mm-hmm. And same as you, he exhibited no clinical or radiographic evidence of neural damage. He was a successful engineer, won the Soviet State Prize. All while walking around with a bullet in his neck for . . . what would that be? Eighty-two years."

"So did they remove it?"

"Nope. Didn't seem to have done him any harm."

I shifted on my chair. "But you think I should remove mine."

"Look. Let me put this simply." His fingers raced along the edge of the desk between us, back and forth, constant motion. "There's a big difference between you and that Russian engineer. His bullet wasn't bothering him. Yours is. Plus, you're young and healthy. A much better candidate for surgery."

He walked me through what surgery would entail.

One operation, lasting four to five hours. I pressed him for details, best- and worst-case scenarios. We talked for another thirty minutes.

As I stood to leave, I posed the question that doctors must dread: What would he do if it were him? Or his daughter, or his wife?

Marshall Gellert did not mince words. "If it were me, I'd want it out."

"I thought you would say that."

"Sorry to be predictable. You know what they say. Show a surgeon a problem, he'll want to operate on it. It's what we're trained to do. But, Ms. Cashion? As an added bonus in your case, it's also the right thing to do."

I studied his eyes. Studied his hands. Felt myself arrive at a decision.

"Will it come out intact? I'll be able to keep it?"

He looked at me strangely. "As a souvenir?"

I thought of Beamer Beasley. Of the little house on Eulalia Road, and the horror that had played out there. As I'd slept on the plane this morning, I had dreamed of Sadie Rawson, of her smile—so like mine—beaming out from the faded newspaper photograph.

"Something like that," I said.

Twenty-two

I spent the weekend alone.

I had let everything slide, and now I devoted myself to restoring a semblance of order to my life. Mail was sorted, houseplants watered, bills paid. I got the car washed and collected my dry cleaning. Will and I texted each other, flirty "thinking of you" messages. I phoned him on Saturday, but he did not come by, and I found that I was fine with that. The thing about being an introvert is that people get on your nerves after a while, even people you like. Whether Will could sense this, or whether he was just busy, I didn't know. But after the demands of interacting with so many new people in Atlanta, I was grateful to retreat and spend time on my own.

The exception to this—and one of the reasons I'd always considered myself closer to them than to anyone else—is my parents. They didn't exhaust me the way other people did. Sunday afternoon I drove over and let myself in the kitchen door as usual. My mother cooked; my father leaned against the counter, scratched Hunt behind the ears, and chatted about the Le Carré novel he was reading. They seemed determined to carry on as though nothing had happened. To preserve the rhythms of our prior life. I understood. Informing this display of nonchalance was a desperate, almost tangible current of love. You could read in their eyes the words they were not saying out loud: *You are our daughter, this is your home, nothing has changed.*

I watched my mother shake an ungodly amount of salt into a bubbling pot. She glanced around, held out her hand, said nothing. I passed her the pepper grinder. When you've cooked beside someone for thirty years, you know what ingredient she wants before she knows it herself. My mother scowled at the pot. Stirred, sniffed, hesitated. *Nutmeg.* I passed it over. The glorious smell of chicken browning in butter filled the kitchen. For the thousandth time I marveled at how she stayed so slim when she cooked like this every night. Seventy-four years old, but from the back you would mistake her for a girl. Her movements had a lightness, a nervousness, like the skittish peck-and-hop of a sparrow. So different from the way I moved. I had never thought about it before. She held out her hand. *Paprika.*

Over bowls of chicken and dumplings, I shared a heavily edited account of my trip to Atlanta. They already knew the headlines. I told them about my visit to Sibley Hospital, about Marshall Gellert and my decision to go ahead with surgery. They seemed to take this as a given. Apparently I was the only one who had needed time to come round to the idea.

My mother's chief concern appeared to be timing. Were the surgery and the convalescence going to conflict with my birthday dinner? My birthday fell late next month. The Cashions do not take birthdays lightly. My brothers, their wives, all my nieces and nephews, would be under strict orders to appear.

"Do you think we should push the date for the party forward?" Mom asked. "I need to know to get the food ordered. I'm planning a surprise for dinner." If the last twenty years of birthday dinners were any guide, that meant baked potatoes and grilled T-bones. Mom is an excellent but exceedingly predictable cook. Creative menu planning is not her strength.

"I'll pick up some merlot to go with the steak," said my father.

"Tom! It was supposed to be a surprise."

From across the table he winked at me, then said, "Change of subject. I found a great new running trail down along Rock Creek. Four-mile loop. You should come with me one of these days."

That was what he said.

What he meant was *I love you, I will take care of you, I am so sorry*.

Twenty-three

I wondered whether I'd hear from you."

"I figured you'd been waiting thirty-four years, another three days wouldn't kill you."

On the other end of the phone line Beamer Beasley chuckled. "Fair enough. How you holding up?"

"Okay. Considering. I've been thinking." I had turned things over in my mind as I drove home from my parents' house, had called him the moment I walked in my own front door. "I'm going to get the surgery to remove the bullet."

"Course you are."

"Why does everyone keep saying that? I could end up paralyzed. In fact, that's probably a bigger risk if I go ahead with the surgery than if I leave things alone."

"I don't know about surgical risks and whatnot," he replied in that even, steady way of his. "I was just reckoning, if it was me, I couldn't live with knowing where that bullet has been."

Exactly. Beasley had articulated my reasoning better than I had myself, at dinner tonight with my family. You could analyze the medical pros and cons until you went blue in the face; the fact remained that the slug of metal in my neck had been responsible for the death of my biological mother. You couldn't just *leave* it there.

"The surgeon says he'll try to extract it, intact. So I was thinking, maybe you would want to take a look?"

"As evidence, you mean?"

"Well, you tell me. Would it be of interest to the police? I mean, given how long ago everything happened?"

"Absolutely. Unless and until you get a conviction, a murder investigation remains open. New evidence is always of interest. There's a Cold Case Squad, that's what they do."

"What about the statute of limitations?"

"Isn't one. Not for murder."

"And how does it work?" I asked with genuine curiosity. "What would they do with the bullet?"

"Run all kinds of tests on it. Measure it. Weigh it. Ideally, they'd have something to try to compare it with. A gun seized from a suspect, say. Or another bullet taken from the crime scene."

"But you don't have that, right? You said the bullet that killed Boone Smith was dug out of a doorframe, you never found it."

"True. I'm just telling you the ideal scenario. A good ballistics tech could still do something with your bullet, though. Check for distinctive grooves on it. Maybe tell you what kind of gun fired it."

"That's something, I guess."

"Sure. But, Ms. Cashion?" He hesitated. "What are your expectations here? It pains me to keep saying it, but

I couldn't catch your parents' killer back in 1979. And that's when the case was fresh, and we had a team working it full-time. I'd caution you against getting your hopes up that anything much is likely to happen now."

"Oh, I know that. I'm not expecting some dramatic arrest."

"Mm-hmm. Still. You never know. I'll make a call or two, find out what's left of the file on your family."

"What's left?"

"Safe to say those files would have been shifted off-site many years ago."

"You mean stuff might have gotten thrown away."

"Let's say *misplaced*."

I ran my good hand through my hair. "One more thing. The suspect you arrested. Or not arrested, but questioned. Cheral Rooney says he's still alive. She gave me an address for him."

Beasley sighed. "Did she now."

"I'm wondering if you should go talk to him."

"Why?"

"She's convinced it was him. She told me—"

"Ms. Cashion." Beasley's voice turned stern. "I'm sorry your mama's old neighbor has got you riled up. And I don't blame you, Lord knows, stumbling on this mess after so many years. But he didn't do it. The suspect, the one she wanted us to question—he didn't do it. He had an alibi, couldn't have been over on Eulalia Road that day. We never had diddly on him. Nothing but her say-so."

"You had me. I pointed to his picture."

Beasley made an exasperated clicking sound. "Yes, ma'am, you did. Right before you started pointing for a lollipop and your dolly. I've seen more reliable witnesses, is my point. You were *three*. You were a *baby.* There's not a prosecutor in the whole great state of Georgia who would hang a murder case on the testimony of a three-year-old. Certainly not one who's been scared so bad she won't speak."

Twenty-four

In the morning I woke early and walked to Saxbys. It's not my favorite breakfast spot—that honor belongs to Pâtisserie Poupon—but I have to walk right past it to get from my house to the library. So does half the student body of Georgetown; by midmorning, the line of students jostling for lattes and chocolate muffins would be out the door. At six, though, when Saxbys opened, I had the place to myself. I grabbed a table in the window, an enormous mug of Darjeeling, and settled in to work.

I have never lost my sense of wonder that I get paid to read all day, to steep myself in the literature of another country, and another century. It is a scandalously pleasant way to earn a living. I sat marking papers until nearly nine, then pushed my glasses back on my head and looked up. My cell phone was ringing. An Atlanta number, area code 404, lit up the display.

"Hello?"

"Sweet Caroline." The oleaginous voice of the *Journal-Constitution*'s managing editor oozed into my ear. "This city is a sorrier place for your having left us, I'll tell you. Like a light's been turned out."

"Hi, Leland."

Oddly, he began to hum. I pressed the phone closer, straining to make out the tune. "Tell me you're not humming Neil Diamond."

"You must get that a lot."

"Thankfully, no. First time in quite a while."

"I've been sitting here dreaming up ways to lure you back," he drawled. "We never did get that drink together."

"We never will, Leland. Was there something I can help you with?"

"Got a few messages to pass on to you. More calls coming in, people who read our article. One man says he flew with your daddy, for Delta. And a lady called—think her name was Susie. Says she and Sadie Rawson were sorority sisters, up in North Carolina. I said I'd let you know. I'll send you all their contact information."

"Thanks. That would be great. Hang on a sec." I cranked up the volume on my phone. In the hours I'd sat working, Saxbys had filled. Rihanna blared from the ceiling; three baristas sweated over the hissing espresso machine. The entire varsity soccer team appeared to be here, dressed in matching gray-and-navy shorts and logo sweatshirts, 2012 BIG EAST CHAMPIONS—BLEED HOYA BLUE!

"Where are you?"

"Coffee shop. Trying to get work done."

"Sounds more like the Kappa Alpha frat house on a Saturday night. Anyhow, listen. I spoke to Cheral Rooney."

"Did you?" I sat up. "Why?"

"Follow-up story. People are intrigued. We got such a big response to last Thursday's piece. I *told* you that running it was a good idea."

"Oh, no. Please. I don't want to be in the paper again."

"Just a little story this time. Inside pages, most likely."

"But what's the follow-up? There's no news."

"You know—'Community Comes Together,' that type thing. We'll mention all the folks who knew the Smiths, how delighted everybody is to learn you're alive and well. I got a nice quote from Cheral about how you're the spitting image of your mama. How she couldn't believe her eyes when she saw you walking up her driveway. 'Like watching a ghost,' she said."

"Did she say anything about the investigation? Into who killed my parents?"

"Noooo." He stretched the word out. "Why? Is there anything to say?"

"Not that I know of. Just wondered." So Cheral had not shared her infidelity theories with Leland Brett. That was one thing to be grateful for, that a lurid account of Sadie Rawson Smith's love life would not be plastered across the front page.

"People are asking about the bullet, though. Whether you're going to leave it be or get operated on."

I hesitated, could think of no reason not to be honest. "I'm scheduled for surgery next week. Here in Washington. Cross your fingers for me."

"I'll send the biggest bouquet of get-well flowers you ever saw. Which day, you reckon?"

"A week from Wednesday. The thirtieth."

"And you sure I can't tempt you down to Atlanta for a drink in the meantime?"

"Good-bye, Leland."

"I'll let you know when the link to this story goes up. Bye for now, pretty girl."

I hung up and looked around. Rihanna had given way to Radiohead on the speakers above me. A stink of scorched bagel hung in the air. The soccer players stood huddled in the corner, scarfing down bananas and super-size cinnamon buns.

I gathered my papers and relinquished the table. In fifteen minutes, I was due to meet Madame Aubuchon.

TO SAY THAT I was dreading this would be an understatement.

Hélène Aubuchon intimidated me at the best of times. Which, needless to say, this was not. She sat waiting for me in her office, immaculately dressed as always. Tastefully rouged lips, a silk scarf knotted around her shoulders. At her ears and throat were pearls. The head of Georgetown's French Department was not a classic beauty. She was bone thin, with a severity to the set of her jaw. But she was elegant, in that manner particular to Frenchwomen of a certain age. It required money. I suspected it also required weekly visits to the hairdresser, devotion to all manner of mysterious skin creams and potions, and—above all—fanatical vigilance to never put on a pound. I wondered when a cheeseburger had last crossed those crimson lips.

"*Alors, Caroline, ma pauvre.* You have had quite a week, I believe." She arched perfectly groomed eyebrows. "And you discovered more than you bargained for in Atlanta?"

That was certainly true.

"It is shocking. *Tout à fait affreux*, about the bullet in your neck. I am so sorry."

Madame Aubuchon and I had never discussed our personal lives. Aside from the occasional polite inquiry into my summer vacation plans, she had never asked about my life outside work. We were colleagues, not friends. So I was surprised to hear real concern in her voice. I seized the moment. "I went to see a surgeon at Sibley. About removing the bullet. He wants to operate next week. On Wednesday. And after that he's told me to allow at least ten days to rest and recover at home, before returning to work."

"Ten days?"

"I'm afraid so. I realize the timing is awful, midsemester. I would put it off until Christmas break, but the doctor says the sooner, the better."

"*Oui, oui, bien sûr.*" She waved her hand dismissively. "That will be fine."

"It will?" Had I heard her correctly?

"*Pas de problème.* In fact, I've spoken already with Robert." Robert was one of my more capable graduate students; he had already subbed for me twice last week. "He can handle your classes for the rest of the term, under my supervision. That way you can rest."

"Oh, no. That won't be necessary. I'll be back by—"

"It is easier this way. *Vraiment.* Less disruptive for everyone."

"No, really. I'll be back by mid-November. And I want to teach. Those students are my responsibility."

"And the smooth functioning of this department is mine." She smiled in a way that made clear the matter was not open to further discussion. "Surely you can see it is not in your students' best interests to have a new professor every other week."

"Of course not. But we're not talking about a new professor every other week. We're only talking about ten days—"

"That's if your surgery proceeds without complication, and you don't require additional time to convalesce. *Franchement,* ten days sounds optimistic." She crossed trim ankles sheathed in sensible, beige support stockings, a rare concession to her age. "Robert did well teaching last week. He's happy to help. He will follow your syllabus."

I sat seething. How could she have turned my course load over to Robert? Before even consulting me? Could she really just banish me from doing my job?

"Your salary will continue as usual. I checked the records. It appears you've never taken a single sick day. You've accumulated weeks of paid medical leave, so there's no issue there."

"It's not my paycheck that concerns—"

"It's settled then," she cut me off firmly. "Consider it sabbatical. You will rest and recuperate. And then return to us, healthy, after winter break."

Unbelievable. "This is effective immediately?"

"That might be best, yes. Tie up any loose ends directly with Robert. Now, do you have someone to look in on you every day, after the operation?"

"My family lives nearby," I muttered through clenched teeth.

"*Très bien.* I'll visit you as well. We are neighbors, you know. *Voisines.* Jean-Pierre and I live on R Street."

Oh, great. That was all I needed, to have my boss popping over for coffee. The social custom of calling on people when they are unwell has always mystified me. By definition, you're not feeling or looking your best. Why on earth do people assume you might want visitors? That you would enjoy nothing more than to play hostess and chitchat? I could picture the scene: Madame Aubuchon, perfumed and pristine in full Hermès splendor; me, sore and sedated and still in my nightie.

I forced a weak smile and stood to go.

Madame Aubuchon watched me cross the room. "I read the article in the Atlanta newspaper. I pulled it up online. Your parents' murder was never solved."

"No." I stopped with my hand on the doorknob. "It wasn't."

"Will the police want to interview you? Formally, I mean?"

"I don't know. I was so young—I don't remember anything."

"But the bullet in your neck might be evidence, *n'est-ce pas*?" The perfect eyebrows shot up. "*Merde. Quel bordel. C'est dingue.*"

My jaw dropped. Madame Aubuchon had just uttered a vulgarity that, loosely translated, meant something along the lines of "Shit, what a goddamn mess."

"Hélène?" I had never addressed her by her first name, but this seemed a reasonable time to start. "Did you just say—"

"Wouldn't it be incredible if they found something? After all these years? *J'espère qu'ils arrêtent le salaud.*"

Good Lord. Not again. Still, she had a point. I hoped they caught the bastard, too.

AT LUNCHTIME, MARSHALL Gellert called from Sibley. "No need for alarm, but I wanted to let you know about a security incident that took place here over the weekend."

"Oh. Okay. What kind of incident?"

"Unauthorized entry. Somebody gained access to the medical building yesterday morning. Building security is still checking things out, but the lock on our office door was definitely tampered with."

I tried to think why anyone would bother breaking into a doctor's office. "Was it somebody after prescription drugs, do you think? Narcotics?"

"That's a possibility. There's a pharmacy on the ground floor, as you may have noticed. And various samples and supplies locked up in cabinets all over the building. The good news is, it doesn't look like any of our computers were compromised. But I've got my receptionists calling around to patients, so they can watch out for unusual activity on the credit cards we keep on file for billing purposes."

"Right. Well, thanks for the heads-up."

Dr. Gellert coughed. "I'm reaching out to you myself

because of . . . uh . . . an additional irregularity. Your chart seems to have disappeared."

"My chart?"

"That purple folder that I was taking notes in. You didn't happen to take it with you, did you?"

"No, of course not."

"Weirdest thing. I'm sure I left it on my desk, so I could review my notes and follow up today. Not to worry. Your test results are backed up online, and I can re-create everything else."

"Maybe one of the nurses filed it?"

"They say they didn't. They all know not to touch papers on my desk. Anyway, sorry to have disturbed you. I'll be in touch in the next few days. Everything's on track for your surgery next week."

I sat thinking. "You'll let me know if my file turns up?"

"Absolutely."

"And if they find the guy who broke in?"

"Sure, if you like. Security thinks they caught him on a CC camera as he exited through the parking garage. Heavyset guy with dark, curly hair. Couldn't see his face."

AT HOME THAT evening, I kicked off my shoes and collapsed on the sofa. It would be hard to pinpoint which of the day's events I found most unsettling. The news that Dr. Gellert's office had illegally been entered and my chart was missing? The revelation that my elderly boss could outcurse a Marseilles dockworker?

It was infuriating, meanwhile, to admit that Madame Aubuchon's judgment in ordering me to take time off was probably sound. I was in pain. My wrist hurt steadily, exhaustingly. The throbbing in my neck was less reliable but more frightening when it came. Even if the surgery went beautifully, I would need weeks to heal. And there was no denying that I was emotionally drained.

I made it upstairs to my bedroom and was changing into my oldest jeans and a soft, dove-gray cardigan when a knock sounded at the front door. I frowned. One of my brothers, stopping by for a drink on his way home from work? I peeked out the window, expecting to spot the blond head of either Tony or Martin.

It was Will Zartman.

I had not seen him since we'd parted ways at National Airport on Friday. I swiped a brush through my hair and ran downstairs. Neither of us spoke right away. We stood a few feet apart, me in my front hall, just inside the door, Will still out on the front step. His hands were stuffed in his pockets, and on his face was the same mix of sheepishness and defiance that I remembered from the last time he'd shown up unannounced, in the hotel lobby in Atlanta.

"This is a nice surprise. I would have changed if I'd known you were coming." I tugged the sweater tighter around my faded jeans. "I was about to open some wine, if you wanted to—"

"You would have changed if you'd known I was coming? If you'd *known* I was coming?"

"Well, yes, I would have put on—"

"Check your phone."

"My phone?"

"Check it."

"Oh. I see. You did call?"

"Twice. In the past hour. To ask if I could take you to dinner tonight. Caroline, I swear to God. Maybe we should switch to a more modern, reliable form of communication. Say, carrier pigeons?"

"All right, all right. I'm sorry."

"Or maybe smoke signals?"

"It's because I turn the ringer off when I'm in class, and then I always forget to—"

"What about Morse code? That could be fun." He was starting to smile. "Or semaphore flags. The yellow and red ones, like they used to wave to signal trains. Doesn't the navy still use them on ships?"

"I'm about to slam this door on you. Get in here before I whack a semaphore flag over your head."

I reached for his jacket, grabbed the edge of a pocket, and pulled him in. It was dark in the hall after I shut the door against the streetlight. An October chill rose off his clothes, and I caught his scent, the now-familiar mix of soap and maybe a warm animal waiting at home. I thought he might kiss me and I felt suddenly, unexpectedly shy.

Instead, Will bent down and pressed his forehead to mine. "I've been trying to give you your space," he whispered. "I know you needed to spend the weekend alone. But I've been going crazy, wanting to see you."

We stood there, heads touching, not speaking, until my breath slowed to match his own. His fingers brushed mine in the dark. Then his hand climbed my arm, circled it, teasing, lingering in the velvety crook of my elbow. It took Will a hundred years to reach my shoulder, to stroke my throat, to round my chin. His thumb, the thick pad of it, on my mouth. Pressing. Bruising. My lips swelling under his touch. I began to shake.

"Beautiful girl," he whispered.

For a man who was not my type, Will Zartman was definitely growing on me.

Twenty-five

W ord of my possible inheritance came before breakfast.

"Good morning," trilled Jessica Yeo. "Are you awake?
Got a minute?"

"Sure. Just making toast." She had in fact caught me
cracking eggs for an omelet that I was planning to stuff
with chorizo. Will and I had never gotten around to dinner last night; we'd found too many other ways to pass
the time. When I woke, he was already gone.

"You're up early. Already at work?"

"God, no. You've clearly never worked in a newsroom.
Nobody shows up before ten. It's like some unspoken
but unanimous pact among the reporters." She giggled.
"I have got your article open on my laptop, though. It
looks good."

My article? "You mean the follow-up that Leland
Brett was writing? It's already finished?"

"It's on the front of today's Metro section. He might
be a horny old bugger, but he writes fast."

"Jessica!"

"Sorry. But I speak the truth. Both about Leland being a horndog, and about the story looking good." She blew her nose loudly. "Excuse me. It sounds like your parents were really nice folks. Ever since the first article ran last week, people have been calling the paper, to say kind things about them, and to wish you well. Leland quotes a bunch of them in today's story."

"He told me he was planning to. I'll take a look when we hang up."

"Cool. Anyway, a couple of developments. I've been following the money. Your money."

"Not *my* money. My birth parents' money. Whatever there was of it."

"Kinda fascinating, actually. The cemetery wouldn't tell me anything. Just the date your parents were interred and the location of their graves."

"I know. I already went out there to take a look."

"It was a long shot, but I was hoping your paperwork would still be in a file somewhere. That it might show who paid for their plots, what bank the check was drawn on, that type thing. It sounds like that stuff got dumped ages ago, though, and it wouldn't be public record anyway. In better news, I'm making progress on Boone and Sadie Rawson's Social Security numbers."

"Yeah, about those—"

"Listen to this," she said, ignoring me. "Officially, it takes weeks to find out a dead person's number. You have to pay twenty-nine dollars and fill out this form. I've got one here, hang on." I heard her shuffling papers, then the sound of something heavy, a book maybe, crashing onto a hard floor. "Damn it." She came back on the line. "I need to improve my filing system. Complete chaos. But here we go: form number 711, 'Request for a Deceased Individual's Social Security Record.' You mail it off and then you're supposed to wait four to six weeks for a response."

"Jessica—"

"However, since I am a rock-star researcher"—she paused theatrically—"I think I can get them for you by the end of the week. The stupid public-affairs lady gave me this lecture, about how it's impossible to expedite a search, and how I had to wait my turn, and blah, blah, blah. But I went over her head and—"

"I already found them."

"You what?"

"I found the numbers. On Ancestry.com."

"Really?" Jessica sounded stunned. "Everyone's Social Security numbers are just sitting there?"

"Well, at least, dead people's are. My parents popped right up. You could have found them yourself in five minutes. The Social Security Administration keeps something called the Death Master File. Grim name, but useful. It lists everybody whose deaths were reported to the government, all the way back to 1875."

"Jeez. I feel like an idiot."

"Not at all. I had time on my hands over the weekend. I pulled up the state records, too. Every death recorded by the Georgia Health Department from 1919 to 1998. I already ordered copies of their original death certificates."

"Great," said Jessica, sounding deflated.

"There is one thing I can't do from here, though."

"The property records, right?" She perked up. "I was getting to that. It's taken me a few days because I can't search online. The database only goes back to 1980. But so far, lunch today is looking quiet, so I was going to drive down to Fulton County courthouse. Apparently they keep books—I mean, actual books—in the Deeds and Records room."

"And the books would show . . . what? Who bought my parents' house? The purchase price?"

"The deed itself. Who sold the house on your parents' behalf, I'm hoping. I've got the lot number on Eulalia Road. So, that should be easy." She clapped her hands. "While I'm there, guess where else I was going to go?"

"Umm . . . no idea."

"Probate court!" she crowed with improbable delight. "It's right there in the same government complex. If your parents had a will—and let's assume they were organized, responsible citizens, and that they did—it should be filed there. And wills are public record, isn't that cool? We can just walk in and ask to see them. I learned that yesterday, from one of the political editors."

I set down my mug of tea on the counter and considered this. "I would have thought that wills were . . . private. I mean, mine certainly is. A stranger couldn't stroll into some government office and browse through it."

"Right, but you're not dead, are you? Your will hasn't been probated."

"Okay, but surely even dead people have some right to—"

"Nope. 'The dead have no rights and can suffer no wrongs,'" recited Jessica. "I'm quoting—oh, what was his name? Some English judge. They taught us all this in journalism school. How you can't libel a dead man."

"Huh. But you can read his will."

"Exactly!"

"Well, if you're right—if we really can read Boone and Sadie Rawson's wills, we might be able to figure out what happened to the house. And why nothing ever passed to me."

"If we can get our hands on your parents' wills, then we might be in business."

THE NEXT TIME my phone rang, the conversation was more tense.

"You need to stop talking to the press," ordered Beamer Beasley. "Next time that Leland Brett calls, you tell him bye-bye and send him straight to me."

"With pleasure. But why? Did I do something wrong?"

"No, ma'am. It's a nice story in the paper this morning. But from a police point of view, it's time to shut down the conversation. The press has served its purpose."

"If it weren't for the press, you wouldn't have known about my coming back to Atlanta."

"That's true. I don't deny a little media coverage can work wonders. Helps jog people's memories, for one. But you also got to remember, whatever gets printed, it's out there for anyone to read. So information about evidence might be best kept to yourself."

"You mean I should shut up about the bullet and my plans to get it removed?"

"I mean exactly what I said. Information about evidence might be best kept to yourself."

"Speaking of which, there's something I should mention." Beasley listened while I described the disappearance of my chart from Dr. Gellert's office.

"I don't know what to make of that," he said when I was done. "Could be something, could be nothing. But I'm sure it's occurred to you, as it has to me, that that bullet in your neck might be of interest to any number of people. So be smart. Keep your doors locked, don't open up to anyone you don't know, don't go out on your own if you can help it." He hesitated. "I suppose this would be an opportune moment to tell you that your case here is being officially reopened."

"No! Really?"

"That's another thing the press is good for, putting pressure on us. Between those news stories and the possibility of new physical evidence, it was inevitable. The decision's already made. They want to go back over all the old files."

"My God." I tightened my grip on the phone.

"We'd also like to do a formal interview with you. Just to set down for the record some of the things you and I've already gone over. If you like, I'll sit in on that."

"It won't be you asking the questions, though?"

"Likely it'll be the current head of the Cold Case Squad. He's good. You want a young guy; it's been a while since I led an investigation. I've been part-time for years now. But given my history with the case, and the fact that I already made contact with you, I've agreed to work this full-time. See if I can spot anything the young guys miss."

"I'm glad to hear that."

"I'm glad, too. But let me say it again: don't get your hopes up. Please. All this means is me and a couple junior detectives will reread the old folders. The answer wasn't in them thirty-four years ago, and personally I doubt it is now."

"But you said yourself there's new evidence. If the bullet in my neck—"

"If the bullet in your neck comes out intact, and if the techs can do anything with it, then we might have ourselves a lead. But let's cross that bridge when we get there. All right?"

"All right." Deep breath. "All right."

"Ms. Cashion," he said in a gentler tone, "chances are whoever killed your parents is dead himself by now."

"I know. You must . . . you must think there's a *chance* of solving it, though, or you wouldn't be taking this on."

After a moment's hesitation, Beasley said, "Let me answer that indirectly. This past spring we charged a guy named Daniel Wade with rape. Actually, five rapes. Possible ties to two dozen more. He was known as the Maintenance Man because he attacked women in their apartments, pretended to be there to do repair work. One lady, he poured water under her front door. Then he knocked and told her he was checking on a leak."

"That's awful."

"It is. What's interesting is these rapes were committed nearly thirty years ago. Back in the mideighties. Not quite as long ago as your case, but close."

"What changed? Why charge him now?"

"DNA evidence. There wasn't a national database thirty

years ago. DNA from the rape kits of several victims indicated it was the same guy. But we only had his DNA profile, not his name. In May, Wade popped up as a match."

"So you've arrested him?"

"No need," Beasley said wearily. "He's already in federal prison in Kentucky. Locked up on unrelated robbery charges, until at least 2021. After that we'll aim to extradite him back down to Georgia."

I was quiet.

"Not a fairy-tale ending, by any stretch. But I raise it because at least those victims get some closure after all these years."

"Closure." I rolled the word around my tongue. "No disrespect to those women, who I'm sure went through a horrible experience. But I don't know that there is such a thing as closure. Not in a case like mine. My parents were murdered, right in front of me." My voice cracked. "Even in the one-in-a-thousand chance that somehow, after all this time, you could find the man who killed them, it wouldn't—it won't bring them back."

"Course not. No power on this earth's gonna bring back your family. But you're confusing two things. Closure isn't about raising the dead. It's about providing the victim with a sense that—that justice has been served."

"I guess."

Beasley heaved a heavy sigh. "I know it comes too late, and that it's not enough. But in a case like that—in a case like yours—that's what we aim for now. Justice."

Twenty-six

J essica Yeo hit pay dirt at the Fulton County courthouse. She dug out the deeds for the house on Eulalia Road within ten minutes. They showed that my birth parents had bought the house for $45,300 in 1975. It had sold four years later, in December of 1979, for $99,500. A tidy profit back then, especially for a young couple barely out of college. I felt a stab of pride for them. They had been on their way to building a comfortable life for our family, before it had all been snatched away.

Boone and Sadie Rawson's wills had proven equally easy to lay hands on. The clerks in the Records room had needed only their full names, and the year they had died.

"Bingo!" said Jessica, when she reached me that afternoon. "Guess what I'm holding in my hot little hands? All freshly photocopied and stapled? They've got all the wills lined up on open shelves, just sitting there in white plastic binders."

The wills were straightforward, two pages each. There were no complicated assets to dispose of. The documents were mirror images of each other. Boone left everything to Sadie Rawson; she left everything to him. Should they not survive each other, then their daughter, Caroline Smith, was to be the sole beneficiary of their estate.

My breath caught. So strange to hear my name, rising up from pages drafted decades ago, by two people I had loved and then forgotten.

I had Jessica read my father's entire will out loud, down the phone line. Three details stood out. The first was the name of the executor of my parents' estate. The person they had entrusted to carry out their wishes. They had both named the same man: Mr. Everett A. Sutherland, of Charlotte, North Carolina. I had never heard of him.

The second was a savings account number.

The third, intriguingly, was a reference to a safe-deposit box.

Both the box and the savings account were held somewhere called Trust Company of Georgia.

"Trust Company?" I asked. "Is it headquartered in Atlanta?"

"It was. Come to think of it, maybe it still is. But it's like all the big Southern banks. Lots of mergers and name changes over the years. I did some research, right before I called you. Trust Company of Georgia merged with a Florida bank back in 1985. Then they acquired a bank in Tennessee, and then other assets. They all consolidated, changed their names to SunTrust in the mid-1990s."

"Oh, we have SunTrust banks here in Washington. There's one inside Safeway. My grocery store." I tried to clamp down my excitement. "I wonder—I guess we can just call them, right? Find whoever would know where old records are kept, for dormant accounts."

"Yeah. I don't know how complicated that process is.

I'm guessing they'll need to see the wills, and maybe your parents' death certificates, and any other documents we can dig out. As for the safe-deposit box . . . that's interesting. I don't know what physically would have happened to it, after thirty-four years of inactivity. Like, whether the bank would be required to hang on to it, or what."

"No idea. I'll make a call to SunTrust. See what I can ferret out."

"Oh, I can do that. I'm having fun." Jessica was breathing faster, as if she had started walking. "I've got to race back to my office. Show my face, since this has been, like, the longest lunch break ever. Tonight, though, I'll nose around. See what I can find out about this Mr. Sutherland. The executor."

But I was starting to question the wisdom of our arrangement. "Thanks for the offer. You've been amazing. Really. But I'm thinking I should take it from here."

"Why?" She sounded hurt.

"Because you're a journalist, and I seem to keep ending up a story in your newspaper."

"But that's Leland's doing! You're paying me off the books—"

"I know, but what if you dig up something newsworthy? What if—I mean, this is incredibly unlikely—but what if you discovered that my parents left me a million dollars? Wouldn't you have an ethical obligation to report that to Leland?"

"As you say, that's incredibly unlikely."

"But you're a terrific researcher, and I'm betting you dig up *something*. And whatever it is—whatever is out there to be found—I don't want it in the paper anymore.

Why don't you e-mail me copies of everything you've turned up? And tell you what," I teased her. "If I stumble into a fortune of a million dollars, I'll split it with you."

AS I WAS closing my bedroom curtains that night, a car caught my eye. A compact gray car, parked diagonally across the street from my house.

Nothing remarkable about that, other than I'd never seen it before. I knew most of my neighbors' vehicles by sight, and we lived far enough up the hill from George-town's restaurants and shops that few tourists parked on the block.

Inside the car, the outline of his head lit by the tiny screen of his cell phone, sat a man. Again, nothing remark-able there. He could be waiting for someone. Or killing time until he had to be somewhere. Under normal circum-stances I wouldn't have given him a second thought. But Beasley had spooked me. I went back downstairs and dou-ble-checked the locks on my doors and windows, before crawling into bed to read.

Around eleven, when I rose to turn off the lights, I peeked out.

The gray car was still there.

Inside, the man was still sitting. His phone was switched off now and I could make out no distinguishing features other than a head of dark hair. I could not see his eyes. Only that his face, a pale smear beneath the streetlights, had been turned in the direction of my front door all evening long.

Twenty-seven

In the morning I was awakened by an insistent knocking.

I ignored it.

It came again.

I opened an eye. The sun was up. My bedside clock read 7:49. Too early for a package to be delivered. Definitely too early for a friend to stop by. Who then? Beasley's admonition to be careful ran through my mind.

Bang bang bang bang bang bang bang.

I pushed back the covers and padded to the window, cracked the curtains, and squinted down. No. Surely not. I rubbed my eyes. Madame Aubuchon was standing on my front step. She was alone, and at her feet rested what appeared to be a large pot. On her hands she wore chunky, garishly colored gloves.

She must have sensed me staring, for she looked up, shielded her eyes from the sun, and waved. I glanced across the street. The gray car was gone.

When I opened the door, she hoisted the pot and held it out in front of her, stooping slightly against its weight.

Steam curled from under the shiny lid. The gloves were not gloves at all, but oversize, crudely knitted, green-and-purple oven mitts. They clashed against the soft rose silk of her suit.

"Hélène?" What on earth?

"Bonjour, Caroline. Ça va?" Are you well? "Here, take this." She thrust the pot at me.

I tried to lift it from her outstretched arms, but pain shot through my right wrist.

She noticed me blanch. *"Ah, je m'excuse. Elle est où, ta cuisine?"*

She marched past me toward the kitchen. I trailed behind. I had not expected my premonition to come true quite this quickly. Here I was, groggy and rumpled and still in my nightgown, and here was Madame Aubuchon, charging into my kitchen, dressed as if she were headed next to high tea at the Ritz.

"You can keep the pot," she was saying. "But my grandsons made these." She tucked the cartoon pot holders away into a Cartier bag.

"Hélène." I pointed at the humongous pot now resting on my stove. "What is this?"

"Bouillon de poulet." Chicken soup. "Properly made, with plenty of garlic and white wine. It needs to cool. Do you have Tupperware?" Without asking permission, she opened a cupboard, peered inside.

I nodded, mute. I have spoken French as fluently as English since high school. More than half my life. But it was so bizarre, the sight of her rooting around my cabinets in search of stackable, plastic bowls, that words failed me in both languages.

"*J'en ai fait une quantité énorme*"—I made a huge batch—"so you would have enough to freeze and warm every day. While you rebuild your strength." She banged shut a cupboard door, apparently abandoning the Tupperware quest, and studied me. "Caroline, forgive me, but you look dreadful."

"*Je dormais,*" I protested. "I was sleeping."

"It's important to keep up your routine," she scolded. "Do your hair, put on your makeup. Get out of the house. It helps when you're depressed."

"I'm not depressed." Not that it would be any of her business if I were. "And I'll get dressed in a minute. It's barely eight o'clock." Harsh morning light slanted through the window above the sink. The scent of garlic mixed with chicken grease filled the air between us. It must have been seeping into the curtains, the dish towels, my hair. She was right about one thing: I would need both a shower and a generous spritz of perfume before I would be fit to leave the house.

My manners kicked in. "You're thoughtful to drop by. *Merci bien*, thanks so much, for the soup. Would you care for a cup of tea?"

"*Non, merci.* I'm running late. But allow me to make one other suggestion."

It was tempting to point out that she had forfeited the right to make suggestions for the rest of the semester, but I held my tongue.

"Paris," said Madame Aubuchon. "Once you're well enough to travel, you should go to Paris. A change of scene would do you good, don't you think? You may use my apartment."

"That's very kind. I couldn't possibly accept."

"*Pourquoi pas?* Don't be so damn polite. Jean-Pierre and I won't get there again until spring. It's near the Bois de Boulogne, *dans le seizième.*"

Of course it was. Paris's sixteenth arrondissement is where people live when they have plenty of money and no interest in being hip. It's the equivalent of the Upper East Side in New York, or Mayfair in London.

She air-kissed my cheeks twice and turned to leave. "The next time I stop by—"

I bit my lip to avoid groaning out loud. *The next time?*

"—I'll bring you a set of keys. Use them or not, as you wish."

"I BROUGHT EXTRA," said Tony, barreling through my front door with his tie flung over his shoulder and four six-packs of beer under his arms.

For the second time today, I stood aside and watched someone cart provisions into my house.

"I know it'll be tough for you to get to the store after the surgery," my brother called over his shoulder. "This way you're fully stocked."

I followed him into the kitchen. "Um, thanks. But I don't drink beer."

"Yeah, I know. One of many areas in which you do persist in demonstrating bad taste." He yanked open my refrigerator door and began whipping bottles of Brooklyn lager out of their cardboard carriers, then dumping them into the empty produce drawers. "These aren't for you, though. They're for Martin and me. So we'll have something decent to drink when we come visit you in your sickbed."

I burst out laughing. "How considerate."

"Don't mention it. You can pay me back later."

"You're too kind."

"I know. My chivalry knows no limits. I was also thinking . . . ugh." Tony inhaled, wrinkled his nose in distaste. "What are you doing in here, Sis? Warding off vampires? Your house reeks of garlic."

"Damn it." I lit another scented candle. I'd spent half an hour this morning digging out Tupperware and Ziploc bags and transferring the contents of Madame Aubuchon's enormous vat, ladle by ladle, into my freezer. There was enough soup to last me weeks. "Somehow I've got to get rid of that smell before tonight."

"Why? What's happening tonight?"

"I've got a date. I'm cooking."

My brother heaved himself up to perch on my countertop and sniffed again. "I hope that's not what's for dinner."

I glowered at him. "Actually, I'm serving steaks. I bought *two*."

"Hint taken. Don't worry, I'll scram." He sat swinging his legs, rubbing scuff marks from the heels of his black dress shoes onto the pale wood of my cabinet door. He knew this drove me crazy. He knew that I would leap to scrub off the marks the minute he exited the room. He also knew I would never give him the satisfaction of asking him to stop. I pointedly fixed my eyes on the ceiling, away from his feet. He pointedly kicked faster. Honestly, sometimes we behave exactly as if we were still ten years old.

"Anyway." *Kick. Kick.* "How are you holding up?"

"I'm fine. Fabulous."

"Seriously." The kicking slowed. "You've had a hellish week."

I blew the hair out of my eyes. "That I certainly have."

"The surgery is a definite go? One week from today?"

"Yes."

"Sis. Anything I can do to help?"

I met his gaze. There was no longer any trace of mischief, nothing but love in his eyes.

"I don't know. I may need your help eventually with some of the crazy stuff I turned up in Georgia. I'm not quite sure where things are going to end up."

"What things? What crazy stuff?"

I had not yet confided in my family that the police were reopening their inquiry into Boone and Sadie Rawson's murders. There seemed no point in prompting alarm, when it would likely come to nothing. I had resolved to follow Beasley's advice: lie low, don't get my hopes up, let the investigation run its course.

I waved my hand dismissively. "Doesn't matter. I think the key thing for the moment will be to get this operation over with, and then to get well. Knock on wood." I glanced around, spotted a wooden salad bowl, rapped it twice for luck. "And after that I need to keep busy. I'm thinking I'll write a book."

"Why not."

"I should already have one under my belt, at this point in an academic career. If I ever want to get tenure.

I wrote a paper this fall, on the politics of divorce in working-class, post-Napoleonic France. It was well received. I could easily expand it."

He scratched the stubble on his cheeks. The glint was back in his eye.

"What?" I demanded.

"Nothing. I mean, obviously, the world's been waiting for that book. I'm thinking huge initial print run—"

"The intended audience would be other academics, you cretin. I didn't say it would be a page-turner."

"No, no, don't undersell yourself. That's got bestseller written all over it."

I threw a tea towel at him. "You are such an obnoxious ass."

He grinned, hopped off the counter, and wrapped me in a fierce hug. Then, without prompting, he grabbed a wad of paper towels and kneeled to polish the marks off the cabinet door.

I was watching him in amusement when the doorbell rang.

TONY AND WILL Zartman got on like a house on fire.

This irritated but did not surprise me.

I perched on the end of the sofa, sipping white wine, while my brother and Will clinked beers and conversed in a language as impenetrable to me as Swahili.

"I can't help thinking the DH situation is going to screw the Sox," said Tony, his eyes glued to the television screen. "Because if they want to use Ortiz, they'll have to take Napoli out of the lineup."

"That'll hurt," Will agreed. "And getting Allen Craig back, that could be huge for the Cards."

"I don't know, do you really think he's their best clutch?"

"Are you kidding? Craig on a good day—"

"What's the DH situation?" I cut in. If I was going to have to sit through this, I was damn well going to participate.

"Designated hitter," said Will, patting my leg.

"And what's that?"

"What's what? A designated hitter?" His expression suggested this was the equivalent of asking what was a sandwich. Or what was the sky. As in, a concept so basic he'd never had to explain it before.

He turned to Tony. "I promised to teach her about baseball, how the rules work and everything."

"Mm-hmm. Good luck with that." My brother smiled in a way that conveyed he grasped the futility of Will's project at a level Will had not even begun to understand.

I ignored them. We sat watching. After a minute, I ventured, "What's with the Boston players? Why do they all have beards?"

"Tribal thing. Team solidarity," said Will.

Tony nodded. "I read that Napoli's is so bushy now, he has to use shampoo and conditioner on it."

"Whereas the Cards pitchers might be too young to grow facial hair."

"Ha! Probably true. But could you believe the fastballs that Wacha was throwing the other night?"

And they were off again, yammering away in Swahili.

As the third inning wound down, after I had fixed my brother with an evil stare and made a pointed comment about how *both* steaks, all *two* of them, were nearly ready, Tony finally stood to leave.

At the front door he leaned close and whispered, "Great guy."

"Thanks."

"Not your type, though. He's disturbingly . . . normal."

"Shhh, you're just worried you won't have an excuse to bust out your 'Sprockets' routine at Thanksgiving."

"Oh, I'll find a way to work it in." Tony studied my face. "Look, I have no interest in your sex life. But is he likely to stay over tonight?"

"Tony! That is so none of your—"

"I'm just thinking you shouldn't be alone. If he's not staying, I could swing back by later tonight, give you a lift up to Mom and Dad's."

"What? Why?"

"Because I'm worried about you. I can tell you're in pain. And I didn't like that reference you made earlier, to 'crazy stuff' you turned up in Georgia. Tomorrow you're going to tell me what you meant by that."

Despite myself, I glanced over my brother's shoulder. The street was quiet. No gray car in sight. "Sure. I promise. I need to get back inside."

"So?" Tony inclined his head toward where Will sat in my living room.

"For God's sake. He's staying. Now good night, you." I shoved my brother out the door. Smoothed my hair. It occurred to me that I must really like Will; I couldn't wait to get back to the sofa, snuggle in, and listen to him hold forth about baseball.

But in my absence, Will's mood seemed to have darkened.

At first, I assumed he was annoyed that I'd stood whispering with Tony on the front step for so long. Will shook his head no when I dangled another beer. He didn't lift a finger to help as I made up plates and carried them through from the kitchen. I plopped down beside him. "What's up?"

"Nothing." He fake-smiled at me, then returned to staring at the screen.

For the next hour we sat on the sofa like strangers, not snuggling, not even touching. Politely chewing and swallowing steak and salad. Every few minutes he offered a point of incomprehensible sports commentary, and I pretended to sound interested. We spoke less and less as the game ground on.

Eventually, I'd had enough. I laid my hand on his. "You okay?"

"Me? Yes. Bit tired. I should get going."

He should get going? This was not the way I had envisioned the evening unfolding.

"Thank you for cooking." He stood up. "Delicious marinade on the beef."

"Will. What is it? What's wrong?"

"Nothing, nothing. Sorry."

"Then why won't you look me in the eye?"

He did then, miserably. "Caroline. I don't know how to . . ."

"Just say it."

"I'm an idiot. You are amazing. I just—you and me—this is a mistake. I'm your doctor. I should never—"

Ah. So that was it. "It's okay. I've been thinking about it, too. The ethics of our situation."

He looked stricken. "You have?"

"I'm guessing doctor-patient sexual relationships aren't exactly smiled on in the medical profession."

A pause. "No. They're not."

"But we're grown-ups, and this is consensual. The situation is what it is. I don't want to presume anything, but . . . if this is something we both want to continue after my surgery, then I'll just switch doctors. *Et voilà*, no more conflict of interest."

"Caroline—"

"And I promise not to subject you to my stupid brother again until we've had a chance to figure out where things between us stand."

This drew a small smile. "I liked him, actually."

"He liked you, too. Now stop talking about Tony and kiss me."

"I would love to. But I need to go home. " Will shook himself, a forceful, involuntary movement, the way a dog shakes dry after a swim. "I'm—I'm sorry everything's gotten confused."

"What are you talking about? Everything's gotten confused—as you put it—because *you* chased *me* down to Atlanta. Are you now professing that your interest was purely medical?"

He bowed his head. "No."

I gaped at him in fury and bewilderment. "So did you come over here tonight as my doctor or my—or my—or what?" I sputtered. "Is this your thing? Are you in the habit of seducing all your female patients?"

"Whoa. Whoa, whoa, whoa. *No.* Jesus. This has never happened before. It won't happen again."

"*Shit.*" I never curse. Madame Aubuchon must have been rubbing off on me. "Shit. Will, wait."

But he was already striding out of the house, the door slamming shut behind him.

Twenty-eight

They say we are born with five basic senses.

Remember, you learned this as a child, from picture books: *What does the bunny see? What does the bunny smell?* And so on. Sight, smell, taste, touch, and hearing. Five. But some people have more. Some people can sense when rain is coming. Some mothers of soldiers swear they sensed a chill, an arrow of foreboding, hours before the telegram bearing the unthinkable news arrived. I believe them. There are bonds that surpass the capacity of modern science to explain.

Then there are the curious solutions that nature devises, to counter a deficit. My great-aunt, deaf from childhood, could sense vibrations, could determine the location of a sound, through her feet. She would curl her toes, bony and freckled, onto the warped boards of her front porch, then she'd jerk upright and point, a full thirty seconds before the rest of us heard the mail truck rumbling up the drive. One sense falters; the others sharpen.

So it is at night.

At night it is the sense of sound that will save you.

By which I mean, you could not see the man's shadow outside, waiting. Could not touch it, as it slipped to the back cellar window, where the black was absolute, where the moonlight did not reach. You could not smell his fingertips as they closed around the doorknob. Could not taste his sweat beading, salty and glistening, under wool.

No, but you could hear the glass shatter.

You could hear the bolt scrape as it slid back. Hear the floorboard creak, protesting the weight of the foot that *should not have been there.*

I was asleep when he came.

AT FIRST, I thought it might be Will returning. Will, having turned around, having decided he wanted to stay the night after all.

I lay suspended, halfway between dreaming and awake. My pillow was warm. I would make him apologize. He would have to grovel. Then I would scoot over, let him slip naked between the sheets, let him curl against me. I made a purring sound, turned beneath the blankets. Hurry up, silly boy. What was taking him so long? Why had he made such a clatter letting himself in? Why was he not padding up the stairs? And something else was nagging, some detail not right, swooping and buzzing at my sleepy brain like an insistent insect.

At last I caught it: Will did not have a key. Will could not be in my kitchen. I sat up.

Listened.

I had imagined this moment. Every woman who lives alone must harbor her own private night terrors. In my nightmares these confrontations always unfold in black and white. Grainy, like a Hitchcock movie. Me, willowy and bearing a distinct resemblance to Ingrid Bergman, my floor-length white satin dressing gown cinched in a bow around my waist. Something—not a specific noise so much as a nameless but urgent sense of menace—routs me from bed. I slide on fur-trimmed, kitten-heeled mules and light a cigarette (still channeling Ingrid here). Inhale for courage. Then Ingrid/I crack my bedroom door, flick on the hall light, tiptoe to the landing, and call down in a throaty, trembling voice—the trembling voice is key—*Is anyone there?* Around this point in the dream I usually snap awake. I never see the intruder's face.

The reality, when it came, was less elegant. My hair in tangles, my breath sour from last night's wine. In reality there was no time to tiptoe. Certainly no time to light up a smoke. And no power on this earth that would tempt me from the safety of my bedroom, toward the yawning, dark mouth of the stairs.

From below, a thump. Someone unfamiliar with my house, bumping softly against a table or chair. Someone moving in the living room. *Out of my bed cross the room slam the door turn the lock.* But the lock on my bedroom door was useless. Flimsy, the keyless kind that spins inside the door handle. A determined child with a paper clip could pick it in ten seconds flat. Something to brace the door, then. Against one wall leaned an antique, mahogany chest of drawers stuffed with jeans and sweaters. My house was built a century before people decided they needed closets. I leaned in and shoved. Slipped. No traction on the waxy floor. Under the bed were a grotty pair of UGGs, suede ankle boots, the ones I wore to bring in the newspaper and roll out my trash bin. Yank them on, *hurry up*, push, the chest gouging tracks into the floor.

There. The chest was square against the door. I pricked my ears.

All was still.

Nothing but the wind rustling leaves outside my window. My heart slamming in my chest. Whoever was downstairs did not want to be heard. Adrenaline shook my hands as I cast about for my cell phone. *Please, God, please, God,* let me have carried it upstairs last night. Not on my desk. Not on the nightstand. I found it in the pocket of my jeans, slung over the back of a chair. My fingers would not cooperate, kept mashing wrong buttons, backing up, fumbling. Finally, ringing. A second went by. Two. Enough time to curse the burglar-alarm panel, winking green on the wall. Mocking me. I had been so upset after the fight with Will that I'd stormed off to bed without remembering to turn it on.

The 911 operator was calm, told me to slow down and repeat my address. I tried. Croaked out my cross street, spelled my name: *C-A-S-H-I . . .*

I was spelling when the stairs creaked. Specifically, the second stair. Then the fourth. I know every loose board. Whoever was climbing was taking the stairs two at a time, and stepping smack in the center, not sticking to the quieter, more stable edges. Whoever was climbing no longer cared if he was heard.

"He's upstairs," I whimpered into the phone. "Please hurry. How long—"

"Ma'am, an officer will be right with—"

"No, now! You need to get here *now*!"

I threw the phone down. Trained my eyes on the crack at the bottom of my bedroom door. The intruder did not turn on a light. On the top step he seemed to hesitate, then he began moving toward my closed door. He was panting. Winded from the stairs. No more than a dozen feet from me. Only the door and that chest of drawers separating us. I could whisper and he would hear every word.

My doorknob rattled. He was testing it. He would give up, turn around now, surely. He would not break the lock. This was not personal. A dozen burglaries occur every night of the week in the District of Columbia. He would grab whatever burglars come to grab—a camera, my laptop, an expensive and never-used tennis racket?—and then he would go back to wherever he had come from.

Another creak. Retreating footsteps. He had turned around, was tracking back down the hall, away from me. I slumped. Air slammed into my chest, sweet air, as though I were surfacing after a long time underwater; I had not realized I'd been holding my breath.

Then the crash. The deafening, savage, booming crash of a man running at the door, lowering his shoulder, trying to break it in. *Oh, sweet Jesus.*

There was only one other way out. My bedroom window looks onto the street. The drop is maybe ten feet, maybe more, onto scrubby azalea bushes and brick sidewalk. I undid the latch, pushed up the window, leaned out, and howled, *Help! Help me!* No one below, the street deserted.

Behind me the sound of wood splintering.

One leg over the sill, then the other, trying to lower myself, but I had no upper-body strength. I'd never done a pull-up in my life. My nightgown snagged. I ripped it free and crashed to the ground. Sting of cold on my skin, scrape of knees against brick, pain beyond words in my neck. I scrambled upright. Swayed. Stumbled. My right arm—the bad one—instinctively mashing down my breasts, stopping them from swinging unsupported under my gown.

Running. Really running, lungs burning, legs churning. Too frightened to stop and look back.

It turned out I have been running my whole life. I just never knew it.

Twenty-nine

They fingerprinted the entire house before they let me back inside. A frizzy-haired, wide-assed woman around my age arrived with a forensics kit and set to work on the front door. I watched her from the backseat of a squad car, a bulky Georgetown University Police Department jacket draped around my shoulders, another one covering my legs. Blue lights mounted on the car roof flashed on-off in jerky rhythm.

I had run straight for the front gates of the university. At the corner of Thirty-Seventh and O Streets, there's always a police car parked, standing by for emergencies and also as a visible reminder of the security presence on campus. I caught the startled look of the officer in the driver's seat as I hurtled in his direction. University cops must see some weird stuff, but hysterical women in UGG boots and torn nightgowns, blood streaming from both knees, probably didn't come along every night. I flew into his arms while he was still disentangling himself from the car, one boot planted on the asphalt, the other midair. Both a gun and a truncheon dangled from his belt. I'd never been so happy to see weapons.

The cop half-walked, half-dragged me into the guard station attached to the gates, a stone hut I'd marched past a thousand times and never given a second glance. He sat me down. Offered a tissue and motioned for me to wipe the snot and tears off my face. It was still dark outside. I had no idea what time it might be.

"You okay, ma'am? You hurt?"

"There was a man," I gasped.

"Okay. You're okay now. Deep breaths."

"In my—in my house."

"And where's that?"

"Q Street."

"Q Street? All right. Take it easy, there you go." My teeth were chattering so violently it must have been audible. He snatched a navy police jacket off a hook and wrapped it awkwardly around me. "So, this guy. In your house. You know him?"

Did I *know* him? But it was a logical question. Women who turn up bloody and weeping in the wee hours must often turn out to be domestic-violence victims, their wounds inflicted by their husbands or boyfriends.

"No." I shook my head for emphasis, and the simple gesture scorched such pain through me that my vision went white. Pinpricks of light danced behind my eyelids. When I forced them open, the cop had folded his arms over his gut and was regarding me with an expression somewhere between pity and wariness. I must have looked frightful. Like a madwoman off her meds.

Snarled hair, skinned knees, mangy boots, the hem of my nightgown ripped and dirty. Embarrassment spurred me to pull rank.

"My name is Caroline Cashion. Professor Cashion. I'm faculty."

"Really."

"French Department. Faculty of Languages and Linguistics."

His eyebrows bounced up. Then, recovering, "Professor, okay, I didn't . . . hang on." He reached behind him, felt around on the counter for a spiral-bound notebook. "Let me take down your address, call this in."

"I already called it in," I snapped. "I called 911 from my house. But the guy, the *guy who I don't know*, the burglar, he was inside. He came upstairs. I had to run."

The cop was nodding, scribbling, a new urgency to his movements, when the hut door slammed open. I jumped, ready to flee. But it was only another uniformed police officer. Flabby, older than the first.

"Evening, Al. Goddamn freezing out—" He spotted me, checked himself. "Evening . . . miss." He looked me up and down, then turned to my cop. "Whaddawe got here?"

"This is, um, Mrs. . . . Professor . . . Cashion. I was just . . ." The one apparently named Al had slid out a keyboard from an underdesk tray and was pecking at the keys. I knew what he was searching. I doubted that at that moment I remotely resembled the smiling, poised ID photo that he would pull up in the university database. But the age, race, and gender would match. The photo must have passed muster because the two cops exchanged nervous glances and began barking at each other.

"Why haven't you cleaned her up? Where's the first-aid kit?" The older one.

Al swatted him away. "I'm calling over to Idaho Avenue, see what they know." Idaho Avenue is the closest DC metropolitan police station. Second district, the one responsible for Georgetown.

"Here we go. Just a little sting." The older officer again, leaning over my knees, swiping at them with an antiseptic wipe that stung like hell. He lowered his voice. "Do you need a rape kit?"

No, thank God.

"You said you called 911? Were they sending somebody over to take a look?" asked Al, one hand cocked on his hip and the other squeezing the phone to his ear. Before I could answer he held up a finger and mouthed, *Wait*. Then, to the phone: "Georgetown DPS here. Main campus. I got a lady here . . ."

Half an hour later I was back on Q Street. Back in front of my house, climbing out of Al's GUPD vehicle, being handed off to a DC police detective. The big boys would take it from here. The sky was beginning to streak gray. My father was on his way. The fingerprint lady had finished out front and moved inside. Al squeezed my shoulder, told me not to worry about the jackets, I could return them anytime.

Then he was gone and a new detective stood before me. The new guy was wiry with beady eyes and a thin, rodenty nose that started too high on his forehead. He addressed me with what sounded like a stock speech: I must be exhausted, but anything I could tell them was helpful and it was important to do it now, while the details were fresh.

My front hall looked just as it always had. Every lamp blazing. A shadow moved at the top of the stairs, causing me to shrink back against the front door. But it was only the fingerprint lady, wrapping up, calling down to us, "All set."

"Ready?" The detective turned to me. "Ready to show me exactly what happened?"

I TOLD MY story.

The detective listened, jotted it down in careful block letters. Ballpoint pen scratching across a carbon-copy form, filling in boxes in smeary pink-and-yellow triplicate. Hadn't these guys ever heard of iPads?

But I sensed he wasn't quite buying it.

He kept pressing me on what I had actually seen (nothing, I'd actually seen nothing, I was behind a locked door the entire time) and what exact noise had awakened me (maybe glass breaking? Or a creaky floorboard?) And what exact time I had heard this alleged noise (um, 3:00 a.m.? 4:00? 5:00?) And, if I never saw him, why was I so sure the intruder was a man? (Because. Because, *jackass*, what woman goes around breaking into houses, charging at doors trying to bust them open with brute strength? For fuck's sake. I never swear, but *come on*.)

At some point during this inquisition my father arrived, followed in short order by Martin and then Tony. We Cashions believe in traveling in packs. Martin and

Dad wore jeans; Tony was incongruous in a pin-striped, dark suit and tie. I gathered this was so he could head straight to his office afterward, but the effect was imposing, as though he were ready to indict the prowler on multiple charges right then and there.

"So let's walk through this one more time." The detective was tapping his notes with the tip of his ballpoint. "You were asleep. Your burglar alarm never sounded because you had it switched off. . . ."

"Sis. For Christ's sake," muttered Tony, shooting me a how-dumb-can-you-get look.

"Not the moment, Tony." Martin laid a supportive hand on my shoulder.

"Burglar alarm wouldn't stop somebody determined, anyway." The detective twitched his rodent nose at me. "But what makes you think it was? What makes you think this was more than a run-of-the-mill burglary? I mean, I get that it was scary, being home alone and a woman and everything, but what makes you think he— let's *say* it was a he—that he wanted to hurt you?"

Was this guy an idiot? "He *ran*. At. The. Door." My words punched out like angry fists. "Did you not see my bedroom door?" The wood had splintered around the lock; one of the hinges had been ripped loose from the frame. The sight had made my stomach heave; I had had to turn away.

"Sure, I saw. Somebody tried to bust it open all right. Probably looking for your jewelry box."

"Oh, please. Last night was not about someone looking for gold brooches—"

"Well, now, you keep saying that. And I'm just saying,

what's the evidence? He smashed a window downstairs, to reach in and flip your basement dead lock. And he bashed the lock on that cabinet there, where it looks like you keep your booze." The detective pointed at a mirrored cabinet in the corner of the living room, where I did indeed store liquor, and where the lock had indeed been bashed in. "We don't appear to be dealing with a master lockpicker here. We appear to be dealing with an unskilled guy who was in a hurry. He wanted your jewelry, and he wasn't opposed to breaking a few things to get in, get out, get the job done."

"No. For starters, no normal burglar would *charge* the homeowner—"

"Burglar off his head on crack would. Trust me. People on crack do crazy shi—" He caught himself. "Crazy stuff."

I scowled.

"Look, I can't rule anything out. We'll investigate every possibility. But it might actually put your mind at ease to know there were two other burglaries reported in the neighborhood this week. Both here on the west side of Wisconsin Avenue. Both involving forced entry at the back or basement door. Windows broken. You see where I'm going? Same guy, on a roll. He wasn't after *you*."

Martin looked at me. "Should you mention the . . . ?" He touched his neck. Martin was the only member of my family who knew that an Atlanta police officer had questioned me about the bullet. "Think it might be relevant?"

I steeled myself.

Yeah. I did.

• • •

I HAD BEEN dancing around this point, trying to avoid staring it in the eye. The idea that events of thirty-four years ago, however terrifying, had some bearing on my present safety seemed, frankly, ridiculous. I might never know for certain what motive someone had had, all those years ago, to turn a gun on Boone and Sadie Rawson. But whatever it was, I appeared to have been an accidental victim. Collateral damage. The killer hadn't bothered to finish me off then, when it would have been easy. He had not considered me a threat. And then he'd gotten away with murder for more than *thirty years*. Why come after me now? Anyone who'd read a newspaper in the last week understood that I remembered nothing, could identify no one.

I know, I know. The bullet. But Beamer Beasley had implied that it wouldn't be of great use to investigators without some sample to match it against. And Beasley himself hadn't seemed terribly concerned about my safety. So, yes, I grasped that the bullet posed a threat. But surely the most urgent threat it posed to my health and well-being was the damage it was currently wreaking inside my body.

And yet.

The DC homicide detective's face betrayed both irritation—I was *ruining* his burglar-on-a-roll theory—and grudging interest, as I laid out the events of the last two weeks. My family's facial expressions would more accurately be described as appalled.

"Let me get this straight," said Martin. "The Atlanta

police are reopening a murder case because of evidence *inside your neck*."

"They want to interview me," I agreed. "Old case, new physical evidence."

"Jesus frigging Christ," roared Tony. "This is the 'crazy stuff' you were hinting at? You're at the center of an active homicide investigation? You didn't think that was worth outright mentioning?"

"Tony," my dad warned.

"And as for these Georgia police bozos," Tony roared on, "who's running things down there? Sheriff Rosco P. Coltrane? Has it not occurred to them that someone else might be interested in the new evidence? Someone with a personal stake in making sure that bullet never finds its way into police hands? Did it not occur—"

"Stop it. Just stop it. The police officer I met with in Atlanta is a good guy. Not a bozo. His name's Beasley. He was on the original team that investigated, back in '79."

"Well, that's a ringing endorsement," snorted Tony. "Although I might be more impressed if they'd, say, solved the murders or caught the guy."

I ignored this. "I didn't say anything because I didn't want to hype this into a bigger deal that it is. When they reopen an investigation, all it means is that a couple of people get assigned to comb over old files. There's a Cold Case Squad—that's what it's actually called—that takes a look if fresh evidence comes to light. They've cautioned me not to expect much. And anyway," I added, clinging to what Beasley had said, "whoever killed my birth parents may well be dead himself, after all these years."

"Unless he's not," muttered Tony.

My dad and Martin nodded in apparent agreement.

I turned to where the DC detective sat perched on my sofa, looking a bit stunned. "Atlanta police will verify everything I've just told you. It's been all over the newspaper down there."

He sighed, as if this were the worst news yet. "You got a number for this Beasley that you can give me? I'll check it out."

"You do that," snapped Tony. "And when you're done, you can turn your attention to sorting out some police protection for my sister. As should have been done several days ago. Which, if it had been done, might have prevented her from being scared shitless last night. Meanwhile"—he swiveled back to me—"meanwhile, I'm taking you to buy a gun."

"Tony! Will you stop being so dramatic?"

"I'm not being dramatic. I'm being practical."

We sat glaring at each other.

Martin flicked his gaze back and forth between us. A good thirty seconds passed. Then, under his breath, he muttered, "Nice Rosco Coltrane reference."

"Butt out," Tony growled.

"Sure. Seriously, though. Skillfully done." Martin leaned back, drummed his fingers on a side table, whistling softly. I hadn't heard the tune in a long time, "Good Ol' Boys."

It took another half minute, but Tony cracked. A smile began to play around his lips. "Enos," he whispered, in what sounded like an outrageous Southern accent. "Enos?"

Martin's shoulders began to shake.

Tony, warming up now: "This is your superior officer, Sheriff Ros-*cohhhhhhh* P. Coltrane . . ."

Dad studied his sons in bewilderment. "What the hell are they talking about?"

"*The Dukes of Hazzard*," I ventured. "That TV show they used to love. Wasn't Roscoe the sidekick to, what's his name, Boss Hogg?"

"Breaker One, Breaker One," Martin drawled. "I may be crazy, but I ain't dumb!"

I giggled. I couldn't help it. Even Dad started to smile. The detective looked as if he wanted to flee.

I had never loved my brothers so much in my life.

Thirty

A decision was made that I should pack a bag and sleep at my parents' house tonight. I didn't resist. No way was I sleeping alone behind that broken bedroom door. My parents had a burglar alarm with motion detectors, and the beagle barked if a leaf so much as rustled in the yard. I would be safe.

Dad waited while I threw a toothbrush, makeup, and a change of clothes in a bag, then drove me up to Cleveland Park. Mom was standing on the front step. She folded me in her arms, kissed my hair, whispering, over and over, *Sweet baby girl*. She insisted that I follow her into the kitchen and take some soup. It was only nine in the morning, but I submitted. Hot lentil with lamb and cinnamon. Delicious.

I excused myself and climbed to my old room on the top floor. I stripped and stood beneath a scalding shower, until my skin bloomed pink and my fingertips shriveled white and wrinkly. The ache in my wrist eased a little. The adrenaline that had carried me these last several hours was depleted. I needed sleep.

Before I drew the curtains, I pulled out my phone and

dialed Will. It went straight to voice mail. He might be with a patient, I mused. Or he might still be angry from our argument last night. Or punishing me for never answering my own phone.

The phone beeped, indicating it was recording.

"Hi. Call me." I couldn't think what else to say, couldn't think where to begin an accounting of what had happened in the hours since we'd parted.

I fanned my still-dripping hair across the pillow, drew up the covers, and sank into dreamless sleep.

WHEN I WOKE, the clock read four o'clock.

My phone showed three messages. The first was from Madame Aubuchon, a stiffly formal message inquiring as to my health and adding that she had changed her mind, she wanted her soup pot back. Next came messages from Beasley and from the surgeon Marshall Gellert. These were both short, stating only their names and asking me to call back at my earliest convenience.

I called Beasley first. Washington Metropolitan Police had already been in touch and filled him in on last night's drama, but he made me retell what had happened, in painful detail.

"I surely am sorry you had to go through that," he said after I finished. "You're the last person on earth I would wish it on. And I'm sorry to make you relive it again right now. But I needed to hear the details firsthand from you, make sure nothing important got left out."

"Of course."

"I don't know—I'm being honest with you—I don't

know whether what happened last night has anything to do with what happened back in '79. But say somebody does want to get his hands on that bullet. Coming after you, when you were home alone at night, would make sense."

I shivered.

"Tonight you're staying with your parents, correct? They'll be with you the whole time? You're not going out?"

I glanced at my reflection in the mirror on the bedroom wall. My hair had dried in a weird cowlick while I slept, my eyes were ringed by dark circles, and I was wearing saggy sweatpants and a Duke basketball T-shirt filched from an ex-boyfriend. "If you could see me, you'd know I'm not fit to be seen in public."

"Good. If they haven't been already, local police will be in touch. They're arranging a cruiser to drive by your house throughout the night. But they can't watch you every second, so it's best if you stay inside and keep people around you."

"You really think I'm in danger, then."

"I think I would never forgive myself if anything else were to happen to you." Beasley was quiet for a moment. "In better news, I can tell you that last night has lit a fire under people here. I've been pushing all week for your family's files. Kept getting told they couldn't find them. Then, lunchtime today? Not three hours after Washington MPD got on the horn asking about you? Two big, fat boxes appear on my desk. They must have finally sent somebody with a brain out to off-site storage."

"What's in the boxes?"

"Stuff. I'm going through it. That's about all I can say at the moment."

"Because you're not allowed to say or because you need time to—"

Beasley acted as if he hadn't heard me. "Your formal interview. I'd prefer to do it in person. But in the interest of time, let me see if I can schedule a slot in one of Washington MPD's interview rooms. We'll send a car for you."

"Can't we just do it by phone?"

"No, we need it videotaped. Let's aim for first thing tomorrow."

I chewed my lip, weighed what to say next, decided what the hell. "My brother wants to buy me a gun. For self-defense."

"You know how to shoot?"

"No." I didn't add that I've never handled a firearm in my life. "I'd have to get some instruction."

Beasley made a doubtful noise. "You're talking a handgun, I assume. Takes a while to get comfortable with one, feel like you know what you're doing. My advice, my official advice, would be to leave the guns to the cops. Local police will do fine looking out for your security."

"Hmm. You said that's your official advice. What about unofficially?"

He hesitated, then sighed. "Off the record . . . speaking as a father . . . I'd say something small, maybe a nine-millimeter Baby Glock, might not be a terrible idea."

●　●　●

"I HEAR YOU'RE agitating to move up the surgery by a few days."

"Am I? Where did you hear that?"

Marshall Gellert and I had played phone tag the better part of the afternoon. He finally caught me as I was setting my mother's table for dinner.

"Oh," he said, taken aback. "I thought—I assumed—I got a call at lunchtime from a police detective down in Georgia. Saying that bullet in your neck is relevant to an investigation, and they want to examine it sooner rather than later. He wouldn't give me details, but I assume that isn't news to you? I thought you must know he was calling."

"I didn't, but I'd welcome getting the surgery over with." So Beamer Beasley wasn't messing around. "When, then?"

"I'm closing in on next Monday. Instead of next Wednesday. Would that fit your schedule?"

What schedule? My current "schedule" consisted of hiding out at my parents' house, being force-fed lamb-and-lentil stew, and being ignored by my boyfriend. If that was what you could call Will Zartman.

"As it happens," Gellert continued, "bumping it up is preferable from a medical point of view as well. Every day might be critical if the foreign object, meaning the bullet, really is shifting. Monday's the earliest I can get the hospital facilities booked at Sibley. And the cameraman is on board for then, too."

"Did you say the *cameraman*?"

"Ah." Gellert had the decency to sound embarrassed.

"I did explain already, it's quite unusual that someone with your specific injury would survive—nay, thrive—into adulthood. A few of my peers started blogging about you last week, when the *Journal-Constitution* article went live. You haven't seen the posts?"

No, I had not.

"Everyone's hoping you'll consent to having the operation filmed. For teaching purposes. You're something of a celebrity in neurology circles."

I'm something of a celebrity in neurology circles. Into my head popped an unpleasant image, a circle of erasable-pen-wielding geeks, thick spectacles sliding down slickly pimpled noses, salivating to watch my neck being sliced open.

"For what it's worth, Dr. Zartman is in agreement. Both that we should film the surgery, and that we should proceed as soon as possible."

My breath caught. "When did you speak with Dr. Zartman?"

"This morning. We conferred before I called you."

So Will was alive and well and conferring about my surgical options. Just not taking my calls.

"I'll have my nurse follow up with you. She can explain the pre-op protocol. In a nutshell, we can give you Vicodin if you're in pain. But no food, no Advil, no other anti-inflammatories after six p.m. on Sunday. I'm writing you a prescription right now."

"Thanks. And, um, did you ever find my chart? Did they find that guy who broke in?"

"Negative. Don't worry, we've reconstructed your

chart. Everything's in order. And I can't figure out what that intruder business was all about. Guy didn't seem to take a damn thing."

For several minutes after we hung up I sat still, imagining those impossibly blue eyes boring down on the clean, white prescription pad. Then his hands, the hyperactive fingers, darting across the paper, twirling, weaving like spiders. A lot about my present circumstances frightened me. But for some reason I felt safe in those hands.

Thirty-one

Calling me the worst shot ever to pull a trigger at the Chantilly Rifle and Revolver Range is an exaggeration, but I was probably the worst shot they'd seen in a very long time.

The gun range was half an hour's drive straight west. You took the Key Bridge across the Potomac River into northern Virginia, got on I-66, and kept going. The building was ugly, its low-slung, yellow stucco facade set across a busy road from a strip mall. Plastic letters stuck to the glass doors spelled out OPEN TO THE PUBLIC and NO LOADED GUNS! Inside it was clean and quiet. Guns of every shape and size were laid out in glass display cases. On the walls hung framed posters. One showed a middle-aged man aiming a pistol at the camera, beneath an invitation: *Stop by for a few SHOTS after work—bring your friends along for a different kind of happy hour!* Or, my personal favorite: *Anger management issues? Relationship problems? Try our therapeutic solution.* This was accompanied by a photo of a woman firing at a human silhouette. She had ignored the red target marked on the chest, but fifteen bullet holes were pierced clean through the crotch.

Learning to shoot was surprisingly cheap. Ten dollars per person, per lane, per hour. Paper targets cost a dollar, same again to rent the mandatory ear and eye protection. You could try out as many handguns as you wanted for $10. Hell, you could rent an AK-47 for $19 for the entire day.

Tony marched up to the counter, explained that I was a beginner and that I wanted to learn to use a handgun.

"Never handled firearms before?" asked the woman. A name tag identified her as Irene. Her skin was bad and her black hair hung in an unflattering bowl cut, but—from what I could see of her jeans behind the counter—she had a fantastic figure.

"Never," I confirmed.

"You looking for a revolver or a semiautomatic?"

"What's the difference?"

She and Tony exchanged glances. "Why don't you try 'em both out, see what you like. Personally, I love me a revolver. Just as accurate, won't jam on you." She took out a gun, spun it open to demonstrate it wasn't loaded, laid it on the counter. "Is this for carrying in your purse or keeping in your nightstand? Picking the right gun's all about trade-offs."

I glanced down at my purse, a black Chanel clutch that I'd bought in Paris years ago. It had taken months to pay it off on my credit card, and it was barely big enough to fit my car keys and a lipstick. "Nightstand, I guess."

"So you could go with a bigger gun. Less kickback."

"Wouldn't a bigger gun have more kickback?"

"I knew you'd ask that." She smiled sweetly. "Beginners always do. But think about it. You fire the same bullet from a big gun and a small one, the bigger one's gonna absorb more of the recoil. Basic physics. Let me get you two set up. I'm not busy, it's quiet as a church in here today."

Irene strung a target halfway down the firing range. She showed me how to hold a gun, how to load it, how to aim. Easy. The target had a blue bull's-eye and a helpful Shooter Tutor. If your shots were going wide to the left, it told you to adjust your trigger finger. If they all went low, you were anticipating recoil. And so on. But the only thing consistent about my performance was that every shot missed, by a mile.

After my first ten attempts, Irene reeled in the target to a mere five yards away. "Doesn't need to be too far, don't worry. Let's be real, you want a gun for personal protection, you're not gonna be shooting the guy from twenty-five yards, are you?"

The trouble may have been my utter lack of athletic ability, I don't deny it. I had demonstrated lamentable hand-eye coordination convincingly and humiliatingly in year after year of childhood sports events. But *you* try shooting left-handed when you're not. My dominant right hand dangled in its brace. At the start I had tried to wrap it around my left, for stability, but the kickback hurt too much, no matter which model gun we tried.

After half an hour, all three of us could tell it was a lost cause. I paid and tipped Irene. She handed over my Shooter Tutor as a souvenir.

In the parking lot, I crumpled it into a ball. "Well, that was embarrassing."

"You did fine," Tony said. "It's my fault. I should have taken into account how hard it would be to shoot with one arm in a brace."

"You looked ready to disown me as your sister in there."

"Only when you were asking genuinely idiotic questions, like whether there's a difference between a revolver and a semiautomatic."

"Well, is there?"

"For chrissake."

"If it makes you feel any better," I said nastily, "you can disown me anytime you like. Since we're not actually related."

He spun around. His face was purple. "Don't say that again. Ever."

I jerked open the car door, threw myself inside, and slammed it shut. He stood frozen in the parking lot, watching me through the window the way you would watch a rabid possum.

We drove home in silence, Tony at the wheel, staring grimly out the windshield.

As we crossed the Key Bridge into Georgetown, I stretched my left hand to rest on his shoulder. He did not swat it away. That's as close to saying sorry as Tony and I tended to get.

AT LUNCHTIME BEAMER Beasley telephoned. Again.

I was surprised to hear from him so soon. The formal interview had gone fine this morning. An unmarked police car had delivered me to and from the session. Both Beasley and Gerry Fleeman, the head of the Cold Case Squad, were on the video linkup asking questions; I'd thought I'd answered them satisfactorily.

But apparently, not until afterward did Beasley finish digging through the boxes. He had found evidence bullets. Several, fired from two different guns. They would have something to compare my bullet with after all.

"I thought you didn't have sample bullets," I said, shocked. "The one that hit Boone, I thought the killer gouged it out of the doorframe—"

"These aren't from your crime scene. These are bullets collected as a precaution, for the purpose of comparison."

"I don't follow."

"Easiest way to match a bullet isn't against the gun that fired it. It's against another bullet. You compare like to like. You know what rifling is? It's the spiral grooves, on the inside of a gun barrel. Every rifle, every handgun, has rifling almost as unique as a fingerprint. Even ones made in the same batch, in the same factory. And the differences get more pronounced over time, as the gun gets cleaned and fired. So when you fire a gun, it leaves its signature on the projectile. We're talking tiny markings. Microscopic. But a good lab tech can spot them. With homicide cases, you always fire sample shots from a weapon recovered from a crime scene."

I was still struggling to follow this. "The point remains that you didn't find a gun in my parents' house. Or a bullet."

"True. We did have suspects, though. Remember? I told you about three separate men who we brought in for questioning, for one reason or another. Two of them owned guns. Nothing illegal about that. We didn't have cause to seize the firearms. But we did fire test bullets from them, into ballistic gelatin. Just in case. Just in case another bullet ever came along to match."

I sucked in my breath. "You've been hoping all this time to get your hands on the bullet in my neck."

"That's an ugly way of putting it."

"But—but why didn't you tell me about the other bullets before?"

"I didn't know. I've worked homicide on and off for forty years. We're talking hundreds, maybe a thousand murders. Not making excuses, but that's a lot of evidence to keep straight in your head. And like I told you, back in '79 we were getting slammed by a new murder nearly every day here in Atlanta." Beasley swallowed. "I was praying we'd had the sense to collect evidence bullets during your mama and daddy's investigation, but I wasn't sure. Couldn't remember. Nothing in the paperwork that I had kept indicated one way or the other."

I sighed. "I suppose it's a miracle they weren't thrown away. That you were able to lay hands on them after so much time."

"If you could see what passes for a filing system down here, you'd know that that's the truth." He harrumphed. "Meanwhile, I gather your operation's been bumped up to Monday."

"Yes, and I really wish you hadn't hassled my surgeon without checking with me first."

"Ms. Cashion. It's my job to collect the evidence. And to do what I can to protect you. Trust me, it's in your interest to hurry up and get that bullet out. If I had my way, they'd be wheeling you into the OR this very minute."

Thirty-two

Beasley's news shook me.

Perhaps the most frustrating aspect was that I could do nothing but wait. Wait for next week's operation, wait to see if I ended up paralyzed, wait to see if the bullet proved useful. I paced my bedroom. Picked up a book, tried to concentrate, snapped it shut after I found myself reading the same paragraph on Jean-Paul Sartre a fourth time. I resumed pacing. Feeling frightened, furious, and at loose ends—all at once—proved a dangerous combination. By six that evening I gave in to temptation.

Will's cell did not answer, and his work phone went straight to an answering service. His house, then. It surprised me to realize I had only a vague notion where he lived. Helpfully, Zartman is an unusual name. The white pages online listed a phone number and a home address. Lorcom Lane in Arlington, Virginia. Just across the river.

I could hardly drive there myself. Not after the burglary, not after what Beasley had told me. I was a prisoner in my childhood home. I sat pondering the problem. Then I called Martin and told him I needed to see someone, that we were headed to Arlington, and that he would have to wait in the car.

He picked me up an hour later. "Let me guess. Your Dr. Sprockets." Martin smirked.

I shot him an annoyed glance, said nothing.

"Tony said he's a great guy. Why don't you just invite him up to the house? Are you hiding him from Mom and Dad for some reason!"

"As it happens, he's not returning my calls."

My brother cocked his head sideways. "I hate to break this to you, but generally speaking, that's a sign that a guy isn't interested."

"Thank you for that deep insight into the male mind," I retorted. "I know what it usually means. But I think— I'm hoping—he's avoiding me because he's trying to do the honorable thing."

I explained about doctor-patient relationships being verboten. About Will's squirming and then storming out the other night.

"You could switch doctors," Martin said.

"That's what I told him."

It was quiet on Lorcom Lane. The streetlights had switched on to illuminate two- and three-story brick colonials, well-kept, typical American suburbia. I felt uneasy. I had imagined Will living in a condo, maybe a converted loft, all exposed brick and soaring ceilings.

When we reached the right address, Martin swung the car into the driveway.

His headlights picked out Will's Jeep. A basketball hoop hung suspended above the garage. Below it a child's bike lay on its side.

All of a sudden, I understood.

YOU WANTED A scene? You wanted to read about me bursting into tears, about the clichéd confrontation with the pretty wife who answers the door, about who slapped whom first?

I'm not that girl.

I told you already: I'm not prone to outbursts, not a volatile person.

Martin, on the other hand, was outraged. He trained his brights on the child's bike, trying to make sense of what this object could be doing in my boyfriend's driveway. He took a second or two longer than I had to figure out that Will must be married, that he was a *father*.

"Do you want me to kneecap him?" Martin asked. "Spell out *dickwad* on his lawn?"

"Just turn around. Hurry up. Before someone comes out of the house and sees us."

We drove home in silence, me staring out the window, clutching my right wrist, wishing I'd let Tony buy me that 9 mm Baby Glock after all.

MARTIN WALKED ME up our parents' front steps and onto the porch, muttering, "He's a dickwad, whether we trash his front lawn or not. You are *so* out of his league. Christ, do I want to call Tony and invite this guy to join us for a friendly beer. Give him a little education on how to treat our sister."

"Thank you, but I'm fine." I was turning my cheek for him to kiss me good-night when I saw it. The gray car. Parked just as before, across the street and a few spaces down. How could such a nondescript car be so noticeable?

"Martin," I whispered. "Do you see that car?"

"An education that would leave him unable to walk for the next week." My brother was still muttering.

"Martin! That gray car. Do you see it!"

He turned, shaded his eyes against the porch light. "What about it?"

"It was parked outside my house on Q Street the other night. The same car."

"Are you sure?"

No, I wasn't sure. It was your run-of-the-mill, gray, compact car. Utterly unremarkable. But either I was going crazy or I had seen this car before, and I went with the latter. "I—I think so. There was a man inside."

My brother scowled, squinted across the street again, started loping down across the lawn.

"Martin!" I hissed, "Stop!"

The car's ignition started up. The headlights blinked on, and suddenly it was reversing. It knocked into the bumper of the car parked behind, then lurched into the street, engine roaring, tires squealing.

"Get inside," said my brother.

I stood frozen, glued to the porch.

"Sis! Get inside!"

I didn't wait for him to tell me a third time.

Thirty-three

D r. Gellert commenced operating at 11:07 a.m.

He was assisted, I was later told, by the on-duty anesthesiologist, two nurses, and three residents who had had their plans for a lazy weekend morning rudely interrupted by urgent summonses from the hospital. The procedure was not filmed. No cameraman could be located on such short notice.

The gray car had achieved what Beasley had wished for but had not been able to achieve: instant surgery.

Last night, within minutes of my phone call to 911, three police cars had swarmed the street in front of my parents' home. Sirens wailed to wake the dead, blue lights blazed, cops muscled their way through the front door. Phone calls had been exchanged with Atlanta, most of which I was not privy to, other than one short exchange with Beasley, during which, as usual, he made me walk him step-by-step through what I had seen.

The result of all this midnight conferencing had been that Mom and Dad, white with worry, drove me to Sibley Hospital's emergency room. A police car—sirens mercifully silenced, but blue lights flashing in full glory—had led the way. We arrived before dawn. I was transferred from the car to a wheelchair and then to a gurney. A plastic bracelet was strung around my good wrist. More phone calls were made. My clothes were removed and replaced by a paper surgery gown. A somber, whiskery anesthesiologist appeared, introduced himself, explained his plans to make me comfortable. I forgot his name before he even left the room.

Drugs, I was thinking. Please just give me the drugs. Give me everything you've got. During the long, long night we had just endured, pain had seized my neck and my shoulders, pain so severe it had felt my body would break in two. This was not the sharp pulsing I had grown used to. This was more dense. Heavy. Like an apron of lead, the kind they swaddle you in before taking an X-ray.

Smiling nurses appeared. Guardrails on the sides of the gurney swung up and locked into place. The gurney began to roll. A mask came down over my face, *Breathe deep,* said the smiles. My mother was walking beside me, still holding my hand.

DARKNESS.

I came to in a postsurgery recovery room. Cold. I was so cold. I had never been so cold. My legs would have to be amputated, they would not survive, the frostbite was turning my skin to wax.

I sensed someone beside me. "Blanket," I tried to tell them. It came out mush. "Bl-shhh-ont."

The person leaned down. "Caroline?" Will's voice. Soft, worried. He laid a hand on top of mine.

Noooo.

I wanted to turn my head away. It would not obey. "Blanket," I said again.

He would not listen. "Caroline. It's me. Everything went fine. You're going to be fine."

Something scratchy was wrapped around my neck, the only part of me that was warm. I willed myself to go under again, to sleep.

Thirty-four

They only kept me in the hospital for one night.

The surgery had gone beautifully. The bullet had popped—Dr. Gellert pursed his lips and made a loud *pop* as he recounted this to me—*popped* right out.

"Like squeezing a boiled tomato from its skin," he added, clearly pleased with himself. "Big old thing. Half an inch long." He held up his thumb and forefinger in approximation.

"Where is it?"

"I cleaned it up, sealed it in a sterile envelope. Handed it to the police myself." His fingers were sliding up and down a Perspex clipboard, rising and then striking the edge as if it were the keys of a baby grand. "They rushed the bullet straight to the lab. It was an Atlanta cop who turned up to get it. Flew up here specifically for that purpose, warned me not to let DC police anywhere near it." Gellert eyed me with curiosity, but did not ask.

I nodded. Tried to nod. The bandages made it impossible to move.

"At any rate, the headline is—we got it out. You did

great. The incision on the back of your neck is less than two inches wide. You'll have a scar, but it'll fade, and your hair will cover it."

"I don't care about that. What about my—my spinal cord? Will I have full range of movement?" At the moment I felt no pain at all, but I was pumped so full of painkillers that it was hard to say whether that meant much.

"We'll have to wait until the swelling subsides. And it will take time for everything internally to knit back together. But so far, so good. I'll see you tomorrow, in my regular office, to check the stitches and make sure everything's draining properly."

At my parents' house, they had made up a bed in the living room so I wouldn't have to climb the stairs. All afternoon I dozed. Dad sat vigil in an armchair by the window, answering e-mails and cursing at the *New York Times* crossword puzzle. Hunt lay flopped across his feet. Mom wandered in and out, inventing ways to make herself useful. I was hungry. Starving. I had been forbidden from consuming anything except liquids until I either produced a bowel movement or passed gas. I achieved this milestone—the latter—as twilight fell. I felt undignified, to say the least. But I was rewarded with crackers and a cup of Mom's homemade beef noodle soup.

Thirty-five

M y neck felt better. That's the only way to describe it, just as simply as that. My parents' living room had no curtains—the house was set well back from the street—and I woke early with the light.

I was stiff from the lumpy, makeshift bed. My bandages itched. But I had slept unexpectedly well.

I wiggled my toes. Clenched and unclenched my buttocks, shifted my hips. Then, cautiously, I tested my shoulders. They were sore but loose. Finally I shut my eyes, held my breath, and flexed my right wrist.

I had not taken Vicodin since dinner last night. Twelve hours ago.

I felt no pain.

WILL ZARTMAN HAD left five phone messages in the thirty hours since I'd left the hospital. I wish I could tell you that I found the willpower to delete them without listening, but I did not. Not that they said much. *Call me, would you please call me?* Each new message sounded less hopeful than the last.

When the phone buzzed again in the late afternoon, I screwed up my courage and answered.

"Hello, Will."

"Caroline! I've left you half a dozen messages."

"Five, actually."

"Right. I gather you're back to never answering your phone." He sounded uncertain, trying to gauge how mad I was.

"That's right. I guess two can play that game." *Pretty damn mad, you cowardly, lying turd.*

He cleared his throat. "Marshall said the surgery went very well. How are you feeling?"

"Oh, just dandy."

A moment passed.

"Look, I know I owe you an apology. Make that several apologies. I heard about the break-in. At your house. I feel awful. I shouldn't have left you. I'm so sor—"

"I drove by your house, Will."

"My *house*? When?" There was no mistaking the terror in his voice.

"Don't worry. I didn't ring the doorbell." Pause. "So. How many children do you have?"

Long pause. "Two."

We didn't have much to say to each other after that.

Thirty-six

By Tuesday I was up and walking around.

For the first time in days I got dressed. My jeans hung loose on my hips. My belly was taut and flat. Major surgery and an all-liquid diet were apparently good for five pounds. At breakfast I peeled three kiwis and ate them with a soft-boiled egg.

As I chewed, I practiced turning my head to the right, to look out the kitchen window, onto the magnolia tree that dominates the front yard. Then left, in the direction of the stove and sink. Right and left, back and forth. Dr. Gellert had removed the bulkiest bandages yesterday. All that remained was a thin gauze pad, held in place with flesh-colored first-aid tape. The tape pulled at the hairs on the back of my neck. Otherwise I felt no discomfort.

I checked my e-mail. A message from Georgetown University police alerted students and faculty to a reported theft on the ground floor of Lauinger, the undergraduate library. We were reminded not to leave laptops or other personal items unattended on campus. I wondered whether Al had been on duty. Lauinger sat on the main quad, not a hundred yards from his stone police hut. It occurred to me that I needed to return his jackets.

There was also a brief message from Beasley. The bullet had arrived safely back in Atlanta over the weekend. Lab technicians were working on it. He would keep me posted.

As I cleared my dishes, I caught sight of my reflection in the glass door of the microwave oven. I looked nothing like myself. My face was thin, my skin was pale, and my hair had seen better days. When had I last washed it? Friday? I was not supposed to get the stitches wet, not yet, but I was allowed to wash from the chest down. It would be better than nothing.

In the bathroom, I dropped my clothes on the floor and peeled back the gauze pad. Gingerly I raised my hand to touch the back of my neck. The stitches were raised, lumpy knots beneath my fingertips. They would dissolve on their own as the incision healed. The skin on my neck, meanwhile, was numb. I could not feel my fingers pressing down. Dr. Gellert had told me the area might stay numb for weeks, or it might stay numb forever.

I wondered about the arteries in my neck. The muscles. Whether they were shifting by fractions of an inch, filling in the space where the bullet had been. After a minute I sat down on the edge of the bathtub, loosened the straps holding on my wrist brace, and took it off. My right forearm was visibly thinner than my left. The muscles—never impressive to begin with—had shrunk over months of disuse. I picked up the brace, refastened the straps, folded it in half lengthways, and tucked it in the cabinet beneath the sink. I had the feeling I would not be needing it again.

Thirty-seven

My house on Q Street smelled heavenly.

I moved back to my own home four days after the operation. By then it was obvious to everyone, even my mother, that I was perfectly capable of caring for myself. In my absence, Martin's wife, Laura, had let herself in and scoured the place with Windex and Pledge. The table in my kitchen gleamed. She had vacuumed the carpets, scrubbed the windows, even laundered the sheets and made up my bed. The heavenly scent floated up from vases of flowers that she had arranged in every room. Peonies. The dark pink ones, my favorites. Where on earth had Laura found them in October? I resolved to be nicer to my sister-in-law; I would owe her some serious babysitting time for this.

Dad had also been busy. He had hired a locksmith to install new dead bolts on all the doors, and a glazier to fix the basement window. My bedroom door he had replaced himself, adding a sturdy lock that could be opened only from the inside. He presented me with a new ring of keys and two spare sets, adding that he would be back in the morning, both to look in on me and to meet the electrician.

"The electrician?"

"Thought it might be wise to put in floodlights. At your front door, and around the back of the house. I ordered the motion-sensitive kind. Anybody steps within a few feet of the house, it'll trigger them."

He looked so worried that I put my arms around his waist and kissed him. "Dad. I'll be fine now."

"Call before you go to bed tonight, let us know you're all right?"

"Promise."

"And set your burglar alarm."

I gave a sharp, rueful laugh. "Don't worry."

After he left, I made another tour of my house, checking every lock, turning on every light. All was in order. There was no trace of last week's nightmarish events.

The doorbell rang as I was climbing up to my bedroom to unpack. I froze. Crept back down the stairs and tiptoed to the front door. Through the peephole I could see only the bald top of a man's head. He was holding something large and shimmery; I couldn't make out what it was.

Ding dong ding dong.

"Who is it?" I called, my voice squeaking with fear, not sure if I could be heard through the locked door.

"FTD. Delivery."

"Just leave it on the step."

"Need your signature, ma'am."

I coughed loudly. "I'm sick." *Cough.* "Contagious. And, um . . . I don't want the Dobermans to get out." In addition to my father's security precautions, I was going to go online tonight and order a bunch of those BEWARE OF GUARD DOG stickers to slap on every window.

I thought I heard the man sigh. He bent down, and then my peephole view was blocked by the shimmery blob. What *was* that? From the curb came the sound of a car engine starting and pulling away. I waited several seconds, then sneaked into the living room and peeked out the window. No one was on the front step, or anywhere in sight. I yanked the door open to find a huge bouquet of silver balloons, weighted down by a basket stuffed with chocolate. Inside the basket was a note:

> *For Sweet Caroline*
>   *Get well soon and then come see us.*
>
> *Your Devoted Admirer,*
> *Leland Brett*

I WAS SMILING and carrying the balloons into the living room when I noticed a bag tucked in the corner of the hall. A paper shopping bag, the kind with handles, half-filled with mail. Laura must have tidied up everything the postman had pushed through the letter slot this past week.

I dumped the contents on the coffee table. Four catalogs from Pottery Barn, a store where I had never shopped. A coupon for a free entrée on my birthday from Mai Thai, the neighborhood Thai restaurant. Bills from Washington Gas and AT&T. And a thick manila envelope, postmarked Atlanta and mailed five days ago.

I ripped it open. Inside was a handwritten note from Cheral Rooney.

Dear Caroline,

I am writing and hoping this finds you well. I expect you saw my quote in the newspaper, about how much you and S.R. look alike. I enclose the article in case you missed it. I was embarrassed to be interviewed, to tell the truth. My mother always said a lady should only appear in the newspaper three times: when she's born, when she marries, and when she dies. Times change though.

You asked to see a photo. You said you deserved to know the truth, even the bad parts. I went back and forth on whether to send these to you. Then I decided you are right.

Sincerely,
Cheral

P.S. Your mother loved you very much. Don't you ever forget it.

From the envelope I shook a crumpled newspaper clipping and several faded photos. These, small and square, had a wide, white border, the way photographs were printed when I was a child. I picked up the first one and studied it. Blinked.

Standing there, with his arm around Sadie Rawson Smith, was a man I recognized.

Thirty-eight

I had to squint. I'd only met him the one time.

Ethan Sinclare looked young in the photo, but his features were unmistakable.

The second picture showed Sadie Rawson and a young Cheral, posing in profile with matching pregnancy bumps. The third was the original of Boone and Sadie Rawson flipping burgers at a backyard barbecue, the one that ran in the *Journal-Constitution* in 1979, the one that had brought tears to my eyes two weeks ago, when Jessica Yeo had unearthed it from the archives. It must have been Cheral who provided it to the newspaper in the first place. The last image was blurry and shot from a strange angle, as though the photographer had not wanted to be detected. It showed Sadie Rawson lounging on the sand in a bikini, reading a magazine, her eyes hidden behind huge sunglasses. A few feet away, a deeply tanned man sat watching her. I couldn't swear to it, but it looked like Sinclare.

I fanned out the four photos, the clipping, and Cheral's note on the table.

It didn't make sense.

I fetched a glass of water from the kitchen, then sank

back onto the sofa. It took a minute to locate Cheral's phone number.

"Hey, honey, I'm glad to hear from you. Did you get my—"

"You said Sadie Rawson's lover was named Tank."

"He was."

"But this photo you mailed me . . . I know this man. His name is Ethan Sinclare."

"I know that, honey. I told you, Tank was his high school nickname. From the football team. It's what we all called him. I don't know whether he still goes by it. I'm happy to say I haven't seen that psychopath in thirty years. But . . ." She stopped. She seemed to have just processed what I had said. "But, Caroline, did you say you know him?"

"He came to my hotel. In Atlanta. The same week I met you."

She gasped in horror. "Did he try to hurt you?"

"No! He was nice. He bought me breakfast. He actually—I wouldn't have let him if I'd known—but he picked up the entire bill for my hotel room. Three nights at the St. Regis."

She grunted. "I didn't say he was poor. I said he was a damn psychopath."

"Cheral, you must know that the police checked out Sinclare. It wasn't him. Couldn't have been."

"Sure, sure. Why, because there's no proof that he and Sades were having an affair? And because he had an iron-clad alibi?"

I raised my eyebrows. "Those aren't trivial points, Cheral."

"I gave the police that photo of him ogling her on the beach. He was in love with her, it's totally obvious."

If she was talking about the picture I now held in my hand, I was not convinced. All it seemed to prove was that he appreciated a woman who could fill out a DD-cup bikini. If every man who fit that description was a killer, I was in trouble.

"The whole alibi thing . . . I don't know how he pulled that off," she admitted.

"What was his alibi, anyway?"

"He said he was with a client all day. You know he's a prominent lawyer here? At one of the big Atlanta firms?"

"Yes. He told me that."

"God, I can't believe you *spoke* to Tank. That arrogant, lying *pig*," spat Cheral. She took a moment to collect herself. "Anyway, his story was that he was in his office downtown, with a client, at the time the murders were committed. The client backed him up. It was . . . What was his name? A banker or something. Some sort of businessman."

"So, your theory . . . your theory is that they were both lying? Sinclare, and his banker client, too?"

"I don't know. I just know—I *know* this, Caroline—it was Tank Sinclare that killed your mama and daddy."

Beamer Beasley was right. Cheral's theories sounded harebrained. They wouldn't stand up in court for five minutes. Certainly not against a silver-haired, silver-tongued attorney such as the man she was accusing.

So why was I now sitting here, turning things over in my head, going back over every word I had exchanged over scrambled eggs and sriracha sauce with Ethan Sinclare?

• • •

"I'M NOT SURE how this changes anything," said Beamer Beasley, when I tracked him down buying waffle fries at a Chick-fil-A on Howell Mill Road. "I mean, I know your mama's ex-neighbor thinks Ethan Sinclare did it. She's been yammering on about it for thirty-four years."

"I *really* wish you had told me that," I complained. "All you said was that Sadie Rawson might have had an affair. You never mentioned his name."

"You never asked," he barked down the phone line. "Last thing I want to do is drag a respectable man's name through the mud, drag him into Ms. Rooney's loony conspiracy theories. Ethan and Betsy Sinclare are well regarded here. He's on the board of directors of the Alliance Theatre, and the Atlanta Botanical Garden. He organizes an annual golf tournament to benefit veterans, for God's sake. He said he didn't do it. He has an alibi. We checked it out. There is *nothing* to indicate he was at the Smiths' house that day. End of story. Frankly, he was probably out of your mama's league."

I bridled at this last comment, but held my tongue. "Was he one of the suspects who had a gun?" I demanded instead.

"Was he what?"

"Last week, you told me that back in 1979 you questioned two suspects who owned guns. Was Ethan Sinclare one of the two?"

"Ms. Cashion." Beasley sounded weary.

"Call me Caroline, for Pete's sake."

"With your permission, I'll stick with Cashion. Police protocol. To do with respect and professional distance and all that. And to answer your question—"

"Doesn't matter. I think I already know the answer. Do me a favor, though? Check where Sinclare was last Wednesday night. The night my house got broken into."

Thirty-nine

My mother arrived before nine, bearing lasagna. Two deep pans of it, one sausage and one spinach. What I was in fact craving for breakfast was a *croissant jambon fromage* from Pâtisserie Poupon. If I'd known she was driving over, I would have asked her to pick one up on her way.

I wouldn't have said no to a Vicodin, either. I now regretted having told Dr. Gellert not to bother refilling my painkiller prescription. Last night I had tossed and turned in bed, feeling as though a thousand tiny needles were stabbing my neck. I decided to view this not as a setback, but as a positive development: the numbness must be receding. My skin and nerves were knitting back together. Still. This morning I was tired and sore.

I was also worried. The photos of Ethan Sinclare were unsettling. During the night, as I'd writhed around on my mattress trying to escape the needle-knives, I had homed in on the weirdest part of my breakfast with him. He had denied knowing Sadie Rawson well. He had presented himself as a tennis buddy, closer to Boone. But Cheral Rooney had told me that Ethan and his wife socialized with my birth parents. Even if Cheral was flat wrong about there having been an affair, even if she was loony, as Beasley seemed to think, I'd seen the beach photo myself. Sadie Rawson resplendent in a bikini. There isn't a beach within a hundred miles of Atlanta; at the very least they'd all taken a weekend trip to the coast together. Why had Sinclare lied?

With supreme effort I put a smile on my face. Mom was burrowed into my freezer, trying to clear space for one of her lasagnas.

"Your freezer's packed to the gills," she muttered. "What is all this stuff?"

"Here. Let me help." I squeezed past her and started rearranging Tupperware tubs of chicken soup.

Mom stood watching. All of a sudden, she squealed. "You're using your right hand!"

I looked down in surprise. It was true. I was throwing frozen soup blocks around as though it caused me no trouble at all. Tentatively, I stretched my right arm straight and rotated my wrist in a full circle clockwise. Then counterclockwise. I hadn't been able to do that for more than a year.

Mom and I grinned at each other.

"I'm going to call your father," she said. "He'll be thrilled."

I headed upstairs to change out of my pajamas. When I returned twenty minutes later, teeth brushed and hair twisted back in a bun, she was seated on my living-room sofa. Cheral's photos were still spread across the coffee table. My mom had picked one up by the edges and was studying it intently, a strange look on her face.

I thought I understood. Had Mom ever seen a photograph of Sadie Rawson? She must be upset. The resemblance to me was staggering.

She waved the photo at me.

"Mom—"

"Darling," she said. "I didn't know you knew Ethan."

Forty

My mouth hung open. I thought my legs might buckle. I steadied myself on the arm of the sofa. "What are you talking about?"

"I didn't know you knew Ethan. Such a lovely man."

"You've *met* him?"

"Of course. We've known Ethan and Betsy for years. We got to know each other at the ABA convention. Let's see, the time it was in Dallas." The ABA was the American Bar Association. "That must have been . . . goodness . . . sometime in the eighties. Twenty-five or thirty years ago. Ethan was seated next to me at the banquet. Which was a relief, I can tell you, because there are some exceptionally boring lawyers in this country, and I always seem to draw them as my dinner partner at these things."

I stared at her, my mouth still open.

She seemed delighted that I was so interested. "Ethan was great fun, though. Knowledgeable about the theater. And tennis. He and Betsy would fly over to England for Wimbledon every year. Remember a few summers ago, when Dad and I had tickets for Centre Court? We talked about how fun it would be if we bumped into the Sinclares there. But the week before, your father insisted on going out jogging, even though it was raining—"

"And he slipped and broke his ankle and you never let him forget it, I know, I know."

"Well, I just think he should have shown better sense. We had to cancel the whole trip. Nonrefundable flights to London." She sniffed. "Anyway, we used to see the Sinclares every year at the convention. We still trade Christmas cards."

My parents must receive a hundred, maybe two hundred, holiday cards each December. They display them from tartan ribbons, tied in bows and trailing down from the spindles of the stairs in their front hall. My brothers and I race each other to read aloud the obnoxiously self-congratulatory family newsletters; we never bother to glance at the cards from Dad's professional acquaintances.

"You didn't answer me. How do *you* know Ethan?" Mom was sensing that something was wrong.

I raised my hand to shush her. "Hang on. This is important. When did you last see him?"

She looked uncomfortable. "It's been years. We stopped going to all those ABA events when Daddy retired. But . . . but Ethan called the house just last week."

"He *what*?"

"Let me think. It was the day I had the girls with me."

The girls would be Hayley and Keira. Tony's little girls. Mom counted backward on her fingers. "Last Monday. The twenty-first."

"What did he want?"

"Caroline, he was just being friendly. Just saying hi. He talked about how he was thinking of following your father's lead, maybe start easing into retirement himself. He asked about you kids."

I felt queasy. "Why? Has he ever met us?"

"No, I don't think so. But why do you have his picture?" She gestured at the coffee table. "And what's he doing standing there with . . ." Her lip trembled. "I assume that's her? Your birth mother?"

"Mom. It's okay." I moved to wrap my arm around her. "What did you tell him? About me?"

"Only that you'd grown up into a beautiful young woman," she pleaded. "People ask after each other's children, Caroline, it's what parents *do*. All I said was how proud we are of you, and how well you've done teaching at Georgetown. And that . . . that you were going to take some time off. To have an operation."

I closed my eyes.

That Monday was the day Madame Aubuchon had ordered me to take sabbatical for the rest of the semester. Wasn't that the night that Will had slept over? I had already met Sinclare by then. But Leland Brett's follow-up article, confirming my plans to get surgery, hadn't run until the next day. Tuesday the twenty-second. That Monday it was not yet public knowledge whether the bullet was about to be extracted, or whether it would stay in my neck forever.

Ethan Sinclare had been checking up on me.

"HE KNOWS MY parents, Beamer." To hell with last names, with police protocol and professional distance. I was too upset. "Sinclare called my mom last week."

"Back up. What are you talking about? How could he call your mama—"

"Not Sadie Rawson. *Frannie*. He knows the *Cashions*."

"What? You sure?" asked Beamer Beasley down the phone line from Atlanta.

"My mother—my mother *Frannie*—just recognized him in a photo. She says he called their house last week. He asked about me, Beamer."

"All right, all right, hang on. Let me conference in Gerry. You can tell us both what happened."

It took ten minutes to recount my conversation with my mother. When I had finished, Beasley cleared his throat. "Sinclare and your daddy are both lawyers. Trial attorneys, roughly the same age, at the end of successful careers. I suppose it's not shocking that their paths might have crossed."

"My thoughts exactly," said Gerry Fleeman. "Makes sense that they would attend the same conventions." I had liked the head of the Atlanta Police Department's Cold Case Squad when he conducted my formal interview over the phone last week. He seemed smart, competent. Now, from six hundred miles away, he was getting on my nerves.

"There must be, I don't know, half a million litigators in the United States," I snapped. "It's not like they're all buddies, hanging out and smoking cigars together at Ye Olde Litigators' Club. And to my knowledge, none of the rest of them has been calling my mom in Washington, inquiring after my health. You don't find that a strange coincidence?"

"Let's think this through calmly," said Gerry. "You said your parents originally met Ethan Sinclare because he sat next to your mom at a dinner back in the 1980s. You're not suggesting . . . what, that he engineered that, are you? As a way of getting to you?"

"I'm suggesting you consider the possibility."

"Ms. Cashion, that would mean he'd been stalking you for the last *thirty years*," scoffed Gerry. "Thirty years! If he means you harm, he's certainly taken his time about it."

"Fine, not stalking me, but keeping tabs on me. Keeping tabs on whether I was healthy. Whether I had remembered anything."

"What, with an annual Christmas card swap? I'm sorry, I just don't think—"

"It does make a crazy kind of sense," said Beasley, just when I thought I might scream. "Whoever the killer was, he would have wanted to know whether the sole surviving witness remembered anything. And he couldn't just call and ask to speak to a little girl. He would have had to go through her adoptive parents."

"Precisely," I said.

"But I still don't think Sinclare had anything to do with it," said Beasley. "I also don't think he had anything to do with the burglary of your house, Ms. Cashion."

"Okay. How come?"

"Because he was at his cabin, out on Lake Burton. His wife says they were there together all last week. They're still there. Sounds like she's attempting to persuade him to spend less time at the office."

"Where's Lake Burton?" I demanded. "When did you talk to her?"

"North Georgia. Rabun County." Beasley sighed. "You asked me to find out where Sinclare was last Wednesday. I can't say I credit your suspicions about him, but I figured we owed you an answer. Also figured we owed him the courtesy of not hearing secondhand that we're taking another look into the Smith murders. So I called his law firm yesterday. They gave me the phone number for the lake house."

"And he's definitely there?"

"Yes, ma'am. Betsy—that's his wife—she said he'd walked out the door five minutes before I called. Out on his boat fishing all afternoon yesterday."

"Great bass fishing up at Burton," Gerry chimed in. "Although getting a little cold for it now. Anyhow, if we're done here—"

"We're not done here," I said, irritated. "She could be lying about where he was last week."

"Possible," said Beasley evenly. "But I had his secretary check his calendar. She agrees he was at the lake house last Wednesday and Thursday."

"Did she lay eyes on him there? Or is that just where he told her he—"

Beasley cut in, "And we checked the flight lists into National, Dulles, and BWI. All three DC-area airports. Ethan Sinclare didn't fly to Washington last week."

"Maybe he drove."

"Also," added Gerry, "local police got the fingerprinting results from your house. And we already had Mr.

Sinclare's on file from way back. We compared them. No match."

"So the man owns a pair of gloves!" I exploded. "Look, please tell me that one of you is going to follow up. Press Ethan Sinclare on how he happens to know *both* my families—"

"I thought we'd already agreed, he had good reason to attend the same Bar Association meetings as Thomas Cashion," Gerry grumbled.

"Absolutely," I shot back. "But why didn't he mention the connection when he met me for breakfast at the St. Regis? He acted as though he had no idea that the man who adopted me was a lawyer."

"I have to agree with her there," said Beasley. "I thought of that, too."

"Thank you." I relaxed a little in my chair. "Meanwhile, any news about the bullet? The lab's had it four days now."

"We'll keep hassling them," said Gerry. "These things can take time."

After he signed off, Beasley stayed on the line. "Sorry about that. Gerry's a good guy. Skepticism and mistrust are part of the job description."

"What about being a complete jerk? Does he throw that in for free?"

Beasley chuckled. "And I take your point about Sinclare not acknowledging that he knows the Cashions. It's odd. There must be an explanation, but I'll be damned if I can think of it. Maybe I'll drive up today, pay him a visit at his cabin. It'd do me good to get out of the city."

"Thank you. One more thing. His alibi. Back in '79. Who was it?"

ON MY DOORSTEP stood a woman with flaming red hair. "Hey there. Hi. Sorry to disturb you," she called through the door, waving a business card in front of her. I couldn't read it through the narrow tunnel of my peephole. "Hello? Rhonda, from your office, said I would find you here."

Rhonda is the administrative assistant for the Faculty of Languages and Linguistics at Georgetown. Cautiously I cracked the door. "Yes?"

"Thanks. Hi." She trained a warm smile on me. "My name's Alexandra James. I'm a journalist. Wait!" She jammed the toe of her boot in the door before I could slam it shut. "I know, last person you want to talk to, right?" The megawatt smile tipped up at me. "Just hear me out. Two minutes and I'll go."

I studied her face more closely. She looked a few years younger than me, perhaps in her late twenties. She wasn't beautiful, not exactly, but she was striking. Well dressed. I glanced down. Great legs. "I remember you. You write for that Boston paper, right? You broke the big terrorism story at the White House last year."

"Yeah." She grinned. "Still recovering from that one. I got this for my troubles." She lifted bangs off her forehead to reveal a thin, white scar.

Alexandra James had been all over the news herself for a while. She had broken the mother of all stories, had been nominated for a Pulitzer Prize, as I recalled, but questions had been raised about her ethics. Whether she'd crossed red lines in dealing with sources. She was rumored to have slept with a British spy; I couldn't remember the details.

"I'm based here in Washington now. I read your story, about the bullet, and what happened to your family. Were you pleased with how the *Journal-Constitution* handled it?"

I was caught off guard. "Er . . . Yes. More or less. Look, I really—"

"Good. I thought the reporter was respectful, the way he wrote about the deaths of Boone and Sadie Rawson Smith. I did wonder, though . . . I mean, obviously, the *AJC*'s an Atlanta operation, they're going to want to play up the Atlanta story. But I did wish they had also interviewed your family here. The Cashions."

"Oh, we don't want any more publicity."

"Can't say I blame you. But it would be nice, you know? To hear from the family that you grew up with. They got . . . sidelined by the story, the way it was written. Left out. Kind of a shame, because if I read between the lines correctly, it sounds like you're close. I'd love to see a story where you had the opportunity to thank them. Talk about how much they mean to you."

A shrewd pitch. She had zeroed in on the one angle I'd be happy to talk about all day.

"Anyway." The smile again. "I promised to shut up after two minutes. May I leave you my card? My cell number's on it, in case you ever want to talk." I accepted the ivory rectangle from her outstretched hand, intending to chuck it in the trash the second she left.

"Oh!" She twirled around. "I almost forgot. Here. For your convalescence."

Alexandra James held up a white box tied with string. I recognized the elaborate, cursive *P* of the Pâtisserie Poupon logo.

My eyes narrowed. "How did you . . . ?"

"Like I said, I called the university before I walked over here. To check when they were expecting you back at work. I didn't want to disturb you if you'd just been released from the hospital an hour ago or something."

"And Rhonda gave out my home address?" I would need to have a word with her.

"No, no. I already had it. You're in the phone book, you know. Rhonda didn't tell me anything except that you're on leave for the rest of the semester. And that if you weren't at home, I might find you here." She tapped the *P* logo on the pastry box. "I share your addiction, by the way. I'm a fiend for their lemon tart."

I bit back a smile. Say what you would about the woman's journalistic ethics, she was clever. I carried the box through to my kitchen. Lifted the lid. Bacon quiche. Still warm.

You are not supposed to accept food from strangers. That must be one of the earliest lessons that my mother—hell, probably both my mothers—had drummed into me. But they also taught me to trust my instincts. Right now mine were telling me that Alex James wanted to interview me, not poison me.

I opened a drawer and pulled out a fork.

• • •

I HAD POWERED my way through two slices of quiche and was eyeing a third when the doorbell rang again.

What now?

It was a tiny skeleton. In plump hands it clutched a hollow, plastic pumpkin. "Trick or treat?"

I had forgotten it was Halloween. Bizarre holiday. Dressing children up as witches and vampires, telling them stories about monsters and ghosts. As if real life didn't pack enough nasty surprises.

Forty-one

For many years, if you wanted to make a phone call in Atlanta, you were routed through the switchboards of Southern Bell.

In the early days, the 1880s, the only long-distance call you could place was from Atlanta to Decatur, six whole miles away. That would set you back fifteen cents for a five-minute chat. It was 1915 before the first trans-continental call, voices dancing from the East Coast to the West across thousands of miles of suspended copper wire; 1951 before you were allowed to dial long distance without the assistance of an operator; 1956 before the first transatlantic phone cable was laid. Southern Bell thrived through the changes, survived a dizzying number of mergers and spin-offs and splits, until the company name was finally retired in 1998.

I mention all this by way of backdrop. Backdrop to what, for our purposes, is by far the most interesting date in Southern Bell's corporate history: March 25, 1971. That's when a Mr. Verlin Snow walked through the doors. He was hired as a senior vice president, poached from a Boston bank, forty-five years old. Technically he was brought in to oversee the completion of the transition to touch-tone phones. They'd been available to subscribers since the early sixties, but folks seemed slow to catch on. But Snow's real talent was as a rainmaker. He possessed an exceptional knack for greasing political connections to increase profits. A columnist for the *Atlanta Business Chronicle* noted that most weekdays you could watch him in action at the Coach and Six, the Peachtree Street power-lunch spot favored by the city's old guard. Verlin Snow stood out, the columnist added with a trace of suspicion, not only for his Yankee accent but for his puritanical habits. Snow conducted business stone-cold sober, in a town where men were disposed toward downing a second martini before the food arrived.

Sometime in the late 1970s, though, he had gotten into trouble. He had hired a young lawyer by the name of Ethan Sinclare, a rising star in one of Atlanta's white-shoe firms. I couldn't tell quite what kind of trouble Snow was in. Beamer Beasley didn't seem to know either, and whatever it was, Sinclare appeared to have earned his fee and succeeded at making it disappear. A *Forbes* magazine profile of Snow in 1981 ("The Man Who Killed Off the Rotary Phone") alluded only to an extended leave of absence, taken at his summer home on Nantucket, from which Snow had returned to work energized and more bullish than ever.

What Beasley did know was that late in 1979, when Sinclare was questioned about the murders of Boone and Sadie Rawson Smith, he had had an impeccable alibi. He had been locked in a conference room at his downtown office, conferring with his client Verlin Snow. Snow confirmed this when police followed up. Yes, he was absolutely certain about the date and hours in question. No, Sinclare could not have slipped out for any length of time. Lawyer and client had been hunkered over stacks of documents, heads bowed together, the entire afternoon. Snow was a pillar of the business community, a member of the right country club, on the executive committee of the Commerce Club. His word was gold.

I was able to piece together most of Verlin Snow's background from my kitchen table. Astonishing what you can accomplish these days, armed with a laptop and a fast Internet connection. But the press clippings petered out after his retirement in the early nineties. He was quoted a few times, trotted out for expert analysis, in news stories covering various telecom antitrust lawsuits. The last reference I could find was from 1997—sixteen years ago— when the student newspaper for Northwestern University mentioned that Snow would be guest-lecturing at the Kellogg Graduate School of Management.

I couldn't tell where he might be now.

I couldn't tell if he'd kept in touch with Ethan Sinclare, or if he knew anything that might help me.

I couldn't even tell if Verlin Snow was still alive.

IT CAME TO me when I stood to put the kettle on and warm the last piece of bacon quiche in the microwave.

Snow's summerhouse. Nantucket.

Finding him turned out to be easy. On my laptop an address and a phone number for a V. R. Snow in Nantucket, Massachusetts, popped right up. When I dialed, no one answered. I speared a bite of quiche, chewed, and tried again. Let it ring seven times. Eight. Nine.

"Hello?" said a surprised-sounding voice, the way one would answer a phone that rarely rang.

"Hi, I'm calling from Washington. Trying to reach a Mr. Verlin Snow. Do I have the right number?"

A longish pause. "Yes," said the voice, still surprised. A woman.

"This is Caroline Cashion. May I speak to him please?"

"But he can't speak on the phone," she said, now indignant, as if this were an obvious point that I had stubbornly been resisting. Her accent was Caribbean, possibly Jamaican.

"Um, you mean not right now? Might he be available later?"

"No. Mr. Snow's not well. What did you say your name was?"

"Sorry. Let me back up. My name is Caroline. I was hoping to come see Mr. Snow"—I was surprised to hear my voice forming these words—"maybe tomorrow."

"Oh, no, no, no" came the reply, now stern. "I wouldn't think so. He doesn't see visitors anymore." Her voice dropped to a whisper. "He's an invalid. Do you not know? Cancer of the throat."

I had done the math before I called. Verlin Snow would be eighty-seven years old. I dropped my voice to match hers. "Can he still hear well enough? He can understand questions? Yes? . . . Okay, tell him something for me. Tell him Caroline Cashion is on the phone. When I

was a girl, my name was Caroline Smith. Tell him it's regarding a lawyer from Atlanta, named Ethan Sinclare.
About time they spent together in November 1979."

The woman was gone a good five minutes. I could
hear pipes running in the background, and the barking
of a distant dog. When she came back on the line, she
said simply, "He'll see you. He's best in the afternoons."

THERE ARE NO direct flights from Washington to Nantucket, not in the off-season.

I would have to fly through Boston, connecting onto
a ten-seat puddle jumper flown by Cape Air. Still, if I left
early tomorrow, I could be on the island by 11:00 a.m.,
New England weather permitting. I reached up to finger
the stitches on my neck as I clicked around travel web-
sites. Dr. Gellert would kill me if he knew what I was
contemplating. Beamer Beasley would, too, for a completely different set of reasons.

Booking flights on small planes—booking any travel
at all—a mere seven days after emergency surgery was
stupid, I had to admit. But as I hesitated, I noticed that I
was holding the computer mouse in my right hand. I
had not been able to do that for the past year. I'd made
the switch back without even realizing it.

Something else felt different, too. I think I've mentioned that I'm not known for rash decisions, am not a
taker of spur-of-the-moment trips. Yet here I sat, about
to buy a ticket for a plane that left in eleven hours, to fly
to an island that I'd never seen, to meet a stranger. I
should have felt nervous, but instead, I felt invigorated.

Sometime in the chaos of these last few weeks, I appeared to have developed a taste for recklessness.

I hovered my hand—my right hand—above the mouse. Then I swooped down and clicked on the box that said PURCHASE.

MY MOBILE BUZZED as I brushed my teeth before bed. I picked right up. One of my post-Will resolutions was to be more vigilant about answering my phone. Another was not to fall for any man who listened to country or wore boot-cut jeans. Also, never again to accept a date that involved baseball (although in fairness, I might have arrived at that particular fatwa even if Will Zartman had turned out to be a good guy).

"Everything okay? You safe?" It was Beamer Beasley.

"Yes." I spat toothpaste into the sink. "Why?"

"Good. In for the night? Alarm on, doors locked?"

"Beamer. What's going on?"

"Just checking. Just that I can't, uh, at this exact moment, I can't locate Ethan Sinclare."

I laid the floss back beside the sink and plopped down on the edge of the bathtub. "What do you mean, you can't locate him? I thought he was up at that lake. Lake Burton."

"Well, that's it. I drove up there yesterday, like I said I would. For a number of reasons, but frankly, the main one was I thought it might put your mind at ease. Figured I could talk to him, let him explain some of the . . . inconsistencies I know have been troubling you. But he wasn't there. I talked to his wife—"

"Betsy."

"That's right. A nice lady."

"So she was at the cabin?"

"Yes. Actually, cabin, my rear end," snorted Beasley. "It's not a cabin, it's a compound they've got up there. Boathouse with room for two motorboats, a sailboat, a couple canoes, you name it. Plus a hundred yards of private shoreline, even a barn so Mrs. Sinclare can ride her horses. Anyway, she was real polite. But she said I'd missed him again. Mr. Sinclare had to drive back into town to take care of some business. She said he'd be at his office. But he never turned up at the law firm today, and nobody's home at their house in Buckhead either. His cell phone's turned off. If I were the worrying type, I'd be starting to worry that he's avoiding me."

I could think of half a dozen places where Ethan Sinclare might be, none of them necessarily sinister. His tennis club. A friend's house. The movies. Maybe he had a woman on the side that Betsy didn't know about. If Cheral was to be believed, he hadn't been a stickler for fidelity thirty-five years ago; who knew if the leopard had changed its spots?

"Thanks for letting me know."

"I'll keep trying," said Beasley. "He'll turn up. We'll get this all straightened out. Are DC police still driving by your house every night?"

"No." I frowned. "Not since last week. Not since my surgery. I mean, the bullet's gone. There's no reason anyone would feel threatened by me anymore, right?"

"Speaking of that. The bullet. That was the other thing I called to tell you. They can't do anything with it."

"Nothing at all?" My voice rose in dismay.

"Not here in Atlanta. They did identify the caliber. It's a .38 Special. Full metal jacket, which explains why the bullet passed through your mama's body and on to you. So the firearm in question would have been a revolver, I'm guessing maybe a Smith and Wesson .38 Special. That's what we all used to carry. Standard service cartridge for police departments, for many years."

"Jesus!" I shrieked. "You don't mean the police were involved?"

"No, no, that's not what I meant. Cops carried them, but so did plenty of other folks. They're good guns, work well for everything from personal defense to target practice to popping off rabbits in your backyard. People still buy 'em. The trouble is . . ." Beasley sighed. "Ms. Cashion, the trouble is your bullet from your neck isn't in good enough condition to make a comparison. It's scored in several places. Scratched up. Maybe from back when it was fired, maybe from where the surgeon used tweezers to tug at it, to get it out."

I felt as though I'd been punched in the stomach.

"We're shipping it up to Virginia, to the FBI. They've got a hundred times the manpower and expertise we do."

"The FBI? The FBI is going to examine my bullet?" I repeated incredulously.

"Best crime lab in the country. Out in Quantico. Literally hundreds of firearms specialists, ammo specialists, forensic techs, special agents, you name it."

"Did you send the FBI the evidence bullets, too? The sample ones that you all kept from 1979?"

"Yes, of course. That's the whole point."

"Were any of them .38 caliber?"

"Listen, let's cross that bridge when we get there, okay? I've already bent the rules, telling you this much."

"But, Beamer—"

"Ms. Cashion, I'm hanging up now. We should hear back from Quantico by early next week."

After that I tried to sleep, but every few minutes some noise snapped me awake. A shutter on my neighbor's house was loose and banging in the wind. Somewhere farther up the block a car alarm went off. When an owl hooted outside my window, shortly after 2:00 a.m., I nearly jumped out of my skin. I checked the settings on the burglar alarm, checked the dead bolt on my bedroom door, then got dressed and waited until it was time to call a taxi for the airport.

PART FOUR

Nantucket

Forty-two

Verlin Snow's house was big and square and built of weathered, gray clapboard. But then, from what I could see through the rain-streaked windows of the airport taxi, all the houses on Nantucket were built of weathered gray clapboard. I had never seen such uniform architecture. My initial impressions of the island were of billowing fog and gusting wind, the air split by the shriek of seagulls and sharp with the tang of brine.

There was also the smell of money. The streets were swept, the gardens tended, wet roses curling over freshly painted picket fences, even in November. I endured the drive from the airport with gritted teeth, one hand pressed to the back of my bruised neck, the other braced against the car door. This morning's back-to-back flights had been smooth; I had wrapped a soft, thick shawl around my shoulders and slept the whole way. But Nantucket's uneven cobblestone streets were torture. The taxi jounced and splashed through puddles, past coffee shops, an old-fashioned pharmacy, a bank, a pretty church. Half the shops looked closed for winter. The sidewalks were deserted.

The Snow house sat near the center of what appeared to be the biggest town on the island, known, with typical New England austerity, simply as Town. After a couple of blocks, the storefronts on Main Street gave way to great mansions, the former homes of sea captains and whaling merchants. Seagulls aside, Nantucket's Main Street bore a remarkable resemblance to the swankier blocks of Georgetown.

"Here we go," said the driver, drawing up near the corner of Main and Milk Streets. Gas lanterns burned on either side of three stone steps and an imposing front door. The brass knocker and letter slot gleamed. I pulled a box of Advil out of my handbag, popped three pills, knocked, and waited.

When the door swung open, the scene was more or less as I had imagined. A dimly lit foyer, fussily furnished but clean. Old rugs, old Audubon bird prints, faded wallpaper, a grandfather clock that looked as if it hadn't kept time for generations. The woman with the Caribbean accent was friendlier and more soft-spoken in person than she had been on the phone. She introduced herself as Marie. I couldn't tell if she was a friend or a nurse or a housekeeper or some combination of the above. She took my dripping coat and led me past darkened rooms.

"He can't talk anymore," she whispered. "Not for months now. But his mind's sharp as a tack."

"How does he—"

"He writes. I've tried to get him to use the computer,

but he prefers his notepad. You'll see." She glanced at me from the corner of her eye. "I was surprised he allowed you to come. He doesn't bother with most folks anymore. Says they wear him out. But he got up and shaved this morning for you."

At the back of the house was an unexpectedly cheerful sitting room. A fire blazed at one end, and before it, in one of those mammoth, corduroy La-Z-Boy recliners favored by old people, sat a man. He pushed the chair upright when I entered and rose to shake my hand. Snow was stooped and shriveled and didn't look as if he'd been tall to begin with. The top of his scaly, bald head barely reached my chin. His skin was sallow and flecks of dried blood dotted his jaw, casualties from his attempt at a morning shave. I felt a wave of pity, imagining him splashing at the sink, the effort it must have required.

Snow gestured for me to sit. He lined his own heels up against the edge of the recliner, stuck out his bottom, and allowed himself to fall backward into the deep chair, the way I remembered my grandmother doing after she got too frail to sit and stand on her own. Snow and I studied each other. He might be in the advanced stages of cancer, but his eyes were clear and lucid. Intelligent. Marie was right: his mind seemed sharp as a tack.

"Thank you for seeing me. Do you know why I'm here?"

He reached toward a wooden side table between us. On it lay a pen and a brown Moleskine notebook.

How do you do, he wrote, then met my eye and nodded formally. On the next line, in a spidery scrawl: *Why don't you tell me.*

So I did. I told him about what had happened to the Smiths in the house on Eulalia Road. About how I had been raised in another city, by another family, and had only recently learned of the existence of my first family. About how I had lived almost my entire life with a bullet inside my neck. He appeared to listen closely, scratching out the occasional *!* at dramatic moments in my narrative, and once a *?* when he seemed to want me to elaborate.

"They never caught my parents' killer," I concluded. "But you know one of the people who was questioned. He was your lawyer."

Snow nodded and wrote, *Ethan.*

"You told the police that you were with him all that afternoon."

Another nod.

"Was that true?"

The intelligent eyes held mine. His hand rested motionless on the notebook. That had been too abrupt a way to ask; I needed to come at the question more subtly. But I felt impatient, and the stitches on my neck itched, and this room felt stiflingly hot.

"Mr. Sinclare came to see me a couple of weeks ago," I tried again.

Verlin Snow had no eyebrows, but the wrinkles on his forehead wiggled in a way that suggested he would have raised his eyebrows if he could.

"He was kind. But some of the things he said—or, rather, things he chose not to say—don't make sense to me." I leaned forward and placed my hand on Snow's emaciated knee. "One other thing that you should know. I was attacked, in my house in Washington, one night last week. Someone tried to hurt me. I think—I don't know, but I think it was someone who knew that the bullet in my neck posed a threat to them. Someone who knew it could send them to prison."

Snow's forehead contracted in a spasm of wrinkles. *!!!*, he wrote.

"Please help me."

Still his eyes held mine.

"I don't care why you had to hire Ethan Sinclare as your attorney. I don't care what kind of trouble you were in. That's not why I'm here." I squeezed Snow's knee, hard. "That day. The day my parents died. Could Ethan Sinclare have been at their house? You swore it was impossible. That the two of you were locked up together in a conference room."

Verlin Snow picked up the pen. Slowly, in cramped, shaky letters, he wrote:

I lied.

Forty-three

I pried the Moleskine notebook from Snow's hands. Rotated it so I could read right side up, ran my finger over his words.

I lied.

"You weren't with him, then? That afternoon?"

He took back the notebook and wrote, *Part.*

"Meaning what? You were with him part of the time, but not the whole afternoon?"

A tired nod.

"So he has no alibi," I whispered. "He never did. He could have been at Boone and Sadie Rawson's house."

Snow flinched and scribbled furiously: *I don't know that.* He underlined the words, four heavy lines.

"Okay, you don't know where he was. Only that he wasn't with you."

Rapid nodding. I narrowed my eyes. "You lied for him. Lied to police in a murder investigation. And you never bothered to ask where he really was? How could you not be curious? What did the guy have on you?"

This was met with a shrug.

"Why did you lie?"

If I was not mistaken, Snow rolled his eyes.

"I suppose that you don't think it matters at this point. But, Mr. Snow . . ." My voice tightened with rage. "Mr. Snow, my parents *died*. I was *shot*. If Ethan Sinclare did that—if he was there—he shot a three-year-old girl and left her to bleed to death. You must have heard about it; you must have seen the newspaper account. How could you live with yourself? How could you lie for him?"

All at once Verlin Snow lurched forward in his seat and made a grotesque, rasping noise, halfway between a croak and a howl. He made it again and then was seized by a fit of coughing. I leapt to my feet and searched the room for a glass of water or a tissue. Nothing. Should I find Marie? But he was quieting now, clutching his chest, tears and snot rolling down his wasted face. He wiped his face on his sleeve and groped around for the pen. He wrote steadily for several minutes before looking up and pushing the notebook across to me.

I was sued. Insider trading, securities fraud. I wd have lost everything!! Fought back. But pre-trial discovery turned up evidence. Record of phone call, typed by my secretary. Ethan required to turn it over. You see?

But that night Ethan came to me. He said—Help me I'll help you. I destroy phone note. If you say I was with you. Easy!! No email then. Long time ago. No electronic document trails. Just the one piece of paper. So he burned it. And I told police we spent that day in conference room. A win-win.

I finished reading and looked up in astonishment.

He turned to a clean page and wrote, *I'm not proud.*

"I should think not."

Assumed it was about a woman. He needed excuse for his wife, for where he'd been. Ethan was always ladies man.

"And what do you think now?" My voice was like ice.

Ladies man. He underlined it. *Not a murderer!!!*

"You don't know that. That's the point. You don't know where he was, what he did that day."

Another shrug.

"I need you to make a statement. Tell the police what you've told me. There's an old detective, Sergeant Beasley, who knows this case well—"

Snow shook his head. He wrote, *Goodbye Caroline.*

With that he tore the pages from the binding, everything that he had written, crumpled and threw them into the fire. The edges caught. Blue flames licked up. Within moments the pages were ashes.

I breathed in sharply. "I can type up what you've told me. All you need to do is sign your name at the bottom. Just the part about Ethan not being with you. Nobody cares about the rest of it anymore. The statute of limitations has probably run out anyway, on the insider trading charge—"

But Verlin Snow had closed his eyes and sunk back into the La-Z-Boy. He looked tiny and old and ill.

"Mr. Snow?" I tapped his leg. "Mr. Snow?"

He opened his eyes to a slit. Whacked my hand away from his thigh. His lips made no noise but formed themselves into an unmistakable round *O.*

No, he said, as distinctly as if he'd actually spoken the word aloud. The eyes snapped back shut.

I found my coat where Marie had hung it behind the stairs and let myself out.

• • •

NANTUCKET IN LATE fall is like a ghost town. A silvery, misty, freezing, prosperous ghost town.

I trudged through drizzle from Verlin Snow's house, back past the church on Main Street, then left and up Center Street. My flight out was not until tomorrow morning, 9:05 a.m., so I'd booked at a bed-and-breakfast for the night.

In the room I scrubbed my face with hot water, kicked off my boots, curled up on the bed, and slept again. Four dreamless hours. When I woke it was dark. I threw off the blanket and wondered how a hotel room could manage to feel both boiling hot and dankly damp at once. I needed to get out.

The boy minding the front desk looked barely old enough to drive. Judging from the full wall of keys behind him, I might be the only guest tonight. He spent a minute reeling off the names of restaurants I should come back in high season to try, and another minute singing the praises of a bar at the tip of the island, if only I had a car to get there.

"Just somewhere close," I pleaded. "Close and open would be good. My standards aren't high tonight."

"Brotherhood of Thieves is thirty seconds that way." He pointed. "Walk out the front door, you're on Broad Street, turn left, and you're there. It's an old whaling bar."

"Perfect."

"Awesome beer on tap. Try the Cisco ale. Or the seasonal Pumple Drumkin, if they've still got it. Brewed here on Nantucket. They add chunks of pumpkin and spices. Awesome." That sounded perfectly vile, but I refrained from saying so.

Brotherhood of Thieves was dark, with low, timbered ceilings and a roaring fire. Lanterns hung from brick walls. Only two tables were occupied, one by an awkward couple who appeared to be on a date, another by four old men who had the air of regulars. Two empty beer pitchers sat stickily on the table between them, and a third looked well on its way to being guzzled. I squeezed into a seat at the bar, caught the bartender's eye, and started to order my usual glass of dry white wine, then reconsidered.

"Double Bulleit, please, neat."

"Nice." He pushed a bowl of pretzels my way.

I held a menu up to a candle to read in the dark. For once I could not face meat. "What are quahogs?"

"Clams."

"Ah. I'll take a bowl of the Island Quahog Chowder then."

"Good choice. Top you up?" He dangled the Bulleit bottle above my glass. I glanced down. I'd already drained my double.

"Yes. Why not. And a glass of water." I should go easy. Neither Will Zartman nor my brothers were here to carry me home tonight. My heart twisted at the thought of Will. The last time I'd been in a bar was the Georgia Grille, the night he surprised me in Atlanta. I held a sip of rye on my tongue and closed my eyes and remembered how it had felt when he touched me, when he had drawn his circles on my wrist, my collarbone, my breast. How difficult it was to breathe when he pressed his hips against mine.

When I opened my eyes, the bartender was placing chowder and a packet of oyster crackers in front of me. "Bowl's hot, watch yourself."

I took a spoonful. It was peppery and creamy and rich. The old men had a fresh pitcher on their table. The beer was a light, straw yellow; they were steering clear of the Pumple Drumkin, too. The couple had gone. On the TV above the bar were pictures of a jubilant crowd waving Red Sox banners. Confetti filled the air behind them.

"Did the Red Sox win again?" I asked the bartender.

"Did they win again? Where have you been? They won the World Series this week. That's the victory parade, today in Boston."

He leaned sideways to watch. The screen showed a caravan of duck boats rolling down a street in Boston, Red Sox players riding on top and whooping. They were still sporting their lucky beards, and when I looked closely, I noticed many of the duck boats had been decorated with matching caveman-style whiskers. A band started up playing "God Bless America." The camera panned to a small girl dancing in the street, her face painted and her blond hair streaked with Red Sox red. Vuvuzelas and car horns brayed.

"Boston Strong," said the bartender, thumping his chest.

"Boston Strong," called the stoutest of the old men. They all clinked smeary glasses at the TV.

"On the house," said the bartender, pouring me what looked like at least a triple. He turned around to grin at the stout old man. "Hey, hey, here we go! Whaddya say, Marty? I think Ortiz and the boys may be going for a swim!" The caravan of amphibious duck boats had turned off the street to take a victory lap in the Charles River.

I sipped my whiskey and watched the men watch the Red Sox. Such simple things can produce such joy. Tomorrow I would have to think about what Verlin Snow had told me. About Ethan Sinclare, about Sadie Rawson and Boone, about what it all meant. Tonight, I allowed myself to sit in a dark bar with a bunch of happy old men, and to believe that the world might be a decent place after all.

PART FIVE

Washington

Forty-four

I felt fine the next day.

It helped that the clocks had changed during the night, buying everyone an extra hour in bed. Or perhaps I was still drunk. Seven shots of rye and I had slept like a baby, my best night's sleep in weeks. On the plane home I popped two Advil, to relax my neck muscles (liver failure, here I come), and devoured both the *Boston Globe* and the *New York Times*. It had been weeks since I'd focused on the news. Politicians who I didn't even know were sick had died, the United Nations was warning of genocide in the Central African Republic, Twitter was about to go public, Amy Tan had a new book out. I read the headlines with the curiosity of someone who has been at sea for weeks or recently woken from a coma; I had missed whole cycles of scandal and redemption.

At home on Q Street, three pieces of mail had been shoved through my letter slot. Pottery Barn, undaunted by my failure to purchase anything, ever, had delivered a fat pre-Christmas catalog. "Let the Holiday Magic Begin!" it trilled, above a photo of a perfect stocking, hung above a perfect fire, glowing beside a perfect cream sofa and a perfect-looking cocktail.

There were also two letters. The first, a handwritten note from Alexandra James: *Lovely to meet a fellow P.P. addict. Hope your recovery continues. Let me know when I can buy you coffee.* She had enclosed another business card.

The second letter was from a manager at SunTrust. We had exchanged e-mails and phone calls, after I rang to inquire about tracing the savings account and safe-deposit box that were mentioned in Boone and Sadie Rawson's wills. The manager had asked me to forward copies of the wills, and of their death certificates. Also, my adoption papers and birth certificate. For good measure I threw in printouts of Leland Brett's two stories in the *Journal-Constitution*. They explained more succinctly than I possibly could why I was suddenly interested in bank accounts that had sat inactive for thirty-four years.

The reply letter that I now held in my hands apologized for having no information on the safe-deposit box. In accordance with the Disposition of Unclaimed Property Act, the box had been drilled after seven years. The entire contents had then been turned over to the state. No bank records survived, nothing to indicate what the driller might have found. I was invited to contact the Georgia Department of Revenue, unclaimed property division, for further information. Here was a handy link to their website.

Tracking the savings account, meanwhile, had taken

some effort. The account number that I'd provided didn't match anything in the computer, and files that old had not been digitized. But a retired clerk had been brought in to go through boxes. They were organized by branch, and my birth parents, unhelpfully, had not frequented the Trust Company closest to their house. Their account had been registered at a branch south of the city, out near the airport; Boone must have found it convenient to hit the drive-through teller on his way to and from work.

I was kindly requested to submit for verification the originals of all the photocopied documents that I'd sent. The manager apologized, again, for the inconvenience. He trusted that I understood, given the length of time that had elapsed and the amount of money involved. I blinked, held the paper farther away, then closer, checking and double-checking the digits and the decimal point.

Sitting in a dormant Trust Company account, opened under the names Boone W. Smith and Sadie R. Smith, was quite a significant sum of money.

Forty-five

The executor of my birth parents' estate was dead.

This news tidbit came courtesy of an e-mail from Jessica Yeo, which I read in the kitchen, perched on the countertop in pajamas and slippers, sipping my morning mug of Darjeeling. I had done a quick search online for Everett A. Sutherland, after his name turned up in Sadie Rawson's and Boone's wills, but hadn't found much. My dad had also professed ignorance, said he'd never looked into the Smiths' estate.

"You're a *lawyer*," I had pressed him. "Weren't you curious about the legal loose ends?"

"No," Dad had answered firmly. "We wanted a clean break from the past. We confirmed, of course, that no guardian had been named for you, that there was no legally enforceable relationship with any biological kin. But as for the question of an *inheritance*"—he had pronounced the word with distaste—"darling, your mother and I were more than capable of providing for you. There was no need to paw around after their money."

Jessica Yeo, however, appeared to have quite enjoyed

pawing around the Smith family finances. Somehow she learned that Everett Sutherland had been Boone's elderly godfather, a family friend from North Carolina. He had died of cancer only a few months after Boone's and Sadie Rawson's murders. Sutherland's funeral had been held at Second United Methodist Church in Charlotte, and he'd been buried beside his wife of forty-seven years.

This explained a lot. Namely, why Everett Sutherland had never tried to track me down. Why safe-deposit boxes and bank accounts had simply been forgotten. Judging by the balance in the Smiths' account, he had steered the proceeds from the sale of the house on Eulalia Road into the right place. But then Sutherland must have gotten sick and been too worried wrapping up his own affairs to put in place proper arrangements for my birth parents' estate. I could only assume he'd meant to contact the Cashions at some point, but had run out of time.

Jessica Yeo didn't apologize for disobeying my request to back off. On the contrary, she pitched a few ideas for what she wanted to look into next. *Pretty, pretty please?* she wrote. *This is soooo much more interesting than the fact-checking junk that Leland keeps assigning me. Do NOT tell him I said that.*

My next e-mail was also from a journalist. Alexandra James reiterated her invitation to coffee, and then, almost as a casual aside, inquired about the bullet. *Did you keep it? I made a couple of calls, and Atlanta police won't comment. But they must be interested, right?*

Reporters. Honestly.

What an exhausting profession, to be professionally

trained to be relentless. In the last five days, Alex James had doorstepped me at my house, delivered a handwritten note, and reached out via e-mail. Next she would be in the street out front, shouting questions through a megaphone.

I nearly sent the last message in my in-box straight to spam. It was from an address I didn't recognize, pierce@ nantuckhotels.com. A guest-satisfaction survey from the bed-and-breakfast? An electronic copy of my receipt?

But it was a personal note. The front-desk minder, the teenager who had looked barely old enough to drive, hoped that I'd had a pleasant stay on the island. House-keeping had found a phone charger and my iPod in the room. Did I want them shipped? He gave the phone number for the front desk.

"So that's where they went," I said when he answered.

"Oh, hey! Yeah, I wouldn't have written if it were just the charger. But I figured the iPod you might want."

"Thanks. That'd be great."

"How was dinner at Brotherhood of Thieves? Did you try the Pumple Drumkin?"

"No. But thanks again for the recommendation. Nice place."

"No problem. That guy ever reach you?"

I frowned. "What guy?"

"Guy called a couple times looking for you, while you were at dinner. Didn't leave a name."

I frowned more deeply. Other than Marie and Verlin Snow, I had told no one I was going to Nantucket. No one else had known I was there, and certainly not where I had stayed. I hadn't wanted my family to worry about my traveling so soon after surgery.

"Older guy," said the front-desk clerk. "Maybe a Southern accent? I wrote down the number from caller ID, after he called the second time, in case it was important. Hang on. Let me see if I can find it."

I chewed the stem of my glasses and listened to him shuffle papers around. When he came back on the line, he read out a number I did not recognize. It began with a 404 area code. Atlanta. I hung up and scrolled through my contacts. Not Beamer Beasley. Not Cheral Rooney. Not Jessica Yeo or Leland Brett. I reached for my wallet. From the fold where I keep receipts, I removed a business card, printed on heavy Crane stock, and checked the cell number.

How had Ethan Sinclare known I was on Nantucket?

I COULD HEAR the bad news in Beasley's voice. Something in his tone, even as we were exchanging pleasantries. "What's wrong?"

"We heard back from FBI forensics this morning. Just got off the phone with the lab. The bullet is inconclusive."

"Meaning what?"

"Meaning they can't match it. Meaning it's in too poor condition. They can't do anything with it. I'm sorry, Ms. Cashion."

"Nothing at all? Did they agree with the techs in Georgia about the caliber, what kind of gun was used?"

"Yes. It's a .38, all right. But too mashed up and scratched to compare with the evidence samples. Not to any degree of certainty. Not even looking at it under a good microscope."

"I can't believe this. What happens now?"

"Well . . ." Beasley let out a deep breath. "FBI's going to send down their complete report. I only got the headlines over the phone. Gerry Fleeman and I'll go over everything and compare notes. But without the bullet . . . It was the possibility of new physical evidence that prompted reopening this case, as you know. Without that, without a bullet match, I'm not sure how much farther we can go."

"So that's it?" I was struggling to take this in. "You're done?"

"I've been over these old files a dozen times, Ms. Cashion. We would need new evidence to justify—"

"Ethan Sinclare didn't have an alibi for that day."

Silence. Then, sounding annoyed: "Yes, he did. I told you. He was at his office, with his client—"

"His client Verlin Snow. I know. Except he wasn't. I went to see Mr. Snow this weekend."

"You *what*?"

Beasley yelled at me for a good five minutes after I told him about my meeting with Snow. I had put myself in danger, I was interfering with an investigation, was I *completely* out of my mind?

"I'll have to see if he'll make a statement," Beasley huffed at last.

"He won't."

"Have to try."

"Sure. Okay."

"And I'll keep trying to get hold of Mr. Sinclare. His secretary says she expects him in later today. Says he's got a bad habit of turning off his cell on the weekend, drives his family crazy, probably hasn't even seen my messages."

I knew that wasn't true. Sinclare's cell phone had not been switched off on Saturday night. He had somehow tracked me down and found the time to call my hotel on Nantucket. Twice. I kept this piece of information to myself. Instead, I asked, "Beamer?"

"Yes, ma'am?"

"The evidence bullets that you collected from the two suspects' guns. Back in '79. Were either of them .38s?"

Beasley hesitated before answering, "Both of them. Different-model handguns. One Colt, one Smith and Wesson. But both were .38 Special. Thing is, so were maybe half the revolvers in Atlanta in 1979. Doesn't prove a damn thing."

MADAME AUBUCHON STOPPED by at lunchtime to collect her soup pot.

As before, she turned up with no warning. Thankfully I was dressed this time, had even put on earrings and makeup.

"*Très belle,*" she said, smiling as she took me in. "You're looking like yourself again. The soup must be working."

"*Ça doit être ça.*" That must be it. "*C'est délicieux.*" It was true. Her soup was delicious, so long as you resigned yourself to stinking of garlic for the rest of the day.

I led her into the kitchen. "*Un café? Un thé?*"

"*Non, merci.* Perhaps something stronger?"

Something stronger? It was half past noon. On a Monday. I walked to the liquor cupboard in my living room and returned with several bottles.

She pointed. "That one, *s'il te plaît.*"

I poured Madame Aubuchon a glass of Armagnac and watched, bemused, as she knocked it back.

"Yes?" Her voice haughty.

"*Rien. Rien du tout.* Nothing. It's just . . . we've worked together for a long time. Ten years, *n'est-ce pas?* But I'm, um, realizing I don't actually know you very well."

She smiled. Shook her head when I made to refill her glass. "Just the one. *Pour la santé.* For good health." She produced an embroidered handkerchief from her purse and dabbed delicately at her lips. "I find it easiest to keep my personal life private. Not to discuss it at the office."

"A wise policy."

"For example, you may not know that Jean-Pierre is my second husband."

"Oh?" I said, to be polite.

"He's only fifty-one," she said with a touch of pride. "*Il n'est qu'un garçon.*" Just a boy.

"I'd love to meet him someday."

"I think not," she sniffed. "He's enough trouble as it is. I don't need him to see the likes of you, *pour l'amour de Dieu.* He would eat you up."

I raised my eyebrows in amusement. "He sounds very . . . French."

She shot me a sharp look. I thought she had taken offense. I was opening my mouth to apologize, when she spoke again. "Jean-Pierre is my second husband because my first one beat me. He nearly killed me. Several times."

My expression changed to one of shock. "Hélène. I'm so sorry. I didn't know."

"No one does. This finger still doesn't straighten properly." She held out a heavily veined but beautifully manicured hand. The pinkie drooped at an unnatural angle.

How had I never noticed?

"And my ribs, cracked three separate times. A punctured lung. Concussions." She said this matter-of-factly, as through she were reciting a list of groceries she planned to pick up on the way home. "After I found the strength to kick him out, I locked myself in the apartment and did not come out for seven weeks."

I didn't know what to say.

"*Sept semaines,*" she repeated.

"How awful."

"Sometimes, to heal, we need time alone." Madame Aubuchon dipped back into her purse and withdrew a heavy ring of keys. "Go to Paris, Caroline. Go hide. Get strong again."

Forty-six

He won't talk," reported Beasley, when he called back midafternoon. "Verlin Snow. You were right. He won't play ball."

"How can you possibly have already reached him? He's out on that island."

"Local help. Nice police department up there. I gather the most excitement they generally get is ticketing folks for expired beach permits."

"You sent Nantucket cops to question Verlin Snow?" I asked skeptically. "About Boone and Sadie Rawson's murders?"

"About Ethan Sinclare's alibi. Way you described Snow, all coughing and wheezing, it sounded like he might not be long for this world. Would have taken me too long to get authorization to go up. Nantucket cops are already right there on-site."

"Sure, but they don't know any of the background. They don't know this case well enough to persuade—"

"I know, and that's why I asked the questions. In an ideal world, we'd open up a grand jury investigation and require his testimony. But we don't have jurisdiction over him up there in Massachusetts, and he doesn't sound inclined to travel to Georgia anytime soon. So in the interest of time, we had two officers drive over to his house and set up a video link. He looked like he could hear me fine. He wrote down his responses, and the whole interview was videotaped, so we've got a record. Not that that'll be much use, because he denied everything you say he said."

I made an exasperated sound. "I told you he would."

"Verlin Snow swears that Sinclare was right by his side the entire afternoon of November sixth, 1979. Just like he's always said."

"That lying weasel."

"He also said he never told you otherwise. Said you must be confused, and we should all go away and leave a dying man in peace."

I snorted. "He's dying, all right. He looked dreadful. Sounds like that's the only true statement he gave you."

"Caroline." Beasley cleared his throat. I registered his switch to using my first name. "I appreciate how difficult all this must be for you. How much you wanted that bullet to lead us to somebody. How good it would feel to achieve closure, feel like you've done right by your mama and daddy. The Smiths. Me, too, trust me. I told you when I met you, this case haunts me every day." He harrumphed again. "Gerry and I have talked it over and—"

"You know what I think? I think you should go arrest Ethan Sinclare. I think he did it. I think he had an affair with Sadie Rawson, and she dumped him, and he went crazy. Shall we recap? Sinclare owned a .38 Special, and the bullet in my neck was a .38 Special. Sinclare doesn't have an alibi, whatever nonsense Verlin Snow is currently spouting. And now he appears to be on the run, he isn't returning your phone calls—"

"Hold on, hold on. Not returning my phone calls doesn't qualify a person as being on the run. If it did, then my daughter was a fugitive for pretty much the entire decade she was a teenager. And let me play devil's advocate on the other things you just said. One, we don't know that Ethan and Sadie Rawson had an affair."

"Cheral Rooney says they—"

"I know she does, and I also know that he denies it. There's no proof either way."

"Verlin Snow said Ethan's always been a ladies' man."

"Oh, Verlin Snow!" crowed Beasley with mock enthusiasm. "Would you mean the same Verlin Snow who gave a statement today, who put it in writing and handed it to two uniformed police officers, swearing that Sinclare was with him at the time the murders were committed? You mean that Verlin Snow?"

"Beamer—"

"Sorry, what was that you were saying? About Sinclare not having an alibi?"

"He's lying, Beamer! Snow lied to you today."

"Prove it."

I was silent.

"Caroline. My point is, there isn't proof. None. Zero. There's no proof there ever was an affair. There's no proof that the bullet that hit you was fired from Sinclare's gun. There's no witness, except for you, and you don't remember a damn thing. Oh, but we *do* have a leader in the business community, a senior Southern Bell exec, who swears that Sinclare couldn't have been anywhere near the crime scene. You with me? We're right back where we were thirty-four years ago. Except that maybe now I'm even more frustrated."

"What about the fact that someone broke into my house two weeks ago and tried to hurt me? Don't you think that might have been Sinclare, trying to get to the bullet before—"

"Sure, it *might* have been. Or it might have been Jack the Ripper. Or . . . Wile E. Coyote. Where's the proof? Come on, you know the standard we have to meet for a felony conviction. *Beyond a reasonable doubt.* We're not anywhere close to that. On the contrary: we've got both his wife and his secretary prepared to swear under oath that Sinclare was in Georgia the night of October twenty-third."

I stamped my foot in frustration.

"You would want to be very, very careful before you brought charges against a man like Ethan Sinclare. I'm not saying that's a reason not to try. But he would be a powerful witness for the defense. He would call in every favor he's ever been owed in Atlanta. And given how generous he and Betsy are in the community, I'd wager that's a few. Speaking of Betsy, he'd have his pretty, blond wife out there, the mother of his children, going on about what a good man he is, what a good husband and father. She'd light up the TV cameras. Betsy would have the whole Junior League lined up behind her, every blond lady in Buckhead insisting her husband must be innocent."

That stopped me short. Not the image of sweet Betsy

Sinclare in front of the cameras. But the image of Ethan as a good husband and father. It was, I had to admit, the same impression I'd gotten. It was difficult to square the kind, fatherly man who'd bought me breakfast with a violent criminal.

Beasley appeared to be struggling with the same disconnect. "I'm not saying rich, white folks get a pass. Even rich, white folks as well connected as the Sinclares. But you're asking me to believe that Ethan Sinclare—an educated, respectable lawyer—went on a homicidal rampage in 1979. Shot everybody in sight, point-blank, left a baby girl for dead. Yet afterwards he went docile as a lamb. He transformed into the perfect gentleman, a loving family man, for more than three decades. Right up to last month, when—*boom!* He snaps again, drives to Washington, puts a brick through your basement window and tries to break down your bedroom door? It's—"

"I know, I know. It sounds completely implausible."

"People can change their ways, I grant you. But those are wild extremes."

We were quiet for a minute.

Then Beasley said, "Mind you. Do you remember last year, that volcano that erupted in New Zealand?"

I waited. Talk about non sequiturs.

"It spewed rocks, sent up giant ash clouds, shut down a bunch of roads. And the volcano experts they interviewed—what do you call them, volcanologists?—they said there'd been no warning. No seismic activity."

"Okay." I was learning that Beasley would eventually get to his point; sometimes he just liked to circle around it for a while first.

"Mount Tongariro, I think it was called. It had been dormant for one hundred and fifteen years. More than a century. And then all of a sudden, no warning, it erupted."

Ah. Now I saw. "Just like that?"

"Yes, ma'am. Just like that."

THAT EVENING I went for a walk along the river. I prefer walking in the woods this time of year; the wind gusting off the Potomac gets icy. But the harbor and the bike paths that run along the water are always crowded, and it felt safer to be surrounded by people. I walked east, past Thompson Boat Center, past the distinctive curve of the Watergate Complex. A pair of scullers flicked their oars across the water. The cherry trees that line the riverbank raised bare branches to the sky. My ears stung with cold. I leaned into the wind, waiting for the tension in my shoulders to ease, waiting for my thoughts to clear.

Somewhere around the Kennedy Center I slowed. A plan of action had revealed itself. I glimpsed the grand sweep of what I should do, and why. I picked up my pace again, pounding the asphalt path. The clarity of purpose sharpened. I examined this plan, spun it around in my mind, feeling around the edges. They were jagged. Too many unknowns. I made corrections. Yes, it could be accomplished.

When I got home, I poured a glass of wine and made two phone calls. The first was to Leland Brett. The second was to Alexandra James. Leland's feeble but relentless sexual harassment campaign notwithstanding, the content of the two conversations was virtually identical.

I told them both that forensics technicians at a Georgia crime lab, and then at the FBI, had examined the bullet from my neck. Unfortunately, it was found to be too damaged to be useful. I directed them to follow up with the Atlanta Police Department for specifics. I gave them Beamer Beasley's direct line.

"I had hoped that the bullet removed from my neck might somehow help to advance the murder investigation, even after all these years," I added, a line I'd come up with on the long loop of my walk back to Georgetown. "But it's not to be. I'm at peace with that. It's time to move on. Whoever killed my parents is probably dead now himself."

I asked both Leland and Alexandra to use my quote in its entirety, and to promise that the story would run in tomorrow's papers. Leland gave his word.

Alex pushed back. "We don't do quote approval."

"What's that?"

"I don't make promises to sources about what portion of their comments will make it into print. But you have my word that I'll quote you accurately."

"Fair enough. And will this definitely run tomorrow?"

"The print edition's tricky. Finite amount of space. I can't control what other news may break, or how that'll affect which stories run and which ones get held. But there's no reason this wouldn't be posted to the website right away. Probably before I head home tonight."

"Excellent."

"One last thing. How are you feeling, postsurgery? When do you expect to be back at work?"

"I'm better. Much better. But the university doesn't

need me back teaching until after Christmas. So I figured I'd plan a couple of weeks in Mexico, to rest and get my strength back. Later this week I'm headed down to Cabo San Lucas."

"Sounds heavenly."

"Thanks. I'm looking forward to a few days of doing nothing more strenuous than hoisting a pitcher of margaritas."

She laughed. "That last bit, I'm happy to guarantee I'll quote."

I put the phone down and topped up my wine.

Then I opened my laptop and booked an 8:00 a.m. flight to Atlanta.

PART SIX

Atlanta

Forty-seven

The Atlanta airport was jammed. On the airport train to the main terminal, people stood shoulder to shoulder, braced against ceiling straps, the scents of hair spray and shoe polish and burnt coffee fogging us in. Someone's roller bag dug into my calves. I threaded through the crowds, making my way toward the now-familiar Hertz outpost, stopping only once, at a newsstand near baggage claim.

Leland's article appeared inside the front section of the *Journal-Constitution*, page A5. He'd been true to his word. My comment about feeling at peace and wanting to move on was near the top, along with a nice quote thanking Boone and Sadie Rawson's friends for their well wishes.

> "It's been amazing to learn how many people loved them, how many people's lives they touched," said Cashion. "I feel blessed—I think that's the right word, despite everything that happened—blessed to have been born into a family with such loving and loyal friends."

Cashion adds that she hopes to organize a memorial service in Atlanta, to remember and to celebrate the Smiths' lives. The date and venue are yet to be determined.

Leland Brett included a line or two about the bullet at the end of the article, almost as an afterthought.

The bullet was too badly damaged to shed new light on the 34-year-old homicide investigation, according to Detective Sergeant Beamer Beasley, of the Atlanta Police Department.

Still, Cashion described her surgery to remove the bullet as "an enormous relief." A spokesperson for Sibley Memorial Hospital in Washington, D.C., where the procedure was performed, confirmed that Cashion is expected to make a full recovery.

Cashion plans to resume her work as a professor of French Literature at Georgetown University, following a trip to Mexico. "I need to take some time to myself, to reflect on everything and to heal.

"To be honest," added Cashion with a laugh, "the best therapy for me right now is probably a margarita, and a couple of weeks of sun and sand."

I paid and tucked the newspaper and a bottle of water under my arm. I would check Alex James's version of the story from my phone, once I picked up the rental car.

It was 10:04 a.m., and I had three appointments to keep today.

• • •

"IF YOU COULD sign here. And here, and here."

The bank manager watched me with ill-disguised fascination across the glass coffee table in his office. He and the bank's vice president for customer relations had greeted me at the elevator bank wearing sober, black suits and bearing a huge bouquet of flowers. These had been presented along with two cards—one reading, *With Deepest Sympathy*; the other, *Get Well Soon!*—signed by more than a dozen members of the bank's management team. I was simultaneously touched and a little embarrassed. After the formalities at the elevator, the bank manager turned and led me through a maze of cubicles. No vase was offered. No kindly assistant materialized to help. There was nothing to do but to follow him, three dozen long-stemmed, pink roses cradled in my arms, ribbons fluttering in my wake, like an aging but still regal homecoming queen.

In his office, fortunately, things went quickly. My identification was verified; original documents were photocopied and stamped.

Boone and Sadie Rawson Smith had not left me a vast fortune.

But their house on Eulalia Road had proved a wise investment. The proceeds from its sale had been pooled with the payout from a modest life insurance policy owned by Boone, which Everett Sutherland had claimed and deposited into the Trust Company account in December 1979. The result was a respectable pot of money. A pot of money that had been all but forgotten when

Sutherland died in May of 1980. For thirty-four years, the phenomenon that is compounding interest had been allowed to work its magic.

The bank manager tidied the edges of the mound of documents that had accumulated on the table between us. From the top, he pulled one last sheet of paper for me to inspect. He made me initial today's date, the current interest rate, and the total balance figure for the account.

"Wire transfer? Cashier's check? We can do either."

I selected the latter.

Ten minutes later, I exited the bank with an armful of wilting roses and a check for $677,143.27.

BEAMER BEASLEY MET me at a Waffle House on Roswell Road.

"If I'd had warning you were coming, I'd have organized somewhere nicer," he apologized, gesturing at the red vinyl booths and the chipped plates, the plastic tubs of jelly and creamer.

"Don't be silly. This is perfect."

The gray eyes took me in. "You look good. Like a different person from when I met you three weeks ago."

"Thank you." I raised my right wrist, waved it around. "No more wrist brace."

He nodded. "And no more bullet."

Beasley slid a padded envelope across the faux-wood tabletop. "Speaking of which . . ."

"No!" I gasped. "Is that it?"

"That's it. Arrived back in the office this morning. Yours to keep now, if you want it."

I tipped the bullet onto the table between us. It was ugly. A dull, misshapen lump, with scratches and dents visible even to the naked eye. And surprisingly small, to have caused such pain. Such grief. I closed my fist around it.

Beasley laid his hand over mine while I collected myself. "I read in the morning paper that you're headed to Mexico. Maybe you could take that with you, throw it out to sea, say your good-byes."

"Maybe." I bit my lip. "About that newspaper article. I should have warned you before I sent the reporters calling. I hope you don't mind my breaking your moratorium on talking to them. Didn't seem to be much point avoiding them anymore."

"That's fine."

"Anyway, I—I wasn't sure if you all would let me keep the bullet. But I was thinking that if you did, I might actually have it made into a necklace." I ran a finger over my stitches. They had nearly dissolved; in the mirror this morning I'd observed that the surrounding bruises had faded from angry purple to brownish yellow. "Aside from a pair of earrings that Cheral Rooney gave me, this is the only thing I have that ever touched Sadie Rawson. I want to keep it close. I suppose that sounds weird."

"Considering this bullet took her life, you mean?" Beasley tapped the metal lump. "I don't think it's weird. It's a physical connection to her. That must feel powerful."

We sat for a time, Beasley stirring a second and then a third creamer into his coffee, me rolling the bullet back and forth across my palm.

"I came into some money today," I said finally.

"Oh? How's that?"

"The Smiths had a savings account. After they died, the money from their house and from Boone's life insurance was stashed there. There's a safe-deposit box, too. I'll fill in the paperwork to dig that out one of these days. The box got drilled, and the contents handed over to the state years ago."

"They'll have liquidated anything personal. Love letters, photographs, jewelry, anything like that."

"So I'm told. And the personal stuff is all I would really care about at this point. There was more cash than I'll ever need in the regular savings account. Enough to . . . Well. Enough to open up some interesting possibilities." I took a sip of weak tea. "I keep thinking about what you said. About justice being what you aim for in a case like this. And it occurs to me that I'm sitting here rolling a bullet between my fingers that ten days ago was inside my neck. Also, I've heard from all kinds of nice people who knew my birth parents and loved them. I'm planning a memorial service in their honor. That's . . . well, it's not a conviction, obviously. Not closure from a criminal-justice point of view. But it's something."

"Mm-hmm." Beasley studied me. "So why do I get the sense this still isn't over for you?"

"What do you mean?"

"Are you really going to Mexico?" His eyes were now suspicious slits.

"Of course. Probably the best therapy for me at this point is a pitcher of margaritas and some sun and—"

"And you're completely at peace and eager to move on. I know. I told you, I read your quote in the newspaper."

"Well, there you go."

"You're also quoted as saying that whoever killed your parents is probably dead now himself."

"I stole that line from you."

We looked at each other. Both of us were working hard not to mention the name Ethan Sinclare.

Beasley caved first. "I'll talk to him. I've set up an appointment through his secretary, for end of this week. I'll raise some of the . . . coincidences that were bothering you. But without the bullet, without any new evidence, I don't see . . ."

"I know. I understand."

Beasley opened his mouth to say something else, then snapped it shut again. Sun streamed through the window, refracting through the jugs of fake blueberry and maple syrup stuck to the table, making them glow like stained glass. A waitress delivered hash browns and country-fried steak to a chubby couple in the booth beside us. From the parking lot outside came a crunching sound, a station wagon backing into the bumper of a dirty, white Honda.

"Well, then." Beasley swallowed the last of his coffee, tucked two creamers into his pocket, and laid a $10 bill on the table. "Then I wish you all the luck in the world, Caroline. And safe travels to Mexico."

"Thank you, Beamer." I leaned over and kissed the grizzled hair on his skull, and then I was gone.

Forty-eight

There is no waiting period to buy a gun in Georgia. No need to secure a firearms permit. You can waltz right in, select the one you want, and carry it out fifteen minutes later in a plastic bag.

There is one catch, though: you have to have a Georgia ID. Gun stores won't sell to anyone flashing an out-of-state license. I sat in the parking lot of Sonny's Sporting Goods for more than an hour, pondering this problem.

Sonny's is a warehouse forty minutes due east of Atlanta. An eleven-aisle superstore, like a surreal Target just for guns. WE BUY AMMO BY THE TRACTOR TRAILER LOAD! announced a banner hanging above the registers.

I had walked the aisles in wonder. Camouflage pants and T-shirts were stacked near night-vision goggles. An entire section was devoted to quivers and crossbow accessories. Plastic bins separated elk whistles from squirrel calls, hog squealers from Canada-goose flutes. I picked up a white tube labeled a Double Reed Cajun Squeal, wondered what kind of swamp animal it was designed to lure.

And then there were the guns.

The entire back wall of the store was lined with them.

Scopes and sniper rifles hung suspended. Handguns were laid out on brown felt trays inside glass cases. Everything from tiny, silver Berettas, to Texas Defender derringers, to an antique Colt .45 with a walnut grip and a stamp from General Custer's Seventh Cavalry. MORE THAN 12,000 GUNS IN STOCK boasted another banner. I couldn't tell how the guns were organized. I only knew that with this many on display, what I was looking for was bound to be here.

"Help you, miss!" A big, bearded man behind the counter.

"Oh, no, thanks. Just browsing."

I walked the entire perimeter of the store, then stationed myself near checkout, watching how it worked, pretending to engage in an involved conversation on my cell phone. Four cash registers were open and humming away. The cashier closest to the doors was ringing up an overflowing cart of trout-fishing tackle. Not of interest. The next was explaining to an irate customer why his 20-percent-off coupon wasn't valid on duck waders. But at the third register, a customer was waiting to buy a gun. He had to fill out a two-page form on a clipboard; the cashier took his answers and typed them in. After several minutes, the official FBI seal appeared on her screen, along with a large green rectangle ringing the word PROCEED. The customer handed over five crisp $100 bills. The cashier ran an orange marker over them. Waited. Looked satisfied and stuffed them into the register. Some sort of anticounterfeit check? The man walked out of the store sixty seconds later, whistling and swinging a plastic bag.

I retreated to my car to watch the front door and

think. Sonny's seemed busy for a Tuesday afternoon. An almost exclusively male clientele came and went, revving and reversing pickup trucks into bus-size parking spaces. My compact rental car sat dwarfed between a Chevy Silverado and a rusted-out Dodge Ram.

Around dusk, a Toyota Tacoma with Rockdale County plates pulled into the spot opposite me. One headlight had stopped working, and the truck bed was piled high with firewood. A lean man wearing a flannel shirt and frayed work pants hopped out. He looked my age, maybe a few years older. He walked around the back of his truck, yanking on the ties securing the wood, tightening them down. I watched how he dragged his feet as he worked, and how he kept his shoulders hunched, like a dog that's used to getting kicked. I scanned his face, hoping to see kindness there, but the light was gone and he was too far away.

Now or never.

I swung my car door open.

"Hey," I called. "Hey there. Could I trouble you for a minute?"

FIVE MINUTES LATER he was bent over my car engine, checking the oil.

"I feel so silly that I couldn't even figure out how to open the hood." I giggled girlishly and clapped my hands together. "When that warning light came on, saying to check the oil, I didn't know what to do. Thank goodness you were here."

He had his sleeves rolled up, his finger looped through

the top of the dipstick to wipe it clean. When he leaned back over the motor to reinsert it, I placed my hand lightly on his arm. He flexed his biceps through the flannel, bulking it up for my benefit. This was going well.

"Everything looks fine, ma'am. Start up the engine again, let's see what she says."

I slid behind the wheel of my perfectly operational car and turned the key. "You fixed it!" I beamed at him.

"Sometimes those dashboard lights act up. I didn't do nothing. Your oil's good to go.

"I'm so relieved," I purred. "How can I thank you?" I slid back out of the car, watched him drink me in. My lips were painted ruby red, and I was wearing a blond wig and hip-hugging jeans tucked into my stiletto boots. The sartorial equivalent of the Double Reed Cajun Squeal, expressly designed to lure the human male.

He licked his lips like he'd been shown the promised land.

"What's your name?"

"Um. Britt. How 'bout you?"

"Tammy." I batted my eyelashes. "I hate to impose on you for another moment. You must be so busy. But I have another little bitty favor to ask."

"Anything," he breathed. He looked as if he meant it.

"You're going in there anyway, right?" I darted my eyes toward the Sonny's entrance.

"Sure. What do you need?"

"Well. It's my boyfriend. Ex-boyfriend. Johnny. He's a horrible man. He . . . he hits me."

Britt opened his eyes wide. "That cocksucker. Excuse my French."

"It's okay. We broke up months ago. But he keeps following me and threatening me and I . . . I'd feel much safer if I had a gun."

"Course you would. Let's go in. I'll help you pick a—"

"No. See, I can't buy one. I don't have Georgia ID. So I was wondering . . . if I made it worth your while . . ."

I watched him register this.

"Oh." He stepped back. "Oh. No, I can't do that."

"Just something simple. For self-defense."

"No, I—that's a felony now. Buying a gun for somebody else. They do a background check at the register, ask whether you're an illegal alien, or a convicted felon, or if you're buying it for someone else."

So lie, I wanted to hiss. "I said I'd make it worth your while." I reached into my back pocket, let his eyes linger on the curve of my jeans. "This is a thousand dollars. Cash." I handed him an envelope with ten bills inside. "You can take it to your truck and count it if you like."

He stared at me as if snakes had popped out of my head.

"And there's another two thousand, when you meet me back here. Easiest three thousand bucks you'll ever make. Britt? Three. Thousand. Bucks. In and out of Sonny's in less than half an hour. I'll give you cash to pay for the gun, too." I forced myself to smile alluringly. "What do you say? You'd be helping me so, so much."

I waited, sweat beading between my breasts, dripping down the small of my back, wondering whether he was about to shout for the police.

He licked his lips again. "What kind of gun?"

• • •

BRITT TUCKED THE envelope into his shirt pocket. "You need ammo, too? Better off with hollow points. They'll mushroom, rattle around inside the guy."

I shuddered. "Fine."

"Fifty rounds'll do you?"

"That's plenty." I was starting to feel as if I'd placed an overly complicated order with a short-order cook, or a Starbucks barista. *Just buy the damn gun, Britt.*

"And you really wanna git .357s instead of .38s," he said thoughtfully. He had a pack of chewing tobacco out now, was working a wad deep down inside his cheek.

"What's that? A different cartridge?"

"Is your cocksucker ex-boyfriend a big guy? You got a three-hundred-fifty-pound guy on crack running at you, you wanna know you're packing maximum power."

I closed my eyes. Was I really standing here, in a rural Georgia parking lot, having this conversation?

"I switched 'em in the gun my wife carries in her purse," Britt added with pride. "Switched her .38s for .357s. She ain't never gonna notice. I'd rather she be firing a .357 when some guy's coming at her."

His wife. Jesus. He'd thrown out that morsel even as he tried to sneak another peek down my blouse. Sleazy. Not, mind you, that I was in a position to pass moral judgment on anyone at this precise moment.

"I'll stick with .38 Specials. The smallest box. I'll meet you right here."

Britt nodded, spat a stream of tobacco juice, and shuffled toward the entrance.

I settled into my car to wait. Locked the doors. Then jumped back out. If flashing blue lights suddenly appeared, or if Britt returned with a security guard, I shouldn't be sitting there waiting like an idiot. I ducked my head and walked to a corner of the lot, near a concrete island of dejected shrubs. From there I had a clear view of the store entrance, the vast expanse of asphalt in front, and the highway beyond. I waited. Shivered. The temperature had dropped sharply with the sunset.

After what seemed forever but was in fact twenty-seven minutes, the doors swung open and Britt walked out. I watched. No one followed him. He wove back toward my car. He was peering into the window on the driver's side, hands cupped around his eyes to cut the glare from the streetlights, when I reached him.

I touched his arm.

He jumped six inches. "Holy crap, you scared me. Where'd you git to?"

"Bathroom emergency." I nodded toward the shrubs. "Well?"

He held out a bag. I glanced around. A woman was climbing into a truck double-parked at the front curb; a car was reversing on the far side of the lot. No one was close. I had seen no security cameras, but to be safe I shifted position, so we were hidden behind the hulking cab of the Silverado in the next parking space.

"Got you a five-shot revolver," whispered Britt. "Smith and Wesson, .38 Special. Made in the 1970s, like you asked for. She's scratched up but she'll shoot fine. Two hundred and forty-nine dollars plus tax. Decent gun for the price."

I handed over the second envelope. "Thank you."

He stood there, smiling hopefully, wide, little-boy eyes above tobacco-stained teeth. "Buy you a beer?"

"Another time." I was already in the car, strapping on my seat belt, shoving the plastic bag deep inside the glove compartment.

Britt leaned in the open window. "Can I git your number?"

"I think you ought to go on home, don't you? You wife's probably got dinner on the table. Use some of your new money, stop and buy her flowers on the way."

BEFORE BED THAT night I did four things.

The first was to write a check for $10,000 to Jessica Yeo. I'd teased her once that if my birth parents left me a million dollars, I'd split it with her. They hadn't, but they'd left enough that I could afford to return a few favors. In the memo line, I wrote, *For being relentless.* I dropped the check into a hotel-stationery envelope and printed her name and the newspaper address on the front.

Next I called Mom and told her that I would be tied up with projects for the next few days. I assured her that I was fine, eating well, and would check in soon.

After Mom, I dialed Martin's number and asked him to keep an eye on my house.

"What's this I hear about Mexico? Dad says you're going to Cabo."

"I want to disappear for a while, get off the grid," I replied, more truthfully than my brother could have realized.

"You'll be okay on your own? Tony said you were be-having a little . . . erratically the other day, when you two drove out to that gun range."

"*Erratic?* That was the word he used?"

"Err, no. *Full-on wack job* was actually the way he put it."

"Can you blame me?" I sighed. "Mother Teresa herself would be behaving like a wack job if she'd been in my shoes these last few weeks."

"I know. I'm glad you're getting away, Sis. It'll do you good to unplug."

"I'm thinking of staying down in Mexico a couple of weeks, maybe a month or so. To rest and clear my head. Think Mom will go nuts if I'm not around for my birth-day?"

"Yep. She'll go nuts, all right. I'll do my best to re-mind her that the wine will keep and the steaks will freeze. Tony and I'll distract her on Thanksgiving, too. Just promise me you'll come home by Christmas? Other-wise I can't be held responsible for her actions."

The last thing I did before sleeping was to slip on boots and a jacket, exit the side door of my hotel, and walk five blocks to a bar. From the pay phone by the bathrooms, I called Ethan Sinclare. He answered on the fourth ring. I kept it neutral and short. I was in Atlanta for a brief visit, I told him. An appointment tomorrow had been can-celed, leaving me with an opening in my schedule.

Might he have time to meet?

Forty-nine

You couldn't plan things this way, you really couldn't, not if you tried. I could have needed the bullet removed in February. Or December. The pain could have slammed me on a breezy, warm day in May. It had happened when it happened, who could say exactly why?

I had been keeping an eye on the date. As the clocks fell back and the nights grew longer, I had watched it creeping closer. But still it felt momentous, to roll over in the morning and to see it—WEDNESDAY, NOVEMBER 6—illuminated in bright digits on the home screen of my phone.

November 6. The anniversary of Boone's and Sadie Rawson's murders. They had died on this date, in this city, exactly thirty-four years ago.

Here's another point to consider: Boone Smith was shot through the brain, his wife through the heart. Only the one bullet ever recovered, as you know. The one pulled from my neck. A .38 Special. And now here I was. Their only child, the only survivor of that day's carnage, back in town with fifty rounds in my pocket and a newly purchased Smith & Wesson .38 Special revolver. You see?

There was a lovely symmetry to it. Even, you might say, a certain inevitability.

BEAMER BEASLEY HAD talked about a volcano. The one that erupted, spewing rocks and ash, after lying dormant for more than a century. The metaphor had given me pause.

But it was a different image that took root in my mind this morning. I thought of a bear. How a hibernating bear will sleep through long winter months, its chest rising and falling, dreaming sweet dreams of honey. But wake that same bear, provoke it, and it will attack with speed and savagery, biting and slashing with claws like knives. There is no way to know which bear you may encounter—placid or violent—when you stand at the mouth of the cave, peering into the dark.

Standing on Ethan Sinclare's front porch felt a little like that.

I had hesitated when he invited me here. His home, his territory, his terms. At least it would be private, I reasoned. On the phone last night he told me that he had been away, traveling. I was lucky to have caught him. He was driving up to his lake house tonight; his wife, Betsy, was already there. Today, though, he was in Atlanta, picking up fresh clothes and running errands. Why didn't I drop by the house for lunch? Something casual, sandwiches and Cokes. He knew a deli that made an outstanding pastrami on rye. He would pick us up a couple, some chips and pickles, too.

Sinclare gave me an address on Tuxedo Road, in the heart of Buckhead. I left the rental car parked at my hotel and took the bus. It dropped me three blocks away, and as I walked, I studied the houses. They were large and set deep in rolling lawns. This was old-money, establishment Atlanta. A van from a pool-cleaning service sat parked in the next-door driveway. From across the street came the whine of a leaf blower. Otherwise the only sign of life was two middle-aged women dressed head to toe in Lululemon, blond ponytails bobbing in unison as they power walked past.

Sinclare opened the door while my finger was still pressing the buzzer. He must have been watching as I picked my way up the prettily curved stone path.

"Caroline." He extended his hand, took mine in a warm grip. "How good to see you."

He closed and locked the door behind us, then led the way past the front stairs, past the living room, into a large and sunny kitchen. A round table in the window was set for two. Bone china, linen napkins and place mats, stemmed crystal glasses. I raised my eyebrows.

"I'm afraid you're still stuck with pastrami and pickles." He smiled. "Betsy would be furious, though, if I didn't at least serve it to you on the good china. Southern ladies and their place settings! Don't tell her I skipped the real silver. Too damn much trouble. You can't throw it in the dishwasher when you're done."

"I'm sorry to miss meeting her."

"She'll be sorry, too, when she hears that she missed you. We keep a cabin on a lake, up in the northeast corner of the state. Lake Burton."

I know, I wanted to say. "That must be nice."

"Good fishing. And quiet, especially this time of year. Betsy spends more and more of her time up there. She tears through three or four books a week, mysteries and romance and that type thing. And of course the dog loves it. He keeps the squirrel population of Rabun County pretty much terrorized to the point of extinction."

"And you? Do you make it up often?" *Were you there last month, like your wife says you were, that night when someone broke into my house?*

"Every chance I get. These gadgets make it easier, don't they?" He pulled his cell phone from his pocket and laid it on the counter. "Client has no idea where you are, whether you're in the office or out tying fishing lines on your dock." He smiled again. His face was tanned and cleanly shaven, if thinner than the last time I'd seen him. He was still a handsome, handsome man. You didn't have to work hard to imagine how attractive Ethan Sinclare must have been in his prime.

"But enough about the lake. What brings you to Atlanta? You look ravishing, if you don't mind an old man saying so. I was glad to read your surgery went so smoothly."

"Thank you. I'm doing well. And I never had the chance to thank you for your generosity at the St. Regis. Picking up my hotel bill. That was incredibly kind."

He waved his hand in a think-nothing-of-it gesture. "Least I could do for the daughter of Boone Smith."

"It's funny, though. At breakfast . . . when we had breakfast that morning, you never mentioned that you also know my family in Washington. The Cashions."

For a fraction of a second, Ethan looked taken by surprise. Then he turned to the fridge and pulled out a pitcher of what looked like lemonade. "Here, set this on the table, would you please? Let's get these sandwiches unwrapped."

I walked the pitcher to the table and filled two crystal goblets, then used a tea towel to wipe the condensation from the sides and handle. When I turned back around, he was at the counter, watching me with an expression I could not read. The atmosphere in the room had sharpened, as though we both sensed that the pleasantries were concluded, and from this moment forward it would be important to pick each word with care.

"My mother—Frannie Cashion, I mean—recognized you in a photograph. She says you've known each other since I was a little girl."

"It's a small, small world, isn't it? That's right. It's been years since we saw them. Thomas and Frannie. Used to bump into them every now and again at legal conferences."

"Why didn't you tell me you knew them?"

"Never crossed my mind. Didn't make the connection until later."

I frowned. "At breakfast we talked about how my father and brother are lawyers in Washington. Cashion is an unusual name. You send my family a Christmas card every year. How could you not—"

"Just didn't. Guess I'm getting old. I was caught up in

the fact that I was sitting there sipping coffee across from Boone's daughter, all these years later. Didn't give any thought to the name of the family that adopted you. I mean, what are the chances I'd know them, too?"

"Exactly. What are the chances?"

"Small world."

I started closing in. "You called our house last month. You talked to Mom—"

"That's right. I called as soon as I figured out the connection."

"But you didn't mention it. You didn't tell her that you and I had met. You didn't tell her we'd just had breakfast together in Atlanta. You acted like it was just a casual phone call to say hello—"

"Caroline." His voice had an unmistakable edge. "You've had a hell of a month. I'm sure it's been hard on you. Shall we get these sandwiches out on plates? Or do you maybe want to wrap yours up to take with you?"

"I went to Nantucket," I whispered. "As I think you know, since you called my hotel twice, looking for me. I talked to Verlin Snow. He wasn't with you the day that Boone and Sadie Rawson died."

"I beg your pardon? What are you talking about?"

"Not the whole day, anyway. You made him lie to the police for you."

Ethan stared at me. "Why would I do that?"

"Because you needed an alibi."

"Now listen here. I don't know what's gotten into you, what all this nonsense is." As his mouth shaped the words, before I understood what was happening, he was around the counter and on me. With one hand he pinned both my arms behind me, and with the other he pressed down on the stitches on my neck, hard.

I cried out in pain.

"Are you wearing a wire?" he hissed in my ear. His hand moved down my neck to my back, searching under my arms, around the underwire of my bra, around the waist of my skirt, down the backs of my thighs. At last he released me and stepped back.

"Why did you come here?" he panted. "What is it you want!"

I had so many questions. What had happened that day on Eulalia Road, I mean what exactly? Why hadn't he killed me, too, finished me off when he'd had the chance? And last month, in my home in Georgetown—what had he planned to do, if my bedroom door hadn't held? If I hadn't leapt from the window and run? Would he have killed me first, or would he have dug the bullet from my neck while I was still alive?

What I heard myself ask was this: "Did you love her?"

His eyes had gone cold. "Sadie Rawson Smith was the most beautiful woman I've ever seen. You don't hold a candle to her, if you want to know the truth."

If that had been all he said—if he had stopped, if he had left it there—I might still have turned and walked away. Walked out the front door, dropped the revolver in the bushes, kept right on going. Perhaps it was enough to know the truth. Perhaps that's all people mean by closure. To understand what happened, to understand you can't undo it, to find the strength to walk away.

Ethan didn't stop there, though. He didn't leave it. "Be careful, Caroline." His voice was so low I had to strain to hear. "Be very careful. I'd hate for anything ever to happen to Frannie."

"You bastard! You wouldn't."

But, yes, he might. Ethan Sinclare stood there, his eyes like dull coal and his lips stretched in a dangerous smile. At my hotel this morning, when I had lain in bed imagining this conversation, it had uncoiled in grainy black and white. It had been like my Ingrid Bergman nightmares: a long buildup, tension ratcheting scene by scene. But I never made it all the way to the end, to this precise moment. His face had kept dissolving. The picture kept fading to black. Before my finger wrapped around the trigger. Before I had to make a choice.

Ethan and I looked at each other and I thought I saw him twitch right.

Now it was my turn to move and I reached for my bag and he reached for me and his hands were on my neck and my finger was on the trigger and I pulled.

It is amazing how steady you shoot when you can hold the gun with both your hands.

I SHOT HIM twice.

Two times.

Bang. Bang.

There would have been a nice symbolism to shooting him once more—one bullet each for me, for Boone, and for Sadie Rawson. But he was already facedown on the kitchen floor, lying on his stomach, black blood spreading like tar across the tiles. I forced myself to count to ten. He did not move.

My hands were trembling and my ears roared and only one thought cut through the noise: *Get out of here*. I grabbed his cell phone and dropped it into my purse. With a napkin I swiped shaky circles along the top and side edges of the counter. I had been keeping track of everything I touched, had been careful to clean my prints from the lemonade pitcher before I'd placed it on the table. I would need to wipe down the front doorbell on my way out. What else?

I glanced down and realized dark droplets were sprayed across my white blouse. His blood. With unsteady fingers I began undoing buttons. One of them was slick and wet and I thought I might be sick. I would have to wear my wool overcoat with nothing underneath until I could retrieve my overnight bag and a fresh shirt. I would wad this soiled one in a plastic sack and carry it with me until I could shove it deep into a Dumpster somewhere. I was still fumbling with the buttons when I heard something. From behind me, from the far corner of the kitchen, came a whimper.

I spun around. Standing in a low doorway, such as might lead to a laundry room, or to the back stairs, stood a woman. A petite, blond, older woman wearing a tennis skirt and white sneakers. Her eyes wide with shock.

Impossible.

"What have you done?" she moaned.

I had a five-shot revolver. I had three bullets left.

I raised my arm and trained my gun on Betsy Sinclare.

Fifty

ow long have you been standing there?"
Her lips flapped like a fish but made no sound.

"How long have you been standing there?" I bellowed again.

Even as I asked, I knew it did not matter. It didn't matter what fragments of conversation she might have heard. She would never fess up to the police about how Ethan had threatened Frannie, or how he had squeezed his strong hands around my neck. No. What she would tell them, what she would be able to describe with gorgeous precision, was this scene before her now: her husband, unarmed and shot twice through the gut; me, leaning over him in a half-buttoned, blood-spattered blouse, the gun still hot in my hand.

She suddenly bent over double, gripped her bare, freckled knees with her hands, and vomited. When she had finished, she wiped her mouth on the hem of her tennis skirt and tucked her hair behind her ears. Then— ignoring me, ignoring the gun in my hand—she staggered to her husband and sank to her knees. "Ethan? Ethan? Please, no, please, no, no, no." Her hands roamed

over him, seeking to stanch the blood. At last she cupped
the back of his head, watching him carefully, just as I had
done moments before, waiting for confirmation that he
was truly gone.

After some minutes she rocked back on her heels and
raised her face to me. I was bracing myself to find grief and
terror there. Instead her mouth was twisted with hatred.

"Betsy?" I breathed. "Mrs. Sinclare?"

"Don't speak to me. Don't you dare speak my name."
This was said with such raw anger that I felt each word as
a brick, smashing against my temples. I was the one
holding a gun, but I wasn't about to shoot a defenseless
old lady, and she looked as if she knew it.

"Do you know who I am?"

"I know you. I knew your whore of a mother." Sweet
Betsy Sinclare hoisted herself to her feet, hawked, and
spat in my face.

Unexpected.

I reared back. Dried my cheek with the napkin and
tucked it into my bag. "I gather you know that your husband and Sadie Rawson were lovers. You know that he
killed her? And killed my father, too?"

"What I know," Betsy snarled, "is that there was an
accident. A mistake. A terrible mistake, that my family
has been paying for, for more than thirty years. And it
was over and no one knows and now *you* show up. And
do *this*!" Her voice rose to a shriek.

I wanted to explain. Wanted to make her understand.
But the drumbeat was back in my ears, cutting across her
words, booming, *Get out of here*.

"Betsy, where do you keep rope?"

She gaped at me as if I were even crazier than she'd imagined.

"Or string? Ribbon?"

"What are you talking about? I'm calling the police."

I raised the gun again. Through gritted teeth: "Where. Do. You. Keep. Rope?" She didn't move. We were standing eight, maybe ten feet apart. "I'm begging you not to make this harder than it has to be." Still she didn't move. Okay, I take it back. Maybe I *would* shoot a defenseless old lady. Just in the foot, just as a warning. It's true what they say. It gets easier after the first time.

In the end we went with duct tape.

I dragged a chair into the laundry room, forced her to sit on it, and went to work on her wrists. Then her ankles, securing them with loop after loop of tape to the legs of the chair. Before slapping a strip over her mouth, I asked, "What are you doing here? Ethan said you were at the lake."

I didn't expect her to answer. But her face crumpled. "I play tennis on Wednesdays. Every Wednesday morning, for years now. I've told him a million times. He never remembers." Tears spilled from her eyes.

And there it was, in twenty words, a portrait of a marriage. Of the toll that decades of jealousy and resentment can take. It occurred to me that she had retched, but she had not actually cried at the sight of his body. What had broken her, what had brought her to tears, was the admission that he didn't care where she was on a Wednesday morning. Or any other morning, presumably, and that he hadn't for years. Had she heard his dying words? About Sadie Rawson being the most beautiful woman he'd ever seen? For a moment, just a moment, my heart broke for her.

But the drumbeat was back: *Get out of here*.

"Are you expecting any visitors today? Betsy?"

She had her eyes shut and her head down.

"Betsy, I'm sorry, so sorry. You can't imagine how sorry. But this is important. When will someone come looking for you or Ethan?"

"I don't know," she sobbed. "I was going to drive up to the lake after I showered."

"When does your housekeeper come?"

No answer.

"Betsy!" I lifted her chin. "Do you have a regular cleaning lady?"

She sniffled. "Thursdays."

"So tomorrow? Are you sure? Is she reliable?"

Betsy nodded.

That meant I had, maybe, eighteen hours before the body was discovered. I wiped Betsy's face with a tissue and forced her to swallow a sip of water. Covered her bare legs and shoulders with towels I found in the dryer, so she wouldn't get chilled. I felt awful leaving her there, far guiltier than I did about having just shot her husband. But what choice was there? I taped her mouth shut and pulled the laundry-room door closed behind me. I wedged another chair under the doorknob, so it would be tough to open from the inside, even should she manage to wriggle free.

Ethan Sinclare's body was sprawled grotesquely across the tiles. I stepped around it in as wide a circle as possible. Turned off the lights. Wiped clean the switch. Stole an Atlanta Braves cap from the hall closet and tucked my hair beneath, hid my eyes behind sunglasses. My head was down and I was thinking fast as I strode up the street.

There was a witness. Everything had changed. I would have to run.

THE FACTS, AS I saw them, were as follows:

I had shot and killed a man.

Murdered him.

He had deserved it. What I had done to Ethan Sinclare represented a pure, shining biblical justice. An eye for an eye. Unfortunately, that didn't make it legal.

I could turn around, give myself up, argue that the shooting had been self-defense. But it hadn't been, not really. I had created this situation all by myself.

I had thought to swipe Ethan's wallet and maybe a knickknack or two. Police would reasonably surmise that an intruder had broken in, that Ethan had come home and surprised him, and that a struggle had ensued. The random-burglar theory. It had the benefit of simplicity. And I liked the parallels to thirty-four years ago. Another kitchen, another gun, another set of police assumptions about a burglary gone wrong. The investigation into Ethan's death would play out in similar fashion to the investigation that he himself had set in motion, back in 1979, back in the house on Eulalia Road.

It was perfect. The very definition of justice.

But Betsy Sinclare had upended this plan. As soon as she was set free—whether that happened in the next hour or not until tomorrow and the arrival of her house-keeper—she would finger me. She would describe how she had watched Caroline Cashion slaughter her husband. Within minutes, my name would be all over CNN. There would be a manhunt, for Christ's sake.

Then it would all unravel. They would trace the gun. They would discover I had bribed a stranger in a parking lot to illegally purchase it for me. They would match the bullets in Ethan's chest to my revolver. God, the irony. I would be charged with homicide. I was no expert on Georgia sentencing guidelines, but it was a safe bet that the premeditated murder of a prominent local attorney wouldn't be looked on kindly.

I didn't want to go to prison.

That wasn't the way this was supposed to end.

If you were suddenly a fugitive, where would you go?

THE TRADITIONAL ANSWER to that question is Mexico. Run for the border.

But in an astonishing stroke of bad luck, I had already told everyone to look for me there. I had a plane ticket booked, to Cabo San Lucas, leaving from Washington Dulles on Friday morning. I'd given my name and credit-card information to a hotel there, a lovely hotel on the beach, where I'd been very much looking forward to staying. I was telling the truth when I said I was planning quality time with a pitcher of margaritas. When I'd made the reservations, my instinct had been that however things turned out with Sinclare, I would need time on my own to calm down. To wait things out. Now those reservations guaranteed that every passport officer south of the Rio Grande would be on the lookout for me. Mexico, alas, was out.

You heard of people in such situations hopping over to Cuba. But you needed a visa to get in, and I didn't have time. Same with Morocco, same with Russia, same with every other country I could think of that wasn't likely to have signed an extradition treaty with the United States. Where could I flee to, tonight, on a direct flight? A city big enough that I could disappear? The answer, when it came to me, was obvious.

I felt around the bottom of my handbag for an object I'd thrown in days ago and forgotten. *Please* let me not have taken it out. There. My fingers closed around cold metal. This would come in handy.

Fifty-one

It's harder than you might think to get rid of a gun.

Sure, you could toss it in a Dumpster, or into thick undergrowth by the side of the road, and hope for the best. But if you want to maximize the chances of that gun's not coming back to haunt you, then the disposal site of choice has to be deep water.

In Atlanta, that meant the Chattahoochee River.

Hunched down on the back of the bus, speeding away from the Sinclares' house, I opened maps on my phone and identified a promising spot. The Chattahoochee River National Recreation Area was only a short drive from my hotel. The website described a three-mile hike called Indian Trail, along the "lesser-frequented eastern banks of the river." There appeared to be a small parking lot, and from there several paths forked off to various vantage points above the river. On a Wednesday afternoon in November, I hoped they might not be frequented at all.

When I eased my rental car into the Indian Trail lot an hour later, I was wearing the blonde-bombshell wig again. Also, a sweatshirt that I'd bought in the hotel gift shop, pale pink with HOTLANTA spelled out across the front in cursive rhinestones. Inconspicuous it was not. On the other hand, if the goal was to avoid being recognized, I could not have been dressed less like my usual self.

Only one other car was parked in the lot. A pea-green Prius. The owner was nowhere in sight. I climbed out and selected the muddiest trail, on the theory that other hikers might be discouraged. Ten minutes later I arrived at a high bluff overlooking a bend in the river. I glanced around. Spotted no one. In the red clay where I stood were boot prints, and paw prints from a dog. They could have been five minutes old, or five hours, or five days. I took a deep breath, hollered out, *"Hello?"*

My voice echoed across the water. No one answered.

I considered, hollered, *"Help! I need help!"*

No answer. Good.

I pulled the Smith & Wesson from my purse and hurled it as far out as I could. The river was wide here and I lacked the strength to hit anywhere near the middle, where the water was presumably deepest. It would have to do. The gun splashed and sank. I held my breath, half expecting a SWAT team to jump out from behind the pine trees and cuff me on the spot. No one appeared. Next I threw the cardboard box containing the remaining forty-five bullets. Then Ethan Sinclare's mobile phone. I'd already had the presence of mind to crush the SIM chip beneath my boot, in case police were already tracking it. In case they were already hunting for me. That left my own phone. I turned it over in my palm, weighing the pros and cons. I needed it until I was away on that plane tonight. But the risk of giving away my movements was too great. I flicked my wrist and sent it flying. It sliced into the water at least twenty feet farther out than my previous attempts. My aim was improving.

My next problem was money.

Thanks to Boone and Sadie Rawson and the wonders of compound interest, I was rich. But once police started searching for me, I would need to stay off the grid. I wouldn't be able to access my bank account. My credit cards would be useless. I couldn't just withdraw half a million dollars cash, throw it in a suitcase, and check it on the plane. So how could I take my money with me?

I mulled this dilemma as I sped back up the trail, turned the car around, and drove to a local branch of my bank. The teller didn't bat an eyelid at the size of the check I was depositing. I asked her to place the money in my checking account, then asked for $10,000 in cash, in $50 bills. That would tide me over for a while if I was frugal. She counted out the money with inch-long, fake fingernails painted hot pink.

"Loooooove your top." She slid the money through the hole at the bottom of her Perspex window. "Are those rhinestones? I like a little bling-bling. You got the whole diamonds-are-a-girl's-best-friend thing going on."

I stared at her. A moment passed.

"You need something else, sugar?"

"Actually . . . yes. Do you have a phone book back there? I want to look up something in the yellow pages."

She drummed her talons on the counter, *click click click*, then nodded and made to stand up.

"And I'm going to need another cashier's check." I tilted my head, running the numbers. "Made payable to me, please. For two hundred and fifty thousand dollars."

TIP-TOP DIAMONDS IS in southeast Atlanta, on a long, dreary road otherwise dominated by car dealerships and drive-through hamburger joints.

I'd selected it because the ad in the yellow pages bragged about having the city's largest selection of certified loose diamonds. Also, because it wasn't Tiffany's. I didn't need pretty blue boxes. I needed a place that knew to shut up and not ask questions when a broad in a rhinestone HOTLANTA sweatshirt rolled in, looking for a bulk discount on a quarter million dollars' worth of bling.

Inside was a waiting area with peach-tinted, wall-to-wall carpeting and a shiny leather sofa. No gems in sight.

"May I speak with the owner?" I asked the woman who had buzzed me in.

"Certainly, madam. Did you have an appointment?"

"I'm looking to make a significant purchase."

"Ah. Okay. Just one minute."

She was gone for nearly ten. I squirmed on the sofa. I needed to be out of here in half an hour if I was going to make it to the airport, drop off the car, and catch my flight. I had no time to try another store. It was here or bust.

At last an exceptionally thin man in a flashy suit appeared and introduced himself as Juan. Affixed to his lapel was a metal button that read BUYING A DIAMOND?

DON'T PAY RETAIL. Beneath this hung another button: CUT DIAMONDS. CUT-RATE PRICES.

Classy.

"Juan." I hit him with my most bewitching smile. "May I cut to the point? I'm interested in buying a number of your best diamonds. In fact, all of your best diamonds. And I'm in a hurry. I need to be walking out your front door with them in twenty minutes. Do you think we can make that happen?"

He looked me up and down, took in the trashy sweatshirt, the muddy boots, the rental-car key fob dangling from my hand.

"You pay cash?" was all he said.

Velvet trays appeared. I selected a two-and-a-half carat stunner of an engagement ring and popped it on my finger right there. The rest I took in loose stones. The female assistant darted back and forth, matching appraisals and lab certificates to gems.

Juan had his calculator out, keeping a running total. When he hit $200K, he looked skeptical. "Keep going?"

I checked my watch. No time. "No, thanks. That'll do it." I turned to the woman. "Would you excuse us for a second?"

She hesitated, glanced at Juan. He nodded.

When we were alone, I patted the padded velvet sleeve in which he'd been placing the diamonds. "I'm not an expert in diamonds, as you've probably guessed. But I will be. One day, when I'm not in quite such a rush, I'll take these and get them appraised. If you have cheated me—if a reputable dealer examines the contents of this bag, plus this ring, and finds them to be worth less than two hundred thousand dollars—I will find out. And I will come back here, and I'll shoot you. Just so we're clear." I smiled sweetly. "Do you need to make any adjustments?"

He blanched. Stiffened. Reached behind him, picked out two good-size rocks from a tray, and dropped them in with the others I had selected.

"Excellent." I pulled the cashier's check from my purse and flipped it over. "Want me to endorse this to Tip-Top Diamonds or to you personally?"

He reached for the check to inspect it. Held it up to the light, ran his fingers over the watermark. "Caroline Cashion's not your real name, is it?"

"Actually, it is. You'll have to trust me on that one. The check's legit. Although I wouldn't wait too long to cash it."

Now he was squinting at the amount. "This check's worth two hundred and fifty grand. I can't make change."

"Consider it commission for a job well done. And for keeping this transaction between us."

He still looked uncertain.

"Juan. I need to go. Do we have a deal?"

He wiped his forehead with the back of his hand and pushed the check across the desk to me. "Endorse it over to my buddy Chuck. He helps with the accounts."

What did that mean, in dodgy-diamond-dealer-speak? That Chuck was the guy who laundered the money? I shrugged and wrote my signature on the check.

Traffic was surprisingly light on the drive to the airport. I squealed into the Hertz return zone an hour and fifty-two minutes before my flight was scheduled to depart. Before climbing out I reset the GPS unit. *Delete all recent destinations? Y/N?* it asked. Yes. A backup file was probably synced to some server, somewhere, but no reason to make it easy to retrace my steps.

An attendant materialized at the window. "Evening, ma'am. Read the mileage for me, if you would?"

I checked the odometer and told him the number.

"Returning it with a full tank?"

"Didn't have time."

Tutting noise. "That'll cost you. Next time select the prepaid fuel option."

I nearly laughed. It would be difficult to explain to this man quite how far down my list of sins having failed to fill my gas tank would rank. Committing murder has a way of putting one's other transgressions in perspective.

As I made my way toward the airport train, a smile lingered on my face. On the one hand: I had killed a man today. A man who, whatever his flaws, was someone's husband. Someone's father. I had terrorized an old lady and locked her in her laundry room. I had deliberately destroyed evidence relevant to a felony. I was about to try to smuggle $200,000 worth of undeclared diamonds out of the country. I was on the run, was possibly looking at life in prison.

On the other: I hadn't had this much fun in quite some time.

IN THE ATRIUM of the main terminal, I stopped to watch a television tuned to CNN. The volume was muted, but judging from the graphics, the anchor was parsing the Dow's having hit another record high today, closing at 15,747. If only I'd had time to sock my money in stocks instead of diamonds.

Next up—Celebrities Caught in "Catfishing" Hoax, announced a banner scrolling across the bottom of the screen. Also ahead, five things you needed to know about New York's new mayor. I was not news yet, then. CNN was headquartered in Atlanta; they would be all over the murder of a wealthy local lawyer. Sweet Betsy must still be locked in the laundry room.

Delta was inviting first-class passengers to preboard when I reached the gate. That meant I had ten minutes or so. I retraced my steps to a cluster of shops that I'd passed. At Emporio Armani I picked up the plainest, beigest sweater I could find. Also two outrageously overpriced white T-shirts and a pair of black jeans that looked more or less my size. At Coach I made a beeline for a pair of sensible, rubber-soled, mahogany-brown boots. No more stilettos for me. Nothing that might attract attention.

The departures screen displayed my flight's status as FINAL CALL. I ducked into DKNY, grabbed an oversize pair of dark sunglasses, threw several bills on the counter, didn't wait for the change.

They were shutting the doors to the gangway as I hurtled up to the desk. A cranky flight attendant scanned my boarding pass, then my passport. No red lights lit up. No alarm sounded. No Homeland Security agent burst forward, screaming for my arrest.

I found my seat. Clicked my seat belt tight. Closed my eyes.

Nine hours and four minutes to Zurich.

PART SEVEN

Europe

Fifty-two

As the plane circled Zurich, I felt myself begin to sweat. Dark crescents soaked under the sleeves of the HOTLANTA sweatshirt. Does it go without saying that I had not slept? That I had passed the entire overnight flight worrying? Of the many images that tormented me, the worst was imagining how Mom and Dad would react when they learned what I had done. I hated knowing I would cause such pain. Hated knowing that I couldn't call to comfort them, or to explain myself. In my life, I've never gone more than a day without speaking to my parents. Now I might be forced to go months, or years, or forever.

We were scheduled to land just after noon in Switzerland. Just after 6:00 a.m. in Atlanta. I had no idea what might have happened in the nine hours we had been in the air. Unless she was an abnormally early riser, the Sinclares' housekeeper would not have entered their house yet. But Betsy might have thrashed herself free, or a friend could have dropped by the house and found the body, or any number of other scenarios could have transpired. It seemed more likely than not that Swiss police would be waiting to drag me off in chains, the moment we touched down.

I had weighed whether to change into my new clothes on the plane, or after landing. I went with the latter. I was stuck with being Caroline Cashion up until the moment I crossed the Swiss border; I needed to match my passport photo. After the border, all bets were off.

The plane bumped down onto the runway. Taxied to the gate. All seemed normal. I stepped off the plane, head down, avoiding eye contact. The throng of passengers shuffled toward passport control. I joined a long line. Around me slumped bleary-eyed, jet-lagged travelers, sneaking glances at their e-mail despite signs banning cell phone use in this section of the airport. I envied their insouciance. Wanted felons such as myself couldn't risk pissing off the guards.

My heart pounded when at last my turn came. I had been hoping for the grandmotherly officer in Lane 7. Instead I was waved toward Lane 5, presided over by a blond man with piggy eyes and multiple chins. He flipped through my passport unhurriedly.

"Purpose of your visit?"

"Tourist." This was always the right answer, no matter what actually brought you to a country. Otherwise there would inevitably be some problem with your visa, some work permit you had failed to obtain, some form you'd forgotten to get stamped.

"How long are you staying in Switzerland?"

"Just transiting en route to Italy," I lied.

He scanned the bar code in my passport. I held my breath. Now he was scrutinizing the main page, the one showing my photo and personal data. Slowly he raised his eyes to mine. *"Alles Gute zum Geburtstag,"* he said sternly.

I am a linguist, as you know. I speak French *couramment*, my accent indistinguishable from a native's. I speak Italian and Spanish well. For reasons that now elude me, I had studied Mandarin for a year in college, and I can still direct a taxi or order the Peking duck in Beijing without resorting to sign language. But German? *Nein.* Barely a word. I'm not even sure I can count to ten.

I spread my hands in a gesture of incomprehension and gave him a shaky smile.

He did not return it. *"Alles Gute zum Geburtstag!"* he said, more agitated this time. The passport officer in Lane 6 stopped what she was doing to peer over.

Was this it? Was he onto me? Had the bar-code scan triggered an alert?

"Sie sprechen kein Deutsch? I saying, happy birthday. Soon you are turning . . . *achtunddreißig.* In English, how you say? Thirty-eight."

He raised his hand and brought it down to crunch a rectangular, red stamp into my passport.

My knees had gone so weak I had to concentrate to walk away.

IN THE LADIES' room of the airport bus terminal I dropped my skirt to the floor. Off next came the rhinestone HOTLANTA hoodie. Hallelujah.

For this next act I had to screw up my courage. I hadn't managed to find proper scissors for sale in the Arrivals Hall, but I did stumble upon a vending machine that stocked travel necessities, from disposable socks to plastic rain ponchos to mini–sewing kits. Inside this last item was a teensy pair of scissors for snipping thread.

I pulled my hair down over my eyes. I should have had a mirror to do this, but I couldn't bear to watch. A hank of glossy, dark hair came off in my hand. I held it for a moment, remembering how Will had wrapped his fingers around these same strands, outside another airport, in what felt like another lifetime. I shook my head to dispel the thought and let the hair drop on top of my discarded clothes. *Snip snip snip.* The scissors were nowhere near big enough for the job; it took ages to work my way around, sawing off my curls to within an inch of my scalp.

When I was finished, I felt naked in a way that had nothing to do with my standing in the stall of a bus station bathroom wearing only my underwear. I bundled up my old clothes, my old hair. Exited the bathroom without permitting myself to check my reflection in the mirror above the sinks.

Ten minutes later, a mousy-looking woman wearing sensible boots and a beige sweater boarded a bus for Freiburg, Germany.

I NEEDED TO make my way west and north across Europe. But it seemed unwise to chart too straight a line. I had booked my flight into Zurich for this very reason: to create a record of me entering a different city, in a different country, than the one to which I was actually headed.

Thus, now, the detour through Germany.

Freiburg is supposed to be a lovely city, with a medieval university and lively market squares and a winding road that leads deep into the Black Forest. I saw none of these. I clambered off the bus, deliberately walked two blocks in the wrong direction and ducked down a smelly alley lined with Dumpsters, before zigzagging back to the *Hauptbahnhof*, the main train station. I had no idea whether this was the right way to go about disguising my tracks. I'm trained as a scholar of French literature, not as some wizard of antisurveillance tradecraft. But I've watched the same *Bourne* movies as everyone else, and Matt Damon's character seems to embrace a pretty basic philosophy: if you're being chased, either find yourself a hell of a good hiding place, or else keep moving.

Inside the train station I purchased a cheap black wool hat and a ticket to Frankfurt. I toyed with riding farther north, continuing all the way up to Antwerp, the Belgian port city that is headquarters to the world's diamond trade. I had visited Antwerp before, had marveled at the diamond district, the Orthodox Jewish traders mingling with Brazilians and Russians, Lebanese and Indians, tens of billions of dollars changing hands every year. Once I identified the right man to approach, I could sell off my stones one by one. If they were worth anything close to what I had paid in Atlanta, the money would last me years.

Antwerp could wait, though. Frankfurt already marked yet another detour. But it is a transport hub, and from there, I could catch a direct train to my final destination.

• • •

TWO HOURS AND twelve minutes later, as the train pulled into Frankfurt's main station, I arrived at a decision. I needed to find an Internet connection and check the headlines. Perhaps I should have done this the moment I cleared customs back in Zurich. But given the choice between dawdling at an Internet café and racing to put as many miles as possible between me and my pursuers, I'd chosen to run. I also felt uneasy about unwittingly creating an electronic trail. Police would easily follow me to Zurich; they would be no more than a few hours behind. Common sense dictated that they would use every cybertool at their disposal. From this point forward, I was determined to leave no traces.

Still.

Separate from the question of whether Ethan's body had been discovered was the matter of his wife. By now twenty-four hours had lapsed since I had tied her up in the laundry room. She had spat at me, she had called Sadie Rawson a whore, and she would do everything in her power to deliver me to prison. But I couldn't just leave her there forever. I needed to confirm that she had been found.

From a kiosk across the street from the station I paid cash for two prepaid phones. I tucked one in my pocket. On the other I launched a browser and searched for Ethan Sinclare. The bio from his law firm's website pulled up first, followed by an article about a speech he'd delivered in Miami, and a squib about a fund-raiser he and Betsy had chaired for the Atlanta Botanical Garden. Nothing more recent.

Puzzled, I checked the *Journal-Constitution* home page. I nearly skimmed right past it. It was the seventh item, only a couple of paragraphs. A body had been found in a private residence on Tuxedo Road. Police stated that the body had gunshot wounds, it had been found on Thursday morning, and they were investigating the death as a homicide. Detectives were seeking to question a person of interest in connection with the incident. The victim's name was being withheld, pending notification of family members. No suspect had been named at this time.

I walked a clockwise loop around the station, stuffing the black hat into a garbage can and donning a pair of forest-green earmuffs that someone had forgotten on the previous train. I reentered the station by a side entrance. At the ticket machines, the woman ahead of me purchased a one-way, first-class trip to Munich. As she turned away, I dropped the prepaid phone I had used into her shopping bag. A nice touch, I thought. On the off chance that my ten minutes online had provided any clues as to my whereabouts, that phone would lead investigators straight to Bavaria.

I FELT A palpable sense of relief as the train crossed the border into France. I spoke the language. I knew the customs. I could blend in. My fingers closed around the keys to Madame Aubuchon's apartment. When I had groped around for them at the bottom of my handbag yesterday, I had known this was where I would run. Hélène had urged me, had practically ordered me, to go to Paris. To heal, and to hide. Her exact words. Of course, she hadn't known that I would be wanted for murder by the time I got here. The police would question her—interviewing a suspect's employer must be part of the drill—and she might reveal I had borrowed her Paris house keys.

But I had a feeling she wouldn't. I couldn't tell you why, other than that she seemed a deeply private person, who would view what she chose to do with her house keys as a private matter. She was also deeply intelligent. She would read between the lines of the press coverage. She would realize it must have been Ethan Sinclare who had killed my family; she would grasp what I had done, and why. Madame Aubuchon had her own history with a violent man. I thought—I hoped—she would not give up another woman in crisis.

The train from Frankfurt did not rumble into the Gare de l'Est until midnight. It would be pushing one in the morning by the time the Paris metro deposited me outside Hélène's building. I took a man's navy scarf from my bag—another item appropriated from the train's overhead bins—and wound it around my head and shoulders. I was cold, and the beige sweater had by now been captured by closed-circuit cameras in transit hubs across Europe. I took a deep breath and steeled myself for what I hoped would be the final leg of this journey. I was nearing a state of such exhaustion that if sirens and police vans were indeed waiting for me outside Madame Aubuchon's flat, I was no longer sure I cared.

Fifty-three

Paris est un véritable océan, wrote Balzac in 1834. "Paris is a veritable ocean. Sound it: you will never know its depth."

Yes, there are bigger cities. Some 2 million people live in Paris proper; it is nothing to today's megacities of Mumbai or Mexico City, São Paolo or Shanghai. But I didn't have the keys to an apartment in those cities, did I? And Paris is big enough. I know some streets here like the back of my hand. The rue Jeanne d'Arc, for example, in the thirteenth arrondissement, home to my favorite butcher shop. The seedy street in the Marais, where I had lived for two years while researching and writing my PhD dissertation. There were whole neighborhoods, though, where I had never walked. Countless streets where I would not be recognized, where I could prowl undetected. Less a woman than a shadow, a silhouette against the sky.

You can scour Paris, Balzac wrote, but there will always be another wilderness. His actual phrase was *un lieu vierge.* A blank or virgin place. A place with no history, at least none of your own, a place where you might assume a different identity altogether.

Few of us ever get the chance to reinvent ourselves. I mean, genuinely reinvent ourselves: new name, new city, new life. I had already done so once. I had been Caroline Smith, and then, with the stroke of a pen, I became Caroline Cashion. That time I had been a child; my new home and new identity had not been of my choosing. This time, though, I had control. Whom would I become, now that I could no longer publicly move through the world as Caroline Cashion? Now that the woman who had used that name for thirty-four years must—for official purposes—cease to exist?

I have always loved the name Simone. Simone Moreau has a nice ring to it. Or Simone Guerin, perhaps. Dubois? Durand? It would need to sound commonplace. An unremarkable name, a name you might forget. I didn't know how one might go about acquiring false identity papers. Presumably such things could be accomplished, if tackled with the right combination of determination, cunning, and cash.

That was a task for tomorrow. Next week, even. Today I slept until late afternoon, and when I woke up, I was ravenous. Madame Aubuchon's pantry was bare. I found a jar of raspberry jam and smeared it onto shards of melba toast so old they were turning to dust. Eventually I gave up and gobbled the jam directly from the spoon. There were tea bags but no milk, tinned tuna but no bread. A strange meal.

Afterward I lay back in bed and watched the stars prick the sky, one by one.

Paris is a veritable ocean. You can scour it, Balzac wrote, but there will always be another wilderness, always "a hidden den, flowers, pearls, monsters." Indeed. The monsters were a certainty. My adversaries would be waiting for me, ready to pounce the moment I was careless, the second I let down my guard. As for hidden dens, as for flowers and pearls . . . Well. We would have to wait and see.

Fifty-four

I did not have Madame Aubuchon's stamina. In her own hour of need, Hélène had holed up inside this apartment for seven weeks. I didn't last two days.

I forced myself to wait until twilight before venturing out. Under normal circumstances, this would not have been a challenge. The flat was spacious and tasteful, the furnishings more minimalist than I would have predicted for a woman in her seventies. Perhaps this was the boy-toy husband's influence on display. The walls were lined with books, mostly in French. On the upper shelves were smaller but still sizable collections in English, Italian, and Russian. The literary canon was well represented, but there was also a suspicious number of mysteries and thrillers. I would have chalked these up to Jean-Pierre, except that Madame Aubuchon appeared to follow a strict labeling system with her personal library. Penciled inside every front cover, in what I recognized as her handwriting, was her full name and a year. Presumably the year she had read the book. Madame Aubuchon had devoured everything P. D. James and Ian Rankin had ever written, along with Lee Child's entire Jack Reacher series. God, it was too good. The prim head of Georgetown's French Department—a leading authority on the seventeenth-century playwrights Molière and Racine—was secretly addicted to page-turners about a testosterone-drenched, ex-army cop. I would have given quite a lot for the chance to drop that into casual conversation in the faculty lounge.

What drove me outdoors wasn't the lack of diversions, but the lack of food. I couldn't face the raspberry jam again. And while I couldn't lay eyes on the source, all afternoon the smell of freshly baked bread had wafted up from the street to torment me. There must be a *boulangerie* on the corner, just out of sight. When the sky at last grew purple, I borrowed a raincoat and hat from the hall closet and let myself out. The coat stretched tight across my chest and hips; the woman was a sparrow.

The bakery was already locked tight for the night, but a corner shop on the next block had everything I desired. A wedge of cheese, the dry French sausage known as *saucisson sec*, half a dozen apples, cans of tomato soup, a liter of milk, a bottle of wine. In a dusty basket near the front I found baguettes. They had gone stale, but I tucked two under my arm, breaking off a heel to nibble as the clerk rang up my purchases.

Ten minutes later I was back in the apartment. I stashed the cheese and the milk in the fridge and chewed a slice of the *saucisson* as I contemplated the nonfood items I had acquired: a toothbrush, a bar of soap, and a box of L'Oréal Prodigy #10, *Blond Très Très Clair*.

Fifty-five

The L'Oréal #10 was a disaster.

It turns out you can't go from naturally dark brown hair to *Blond Très Très Clair*, at least not without making an intermediate stop at ghastly orange. The woman who stared back at me from Madame Aubuchon's bathroom mirror was crowned with what could only be described as a carroty mullet, complete with crooked layers in front and a ratty tail at the back, where I'd left the hair longer to hide my still-vivid scar.

I would have to seek professional help. Vanity aside, I was trying to keep a low profile, and this look would cause young children to run screaming.

On boulevard Saint-Michel was a salon I liked. But they might remember me, and it was unlikely to be open on a Sunday. Instead I borrowed the rain jacket and hat again, lowered my sunglasses, and caught the metro to the Château Rouge stop, in the eighteenth arrondissement.

YOU COULD SMELL and hear the Marché Dejean before you saw it. The unofficial heart of Paris's African community was hopping on a Sunday morning. The stink of meat assaulted you even as you climbed the steps from the metro, wafting over from Boucherie Amar Frères, a halal butcher. Around the corner, pretty housewives from Senegal haggled over the price of yams; street traders hawked fake Louis Vuitton bags; children begging for sticky, honeyed pastries spilled out the door of an Algerian bakery.

I stopped outside a Tunisian restaurant to get my bearings. Surely there was an Arab hairdresser around here. I was gambling that barbers in this neighborhood might be less likely to abide by the rhythms of a nominally Catholic country, where on a Sunday morning everyone was supposed to be either asleep or in church. Judging by the throngs of people squeezing past me, I had guessed right on that front. I was also gambling that someone used to styling women of color might have experience in rescuing brunettes from bad home dye jobs.

A beautiful black woman with platinum-blond hair swept past me on the sidewalk. I caught up with her, paid a compliment, asked directions. She said a name and pointed. It took several wrong turns and another request for directions before I arrived at a brightly tiled establishment fitted with two vinyl barber chairs. The proprietor looked surprised when I walked in. Even more surprised when I peeled off my hat and revealed the mess he had to work with. He held up a finger, signaling me to wait, and disappeared into the back. A minute later he returned with a woman in tow, a baby on her hip and a girl of four or five trailing behind. The two of them consulted in a language I couldn't understand. Hindi, possibly, or Urdu. They were not African.

Then she stepped forward with a surprisingly sympathetic smile. "You did on your own?" She pointed at my scalp.

I nodded sheepishly.

"One hundred euros. I fix for you. Will take some hours."

I handed over the money, plus a generous advance tip. When someone is about to attack your head with bleach and a pair of scissors, it's in your interest for the person to feel warmly toward you.

I was led to one of the vinyl chairs. The girl shyly offered me tea, then sugar cubes, which she dropped into my cup with tiny silver tongs and a look of such endearing seriousness that I accepted three. She disappeared while her mother stood behind me, whipping bleach into a paste in a steel bowl.

"Where is your family from?" I asked the woman, by way of conversation.

"Pakistan. Lahore. And you?"

"Lyons." France's third-largest city. I knew it reasonably well, should she ask questions. But she merely nodded. The girl reappeared, carrying a stack of comic books. She held one up to me, smiling. I smiled back. She held up another one, pointed at the cover and giggled.

Her mother spoke sharply to her, asking a question in their language. Then the mother began to laugh as well. "She says you look like Tintin."

I stared. The Belgian boy adventurer on the cover of her books styled his orange hair in a cowlicky cross between a pompadour and a Mohawk. I made to protest, but what was the use? The girl had nailed it. She crawled into my lap and demanded that I read aloud to her the adventures of Tintin and his dog, Snowy, while her mother rubbed a white paste that smelled of lemons into my hair.

I EMERGED INTO the strong sunlight of early afternoon looking less like Tintin and more like a youngish Mia Farrow. The Pakistani woman had done me right. My hair was dark, golden blond, shaped into a modern pixie cut, spiky on top, with a flirty flip in the back. The hair just covered my scar. She had deftly avoided touching it, had asked no questions.

I walked to a nearby café and ordered more tea. The remaining German phone was in my pocket. It was time, I reckoned. I had not checked the news for three days. I prepared myself to read about the manhunt that must now be under way for me. The press must be hounding my family in Washington; my heart ached at the scandal and shame I had brought on the Cashion name.

On the *Journal-Constitution* mobile site the murder had ascended to the lead story. Ethan Sinclare was now identified by name. His family was described as shocked and grief-stricken. The Atlanta Bar Association was planning a tribute dinner. There was a more detailed account of the wounds that had killed him, two bullet shots to the stomach, fired from close range. Police were still seeking to question a person in connection with the incident. Anyone with relevant information was urged to make an anonymous call to the Crime Stoppers Atlanta tip line, or to text the tip to C-R-I-M-E-S.

There was no mention of my name. Nothing hinting at a motive for the killing. I did not understand it. I sat until my tea went cold, then removed the chip from the phone and crushed it beneath the heel of my boot.

The Marché Dejean had finished for the day, but at the top of the stairs leading back down into the metro, a lone vendor remained. He had a dirty, green sheet spread across the sidewalk, loaded with car air-fresheners, lighters, knockoff designer sunglasses, and a handful of pre-loaded cell phones.

"Combien?" I asked, gesturing at the phones. How much?

He shrugged. *"Trente-cinq."* Thirty-five.

I scoffed and turned to go. But his necklace caught my eye. Rather, not a necklace but a small, leather pouch, hanging from a suede strap.

"Et pour ça?"

"Ça? Non. C'est la dent de mon fils." That's my son's baby tooth.

Not the tooth, silly. Just the pouch.

He looked dubious.

"Cinquante." I held out a fifty-euro note. "For both."

He shook a small, brown tooth from the pouch into his fingers. Unknotted the suede strap and handed it, along with a phone, over to me.

"Code for the SIM card is taped to the back," he mumbled.

Once I'd settled into the plastic bucket seat of the train, I unwrapped the bullet from its tissue-paper sheath inside my purse. Dropped it into the pouch and tied the strap tight around my neck. The leather was still warm from his skin.

THAT NIGHT I became aware of a man watching me.

Back in Hélène's apartment I had found myself restless. The evening was unseasonably warm. The neighborhood cafés would be packed. My cans of tomato soup were unappealing. I paced the parquet floors, weighing the risks, knowing I should stay inside with the curtains drawn and my nose in a book. But I seemed unable to channel my old risk-averse, introverted self. She bored me. Just after dark I exited the building by a back service door, slipping into the soft air and walking east, crossing the Seine, hugging back streets and then the banks of the river itself.

There is an Italian wine bar near the Odéon that stays open late. On a night like tonight it would be busy, knots of people sipping Sangiovese on the sidewalk, waiting for seats at the bar or at one of the red Formica tables. I scanned the wine list and ordered the house Vermentino, a dry white from the hills between Liguria and Tuscany. Then I plunked down on the curb to wait. The crowd was mostly young, mostly locals in expensive denim and leather jackets, lighting each other's cigarettes and chattering in French. I was wearing my sensible boots with black leggings. No makeup, no jewelry, no ornamentation of any kind. My newly blond, cropped hair lay flat against my head. I felt invisible.

From inside the restaurant, though, a man kept glancing at me. He was at a table for two in the window, speaking to another man whose back was to me. I could not see his features clearly in the candlelight, just the flash of his dark eyes. They did not look away when I stared back. Suddenly he was making his way to the bar, speaking to the bartender, pointing outside toward me. My blood froze. I scrambled to my feet, ready to run.

But when he appeared at the door he was holding two glasses. *"Je me suis demandé si vous aimeriez un autre."* I thought you might like a refill. He nodded in the direction of the bar. "He said you liked the Vermentino."

I stepped back. Scanned our surroundings for signs of a trap. A squad of armed Interpol agents might be lurking behind him, preparing to storm us from the restaurant kitchen. He took in my tense posture with a raised eyebrow. "You're not going to run away, are you? *Je ne mords pas.*" I don't bite.

I could have been mistaken, but his black eyes were not watching me like those of a cop closing in on his quarry. They were watching me the way a man watches a woman he wants, outside a bar on a velvety night in Paris, when the evening is still young enough that anything could happen.

I took the wine.

"Comment vous appelez-vous?" What's your name?

"Simone." It was the first time I'd said it out loud. *"Je m'appelle Simone Guerin. Et vous?"* And you?

"François." He smiled and produced a pack of cigarettes, shook out one for each of us. I opened my mouth to tell him I don't smoke, then reconsidered. Caroline didn't smoke, never had. Simone, on the other hand, was still making up her mind about such things.

"Alors, Simone. Parlez-moi de vous." Tell me about yourself.

"Je suis écrivaine." I am a writer. That had a crumb of truth. I thought of the book I'd been so excited to write, not three weeks ago, the one my brother Tony had teased me about in my Georgetown kitchen. The politics of divorce in working-class, post-Napoleonic France. It was as though the idea had sprung from the mind of a completely different person. The topic now failed to interest me in the slightest. I began to talk instead about travel memoirs and fat war histories, slim volumes of poetry and novels with bleak endings that drove you to despair. About all the books I loved to read, and all the ones I wanted to write, and some of what I said was real and some of it I made up as I went along. His black eyes never left mine.

Shall I describe him for you? François was pale with thick, dark hair that matched his eyes. Tall but delicately boned. He wore a black cashmere turtleneck and skinny jeans. But you already guessed that. He leaned down to kiss me and I let him. Smoke curled up from the cigarettes we held against our hips. He was so precisely my type that his lips felt already familiar. I had kissed a dozen boys just like him, on a hundred velvety Paris nights. Paris is a veritable ocean, wrote Balzac, but it is also, he conceded, a moral sewer. *Un égout moral.* This can be a good or a bad thing, depending on how remorseful one is prepared to feel the morning after.

If they ever called my name for a seat inside, I missed it. At midnight the candles on the tables had burned low. Every chair was still occupied. The hum of conversation, of easy laughter and whispered seductions, floated out to the sidewalk. The bartender eventually passed us the Vermentino bottle through the window, and we stood there, kissing and talking and smoking, until it was finished.

When he whispered that his apartment was close by, though, I broke away. I've had my share of lovers, but I've never picked up a stranger in a bar and slept with him. I'm no prude about such things. I simply think a man should have to work a bit harder than that. So much of the pleasure lies in the chase.

I kissed him, on the cheek this time, and said goodnight.

"Attends," he said. Wait. On a scrap of paper he wrote his name and a telephone number. I folded it, discovered I had no pockets, tucked it into the leather pouch at my neck.

Mist was rising off the Seine as I threaded my way home. I stopped every few hundred yards, listening from darkened doorways, making sure that neither François nor anyone else had followed.

Fifty-six

Y ou don't tend to know when you're about to have a momentous day.

Morning dawns like any other morning. You stretch, put the kettle on, feed the cat, pad around in blissful ignorance. Only later, when you unfold the fateful letter, or the knock sounds at the door, do you realize that the trajectory of your life has irrevocably been altered.

In my case, the messenger was a news website.

I bolted upright in bed shortly after 8:00 a.m., startled from sleep by the blaring horn of a city bus. On the past two days traffic had been light, but today Paris was roaring to life in full weekday-morning, rush-hour splendor. Madame Aubuchon lived in an elegant building with leafy views across the Bois de Boulogne. Half a block away, though, thrummed a major artery. You could almost feel the pent-up commuter frustration rising from the streets up to her balcony.

I padded to the kitchen and put the kettle on for tea. Toasted the last of the baguette and spread it with the dreaded raspberry jam. As I chewed, I scolded myself for being careless last night. I should know better. No more nights out snogging strange men. From this moment forward, my raciest evening encounters would be with a mug of herbal tea and one of Hélène's dog-eared Jack Reacher paperbacks.

I had matters to attend to, now that I was rested. I needed to get a fake ID. I needed fresh clothes, the drabber the better. Most pressingly, I should find a new accommodation. Even if Madame Aubuchon did not crack under police pressure, this place was insecure. Staying here was tempting fate. I wanted rooms with no connection to the woman once known as Caroline Cashion.

In the shower I pumped out my usual shampoo dose, to find it was five times as much as my new pixie hair required. I made a mental note to add a razor to my shopping list. At this rate, I would soon have more hair on my legs than on my head. After toweling off I reached for the prepaid phone that I'd bought yesterday from the street vendor. I would check the headlines, crush the chip again, purchase yet another new phone while I ran errands today.

I began to read. At the first paragraph I went pale. By the third, I had crashed down on the side of the bathtub, my eyes twitching, breathing hard.

BETSY SINCLARE HAD given an exclusive interview to the *Atlanta Journal-Constitution*. She was pictured looking frail and wearing widow's weeds. Above the article ran a banner headline: "Bereaved Widow Shares Saga of Terror, Tragedy." The story that followed, written by a reporter whose name I did not recognize, bore no resemblance to events as I knew them to have unfolded.

Mr. and Mrs. Sinclare had been about to sit down to lunch together at their upscale Buckhead home, the newspaper reported, when their lives were shattered. Earlier that morning Mr. Sinclare had driven to Henri's Bakery, where he was a regular customer, to buy his wife's favorite sandwich.

"We love their pastrami," said Mrs. Sinclare, her voice catching. "Ethan always goes out of his way to bring it home for me. And because he'd been out of town on business, he made a special effort. I came sailing in from my tennis match and found he'd set the table with our wedding china and crystal. Forty years of marriage, and he could still be such a sweetheart."

Before the couple could enjoy their romantic meal, however, an armed man burst into the room, according to Mrs. Sinclare.

My mind reeled. I plowed on.

"He came out of nowhere," she said. "He was wearing gloves and a ski mask, like you wear in Aspen, but you could see his eyes were bloodshot. He was yelling for money and he was waving a gun around and Ethan tried to stop him. They were wrestling, and then there was a noise like a clap of thunder."

That noise was the sound of two bullets being pumped into Ethan Sinclare's stomach. He is believed to have died almost instantly, said Atlanta police lieutenant Jeff Packard.

Mrs. Sinclare tried to escape, but the intruder over-powered her, bound her wrists and ankles, and locked her in a laundry room adjacent to the kitchen, she said. She was discovered by the family's longtime housekeeper the following morning. Based on Betsy Sinclare's description, Lieutenant Packard said, police are searching for a man last seen wearing a red-and-black coat and gray pants.

I checked and checked again. Nowhere in the article did my name appear.

What the holy hell was this? There was no room for misinterpretation. No shades of gray. Betsy Sinclare had lied. Outright lied both to the newspaper and, by the sound of it, to the detectives investigating her husband's murder.

The question was, why?

THE STORY MUST have been a plant.

They must have been trying to trick me into thinking I was safe, trying to tempt me from my hiding place. Admittedly, this theory had flaws. The police would blow all credibility if they got caught fabricating a story and shopping it to reporters. The newspaper would blow all credibility if it got caught wittingly printing a fake story. Neither institution would be cavalier about such risks.

Still. What other explanation could there be?

I threw down the prepaid phone in frustration. It was already blinking low on credit, and I'd only been online ten minutes. I borrowed a coat from the hall closet (a fur-trimmed cape this time, not the rain jacket, no point in being predictable) and set off for the Renaissance Hotel. I'd passed it on avenue Poincaré on my way home last night, had noticed the taxi rank and two bellhops in top hats idling outside the entrance. At times in life nothing feels so comforting as the high-end anonymity of a big American hotel. Usually these times occur when I'm in an unfamiliar city and in desperate need of a ladies' room. Today I required a different amenity: the business center.

It was in the basement. As the computer whirred to life, I stole sideways glances at the room's other occupants. Had the woman at the workstation closest to the door—the one wearing a malevolently striped suit and terry-cloth room slippers—had she stared at me longer than necessary? And why had the man beside her jumped up to leave so suddenly? I squeezed my head between my palms, a futile effort to quell the paranoia, and started typing.

The CNN.com story included a few details absent from the *Journal-Constitution* account. A neighbor said she had seen a purple minivan screeching away from the Sinclares' house on the morning of the shooting. The man whom police were searching for was described as African-American, with a stocky build, around five feet ten inches to six feet tall. Ethan's funeral was to be held at the Episcopal Cathedral of St. Philip, this coming Wednesday.

The fundamental thrust of the story remained the same, though. Betsy Sinclare swore that she and Ethan had been attacked by a crazed man wearing a ski mask ("like you wear in Aspen," she had said. Priceless). I surfed around, checking other news sources. Alexandra James had not touched the story, and why would she? Ethan Sinclare may have been prominent in Atlanta, but he had not enjoyed national stature. Reporters outside Georgia had no reason to take an interest. I read every scrap of information I could find and then leaned back in utter bewilderment. After a while I cleared my search history, shut down the computer, and walked upstairs to the front desk. Screw disposable phones. I didn't know where in this neighborhood to buy one, and I didn't have time to run around. Was there somewhere I could make a private call? I asked.

I was shown to a quaint, wooden phone booth in a carpeted hallway running off the lobby. I had had no contact with my family since leaving Atlanta. No way to do so without compromising my security. But I was now frantic to speak with someone who would be on my side, to confirm whether it could possibly be true that Betsy Sinclare had not ratted me out.

Two minutes later Martin accepted the charges. "Sis! You know it's, like, six in the morning here?"

Powerful, childlike relief coursed through me at the sound of his voice. "Martin. I know. I'm sorry, I—"

"It's okay. I was up already. I wasn't expecting to hear from you. You said you were disappearing off the grid for a while."

I frowned. How much farther off the grid could a person get? I had fled to a different continent, cut up my credit cards, shaved off my hair, and changed my name to Simone. I'd converted my cash to loose diamonds and—aside from this call—limited my communications to burner phones. But Martin knew none of this. He didn't even know I was in France.

"Sis? You there?"

"I'm here. Bit of a delay on the line."

"So how's Mexico? Enjoying the beach life?"

"Oh, you know. Mexico's hot," I said evasively. "Is, um—is everything okay at home?"

"Here? Sure. I checked your house over the weekend. Some trash blew into the storm drain, but I swept it out, and everything else looks fine. Haven't actually laid eyes on Mom and Dad in a few days. Work's been crazy. I'm getting slammed by this Abu Dhabi deal. But, let's see . . . Dad's got some new road race he's training for. Not sure what Mom was up to this weekend. I guess church, Flower Guild, the usual."

This all sounded spectacularly . . . normal. The police had not showed up. My family did not yet know what I had done. Incredible.

"This must be weird for you, being out of touch. I know you usually talk to Mom, like, seventeen times a day."

"Slight exaggeration."

"Not much of one. I was thinking about it. How if I were you—if I'd lived through what you have—I wouldn't let Mom and Dad out of my sight, either. I mean, I know you don't remember anything. But maybe deep down you do remember your first parents, and the way that you lost them, and it made you . . . it's made you stick close to Mom and Dad, all these years."

I winced. "I don't know. Maybe. I've tried and tried to remember, but it's all . . . blank."

We were both quiet for a moment.

"On a different note, have you talked to Tony?" asked Martin. "You should call him."

"Okay. Why? Anything wrong?"

"No, no. Only that your married doctor called him."

I did a double take. *"Will?"*

"Yep. Tony threatened to—um, how to put this tactfully—he threatened to cut off Will's dick and feed it to the snakehead fish in the Potomac if he ever came near you again."

Tony would have meant it, too. "But why did Will call Tony?"

"You should ask him. Tony, I mean. I'm just repeating secondhand. But I gather Will's desperate to talk to you and you haven't been answering your phone. So he was trying to get Tony to pass along a message."

I thought about this. I certainly hadn't been answering my phone. It was buried in sludge at the bottom of the Chattahoochee River.

"Will moved out. Out of that house we drove to, the one on Lorcom Lane. That's what he told Tony, anyway."

"Jesus. Fuck."

"Whoa. You really have unplugged. Don't think I've ever heard you swear before." Martin sounded amused. "My offer to kneecap him stands, for what it's worth. Anyway, I gotta run. Drink a margarita for me. And listen, Sis, will you be home for your birthday? Or Thanksgiving? Mom'll want to know."

"I don't know." It was the truth. My birthday was in

fifteen days. Thanksgiving fell two days after that. If the next couple of weeks proved remotely as interesting as the last one had been, I had absolutely no idea where I might be.

ONLY ONE PERSON knew for sure why Betsy was lying.

Contacting her seemed a staggeringly stupid thing to do, but I couldn't see that I had an alternative. I waited until midafternoon, when it would be nine in the morning in Atlanta. I used the time to purchase yet another prepaid phone, this one from a reputable phone store and loaded with a hundred euros in credit. On the off chance that she actually took my call, I didn't want to risk being cut off.

A hushed female voice answered the phone at the Sinclare residence. Mrs. Sinclare was resting and not accepting calls, the woman informed me, but the family appreciated my thoughtfulness at this difficult time.

"I think she might want to speak with me," I insisted. "Could I trouble you to check? Please tell her it's Caroline calling."

The voice hesitated. "I'm not sure. What may I say it's regarding?"

"I'll hold," I said, ignoring the question. "If you could tell her that Caroline . . . Smith is on the line." That ought to get her out of bed.

A long pause followed, punctuated by several clicks, as if an extension in another room was being picked up and the first one disconnected. I heard breathing.

"Mrs. Sinclare? Are you there?"

More breathing, then a hoarse laugh. "Do you know where I'm standing right now? In my laundry room. My goddamn laundry room. It's the only place in the house where I can shut the door and escape all these people who've come to be helpful. And the funny thing is, you're the only person in the world who would grasp the irony in that. In my hiding in here with the dryer lint, to take a call from you."

"I'm sorry. I never meant for you to—"

"Shut up, you little tramp," she spat. "I'll do the talking. We'll speak this once, and then never again, do you understand?"

I was too stunned to respond.

"You'll have seen the newspaper stories by now, I imagine. You'll have read my account of how my husband died." Her voice sounded flayed, raw from weeping. "You will have noticed there was no mention of you. There will never be any mention of you, not in connection with my husband, do you understand?"

No, I did not. "Why did you lie?"

She drew a shuddering breath. "Your whore mother tried to destroy my family thirty years ago."

"Your husband *did* destroy my family thirty years ago," I retorted. "You're not the only victim here."

"That was all . . . behind us. Decades behind us. There was no reason for you to come here. No reason to rip open old scars. And there is nothing—do you hear me?—nothing that would give me greater pleasure than sending you to prison for the rest of your life."

"So why did you—"

"Shut up!" she hissed. "I said what I said because I had

quite a long time to think, tied up and gagged in here on the laundry-room floor. You made sure of that. If I identify you—if I tell that it was you who killed Ethan—everyone will wonder why. Don't you see? Why would some hoity-toity professor with no prior record gun down my husband? The police would want to know the *motive*." She was crying now. "Everything would come out. All of Ethan's affairs. Everything about him and Sadie Rawson. And that something terrible happened that day and that two people died and somehow their baby girl got shot."

"You mean me."

"I mean you," she whispered.

Then she said, "If I tell the police the truth, it would ruin you. But it would ruin me, too. I would be a pariah. Known all over Atlanta as the wife of a . . . a *philandering murderer*. The wife of the man who shot a baby girl and left her for dead. You were so little," she moaned. "Still in your pink pigtails, hiding behind your mother's skirts. Can you imagine the shame if all that came out? It's not the kind of thing that people would forget."

"So you—you made up a story about a crazy man with a gun?"

"It was the only way out that I could think of. People will believe me. They already do."

She was clever. And correct. People would believe sweet Betsy Sinclare. I felt impressed, and a little sick.

"I will not allow my family to be ripped apart. Not now. I will not allow Ethan's name to be dragged through the mud. I swear to God, you'll have to come back with your gun and shoot me first."

"That won't be necessary," I said softly.

After some minutes she sniffled. Coughed and cleared her throat. "Does anyone else know? Have you told anyone?"

"I was about to ask you the same thing."

The hoarse laugh again, even sadder now. "I've lived with my husband's secrets for a long, long time. I can live with this new one, too. Please don't call me again, Caroline. I am asking you—I am begging you—to keep your mouth shut. Leave my family alone."

The phone line went dead.

I wiped tears from my eyes and thought about all the ways we hurt the people we love, and how long those wounds can fester. How had Faulkner put it? *The past is never dead. It's not even past.*

Fifty-seven

The police were not looking for me.

They never had been.

I had embraced the fugitive mind-set so firmly that this would take time to sink in. I found myself doubting, still casting glances over my shoulder. Seventy-nine euros and eighteen cents of credit remained on my phone. I tapped it to make one final call to Atlanta.

"Caroline. I'm glad you decided to call me back," said Beamer Beasley. "You still in France?"

I was sitting on a low, stone wall overlooking the Seine. Bateaux Mouches glided past on the river below, their giant, open decks dotted with tourists. The Eiffel Tower loomed on the left bank. It was late afternoon and the sun was a low, orange ball, warm on my face and arms. Now I felt myself go cold. It was his use of the word *still*. Anyone with caller ID could see the +33 country code and divine that I was speaking from a French phone. But *still* implied that this wasn't news. *Still* implied that Beasley had already known I was here.

"Yes, still in France." No point denying it. "How did you know that?"

"I took the liberty of making a few calls. Once I verified you never got on that plane to Mexico."

"And why were my whereabouts of interest?"

"Well, originally, to inform you about the death of Ethan Sinclare. I assume you've read the news reports by now, though."

"Yes." My leg had begun to tremble. "What a . . . a terrible shock."

"It certainly is. His poor widow is taking it awful poorly. You've never met her, have you? Betsy Sinclare?"

I said nothing, waited to see where he was going with this.

"The thing is," he said. "The thing is, there are a couple of curious details that haven't made their way into the newspaper. A couple of loose ends, I guess you'd call 'em."

"Oh?" My leg jounced up and down uncontrollably. I pressed my palm down against my knee, trying to hold still against the stone wall, trying to fight down the panic.

"Mind you, I'm not working the Sinclare investigation myself. So this is only what I happened to overhear in the hallway. Watercooler chitchat."

"Beamer, out with it," I heard myself rasp.

"Well, Mr. Sinclare was old-fashioned about technology and whatnot. He did own a cell phone, which we can't find. But he didn't keep his calendar electronically. He recorded his appointments in a little, purple leather book. We found it in his back pocket."

"Ah."

"And the day he got killed—the day Mrs. Sinclare

says he surprised her with a romantic pastrami-and-rye on the good china—he had an entry for *Lunch with C*. The time slot overlaps exactly with the coroner's window for his time of death. Isn't that interesting?"

"Not particularly," I hedged. "Maybe he canceled lunch with someone, in order to eat with his wife."

"Betsy Sinclare says *C* meant her. Says he always called her *Carissima*, dearest one, ever since their honeymoon in Rome. Sweet, isn't it?"

I waited. Wary.

"I just mention it in passing. Now, the other curious thing. Two hairs. Two long, dark brown hairs. Caucasian. They were removed from Mr. Sinclare's sweater sleeve. Tech can't find a match for them."

I closed my eyes. The image of Ethan Sinclare's squeezing his hand around my neck swam into focus. My hair sheeting across my face, covering his arm. Two strands of hair, my DNA, at the crime scene. *On the victim's body.* How could I possibly explain that?

"Betsy Sinclare is a blond, as you may be aware. The alleged perpetrator is described as African-American, so the hairs aren't his. We've ruled out the housekeeper."

"Ethan's granddaughters?" I asked weakly. "His secretary?"

"Checking all of them. But you know what, Caroline? You know what my theory is? My theory is, once a ladies' man, always a ladies' man."

"What are you talking about?"

Beasley sighed. "When I overheard the guys discussing the hairs, and how they couldn't find a DNA match in the system, I might have mentioned that Mr. Sinclare had a reputation for occasionally wandering outside the marital bed. I might—Lord forgive me—have suggested that it would be a kindness to the victim's widow not to make too big a stink about another woman's hairs being stuck to his sleeve. I might have even gone so far as to strongly advise my colleague in charge of the investigation that we show some compassion and not add to the poor family's grief."

"But . . . your colleague's job isn't to show compassion. It's to find out who killed Ethan Sinclare."

"Mm-hmm. But we have an unassailable witness—a churchgoing, God-fearing *grandma*—who's prepared to swear on the Holy Bible that her husband was shot by a big, black guy who broke into their house. So that's who we're looking for. My colleagues aren't going to devote a lot of energy to chasing Caucasian brunettes."

I took this in.

"Doesn't mean they won't match the DNA eventually. All these new advances, every year. Like that Maintenance Man case I told you about. Those hairs from Mr. Sinclare's sleeve . . . whoever they belong to would want to be awful careful not to find a reason to get their DNA tested. Not ever to end up in the national database."

"Thank you," I whispered.

"For what?"

"Just thank you."

"You know, it's taken me a long while to grasp this. But sometimes justice is served in ways that have precious little to do with the criminal justice system."

• • •

THAT NIGHT, SITTING cross-legged on Madame Aubu-chon's bed, I laid two objects on the white sheets.

The first was the disposable phone, reduced now to a mere forty-three euros in credit. I had used it to remotely access my old voice mail and had discovered no fewer than nine messages from Will Zartman. The first eight were short, only a few seconds each in duration, presumably of the *Call me, would you please call me* variety. I deleted them. But the last one ran nearly three minutes long. I couldn't bring myself either to erase it or to listen. Next to the phone I unfolded the second object, a piece of paper from inside the leather pouch knotted around my neck. I smoothed it flat against the sheets. Angular handwriting, black ink, the name *François*, and a phone number.

My hand hovered. Hesitated. I reached for the phone and dialed.

"Hey," I said when he answered, then leaned back against the pillows.

"Hello?" came the cautious response. "Caroline? Is that you?"

"It's me."

Will heaved a deep breath. "Thank God. Are you okay? Where are you?"

"In Paris. Long story."

"But you're okay? How's your neck? Your wrist?"

"Fine. Better every day."

"Thank God," he breathed again. "Marshall Gellert said you missed your last two appointments. That you didn't refill your painkiller prescription. I didn't know if you—"

"My brothers said you moved out." I didn't have the patience to beat around the bush.

"Oh," answered Will in a quiet voice. "Yes. We're separated. My wife and me. Caroline? I made a terrible mistake not telling you, I know that. There was never a—"

"Never a good time? Is that what you were about to say? See, because I would argue that before you kissed me that night in Atlanta would have been a good time."

"I know. I know. I thought you'd run screaming for the hills."

"Well, that's true. I can't say I was exactly yearning to get involved with a married man with two kids and a soft spot for Garth Brooks."

"You make me sound like quite the catch."

"Make that a married, middle-aged baseball fanatic, with kids and a house in the suburbs and—"

"Yet you called," he cut me off gently. "Why?"

Why indeed? Why risk my heart on a man with baggage, a man who had lied to me, a man who might—who knew—be lying even now about being separated?

"I miss you," I said. But it was more than that. I had allowed Will to touch me at a level deeper than I had allowed any of my previous, predictable lovers. Perhaps deeper than I had been capable of, just weeks ago. If he came with baggage, then so be it. I was carrying quite a lot of baggage of my own by now.

"I miss you, too. Come home."

NOT UNTIL SOMETIME after midnight did I stir beneath the white sheets, open my eyes, and realize that Betsy Sinclare was still lying.

I had been dreaming of a girl with dark hair tied back in pink ribbons. *Still in your pink pigtails,* Betsy had said, *hiding behind your mother's skirts.* Pink pigtails. That detail had not appeared in the press accounts at the time of the murders. To my knowledge, no photograph of me from that day had been released. Possibly Ethan had described my appearance to his wife, but it seemed an odd detail to have mentioned. So how could she have known? How could she have known the color of my ribbons unless she had been there and seen me?

I sat up in bed and ran my fingers through my now-short, now-blond hair. Watched a shadow crawl across the bedroom wall, cast by the headlights of a passing car. What was Betsy up to?

The phone in Atlanta rang and rang. I was about to hang up and redial a third time when she picked up. She sounded exhausted. "I told you never to contact me again," she rasped. "I'm going to hang up, and if you have the slightest scrap of sense, you'll do the same."

"How did you know I was hiding behind my mother's skirt when she died? Betsy? Or that my hair was tied in pink pigtails?"

Several seconds of silence, then: "I have no idea what your hair looked like. I don't even remember saying that. What kind of crazy questions are these? Caroline, if you keep harassing me . . . God is my witness, I will tell the police the truth. I'll tell them who shot Ethan. Do you hear me? I will call them right now."

"I think you were there. In the house on Eulalia Road that day. I think you saw me."

"You are out of your mind."

"No, I'm not. You were there. You saw it. Tell me what happened."

She was breathing fast, little pants of air whistling down the phone line.

"They're all *dead*, Betsy. Everyone who was in that room, except you and me. Who are you protecting anymore?"

She held out another few seconds. When she spoke, it was in a snarl. "Your mother knew how to provoke a person. You have *no* idea. Sadie Rawson would stand there, all snooty and superior, in her too-short skirt and her too-high heels, wiggling her bottom. Just throwing it in your face, like the floozy she was. I only went over there to make her give me the necklace. To make her stop parading it around all over Buckhead."

"What necklace?"

"The one Ethan gave her. A sapphire floating on a gold chain. Maier and Berkele mailed the bill to our *house*. I had to write them a check for it. To keep our account in good standing. Do you have any idea what that feels like?" Her voice rose to a shriek.

"So . . . you . . . you and Ethan went over to the Smiths' house together? To ask for the necklace back?" But this version of events didn't make sense either. A knot of dread was hardening between my shoulder blades.

"I drove over myself. To make her give it back and to tell her never to show her face again, not anywhere within a hundred feet of my family. She told me to go to hell. She *taunted* me, said my husband had never loved me and the necklace was hers to keep."

From deep within me, something caught. A sapphire.

A sparkle of blue. I could see it. I remembered. Deep blue against a white throat, a cloud of black hair, warm arms holding me close. Female voices raised in fury.

"I didn't go over there to kill her. I'm not a monster. I only wanted to scare her. I had Ethan's gun—the one he kept in his nightstand—and I took it out, to show her I meant it, to make her listen. And then your daddy walked in! In the middle of the afternoon! I forgot he worked those crazy pilot hours. Boone started carrying on and shouting at me to keep quiet and I told him his wife was filth and he came at me and he was going to grab the gun and I just—I just—"

"*You* shot him?"

"It happened so fast. So fast. He fell over and I was going to help him but your mama flew at me. She hit me, she said I would go to jail forever, that my babies would be orphans. That she would make sure of it. I couldn't . . . I couldn't let her do that."

I closed my eyes. Saw the gleam of blue again. There had been noises. Great, cracking explosions of sound and then a pinch in my neck and my mother, sinking soft against me onto a red, tiled floor. Did I in fact remember this? Was I inventing the memory now? Did it matter?

"I didn't know you were hurt. I wasn't thinking about you at all. I was in shock and I called Ethan. He was there in minutes. He dug the bullet out of the door, but he couldn't find the other one. And it was only then that we . . . that we . . ." Betsy drew a great, shuddering breath. "We thought you were dead, too. You weren't breathing, or it didn't look like you were. I wouldn't have left you. I wouldn't have left a child."

"Why did he help you?" I whispered. "You had just killed the woman he loved."

"One of many women he thought he loved over the years," she said bitterly. "I was his *wife*. The mother of his *children*. He wasn't going to let me go to prison, was he?"

My tongue lay thick and heavy in my mouth. I had to concentrate to lift it, to force it to form words. "So he didn't do it. Ethan didn't shoot my parents. You did. He was protecting you, all these years."

"Yes," she said simply.

"Sadie Rawson's necklace. The sapphire. You took it?"

"It won't ever be found, if that's what you're asking."

My mind flashed through the events of recent weeks, struggling to recalibrate. "What about—who broke into my house in Georgetown the other night, then? Who took the files from my surgeon's office?"

"I'm sure I don't have the faintest idea what you're talking about. But one can imagine that a professional might find ways to accomplish all sorts of things for the right price."

A strange, almost comfortable silence settled between us. Two women who had done their worst to each other, sitting alone in our darkened bedrooms, thousands of miles apart.

At last sweet Betsy Sinclare cleared her throat. "I'm going to say good-bye now, Caroline. But let me leave you with this thought: You shot an innocent man and you're going to get away with it. Don't be stupid. Keep your mouth shut. Walk away."

Fifty-eight

There is a café on the rue de Grenelle where you can sit and order a café crème and watch the patrons come and go. It's a humble establishment, not one of the famous Paris cafés. Sartre never held court here. Neither did Hemingway, nor Picasso. They preferred Les Deux Magots, a few blocks farther east.

I've always favored the rue de Grenelle café for precisely this reason. It caters to the neighborhood, not to celebrities or tourists. Old men greet each other. A woman tears pieces of her morning croissant and feeds them to her dog. An elegant couple in their twenties, still dressed in shimmering evening clothes from the night before, sit smoking at a table on the sidewalk. He kisses her and she lifts her face to him and you see that she is tired yet achingly beautiful.

I sip my coffee and watch them. I despise coffee, never touch the stuff. A surprise to find myself craving it this morning. A surprise to find it tastes delicious, rich and nutty. You think you know yourself. You think you know whether you care for coffee, whether you care for cigarettes, whether you like to swear, whether you could kill a man. You think you know what you are capable of. Then one day you discover that, quite literally, you are not the person you thought you were.

Onto the café table before me I shake the bullet from its leather pouch. It rolls unevenly, coming to rest against the raised chrome rim. Ethan Sinclare had not pulled the trigger; had perhaps never pulled a trigger in his life. I had imagined myself administering justice. *A pure, biblical justice.* An eye for an eye. In fact I have murdered a man who—if not exactly innocent—was not guilty either. The true killer is alive and well. She is at this moment ensconced in her Buckhead mansion, poised to live to a ripe old age surrounded by loving children and grandchildren. Anger bristles through me. Justice is not served. Old wrongs are not righted after all. My own action adds yet another notch to the groaning tally of wrongs, but does it cancel out the original act? My instinct is—no. The scales are not yet balanced. Laid before me then, a choice: Follow Betsy's advice and walk away? Or go back and finish what has been left undone? It is mine to decide when this story will end.

For now, I rise. Push back my chair and walk north to the river. Halfway across the Pont Royal, with the Louvre straight ahead and the Musée d'Orsay at my back, I stop. Pigeons flap lightly above my head, circling a bread crust abandoned on the paving stones. The walls of the bridge are low here, barely waist high. I lean forward over the jade water. Hold out my fist.

It takes only an instant for a bullet to split the air and steal a life. Only an instant to wreak such sorrow. The heart breaks and it cannot be mended, not to the shape that it once was.

Today, though, the bullet will drop like a harmless pebble. Like an acorn dropping from an oak. The water will swallow it with barely a ripple, or perhaps with no sound at all.

I stand beneath the vast, pale sky and I open my hand and let it fall.

Acknowledgments

Among other things, this is a book about the bond between siblings.

C. J. Kelly taught me most of what I know about brothers. We are improbably close, considering we were born eight years apart and that we spent much of our childhood bickering over whom Mom and Dad love best (Ceej: just admit it already). My brother is hands down the person I would want beside me in a bar brawl. I couldn't be more proud of the family he is building with his beautiful wife, Jenn, and their son, Cache. Of my early readers, C.J. is the only one to write a comment that made me cry. In the margin of a scene where Caroline hollers at one of her brothers, he scribbled, "This rang so true. I love you."

Our parents' first house was a fixer-upper on Eulalia Road in Atlanta. I have only happy memories of life there, but it was in that white-tiled kitchen that I imagined the murders of Boone and Sadie Rawson Smith unfolding. When I announced my plan to write a novel set in Atlanta, Mom and Dad got so excited that it became impossible to dedicate this book to anyone else. Mom volunteered to conduct stakeouts on Eulalia, and then—purely for research purposes—subjected herself to multiple rounds of margaritas and cowboy shrimp at Georgia Grille. As for Dad . . . let's just say he embraced the project with such enthusiasm that he is now the proud owner of a 1970s-era .38 Special.

My family in Scotland was no less supportive. Marie and James Boyle whisked our boys away to Edinburgh more than once, to allow me peace and quiet to write. My husband's brothers, Anthony and Martin, lent their names to Caroline's brothers. Dot Boyle and Hilary Wilson shared daily updates on their young daughters, which was incredibly useful in helping me imagine the inner world of a three-year-old Caroline Cashion.

Among my girlfriends, I owe special thanks this round to Sasha Foster, whose expertise in criminal justice shaped Beamer Beasley into a richer character. Kate Gellert made a point of buying a copy of my first book every single day, *for months*, in order to boost my bestseller rankings. Does it go without saying that she enjoys a special place in this author's heart? My heartfelt thanks to Kate and to the many other friends who mixed cocktails, addressed invitations, and offered toasts—including Marilyn Baker, Nancy Taylor Bubes, Heather Florance, Heather Hanks, Maggie Hedges, Hannah Isles, Susie King, Val LoCascio, Colleen Markham, Leslie Maysak, Anne Mitchell, Lan Nguyen, Shannon Pryor, Becky Relic, Megan Rupp, Jonathan Samuels, Casey Seidenberg, Linda Willard, and Tammy Mank Wincup. You guys throw a mean book party.

In Italy, as my book deadline approached, my panic

mounted, and I took to typing eighteen hours a day inside the garden shed erected in our living room (literally, a steel garden shed, painted lime green, in the middle of the living room—long story), dear friends Kerstin Jacot, Christina Petochi, and Charles and Christina Hellawell took over the mothering of my children. They delivered the boys to and from school, fed them meals, and I believe at one point were even putting out our trash.

My Florence book group kept me sane by dragging me away from my laptop to read everything from Hemingway to Russian political history. We have a reputation as a drinking club with a book problem, for reasons we can never quite remember the next morning. Certainly it has nothing to do with the leadership of Alison Gilligan and Diana Richman, who organize our ranks with grace and a ruthless efficiency from which military commanders might learn much.

My thanks to Bita Honarvar and Sandra Murray, for access to the *Journal-Constitution* archives. To Carolyn Atkinson of the National Association of Unclaimed Property Administrators, who helped me plot how Caroline might go about tracing her inheritance. To Marc Vinciguerra, who corrected my Parisian slang. To Brian Martin, who not only let me steal his syllabus but who was alone among early readers of *The Bullet* in proposing a psychoanalytic reading of Will's masculinist judgment of Caroline's multiple *boules*. (Editors at the *New York Review of Books*, take note.)

Perhaps my greatest stroke of luck in the book-publishing process was meeting Victoria Skurnick, of the Levine-Greenberg-Rostan Literary Agency. She is a force of nature, and my advice to anyone who ever crosses paths with her is to shut up and do exactly what she says. Trust me: it saves a lot of time. Karen Kosztolnyik is the kind of editor whom writers dream of. She managed both to love this book from the get-go, and to make it a million times better. My thanks to Karen, as well as to Louise Burke, Jen Bergstrom, Jean Anne Rose, and the entire team at Gallery Books and Simon & Schuster.

I share my protagonist's weakness for the Euro look. Happily, my Euro husband favors Italian suits and Scotch over skinny jeans and cigarettes. Nick drove carpool and did grocery runs and learned to cook a formidable chicken curry, to give me time to write. He listened to me ramble about possible plot twists and then came up with some of the best plot twists himself. Peach, I could not do this, or anything else that I do, without you by my side.

Our son James spent much of last winter plopped beside me, penning his own first novel. He already possesses, at the age of ten, both a way with words and an appreciation for the challenges that fiction writers face. ("Mom," he sighed one night, "it's a ton of work when you have to make up all the characters and all the action and the ending and *everything*, isn't it?") Our younger son, Alexander, endured months of suspiciously early bedtimes, so that I could sneak away and continue writing into the night. In the morning he would cock one sleepy eye, wrap warm arms around my neck, and whisper, "Did you finish the chapter?" Yes, lovely boy, I finally did.

THE *BULLET*

MARY LOUISE KELLY

Introduction

Caroline Cashion is a mild-mannered professor of French with a stable, loving family and a happy, if uneventful, life. She never expects that a checkup for wrist pain would lead to the shocking revelation that there is a bullet embedded in her neck, which reveals that she is the sole survivor of a brutal murder that killed her birth parents and changed her fate forever. As she attempts to unravel the mystery of her childhood trauma, Caroline must quickly come to terms with the fact that she isn't the only one with dark secrets. Someone is invested in making sure that a decades-old crime is never solved . . . and he or she is willing to kill to make sure that the past stays covered.

Topics and Questions for Discussion

1. "'We love you. We always will. No matter what, you are our daughter.' I stared at him. Those were the most frightening words I'd heard yet" (page 25). Early on in the book, Kelly sets up a relationship between love and fear. How does this play out as *The Bullet* progresses? Think of several examples in Caroline's life, as well as for the Smiths and Sinclares.

2. Caroline is a professor, dedicated to the pursuit of knowledge. Still, would you say that knowledge makes Caroline happy? Why or why not?

3. Do you find Caroline a likable character? What details signal to us that we can trust her, and in what ways does the author work to endear her to the reader, before the book's shocking end? Consider her appearance, habits, relationships, and hobbies.

4. Look at the beginning of chapter 10, when Caroline first visits the house on Eulalia Road where her parents were killed. Can you relate to Caroline's desire to relive her past, even in its most disturbing and heartbreaking moments?

5. Knowing the details of her parents' lives makes Caroline feel closer to them, yet the book's opening prologue suggests that those intimate details can mask larger truths. Which do you think are more important in this book, in the end?

6. Maternal characters are very important in the novel, from Sadie Rawson (who literally takes a bullet for Caroline), to Madame Aubuchon, to her mother in DC. Compare and contrast these characters, as well as other "mothers" in the text. What do you think the author is trying to say about the complex nature of motherhood?

7. On page 202, Beasley and Caroline discuss the nature of closure. How does Caroline's sense of what this means change over the course of the novel?

8. Should Verlin Snow have been required to confess? Do you understand the reasons for his actions, or find them morally wrong? Discuss with your book club.

9. Do you think justice is served for Caroline and the Smiths in the end? Why or why not?

10. "Sometimes, to heal, we need time alone" (page 321). In what ways does her decision to go to Paris help Caroline? What does she learn or do there that might harm her?

11. Why do you think Caroline decides to let go of the bullet, in the end? Would you have done the same?

12. Author Alice LaPlante praised *The Bullet* by calling it "at once a thriller [and] a medical mystery." Did you find Caroline's story believable, in the way many medical mysteries are? What techniques did the author use in order to heighten this book's credibility and verisimilitude?

Enhance Your Book Club

1. What's in a name? Caroline is relieved to discover that the Cashions did not change her birth name, but she also becomes "Tammy" and "Simone" over the course of the novel. With your book club, find a baby name book or reference website and look up the attributes of several character names from *The Bullet*. Then, look up the meanings of the names for each of your club members, and discuss whether you think they match each of your personalities.

2. Make an appointment to take your book club to a local shooting range. Compare your accuracy: the best shot gets bragging rights!

3. Caroline is a devout foodie. Feed your book club with some of the dishes she describes so delectably in the novel—think sweet potato pancakes, Madame

Aubuchon's garlicky chicken cassoulet, or even Caroline's Parisian go-to meal of baguette with raspberry jam. Top it off with an aptly named rye cocktail, like the Revolver: http://liquor.com/recipes/the-revolver/.

4. Research some of author Mary Louise Kelly's journalism—you might consider playing one of her pieces for NPR at your book club. Compare and contrast her voice in her nonfiction work versus in *The Bullet*. Do you think her personality comes through in both genres of her writing? How can you tell?